Caught in the Middle

-We Kinky Three #1-

by **Kira Barker**

Caught in the Middle

We Kinky Three #1

ISBN-13: 978-1507735053
ISBN-10: 1507735057

Cover art by Mayhem Cover Creations
Edited by Marti Lynch
Interior design by Kira Barker

www.kirabarker.com

Give feedback on the book at:
kira.e.barker@gmail.com

Twitter: @KiraEBarker

CONTENT WARNING: This story contains scenes of an explicit, erotic nature and is intended for mature audiences. 18+

First Print Edition March 2015
Produced and published by Barbara Klein, 1140 Vienna, Mauerbachstr. 42/12/3, Austria

To everyone who made this possible. This one is for you!

-1-

A warm, firm body—pressed against mine. Hands—searching. Lips—finding. Mouths—hungry, exploring, everywhere.

My eyes drooped closed, fluttering lids battling the glare of the neon lights overhead. The cold toilet seat cover under my ass was definitely not helping to jump-start my libido. The knowledge that my beeper could go off any second now wasn't, either. Some people might get a kick out of a semi public environment for their intimate moments, but this definitely wasn't doing anything for me. Maybe because it had become routine too long ago. Maybe I was really overthinking this.

Maybe I should just shut my inner narrative up and get back to rubbing one out?

Snorting at my own antics, I yanked on the drawstring of my scrubs and pretty much shoved my right hand down my panties. Not quite the kind of forceful action I had in mind, but better than not scratching that itch at all.

Where was I? Ah, right.

Lips trailing wet kisses down the side of my neck. Hands, warm and strong, stroke over my arms. I moan, but the sound gets cut off by his hungry mouth on my lips. His tongue thrusts into my mouth, slides against mine, demanding, taking. One hand lets go of my arm to push underneath my shirt, his touch eliciting sensations where it hits the skin of my ribcage.

Under clothes action, seriously? I really didn't have time for this! Why were there even clothes involved in my wank fantasy?

No clothes, just naked skin on naked skin. I can feel the heat of his body so close to mine, getting warmer still as he closes the distance, a muscular thigh brushing mine—and something else, too. His cock is hard and ready, begging to be touched, and he flashes me a cocky grin as I wrap my hand around it. Gray eyes hold mine for a second, then he steals another kiss that deepens, and his hands are everywhere—my thigh, my sides, my tits. I'm burning for more, I need this, I want this so much, and he knows it, is only too happy to give me what I need. His lips leave mine only to kiss a hot trail down my jaw to my neck, blond hair filling my vision as he nudges my head to the side to better reach that special spot that makes me go crazy when he flicks his tongue over it. My head falls back and another breathy moan leaves my lips, followed by his name—"Jack."

What the fuck? Who in their right mind moans names during sex?

But, I had to admit, he would get off on that. Definitely. And while I wasn't opposed to my imaginary hand stroking his imaginary cock, I wasn't up to stroking egos of whatever inclination.

Now, of course, the cocky bastard is grinning at me, and I get annoyed. Annoyance doesn't do a thing for me!

It was always the same with Jack, and the mental image I had of him was so incredibly life-like that even wank-fantasy Jack only took five seconds to get under my skin in that not-exactly-exciting kind of way.

Groaning with frustration, I screwed my eyes shut and forcefully wiped my mental slate clean. This so wasn't working as it was supposed to be!

Taking a deep breath, I let my fingers skim sensually over my clit. Responsive enough, but a quick check lower confirmed what I was afraid of—I was still dry as hot sand in the middle of the desert. Gnashing my teeth, I considered my options, but then decided that dawdling wasn't one of them. I still felt kind of sleazy, and not in a good way, as I stuck two of my fingers into my mouth, then pushed them back into my pants. Ah, much better! A little circling motion and clenching of my pelvic floor muscles, and we were back on track!

That still left that other problem, but thankfully, I had an easy solution for that, too.

Strong hands grab my arms, and I feel my body getting flipped over. I barely have the chance to steady myself with my palms flat against the wall before the front of my body collides with it. He's on me a moment later, his naked torso pressing against my back, keeping me trapped, helpless, at his mercy. He grips my wrists, pulls them up, and transfers them to a single hand where he keeps them locked against the wall, his skin a few shades darker than mine in contrast. He's taller, if somewhat less muscular, and his hard cock rubs over the upper curve of my ass. His lips skim over my shoulder, then there's teeth; a small bite only, but enough to make me hold my breath.

His free hand moves between my body and the wall, sure fingers finding my breast, digging in, claiming, taking. I go still when he finds my nipple and tweaks it, hard. Sensation zings down my body, need, lust, with more than just a hint of pain, but that's what I crave, too. I shiver in response, making him chuckle, a deep, masculine sound that resonates through his chest.

"Spread your legs, slut," he whisper-grunts into my ear, making my breath hitch in my throat.

Then the hand drops from my breast and reaches between my legs, finding my labia swollen and wet. He doesn't dawdle, doesn't tease. Two fingers thrust inside me while his thumb starts rubbing my clit, fast.

I buck against him, feel his hard cock leave a wet trail of pre-cum over my lower back. The hand that holds my wrists lets go, but I keep them crossed. Instead, he threads his fingers through my hair and pulls my head back and to the side, forcing me to look into his face. Dark brown eyes stare unblinkingly into mine. I bite my lip to hold in a moan, but then a third finger joins the other two, and I lose that battle. The corner of his mouth quirks up.

"Ask me."

My eyes want to roll back into my head from the wonderful sensations he creates, but I force myself not to bow down—yet. So I stare back at him, half in challenge, half in silent plea to just get on with it. But, no, that's not how he does things.

"Ask, or I'm going to leave you hanging high and dry."

Not so very dry by now, but I hastily chased that thought away.

I know it's a losing battle that I'm fighting, but fighting is part of the fun, and losing never felt so good.

"Simon, please."

"Please what?"

Swallowing thickly, I resist, but then he bucks his hips, making his cock slip between my ass cheeks, and my resistance crumbles.

"Fuck me!"

His grin widens, but it's that hungry kind of grin that could never irk me in any way and feeds right into my frenzy.

"That wasn't so hard now, was it? And because you're a good little slut, I'm going to fuck you, hard and fast, like you've never been fucked."

Does anyone say shit like that outside of porn? I really didn't know, but the fact that I questioned it now annoyed the hell out of me. I was close, so fucking close, right at that point where I could already feel my vaginal walls clench, the absence of fingers or cock still there, but dwindling to the point where it didn't matter anymore. Just a few more seconds, just—

Beeeeeep!

"Fuck!"

Another orgasm slipped away, close enough that I could already taste it on my tongue—ignoring the fact that I had no fucking clue how a climax should be quantifiable via taste buds, but I kind of liked the idea. I was, once again, thwarted by the job that I loved, but was also sure would be the end of my sanity sooner or later.

Of course, I could have taken those extra twenty seconds to finish myself off, but already that sense of duty that startled my brain awake at random moments of the night—way too many nights—pushed through the haze of lust and got me scrambling for the toilet paper. I tried to tell myself that it was a small triumph for my physiology that this time I'd at least made it to the point where natural lubrication kicked in, but that felt like a very stale victory.

Thirty seconds later I stormed out of the bathroom, my hands still wet from the cursory attempt to get the scent of my own juices off them, if not properly clean. If they beeped me at four in the afternoon, that meant they needed me down in the emergency room, and I wouldn't get into direct contact with the patient before I had scrubbed in, anyway.

Ignoring the elevators, I hurtled down the two floors through the adjacent stairwell, which spilled me out into the chaos of the ER just in time to see two new patients being wheeled into ORs three and five. Eliza, one of my fellow residents, was straddling one of them, performing CPR on the spot. Shit. She'd beaten me down here. Then I saw a nurse fly after them with no less than three blood bags in her hands, and I allowed myself a moment to relax. She might have been first, but it didn't look like she'd get much time logged on that one.

My bet was that they'd need me in the other operating room.

"Slater, you're late. What do you lazy bitches do on your shifts that you need almost two minutes to get down here? You don't even smoke! You're with me."

I quickly fell in behind the blonde fury marching after the trail of EMTs, nurses, and ER doctors. Some people had problems with Zoe Tyne's tone, but she was the best trauma surgeon I'd ever met. I would still have admired her if she'd actually treated me like a piece of shit, rather than just talked trash occasionally. It had taken me the better part of the first two years of my residency for her to even notice me; I was not going to fold now because the woman had a mouth like a sailor.

"Scrub in," she told me needlessly as she swept into the prep room, sending the nurses on standby scurrying.

"What's the situation?" I asked, reaching for the soap to start the thorough cleaning ritual no surgeon worth their salt would ever skimp on.

"How should I know? You want soft, classical music with your well-plotted, finely choreographed, chicken-shit surgeries, you can go right back to where you hid from me the entire day. Here we are in the trenches, and in the fucking trenches you need to actually look at a patient to know what the fuck is going on. If that's too insecure for you, Missy, run now, because I don't need a wimpy dancer; I need a soldier."

"Yes, ma'am," I snarked back, hiding a smile. If anyone but the nurses heard us talk like that, the HR department would chew out our asses—again—but I couldn't help the excitement spreading like a physical wave through me. No one talked shit like that in front of a patient, but taking that extra moment to clear my head usually did wonders for my alertness afterward.

The nurse was ready to help me into the gown, then tied it behind my back while I waited with my raised hands, both eager to get going and wondering how stupid I must look. No need to wonder, really. I just had to glance to the side where my mentor was suffering through the very same last step. She caught my gaze and gave me a curt nod, and then we were off into the thick of the fray.

"Status?" she barked at no one in particular, but then protocol was a useless thing when you were out to save lives.

"Construction worker, thirty-five, fell off a scaffold and impaled himself on a bar. Went clean through. He lost consciousness four minutes ago, BP dropping."

The nurse continued rattling off numbers that I filed away while I got a quick first assessment of the patient. The bar that had pierced his lower abdomen was still inside the wound, practically tamponing it, else the poor bastard wouldn't be alive anymore. If he was lucky enough that it missed any major organs, then his chances were good. If not, Zoe and I would have a hell of a lot of chasing after the next spurting artery to do to keep him alive.

As they say, there was only one way to find out.

Five hours later, I found myself staring bleary-eyed at my phone.

The patient had made it, but wasn't in the clear yet. The bar had punctured his liver and spleen, cracked two vertebrae, and done yet-to-be-determined damage to his spinal cord. He was scheduled for surgery at 5:00 a.m., but I wouldn't be a part of that because Josh was banging the head of Neurosurgery, and she'd penciled him in for assistance before I could have a chance to point out that he was my patient. That grated, but only so much. Getting a chance to sleep instead sounded good after the hell of a week I had on my back already. Technically speaking, I should have left the hospital late Thursday night when I went over the official eighty hours medical staff were allowed to work per week, but Zoe had managed to tweak things to get me on the day shift for Friday. I'd switch to night float tomorrow evening, anyway, and what was left of my circadian rhythm would send me to my knees.

The phone. Right.

Not one, not two, but five text messages and two missed calls were waiting for me. The first was a curt and perfectly spelled reminder of the event I had stupidly agreed to attend tonight. I was sure a part of Simon would die if he ever used an acronym. The other texts were a series of atrocities that likely only a sixteen-year-old could have deciphered, the last consisting of abbreviations only. It was obvious that Jack was messing with me there, but—likely as he'd intended—the last text made me smile. There couldn't be any acronym for "talk to you later" that looked like a dick. At least I thought that was what it should spell, but the meaning wasn't lost on me, either.

Both calls were from Jack, one dated about an hour after the first text, the other I'd missed by only ten minutes.

I considered just turning off my phone and going home straight away, but as exhausted as I was, I doubted that I would be able to sleep. Performing CPR with your hands thrust into an open ribcage for thirteen minutes straight could do that to you. I was way too wound up now, and with twenty hours to go until I had to clock in at the hospital again, I could even allow myself to sneak a shot or two. Besides, my work schedule had forced me to cancel on the guys three times in a row, and I didn't put it past Jack to bring the party to me if I tried to skip a fourth time now.

I wondered for a moment if that would really be the worst thing that could happen to me, but then shoved my silly daydreams away.

It was bad enough that my brain was so starved of actual social interaction—and sex—that the only thing I could come up with for my wank fantasies were my best friend and his roommate, but I couldn't allow myself to let that idiocy seep into my actual conscience. No, as much as the lizard part of my brain might lust after the guys, they had a strictly defined space in my life, and that was for relaxing and booze. Quite frankly, if I couldn't have sex, that still sounded like a tantalizingly good offer.

-2-

I got there just before ten. Didn't people say it was fashionable to be a little late—two hours—and that no real party started before midnight?

I idly wondered who these people were, and if they would still be alive by the time they hit thirty. Watching a gaggle of geese sashay over to the door now, all dolled up, squashed-together and pushed-up cleavage prominently on display, I couldn't help but feel a little old. None of them could have been much past twenty, twenty-two at the most. Were they even allowed to stay out after dark?

They swarmed all over whoever opened the door, and I hastened my step to slip inside before it could close again. By then, the trio of girls was busy verbally—and maybe even physically, in one case—assaulting the host, who looked very pleased with the attention. Until his eyes fell on me, and that lazy grin he'd donned for the girls morphed into a real one.

"Erin!" Jack shouted, drawing out my name as if my mother had given birth to an "Irene" instead. The bimbos looked less than pleased that the apparent object of their adoration was not mutually interested, but instead focused on what was likely a hobo hag to them. That was not the only reason why it was so easy to smile when Jack enveloped me into a bear hug that left my feet dangling off the floor for a few seconds. "Glad you could make it," he added once he let go and stepped away, still grinning like a little boy. If said little boy had had a penchant for all things fitness and spent enough time out in the fresh air to make that tan and beach-blond highlights the real deal, that is. I didn't know many software developers, to be honest, but Jack definitely didn't rock that typical geek image.

"With enticing messages like that, how could I resist?"

Now his grin turned stupid, and I already knew what was coming next.

"Shit, if I'd known that it only takes me texting you a dick for you to show up, I would have done that weeks ago!"

One of the bimbos gasped. Another gave me the stink eye. That was too hilarious to resist. Reaching for my pocket, I made as if to get out my phone.

"Wanna see? But, why bother—I'm sure it's nothing you haven't seen plenty of times before."

How they managed those almost identical sneers I couldn't say, but it was kind of fascinating to observe.

"Someone's in a good mood tonight," Jack murmured under his breath, and when I gave him a sharp look, I got a bright smile for my trouble. "Yup, you definitely need to get laid," he told me succinctly. Oh, finally something we could agree on, but sober I would never admit that. "You know where the booze is. I'll catch up with you later," Jack promised, then off he went to appease the ladies. It wouldn't come as much of a surprise if one—or all—of them would stay the night. And that was just one more reason why I really had to get those stupid ideas out of my head.

At any other place, such a brief welcome might have rubbed me the wrong way, but Jack was right. I knew where the booze was—also the shower, coffee machine, fire extinguisher, and even the spare toilet paper. Except for my own apartment and the hospital, this house was the closest to home that anywhere had felt to me in ages, and, if I was honest, it came a long shot before the other two options.

Swinging by the kitchen, as usual crowded for no other reason than people finding kitchens insanely fascinating, I grabbed a beer and moseyed into the living room part of the shared open space. Not exactly a regular at these shindigs, I still knew a couple of people, and recognized a few more that I'd never bothered to get the names of. Sadly, the wispy blonde I was looking for wasn't around, but then I could socialize like a beast without playing ugly stepsister to Kara's superficial gorgeousness. It still made me wonder where she was—she usually didn't miss these parties, but there were firsts for everything.

Close to the makeshift bar that now also had to make do as a buffet table, I found the other regular inhabitant of these not-so-sacred halls. Unlike Jack, Simon didn't notice me until I'd spent a full five minutes hovering near his right elbow, and even then he just graced me with a smile and offered no other greeting. I knew that wouldn't change until his current conversation partner beat it, which didn't seem likely to happen in the next, say, century, judging from the look of adoration on his face. Typical fan boy, likely an aspiring writer himself.

Most people would have found Simon's attitude rude, but I'd long since become so used to his ways that I didn't even notice. Maybe he simply didn't affect me like that, or perhaps it stemmed from the fact that I'd known him before he'd turned into the man he was now. Simon had always been different, but at eighteen, awkwardness had still surpassed arrogance. Now, there wasn't any of that left in him, of course, and after I'd listened in on their conversation for a while, I decided that befriending the half-empty bottle of tequila held more merit. I couldn't even remember the last time I'd had anything stronger than coffee; it was about time that I changed that.

An undefined while and two glasses of tequila later, I found myself smiling at a guy who I vaguely remembered from somewhere. He didn't look like any of Simon's typical crowd—no pretentious tweed jackets in sight, nor a starved artist look going on—and when he introduced himself as Barry, I tagged him as one of Jack's coworkers.

"You're Erin, right?"

"Uh-huh," I replied at my most eloquent, and nursed my tequila for all the moral support it was worth.

Don't get me wrong—I can be civil, but Barry wasn't really pushing any of my buttons. He wasn't even that bad looking, more like the better half of average, but he was exuding blandness like a good cheese aroma. Maybe it was his haircut, maybe it was the funny slogan on his T-shirt—which should probably have been a dead giveaway regarding his affiliation, unless it was a Fight Club quote I had missed that obviously put him in the Jack corner of the world—but something about him made me want to smile politely and talk animatedly to a potted plant instead.

"Jack talks a lot about you."

Clearly, the message I'd tried to send had not landed with the receiver. Or he was just desperate. That made two of us, but if Barry was the catch of the night, I could easily go celibate for another couple of, oh, years.

"He does?"

"Only good things," Barry was quick to assure me, which told me two things. First, he really was trying to pick me up, and second, he was a hell of a bad liar.

"Is that so? Like what?"

Not happy that this conversation was taking a turn toward interrogation territory, Barry gave an uncomfortable shrug.

"You've known each other for ages, right?"

"About."

I stayed with the most useless affirmative answer I could think of. Taking another sip, I decided that this was fun after all. Not the kind of fun Barry was after, but it beat waiting for either of the guys to have time for me, or wondering just what made normally sensible guys like Jack lust after bimbos like those blondes. The one who'd given me the stink eye was right now glancing over to me and looked way too satisfied about who I was trying to avoid having to talk to. Or maybe that was her signature expression when she wasn't trying to get into some guy's pants. Maybe it was a neural condition. Or psychological. Either way, out of my field of expertise.

Belatedly I realized that Barry had asked me something that I'd droned out thanks to the glory of a momentary bitch-staring contest.

"Sorry, what did you say?"

"I asked what you do for a living?"

And here, ladies and gents, was my chance to either make or break my evening entertainment. If Jack had really told him anything about me that went beyond stupid anecdotes, it probably was a bad idea to lie, but then most guys didn't react favorably to the truth. Something about manic work obsession always threw them off. Why I even considered those consequences, I didn't know, because I still wasn't exactly warming up to the idea of mashing privates with Barry—but then again, I could do way worse. He had approached me, and my baseline hostility hadn't chased him away, either, so maybe...

But no. I didn't exactly consider myself to be a truly honest person, but I was proud of my achievements, and it wasn't like I could shine with anything other than my work.

"I work at a hospital."

No idea why I was so vague, but the words were out before I could take them back. Another sip of tequila helped chase them down. Barry's eyes hung on my lips just long enough to make me grin, not because I wanted to entice him, but simply because it wasn't my first glass, and this was comically hilarious.

"So you're a nurse?"

He ventured a guess that both widened my grin and utterly destroyed any chance of him tapping my ass tonight. Not that there was anything wrong with being a nurse—I wouldn't have a job if not for the army of nurses who kept the hospital running, and like every sane person I tread carefully around Nurse Dana if I couldn't altogether avoid her, but it was kind of insulting to aim for the lower income jobs first. Sure, there was the possibility that he meant it as a compliment, as in pretty girl in a skanky nurse's outfit, but that was one way of thinking my brain simply wasn't wired for.

"Surgeon, or surgeon-to-be, if I survive the remaining months of my residency and pass the board certification exam. If you ever chop off a finger or split open your skull, I'm your girl!"

That was definitely the tequila talking, and I took another drink to hide the wince at the last part. Nothing of mine would ever be Barry's, but it had sounded like a nice way to end the sentence. And that was just one reason why I should have laid off the booze after that first glass of tequila.

"Oh. Well, that's good to know," Barry enthused, not very enthusiastically. I rewarded that with a bland smile that grew exponentially when Jack made a surprise appearance. He eyed my glass critically, then looked from me to Barry and back. The way he clapped Barry on the shoulder was more intimidating than jovial, a sentiment Barry seemed to pick up on immediately from the way he stiffened.

"Barry, my man, you should go harass someone else."

"Hey, I'm not harassing her!" he protested, then shot me a glance that made me wonder exactly what Jack had told him about me. "Am I harassing you?"

The jury was still out on that, but I definitely didn't like the asshole move Jack was pulling just then.

"Of course not. We were having a very pleasant conversation before Jack came barging in."

I might have sounded more sincere if I could have wiped that silly grin off my face, but there was booze! And Jack! And a way out of this fucking stupid conversation!

"I sincerely doubt it," Jack muttered, just low enough that I could have pretended not to have caught that, but of course I didn't.

"What's that supposed to mean?" I complained, then hated myself for playing right into Jack's hand, judging from his snort. "I really don't need you to come riding in on that shiny steed of yours and rescue me like a damsel in need of, well, rescue."

Now Barry started looking really uncomfortable, but that might have been due to the fact that Jack still hadn't let go of him.

"Rescue you? On the contrary. I'm here to save Barry the trouble of getting his ass handed to him." Looking from my face to my glass, Jack raised one eyebrow, a feat I'd always envied him for. "Exactly how many beaker-sized portions of tequila have you chugged down already?"

"That's my third. I think. And it's a normal long-drink glass, not a beaker. Even if it's not rum, I still only get two fingers each time."

"Yeah, I know your two fingers measuring thing," Jack offered, spreading his right forefinger and middle finger as far as they went, the gesture distinctly obscene—but then that might have been just me again.

"It's quality tequila. What can I say?" I shrugged off his criticism, if it even was that. Unless I barfed in his sock drawer again, Jack was usually cool about me drinking a little more than I should. It happened maybe once a year, nowadays usually not even that often. I had a penchant for hangovers and not enough time in my schedule to suffer them in style.

"Anyway. I'm sure Barry is very pleased to have met you, Erin, but he just realized that it's time for him to go fetch something from the kitchen."

"Fetch what?" Barry asked, making both Jack and me stare awkwardly at the floor for a second. Some people just made it too easy.

"Your sense of self-preservation," Jack replied, then turned them both around and started marching Barry in the indicated direction. "If that's her third glass, you only have one more stupid answer left before she goes for your jugular, and I think you just used that up. You can thank me later."

And, just like that, my dear friend deprived me of my only chance to get some tonight. That rankled. Not because Barry would have been such a catch—and it had been a very slim chance to begin with—but the fact that Jack had the audacity to interfere got my temper rearing its ugly head. Like anyone needed protecting from me. Seriously? The gall!

"I'm sure that whatever this most offensive glass has done to you, it does not deserve that gorgonesque glower, even if by now you've scared it enough and I'm sure it won't become a repeat offender."

Pursing my lips to hide a smile, I turned around to fully face Simon. He was a decidedly pleasant change to look at compared to the blandness that was Barry. And better yet, he came bearing gifts!

I held out my glass, which he dutifully sloshed tequila into, but I refrained from doing that spread two fingers gesture Jack had just made fun of. A hint of a frown appeared on Simon's forehead, but he must have figured it was wiser not to point out my uncustomary meekness.

Where Jack was all California sunny boy, Simon rocked that tall, dark, and handsome cliché, mostly thanks to his mother, who could give Sofia Vergara a run for her money on her good days. Over the years, I had seen many a woman succumb to that charm—until he opened his mouth. The only thing about him that surpassed his intelligence was his arrogance and lack of a filter, both attributes I valued highly but that most people couldn't stomach. Jack was pretty much immune to it, and Kara had her own thing going on that made Simon appear civil, but off the top of my head I couldn't think of anyone else who wasn't hesitant about approaching him again after a lengthy discussion. Except maybe for the avid readers of his Friday column, but I still wasn't sure if those didn't already qualify as a cult.

"So are you going to answer my question, or do I have to spend the night tossing and turning, anguished by the lack of knowledge?"

I had to work hard to keep a straight face and not let my brain spew out some alternate options of how to spend that time better—like, with me, against a wall—and once again, a sip of tequila gave me the time to clear my head.

"Jack is being a protective asshole again. The glass is innocent. And I'm not sure if 'gorgonesque' is a word."

Simon deflected that with a smile that should have been easy but was everything but.

"And there it is again, that look on your face. Even if it wasn't a word before, if I send a picture of you looking at me like that for an example, I'm sure it will be officiated."

"Oh, you say the sweetest things!"

"And you always deserve them."

It was moments like these where I was ready to dispute my common sense—or obvious lack thereof—but I couldn't help breaking out into a wide grin at his retort.

"Maybe I do, but that I admitted it has to stay between you and me. Jack can never know a thing."

"My lips are sealed," Simon was quick to offer, a wry grin twisting his mouth as he made a zipping gesture. My eyes probably lingered a moment too long there, but I figured that he'd easily attribute that to the booze. And if not, Simon was the kind of guy who'd come up with a really obscure reason instead of the obvious truth. Calling him a little out of this world was maybe unfair, but his mind did work in mysterious ways sometimes.

"So what did Jack do this time? Not that he needs to do much to get you throwing hissy fits left and right."

"Those are not hissy fits, those are justified expressions of anger. Whatever. He was just Jack being Jack. The usual."

"Come on, give me the details. You know you want to."

And one day in the sadly very near future, a sentence like this would be my undoing. I knew it. It was inevitable!

Licking my lips, I tried to clear my head, but now all that seeking wisdom at the bottom of my glass was turning the tables on me.

"Actually, I'm not a hundred percent sure what happened. It kind of looked like a rescue attempt, because, you know me—I eat guys like Barry for breakfast, but now that I think about it, I think he was cockblocking me."

Simon winced, and chances were that it had nothing to do with sympathy—a normal human reaction—but rather the fact that I dared to use colloquialisms and word repetitions.

"Well, it's been known to happen," he supplied wisely.

"What, me turning into a post-coital praying mantis?"

His smile turned a little dark, hinting at deeper amusement.

"I'm lacking hands-on data for that, but what I meant was that on more than one occasion, I've observed Jack running some guy off because he himself was more than just passingly interested in genital contact with the involved female."

Which brought me about a mile closer to that very special breaking point.

Thankfully, my level of inebriation made me laugh shrilly instead of showing any other reaction, and gave me a very good excuse for the color surging into my cheeks.

"You can't just say shit like that to me!" I complained, or tried to, a few of the words getting mangled in the effort. Simon still understood what I was trying to say, once again proving that he was only dense when it concerned people he really didn't like.

"Why, am I using words that are too big for you again?"

"Yes, that too!" I tried to do damage control, failing horribly, but it didn't really matter. "But, seriously, 'genital contact'? Can't you just use slurs and expletives like everyone else?"

To myself, I could easily admit that I had ulterior motives for provoking him, and judging from the way he looked at me, he knew that. Shit.

"Whatever do you mean by that? Wasn't it you who once held a fifteen-minute lecture on how to perform cunnilingus in proper anatomical terms because Jack used the word 'shlong' ten times in a sentence? I'd even go so far and bet that it was after you killed the first half of the bottle of tequila that you're now polishing off at an astonishing rate."

Ah, fond memories, and the perfect excuse to bring our derailed conversation back on track.

"You mean I have my very own special bottle of tequila? Aw!"

I made a grab for it, even though my glass was still half full and I had no intention of letting myself slide any further into casual alcoholism, but Simon easily plucked it out of my grasping hands and held it out of reach. That incidentally brought us close enough that when he replied, I was the only one who heard.

"Okay. Jack has a habit of scaring off guys when he really wants to fuck the girl they're trying to chat up. Happy now?"

And that, ladies and gentlemen, was an observation I didn't have an answer to—a first, as Simon probably would have pointed out if he hadn't been so busy staring straight into my eyes, unblinking. From way too close, with my hand still on his shoulder as I tried to gain leverage to reach for the damn bottle.

The moment passed, or so it did for Simon, who let that intense look on his face fade into a pleasant smile after he put the bottle back onto the bar beside him. My mind was still stuck, and I had the sinking feeling that it would remain so for the time being.

Looking out over the crowd milling around, Simon's attention latched on to something behind my back, and he wasn't one bit apologetic when he excused himself.

"There's someone I need to talk to. You're staying a while longer, right?" He waited for my confounded nod, then leaned close enough that when he went on, his breath fanned across my cheek. "And, just so you know, he's not the only one."

Then he left me standing there, staring into space with my glass of tequila, wondering what I could possibly have eaten that would give me hallucinations like that. And yes, I was definitely staying a little longer.

-3-

The party wound down around one in the morning, way too soon for some of the hipsters, but to me it felt like a small eternity. Maybe because I'd spent the hours in between trying my hardest to sober up, a mission that failed horribly and just left me feeling slightly nauseated from the greasy pizza and gallons of water I'd decimated. Maybe it was because I'd done a good job avoiding both Jack and Simon, which left me without anyone interesting to talk to. That gave me time aplenty to mull over what Simon had said—and clearly hadn't—leaving me horny, confused, but also convinced that this was all going to turn out to be a huge misunderstanding.

Normally I could take being ridiculed by the guys, or mostly Jack, but this cut a little too close to home for my comfort.

Consequently, I felt ready for war by the time the last guests were more or less evicted and the guys returned to where I had taken up a defensive position in the middle of the couch.

My wank fantasies were one thing, but if Simon had actually meant what I thought he had, we were heading into unfamiliar, possibly dangerous territory. The three of us—four, if I included Kara—had been good friends for a long time, and as much as my sex-starved body was clamoring for release, I couldn't help but feel a certain level of trepidation rise inside of me. With all the stupid things I'd done in my life, I'd always known that none of them could in any way negatively influence our friendship. Would adding sex to the equation change things now?

It was probably unfair, but my worries regarding Simon were much less pronounced than those concerning Jack. I'd been friends with Simon for over a decade now, and while both of us had changed since starting college, our friendship had always been on a mostly mature level.

Thinking back, it was only too easy to still remember the slightly awkward if terribly blunt boy he'd been when he got assigned as Jack's new roommate mid-term of our first semester in college. Of course, back then his accent and the words he used had made him seem like an adult to me, so much so that I couldn't help but develop somewhat of a crush on him. In all fairness, it had always been more of an intellectual attraction than me lusting for the man-child he'd actually been. The feeling had certainly not been mutual, and it had taken a while for him to warm up to me, but once we got over our rocky start, things had been great. Not behaving like any of the scores of girls who kept flirting with Jack had likely helped a lot.

I'd never allowed myself to develop that tiny crush I'd had on Simon into more, although I doubt I would have rejected his advances had there been any in the past. Even when he'd fleshed out and physically became the man he was now, things hadn't really changed. Come to think of it, being Jack's roommate for forever had automatically enveloped him in the pseudo platonic bubble that had surrounded Jack and me since we'd become aware of the fact that, technically, we could have been doing other things together than playing tag and ratting each other out to our parents. Things might have gotten awkward quickly if we'd started something that later went up in flames, so avoiding that issue altogether had always been my prerogative. Simon was my friend, usually hilarious to be around, and while I might on some level still lust after him, I'd never seriously considered him a viable option to physically get off with.

Jack was an entirely different matter.

Maybe it was because I still vividly remembered him as the grinning boy from next door, but if I was honest, my mind automatically blocked any serious sexual thoughts about Jack, even though I was aware that he was a very sexual being. Jack made sure that no one who spent more than a day or two in his vicinity was left unaware of that, and while I liked to pretend to be immune to his charm, things had been a lot more complicated for longer than I liked to admit. While I didn't see it as my right to judge his preferences or actions, I seldom approved of them, and it was kind of hard not to let that affect me more often than not. Someone who hadn't known us for a long time might wonder about the dynamics between us, and thinking about it now made it hard for me to put how I felt about Jack into words.

All his faults aside, he had been there for me when my mom died. He was the only one who joined me in my mission to make life a living hell for my stepmom when my father had finally moved on and fallen in love with another woman. Heck, I even still had the letter he'd written where he'd sworn to avenge my death if she did turn out to be the proverbial evil stepmother. He'd been there to comfort me when I felt pretty much exiled from home when my little sister had been born, and he was likely the only one in the world who knew that, all animosities aside, I loved Jenny more than anything, even if we only shared half our DNA and I had a good sixteen years on her.

He'd always had my back, and it was impossible not to instantly forgive him minor nuisances like his bad taste in tacky girls. Jack was Jack, and on more levels than one I was happy that he wasn't really a commitment kind of guy, because this way there was no one else around who could lay claim to "my" Jack.

Growing up together, both with only one parent left—me due to my mom's death, his father gone after the divorce—in a place and time where most families were still of the nuclear kind and anything else was considered abnormal had created a bond between us that so far no one had ever managed to cut, or even strain.

It had always been like that, and I guess I'd expected things to go on like this forever, stupid as that might sound. Thinking back over the past ten years, there had been a few instances that had made me think, a few remarks exchanged that could have been loaded rather than innocent, but I'd never let myself read too much into them.

Until now.

And as I was already trying to have some kind of honest, if hopefully silent, conversation with myself, I had to admit that, all reasons for seeing the guys as just friends aside, I couldn't think of anyone I knew I'd rather get intimate with than Jack and Simon.

The fact that Jack looked relieved that the bimbos were gone was telling, or so I tried to convince myself, then tried even harder to banish that newfound conviction from my mind. So what? He'd kicked out three very blonde, very perky potential bed bunnies—that didn't have to mean anything. Yet more than five minutes had passed since the last feminine trill had been cut off by the closing door, giving the guys plenty of time to talk between them, if they hadn't done so beforehand. It certainly didn't take that long to load the dishwasher.

Jack paused on the invisible threshold between kitchen and living room, then came over to sag down onto the couch to my left, his customary place when I was, as usual, hogging the corner section. He seemed slightly strung out, but that could have been entirely my misconception. He offered me the fresh bottle of beer in his hand, then chugged down half of it when I declined. Simon's eyes seemed to linger on me a little longer than usual as he sat down on the remaining part of the couch to my right, but then I had to admit that I usually didn't pay much attention to how much he looked at me in general.

I was obviously overanalyzing everything, and that was very soon going to drive me insane! And like that, potentially being laughed at for my silly ideas wasn't that bad an outcome anymore.

"So," Jack started, drawing the word out overly long while his eyes flitted from me to Simon and back again. "Exactly why are you two acting like someone put itching powder into your unmentionables?"

I hadn't even noticed that I'd started fidgeting and promptly forced my fingers to stop. Simon gave Jack a deadpan stare in return that communicated plainly that he didn't think he had been acting differently, but that made me feel a little better about my paranoia.

"No particular reason," I tried to deflect, but it came out too fast.

Jack's brows drew together, but when I wasn't volunteering any more information, he turned to Simon.

"What the fuck did you say to her?"

I hadn't thought Simon capable of a comical, "who, me?" face, but he pulled it off rather nicely. When both of us kept staring at him, he dropped it, donning a wry smile instead.

"Erin was a little angry when you ran off that guy Barry."

"That's it?" Jack asked, then took a swig of beer, likely to hide a grin that might have incurred my wrath under different circumstances. What could I say? It was known to happen. Often.

"Pretty much," Simon replied, and shrugged. "I might have also explained that you likely did it because you want to bone her, and I thought I should include that I'm not opposed to having sex with her, either, mostly for full disclosure's sake."

How he managed to keep a straight face saying that, I had no idea, but Jack did a spit-take with his beer that ended in an impressive coughing fit.

"Dude, you have to warn me when you talk shit like that!" he got out once his airways had cleared up again.

I couldn't help but laugh at him, but the way he looked at me then, partly cautious, partly relieved, shut me up quickly.

"Why? It's nothing that we haven't talked about before," Simon pointed out.

Now that caught my attention, and the somewhat guilty look on Jack's face was easier to latch on to than Simon's smugness.

"Hey, wait... what business do you two idiots have talking about screwing me?"

The guys shared one of those typically male looks that on a good day would have driven me insane, and now was downright infuriating.

"Do I really have to spell that out?" Simon asked, the way he focused on me somewhat unnerving.

My first impulse was to fly into a rage, but I cut down on it. It was the easy way out to accuse them of making fun of me, then storm off before anyone got a chance to get another word in edgewise, but that wasn't really my thing. Besides, if he was serious, that wasn't a door I wanted to slam shut quite yet, at least not before I managed to weasel a few more details out of them.

"I think she's going to hit you if you don't." Jack interrupted our staring match, now fully recovered from his untimely beer inhalation.

"Could be worse," Simon replied, and I somehow got the sense that he said a lot more with it than I could glean from his words. A sidelong glance at Jack revealed that indeed, there was some inside joking going on, and I really didn't like being kept in the dark.

"What's that supposed to mean?"

Settling more firmly back into the sofa cushions, I crossed my arms over my chest, not giving a shit whether that made me look defensive or not.

"Rough sex can be fun. Foreplay, too," Simon informed me succinctly, making Jack cough again.

I really didn't know what to make of Simon's statement, and it was so much easier to focus on Jack's inability to breathe like a normal human being right now.

"You know, you maybe should get that checked if you repeatedly choke on something."

"You're looking at the wrong guy here," he got out between one fit and the next, and ended up with what I thought was laughter now. Simon and I shared a look, but again I got the sense that I only got half of what that might have meant.

"You still haven't answered my question," I huffed once Jack had quieted down.

Simon chose to answer me.

"Which one—why we talk about having sex with you, or why we want to have sex with you?"

I could feel color creep into my face, and suddenly wished for my still-unfinished glass of tequila.

"Maybe you could start with why you always say 'we.'"

His shrug was nothing if not nonchalant.

"We, because obviously we are both interested in having sex with you, and because it wouldn't be our first threesome, if you were up for that."

Who needs sanity, anyway? Completely overrated, if you asked me right then.

I couldn't help but stare at him for several seconds, although I tried to force my brain into jump-starting again, or at least to stop sinking deeper into wank fantasy territory. Simon held my gaze calmly, although his smile got a little more conceited with every moment that passed.

"So that's a thing you do," I hedged, kind of proud that my voice remained somewhat steady.

Now that smile dipped into darker registers that, incidentally, did terrible things to my clarity of thought.

"Among other things, yes."

I opened my mouth to inquire what that was supposed to mean, but because that question hadn't gotten me anywhere the last time I'd posed it, I swallowed it instead. It took a lot more conviction than it should have to tear my eyes from Simon's and look over to Jack. In the meantime, he'd won the battle against the elements and had almost finished his beer, looking very comfy and at home with his feet propped up on the couch table. When he saw me looking, he flashed me a typical Jack grin, bright and kind of leery.

"Don't even think about saying that's so much of a surprise."

"With you? No. You?" I turned back to Simon, a light frown creeping onto my forehead as I considered. "I honestly haven't given that much thought about who or what you do, but I consider myself open-minded enough to say with conviction that I don't give a fuck about it."

I knew that my words held a challenge as soon as Simon's smile widened into a grin, and I didn't need Jack's muttered "Oh, here we go," to realize that my view of one of my oldest friends would likely change any second now.

In typical Simon fashion, he was completely unperturbed by my claim, and there wasn't even a hint of anything but ease about him as he replied.

"I sometimes have sex with men, too, and not in a 'it's just a phase' fashion. I do consider myself bi. And what might concern you more, considering that Jack has so far been a firm believer in loving just the ladies, is that I'm into BDSM. Mostly the 'S' and 'M' parts of the acronym, but it's a wide playing field, and I've spent my time rolling around in the various corners. While I'm not opposed to switching things up sometimes, I'm most at home being on the controlling end of business, if you get what I mean."

"I think I do."

And I think my ovaries just exploded.

I had to admit, there was a flicker of unease that crept up my spine at listening to him explain, but it was entwined with a hefty dose of fascination. For one thing, as I'd said, it wasn't my business what he did in his free time, and I really couldn't care less when it didn't concern me, but considering that he'd only minutes before stressed again that his sex life might eventually, if I wanted to, bump uglies with my sex life, it was something I should maybe spend a little time considering. The problem was that right now my brain was in no condition to do any analytical thinking at all.

"Good," Simon replied, somewhat belatedly. My silence probably spoke volumes, but I honestly didn't know what to say, and it was incredibly hard to even want to look away from him right now.

"If you two don't need me anymore, I'll go catch some shut-eye," I heard Jack say from somewhere to my side, and the irritation his amused tone brought up in me finally broke the spell.

"What do you mean? I don't think this conversation is over yet," I pointed out, only to get another one of those infuriating grins from him.

"No? So you're just drooling all over him, now that you know he's a kinky bastard, on principle?"

"I'm not drooling!"

At least I hoped that I wasn't. Checking now was out of the question.

"So you say," Jack unhelpfully supplied but settled back into his seat.

"I'm not," I repeated, then groaned. "Drooling, I mean. I have a little more self-control than that." Which was a lie, but a white one.

"Yeah, I can see that," Jack continued, but reined himself in when Simon shot him a warning glance. Interesting.

"Okay, I admit, Simon might just have given me some extra material for my wank fantasies, but look at my life right now. I simply can't add anything that has even the potential to add stress or complication to it."

"And that's exactly why you need to get laid," Jack retorted. I was a little surprised that he didn't pick up on that tidbit that had slipped by my inner filter, but I was grateful for that.

"You think?"

"And he's not the only one who thinks so," Simon added, which earned him a sharp look from me. "What? It's true. You're completely overworked, and you just admitted that you're stressed out and don't appear to have any way of successfully relieving all that tension. Why does uncomplicated, no-strings-attached sex sound so bad to you?"

"It doesn't, or else I wouldn't be here anymore," I pointed out.

Simon looked over to Jack as if he were seeking confirmation, and when Jack shrugged, he turned back to me.

"Can I take the fact that you just kept Jack from running off as a sign that you are, indeed, up for a threesome with us?"

"Right now?" I meant that more as a joke, but particularly the lower half of my body was much in favor of the idea.

"Once you've sobered up and slept enough not to doze off in the middle," Simon proposed.

"I doubt that will happen," Jack offered cheekily, but shut up when Simon and I both glared at him.

"Sounds good," I agreed, my voice weirdly thick. On so many levels, I still hadn't quite caught up to the fact that this was really happening.

"When do you have to work tomorrow?" That I was working weekends seemed to be a given, but then that wasn't much of a surprise to me.

"Six in the evening. I should be in the hospital by five-thirty."

Simon gave a cut nod.

"Can you be over here by one? That should give all of us enough time to catch some sleep and eat breakfast."

I doubted that my night would be a restful one, but agreed.

At a pointed look from Simon, Jack got up, grinning like that cat who had just licked the cream. Or was about to. Fuck. If this was any indication of how my mind would handle things if this really was going down as my baser nature hoped, I was going to be in so much trouble.

"See you tomorrow at one, then, bright and horny."

I was sorely tempted to throw one of the couch pillows at him to wipe that grin off his face, but I restrained myself to a pressed smile.

"Good night, Jack."

Snorting, he turned around and slinked off in the direction of the back hallway. That left Simon and me alone, a weird kind of awkwardness coming up between us when neither of us said a word.

Getting up, I straightened my shirt, then did my best to stop my fingers from fidgeting again.

"Well, see you tomorrow then," I offered.

He nodded and followed me to the door, where he stopped me from running off by leaning against the door frame in a way that made it impossible for me to side-step him unless I wanted to walk right into him.

"About that," he started, then waited until I'd caught his gaze. "I understand what you mean that right now you don't need anything in your life that throws you off track, but it doesn't have to be like that. I know you think I'm some kind of egotistical, insensitive asshole sometimes, but I care about you, and I'd never do anything to hurt you in any way."

I considered that for a moment, both amused by his rather accurate self-assessment and by the literal meaning of his words.

"Doesn't that get kind of in the way of being a sadistic, egotistical asshole?"

His answering smile was a thing of true beauty, and not befitting the subject. I definitely dug the intense look in his eyes.

"I probably should have phrased that better, yeah," he amended, his smile splitting into a grin. "Then let me try this again. If you're into it, I have no qualms to spank and flog and cane that sass right out of you, but rest assured, I will take very good care of any physical discomfort I cause, and I will never hurt you emotionally in any way. Pain can be cathartic, particularly when everything else around is closing in on you. Even if your schedule is packed, it's easy to find an hour to chase the endorphin rush when it helps you cope for days afterward."

I could tell that he was speaking from personal experience, and that made it even more tempting.

"Just because something fascinates me doesn't mean that I'm into it."

Now condescension sneaked into his look, and we were back to familiar territory.

"I beg to differ. If it fascinates you, you should give it a try. The only uncertain variable is how much you're actually into it, not whether you're into it. Why not give it a try tomorrow? If I'm not terribly misjudging you, having sex with two guys at the same time is already a venture into new territory for you. Why not go the extra mile and add some spice to it?"

As if the fact that I was actually agreeing to this in the first place wasn't enough to send my mind reeling, but in the best of ways.

"Define spice?"

He shrugged, leaning closer, turning an already intimate conversation into a living wet dream.

"Just some of the standard kink fare. A little role play, a little spanking, a little restriction, some rough fucking. The usual."

"For you, maybe."

His smile was answer enough.

"What about Jack?" I pointed out.

"Jack's pretty much indifferent to most things as long as it involves sex. Don't worry—nothing I'd do to a newbie will squick him out."

Part of me wanted to balk at being referred to like that, but of course he was right. And, if I thought about it as objectively as I could—which wasn't my strong suit right then—it made sense to just shut up and take his offer. Knowing Simon, there would come a time for talking, but still not really sober, and quite worked up as I was, that wasn't right now.

"So just some entirely uncomplicated, no-strings-attached, slightly spiced-up sex, right? Count me in."

"Perfect," he replied, then stepped away after lingering just long enough that I started to wonder if he felt as reluctant about not getting right to it as I was.

"See you tomorrow at one."

"Exactly."

With that, he opened and held the door for me, but called after me before I'd made it down the few steps to the curb.

"Oh, and Erin? Don't be late. You don't want to start tomorrow off on a bad note."

For a warning, that sounded tantalizingly good, but I inclined my head dutifully.

"I'll be on time."

And that was that, as they say.

-4-

Less than eleven hours later, I found myself back on those very steps, just as excited but a lot hornier than before, and, if I was honest, a little intimidated, too. As much as I might have fantasized over the years, I couldn't imagine doing something like this with anyone I didn't trust explicitly, and the guys were right on top of that very short list. Part of me wanted to tell Simon right away that I had second thoughts and that maybe we should keep that extra spice out of what suddenly seemed like an already overwhelming situation, but my ego simply wouldn't let me. I'd always been a believer in jumping right into the deep end, and it seemed that my mostly non-existent sex life was no exception to that.

For the first time ever, I hesitated at the door. I couldn't count how many times I'd traversed this threshold—hundreds, maybe even thousands—and not always as clear-headed and sober as I was now. I'd slept surprisingly well last night, routine taking over, and consequently felt downright chipper today. Of course, that had nothing whatsoever to do with what I expected lurked beyond this door.

I was so full of shit today, it was bordering on ridiculous.

Taking a last deep breath, I squared my shoulders and reached for the door handle, but before my fingers could touch it, the door swung inward, revealing a deceptively nice smiling Simon. He looked almost exactly like yesterday, down to the mussed short hair, but his T-shirt today was black, while yesterday it had been navy—I thought. Quite frankly, I'd never given less shit about the color of clothing than right fucking now.

"See? I can be on time," I offered instead of a greeting. When I'd checked it moments ago, the display of my phone had read 12:56.

"Good for you," he replied, then stepped aside to let me in. I shucked the gym bag holding my change of clothing and emergency rations for my upcoming night shift by the cupboard and kicked my shoes off with deliberation. So what if my heart was suddenly galloping? That didn't mean I had to show just how nervous I really was.

That plan got immediately thwarted when strong, warm arms suddenly appeared around me, pulling me hard against Simon's chest, the shock making me elicit the most unbecoming squeal in my repertoire. It cut off when he clamped his hand over my mouth, his other arm tightening across my middle.

"It really is very considerate of you not to be late. I'm not sure you would have liked starting this off with punishment," he whispered into my right ear, making the fine hairs at the back of my neck stand on end. "I should maybe warn you that I really do take this seriously. It should not come as a surprise to you, seeing as you often point out that I never half-ass anything, but I thought I'd be nice and give you a fair warning."

He let that sink in before he went on.

"The rules are pretty simple. You have a safeword—'red.' You use it when something gets too much for you or when something unforeseeable happens, like cramps, some emotional turmoil, or shit like that. You should never hesitate to use your safeword, but I trust that you won't abuse it. When you use it, everything stops, and I'll make sure that whatever is wrong gets straightened out. Then we decide if we want to go on or call it a day, no hard feelings either way. I can't really do the fun stuff without knowing that you're giving me vital feedback if I need it, and it's a fail-safe for you to rest assured that, everything else aside, you're the one in control and can get yourself out of everything at a moment's notice. Nod if you understand."

My heart was hammering so hard in my chest that I was sure that he must have felt it, but I didn't hesitate a moment to agree.

"Good. For the duration of this scene, you will call me 'Sir,' and you will act respectful. I know that you're a spunky spitfire sometimes, which is a trait I love and respect, and if you feel confident that you can take the brunt of the consequences, please do go ahead and mouth off to me. For today, though, you might consider moderating yourself a little. Don't worry about being bored when I say that I will take it slow at first. As soon as I get the sense that you're on board with something, I'll push a little harder. Should there be a next time, we'll have plenty of time to discuss what to do for that then, but today it's all about you getting your feet wet, among other things."

Despite the tension—or maybe because of it—that really bad pun made me laugh, the sound muffled by his hand.

"Anything else?" Simon mused, the fingers of his free hand drumming an all-too-familiar rhythm on my left hip. "Ah, right. We use condoms for everything that goes beyond oral sex, and on the cupboard over there are our STD tests. I know you regularly get checked, so I'm trusting you. Mine is from three days ago, and Jack's from last week. He said he did have sex with one woman in between, but we both know her and know she's a responsible adult, so I feel comfortable with considering that as a go. If you object, now's the time." With that, he uncovered my mouth.

That definition meant that Jack's last had very likely been Kara. I didn't know how I felt about that, but it wasn't much of a surprise. Better than any of the bimbos from last night. I had thought about asking about test results, but then relied on Simon's general penchant for being a stickler for details. It was very reassuring that he had everything covered.

"No objections."

I wondered if I should have used that stupid appellation, but either he hadn't expected me to, or let it slide.

"Good. You have sixty seconds to undress. We'll be waiting for you in the living room."

He then let go of me, and without another look back walked deeper into the house.

For a moment, I was simply stunned. So, this was it, whatever 'it' was going to turn into. I was so excited that even standing still was a feat. The hint of trepidation from before was gone, but now there was a lump in my stomach that made me rue eating anything for breakfast.

Then Simon's last words finally sunk in, and I started to scramble out of my clothes. A minute could be over damn fast, and although I'd used the bathroom before leaving home, I felt the sudden if likely unnecessary need to urinate. Deciding that his warning was something I wanted to heed at least once, I forced myself to ignore my mind's antics and raced down the hallway and into the living room before I could have any second thoughts.

I'd never felt so damn naked in my entire life.

Simon and Jack were waiting for me, both wearing identical, closed off expressions, standing around at ease as if nothing particularly out of the ordinary was about to happen. For them it maybe wasn't, but my entire system was on high alert, and I had to close my hands into fists to keep them from shaking.

That's when I realized that I didn't really know what to do.

Being naked in front of two fully clothed men felt strange—exciting, yes, but still strange, which was something that I hadn't expected. Sure, they'd seen me in a bathing suit many times in the past, but somehow this made all the difference. I felt vulnerable and exposed, and the irrational need to try to cover at least parts of my body rose in the back of my mind. I forced myself to stand up straight and do no such nonsense, but swallowing was suddenly a monumental task.

And then they were just staring at me, taking all of me in, while my pulse raced and my chest kept heaving with every shallow, fast breath.

Nervously, I licked my lips, then let my eyes drop to somewhere between the couch and Simon's knees. I really didn't know how he expected me to behave—he'd left that out of his instructions completely, and holding his gaze was hard. Then I felt stupid about that because I really didn't want to appear like a demure, shy girl, and looked back up. They were still staring at me, but Jack was trying hard to hide a smile, which kind of helped ground me a little. Taking another, deeper breath, I forced myself to calm down, and this time when my eyes found Simon's, I didn't look away.

He took pity on me about ten endless seconds later, looking over to Jack while he jerked his chin in my direction.

"Hold her."

Then he walked up to me, just as Jack circled around to my back, and before I had a chance to react, Jack had wrapped his fingers around my upper arms and held them steady. Simon made a grab for my left wrist and buckled a thickly padded, black leather cuff around it. Swallowing turned just a little harder still when he did the same to my other wrist, and without needing any further direction, Jack then pulled my arms behind my body and snapped the cuffs together. That position forced my shoulders back and my tits to stand out. My breath caught in my throat, but I forced myself to let it out as evenly as possible.

Simon gave me the barest hint of a smile before his features evened out again, and he reached up to thread his fingers through my hair at the back of my head. I'd left it loose for once, maybe out of some silly notion of trying to appear sexy or something, but instantly rued that decision when he yanked hard on it, forcing my head to the side. I winced but otherwise didn't protest. My heart skipped a beat or two when he leaned in, almost close enough for my eyes to lose focus on his face.

"Are you going to be a good slut today?"

I'd kind of dreaded this part—fantasizing about name calling was one thing, but I normally didn't let anyone use any kind of derogatory term when talking to me. Often, even "girl" drew my ire. With Simon and Jack, my expectation had been different, more in the direction of uncontrollable laughter.

Right then, laughing was the farthest thing from my mind, and there wasn't even a hint of irritation in sight. In fact, him calling me a slut made me feel kind of sexually empowered, as if I'd suddenly morphed into a seductive vixen. If that worked, I might as well give the rest a shot, too.

"Yes, Sir," I tried to offer confidently, but it came out more like a shaky breath.

Simon pursed his lips as if he had to consider believing me.

"We'll see about that."

Without further warning, he slapped my left thigh hard enough to sting, then the other when all I did was give an undignified yip.

"Spread your legs and keep them open until you're told otherwise. Whenever you're lazing around idly, you're going to assume a position like this, knees apart, arms behind your back. Don't make me tell you a second time."

It irritated me a little that he seemed to expect me to guess ahead of his orders what to do, but when I widened my stance, he reached for my pussy, and any protest that had started to form dwindled rapidly. He didn't tease or linger, but brought two of his fingers right to my clit, then eased them downward between my labia and thrust them into me. I made a face at the rather obvious wet sound he caused, but he looked more pleased than smug. As quick as he'd started the maneuver, he withdrew his fingers again, idly rubbing them clean on my naked hip. Even with the contact gone I could still feel the aftershocks of it, and it made me so damn horny that I was almost afraid I'd come right there if he did it again.

He didn't, but instead turned around and walked over to the couch where several things lay on a blanket. I got distracted from trying to make them out when hot, hungry lips appeared on my shoulder and started kissing up a warm trail to my neck right below my ear. My eyes fluttered shut for a moment and I leaned back into Jack, my fingers incidentally touching down on his crotch.

Oh, someone was happy to be here, and that wasn't just me.

Jack chuckled softly, the proximity of his mouth to the sensitive spot on my neck making me shiver, but when I tried to withdraw my fingers, he bucked his hips forward to keep the contact up. Not that I could have done much to evade him, anyway, considering the cuffs and the way he was still holding me. Nor did I want to.

"You can touch me as much as you like. In fact, why don't you open that zipper and reach into my jeans while you're at it?"

I was a little surprised that he suggested rather than told me to, but I remembered Simon's comments about Jack's preferences all too well. For a moment I considered playing coy, but then his mouth went back to kissing and nibbling on my shoulder and neck, and any residual thoughts about propriety fled my mind.

The cuffs were comfortably restrictive but left my wrists enough room to rotate to facilitate the task, and once Jack felt that I was busy getting into his pants, he let go of my arms in favor of reaching around my body for my breasts. Hyper aware of everything as I already was, feeling his fingers stroke over my hard nipples before he closed them around my tits made me moan. Then the zipper gave and I felt warm, soft skin push against my hand, sending my pulse racing even more.

I would have been lying if I said that I didn't have a vague idea of what Jack was packing. Even in college we'd spent many summers camping, surfing, or going for a swim, and I'd never been a modest wallflower who turned around just because someone was changing out of their swimming trunks. Guessing was one thing, but having the hard evidence, pardon the pun, in my hand was quite another. Part of me wanted to savor that moment for whatever insane reason, but that was a part that was very easily shut up and forgotten. He gave me a delicious little growl as I wrapped my fingers around his cock and started stroking him, as much as my current position would let me.

Simon's return on mostly silent feet brought my attention back to him. He seemed faintly amused, but the look on his face turned more stern as he caught my gaze. From the edge of my vision, I could still see that he was carrying a medium-sized flogger in his left hand, the leather strands trailing down to his knee.

"Don't squeeze too hard. He won't like that," he advised.

Before I could make any sense of that, he brought his arm back, then sent the strands of the flogger flying for my leg. They hit me mid-thigh, not very hard, the contact more tickling than actually painful. Inadvertently, I shrank back even thought I tried not to, and my grip constricted, prompting Jack to give my breasts a rather harsh squeeze in between the mostly sensual massage they'd been receiving so far. When Simon hit my other thigh just a little harder, I managed to constrain any tensing to above my wrists.

The next time the flogger made contact with my body, it actually stung, the fourth time the sensation was mildly painful.

I tried to steel myself somehow for it, but my concentration was so frayed between the new sensation and everything Jack was doing to me right then that it was almost impossible. It didn't really matter, I found out with the next, now decidedly harder impact of the leather strands with my leg, because the pain didn't distract me from the need scorching through my body—no, it clearly added to it.

Simon kept going like that for about a minute, regularly looking at my face and judging my reaction between taking aim. I was sure that by the time he stopped, my thighs must have been red—they certainly felt warm with a light burning sensation radiating from them. I relaxed, feeling just a little proud of myself for not uttering a single sound.

I probably looked a little smug, too, because something changed in Simon's eyes, and before I could brace myself, he used his free hand to slap me firmly between my legs.

It was definitely discomfort rather than surprise that made me grunt, but before that had even properly registered, his fingers were back inside me, and not just probing like before. Unlike any other guy who'd ever touched me before, he seemed to know exactly in what direction to move and where to press, causing freakishly strong sensations that threatened to buckle my knees. Jack's hands moved back to my upper arms to support me, and while I immediately missed the contact, I couldn't quite bring myself to care when Simon's thumb found my clit.

"Holy fucking—" I started hissing between my teeth, but cut off when Simon dropped the flogger and wrenched my head back by my hair again. Leaning in, his mouth was tantalizingly close to mine—close enough to kiss—but the way he stared at me told me rather plainly that he had no intention of doing that.

"My, my, aren't you a horny little slut? If I'd thought I'd get you to almost come that quickly, I would have set this up differently."

His fingers didn't still then. No, they sped up, and all I was capable of was a terribly embarrassing sound between a moan and a gasp.

"Do you think I should let her come already?" he asked Jack conversationally, getting a low chuckle in return.

"I don't know. Do you think she deserves to come?"

For that he deserved a harder squeeze from my fingers, but that only made him laugh.

"No, I think she hasn't really worked at all for that privilege," Simon mused, then had the audacity to grin in my face. "But you should know that you only get to come when you beg me. Understand?"

Gritting my teeth, I made the stupid decision not to reply right away, and only got a moment to regret it. Instantly he withdrew his fingers, making me feel terribly empty, but before I could react, he slapped my pussy again. If it had stung before, now it hurt, the next, even harder slap making me cry out as I tried to wrestle myself free from Jack's grasp. Without me really noticing, he'd turned his supporting grip into something very much like a vise and had stepped back far enough to let his cock slip out of my hand.

Simon paused for a moment, and this time I wasn't dense enough to be stubborn.

"Yes, I understand, Sir!"

Part of me wanted to plead for him to stop, but I bit down hard on my tongue to keep myself from that. It was hard enough to manage to keep my thighs apart when all I wanted to do was clamp my legs together, but I didn't doubt that such a maneuver would come with an even stronger retaliation.

"Good," Simon said as if nothing whatsoever had happened, then let go of my hair so he could bend over and pick up the flogger again.

My breath was coming in harsh pants, and it took a few more seconds for the pain to subside, but that left me very conscious of the fact that I was still worked up as hell. How I could be so turned on by something like that was a detail I chose to ignore for now, but then it fell right in line with everything else.

"Turn her around."

At Simon's direction, Jack eased his grip on me long enough to let me flip around at his nudge, coming to face him now. He flashed me a smile as he wrapped his fingers around my arms again, then pulled me flush against his body so that my breasts were mashed against his chest. My chin almost collided with his collarbone before I steadied myself, and I quickly widened my stance when he whispered a soft, "Legs," into my ear.

Then the flogger bit into my left ass cheek, just as hard as Simon had hit my thigh before, making me buck into Jack before I could brace myself. Jack chuckled under his breath and pushed his hips forward, causing his cock to rub against my lower belly.

"That eager, are you, hm?" he remarked, and for a split second the usual impulse was there to bite his head off. Not even the flogger assaulting my other ass cheek helped.

Surprisingly, Jack nudging my face slightly with his nose before his warm lips pressed almost sweetly against mine did the trick.

The intimacy and sheer gentleness of his kiss astounded me, enough so that it took me a moment to react when his tongue moved against my lips, seeking entrance. The flogger hit me just hard enough to make me wince, thus opening my mouth, and Jack took that as a welcome invitation to proceed. My mind caught up then and I deepened the kiss, losing myself in it just for a moment.

Then I noticed that Simon had broken his rhythm and stopped, distracting me again. I really didn't want to break the kiss, and besides, I couldn't really turn my head well in this position anyway, but I was instantly suspicious. That was likely the reason why I didn't jump when his palm came down on my ass instead of the flogger, but the new sensation made me moan into Jack's mouth.

Simon picked up a steady rhythm, hitting each cheek five times before moving to the other. More than one moan and a few grunts escaped me, but Jack swallowed all of them. Maybe it was that distraction, or maybe it was the different sensation that let my body cope much better, but by the time Simon stopped and Jack pushed me away, my mind was once again reeling with need.

Jack looked a little worked up himself as he smiled at me, then flipped me over again so that Simon could grin into my face. I tried not to react, but that was impossible, even more so when Simon took the chance to lean close himself and capture my lips hungrily with his.

Jack's kiss, even when it had become more heated, had still retained that sweetness. Simon's was different somehow, more demanding but also tantalizingly teasing. I made a sound low in my throat when he moved back the second time, only to capture my bottom lip between his teeth and suck on it before letting go.

My erratic breathing rhythm had slowed down somewhat in the brief respite I got, but I knew that was over when I caught the gleam in Simon's eye. No doubt, he enjoyed himself quite a lot when he reached between my legs, and after only a cursory tickle over my clit started slapping my pussy once more.

My first reaction was to try to shy away, until I noticed that he'd moderated the force behind each slap to where it stung, but also felt strangely enticing, almost pleasant. It took me a little while to come to grips with that realization, and a little longer still until I could make myself relax into the steady rhythm. Simon stopped looking away from my face so he could hold my gaze—his aim was steady enough for that—and seeing him watch me with that intensity only added fuel to the flames.

He stopped eventually, which instantly made me yearn for more, but he didn't give me a chance to dwell on that. At his nod, Jack let go of me, and Simon reached for my hair again, if a little less forceful than before as he turned my face up to his. I had to admit that, even though it hurt a little, I really liked that, too.

"I think you've been lazy long enough. Time for you to show some gratitude."

His words confused me, but when he let go and instead reached for my shoulders so he could push me down into a kneeling position, I got an idea of what he might be up to. Sure enough, he reached for the button of his jeans, opened the fly and pushed the denim down to his thighs, letting his cock see the light of day. Unlike Jack, he wasn't completely hard yet, which made me wonder just how much of a distraction coordinating everything must be for him.

Kneeling, with my thighs spread and my wrists still locked together behind my back, there wasn't really much I could do, but I dutifully opened my mouth, because what else was there to do? Besides, he really had a nice cock, and if I couldn't touch it with my hands, it was only fair to give it some attention with my lips and tongue.

"Good girl," Simon muttered, then stepped closer and reached for the back of my head. I was surprised that I felt more puzzled than irritated by the unlikely praise, but then his dick was close enough for me to reach, and I closed the distance quickly so that I could swirl my tongue over the glans and then take him into my mouth as far as I could.

Simon groaned, his fingers threading deeper into my hair, and he pulled just enough on my roots to signal me to get going. I set to the task with as much alacrity as I could muster, which, in all fairness, wasn't that much.

I'd never really given much thought to giving head, mostly because it had never really done anything for me. Sure, most guys expected it, and if they were ready to go down on me I felt obliged to reciprocate, but that had been the extent of enjoyment for me so far.

Today was definitely different and turned even more so when Simon let out a low moan, then bunched up a good portion of my hair in his hands and actively started to guide my head, rather than let me set the pace.

He had a perfectly proportioned cock, and I was happy that, besides a hint of clean sweat, all my nose picked up was that purely masculine musk, but that wasn't it. Physically, there wasn't much difference, but in my head this felt completely detached from any other blow job I'd ever given. Maybe it was because for the first time ever I got to this place already so worked up and horny that I was sure I would come embarrassingly fast the next time anyone stuck anything up my vagina. Maybe it was entirely in my head—the whole setting, the fact that I was restricted in my movement by the cuffs, the knowledge that I had to keep my legs spread because I had been told to. Or maybe it was the simple fact that, technically, I wasn't sucking him off so much as he was fucking my face, now holding my head steady while thrusting his hips forward.

Whatever it was, I really didn't give a shit. It was a fucking turn-on and I loved it, and everything else was secondary.

Then Simon's grip and rhythm changed, and the next time he thrust into my mouth, he went in deeper, bumping into the back of my throat. Immediately my gag reflex came alive, making me want to buck away, but that wasn't quite that easy with the way he kept my head in place. I coughed, or tried to, tears welling up in my eyes. A moment later he eased up, only to try again with similar results. This time he let go completely, giving me a chance to pull away and clear my airway until I could breathe freely again. The use of my hands would have been nice, but since he made no move to disconnect the cuffs, I had to make do with rubbing the spit that had ended up on my chin all over my shoulder.

I didn't get a chance to do more than glance up at him before he caught my head once more and resumed fucking my mouth as if nothing had happened. My pulse was still elevated and only dropped slowly, but before long he told me to take a deep breath and tried again.

I was so not the queen of deep throating, and for the first time ever I actually cared about that.

"I think you need a distraction," Jack said from somewhere surprisingly close to me. Then his hand was on my ass, making me rise into a higher kneeling position, and before I fully registered what was going on, he was pushing his head between my legs while maneuvering me back with his hands on my thighs until I was effectively straddling his face. When I looked down, he flashed me a grin, then grabbed my hips and raised his head. For a few seconds straight, the ability to think pretty much fled my mind.

But, damn, he knew how to work that mouth!

When I managed to get a grip on myself again, I realized that Simon had let off, but when I looked up at him now, he pointedly stared down at his now thoroughly hard cock.

"Suck me off, slut. I don't care how you do it, but you better get the job done fast."

I flashed him what I hoped was a hungry grin, although it got thwarted midway when Jack did something amazing with his tongue on my clit, but Simon didn't seem to mind my indecently loud moan. He did lose patience, though, and grabbed my head, against his previous direction. I really didn't mind.

And when he came down my throat a good five minutes later, I was more than happy to swallow.

If I'd thought I'd been worked up before, I was borderline crazy with need by the time Simon pulled me—rudely—off Jack's face and pushed me toward the sofa, where I ended up in a half-crouched sprawl. How I hadn't come yet was beyond me—likely overstimulation—and Jack had done his part to tease and lick but never quite fulfill what he was promising. He also looked rather smug as he followed us, then plunked down onto the sofa behind me, completely ignoring my death glare. Somewhere along the line he'd lost his clothes, but I didn't really feel inclined to stare at all that muscle, tanned skin, or the black lines roving up his right bicep to his shoulder right now.

Tired from kneeling for so long and with my arms still locked behind my back, I was kind of helpless as he pushed me around and rolled me onto my side, then had me pull my knees up toward my chest. I stopped wondering what that was all about when I felt his finger, cool and slick with lubricant, stroke over my anus.

Reason, and more medical experience than I liked to admit, told me to relax, but instinct made me tense up. It didn't hurt when he started easing one finger through my sphincter, but then the dreaded burning sensation started up, making me clench in earnest.

"Easy there," Jack cooed as he removed his finger, only to return with an even more liberal amount of lube. His other hand found mine, letting me hold and squeeze it, and when he tried again, it went marginally better. "Just bear down on my finger if you can't relax. It will get better soon."

I wanted to snap at him that I knew exactly what I should do, but held my tongue instead. Not because of Simon's warning this time, but mostly because my mind was still too frayed to come up with the eloquence required for our usual banter. That realization made me smile, which turned into a wince when Jack's first digit made it fully inside. But he had been right; it got better from there, also because the wave of need inside me receded slowly, letting me unclench other muscles in the general periphery.

The couch dipped on my other side, and when I opened my eyes, I looked right into Simon's face. He was naked, too, and still soft thanks to my not-quite-superior skills, but I had a feeling that by the time Jack was done with me, that status would have changed, too. He seemed more at ease than before as he settled onto his side, then leaned over me to steal a kiss while his hand skimmed from my shoulder down to my breast.

I tensed briefly when I felt Jack add a second finger to the first, but it didn't take him long to open me up enough to let me enjoy the intrusion. Simon did his part to make me relax, his mouth now kissing a trail down to my breasts while his hand slid over my stomach and between my half-parted legs.

"This isn't your first time anal, now, is it?" Jack ventured a guess as he sped up, and got a low moan from me in return.

"Third. And that's part of the problem, I think."

"We have all the time in the world," he assured me, then laughed when I practically jumped when Simon's roving fingers reached my clit. "Well, we do—you don't."

A terrifyingly true statement, I realized, when Simon didn't linger for long but instead slid one probing finger into my vagina, perfectly in sync with Jack's. Muscles clenched and need surged, and I almost came right there. The problem was, neither of them seemed inclined to stop, and my brain was very happy to inform me just how good it would feel if it wasn't just fingers penetrating me, but cocks.

I realized that I was about to come, and this time I wouldn't be able to hold back anymore. Quite frankly, I felt rather disinclined to try. So far there'd always been something to distract me, but now everything just added up to drive that wave higher and higher. The way the skin on my thighs, ass, and labia was still warm and sensitive from the spanking; Simon languidly sucking on my nipple; their fingers going deeper and deeper, spreading me open while rubbing against each other through the thin layers of skin in between; and not to mention the mental impact all that had on me, and I lost the battle before I even realized that I'd given up on it.

What I hadn't factored in was that other people were keeping better track of my reactions than I was.

I was just about to come—moments, less than seconds away at the most—when Simon withdrew his hand, and Jack's followed suit immediately after. That left me hanging, high and absolutely not dry, an infuriating inch away from my orgasm.

"No! No no no no no!" I muttered under my breath, then tried in vain to somehow wrench my hands free to finish the deed myself, but of course that was impossible. I felt Simon's almost silent laughter against my tit before he bit none too gently into it, then got up in one swift motion.

"I think that's enough."

"No!" I cried out, mostly because it was the only word remaining in my vocabulary. Jack snorted while Simon shot me something between a very amused smile and a glare that had lost a lot of its previous intensity, but when he reached for my arms and wrenched me up into a mostly sitting position, his touch wasn't the least bit gentle.

"Oh yes, and don't you dare tell me what I'm allowed to do, or not," he grunted, but still seemed to fight a laugh. He then sat down beside me right at the corner of the couch that was usually my place, and Jack helped him pull me onto his lap. For a moment I wondered if he was going to spank me now, but they kept pushing me around until I was straddling Simon, with Jack moving in behind me.

Simon's cock still wasn't fully hard but getting there, and I got mesmerized for a second when he wrapped his hand around it and started stroking up and down. With his other hand he held out a condom to Jack, who quickly rolled it down his own dick.

A push between my shoulder blades had me pitch toward Simon, leaving my ass higher in the air, and a spurt of cool lube later, I felt the head of Jack's cock push against my rosette. There was a moment when tension built and I tried to brace myself, but then he slid in with surprising ease, making me feel all kinds of pleasurable sensations I hadn't really thought my ass was capable of. Then again, as close to coming as I still was, anything even remotely stimulating might have felt great right then.

Keeping one hand at his dick, Jack grabbed my hip with the other, then started to ease out and back in, setting a delicious yet infuriatingly slow rhythm. I screwed my eyes shut and nudged my cheek harder against Simon's shoulder, then did my best to just get lost in the moment. It felt so fucking great that it wasn't really a hard thing to accomplish.

I might have come that way if given enough time, but long before that, Simon was ready, prompting Jack to slow, then fully pull out. I mewled my protest, but cut off mid-whine when Simon pulled me down onto his cock instead, sliding easily into my pussy until my thighs hit his. Jack's hand on my shoulder pulled my torso away from Simon's, bringing me into a more upright kneeling position and thus able to look down at him. He offered me a slight smile, then leaned his head more firmly against the back of the couch as he let his hands roam up my body to settle on my breasts.

Then Jack's cock was back, and I exhaled shakily when he started to ease himself back into me. I won't lie—it was uncomfortable at first, but the spreading sense of being filled more than made up for that. A buck of the hips from Simon that got his cock moving in the other direction from Jack's, and I forgot all about it.

"Fuck!"

And that, they did.

Until then, things had worked more or less smoothly, but now they turned appropriately chaotic. For one, I was completely incapable of holding back, and this time neither of the guys seemed ready to stop, so I got a hard pinch in the ass from Simon for my trouble of not being his obedient little slut, but that was the extent of his ire. Instead, he moved his hands up from my breasts over my neck to clasp the sides of my face, then pulled me down into a hungry kiss that stole what little air I had left.

My orgasm, starting kind of slow now that it was finally allowed to consume me, turned into a wildfire when Jack put one leg up on the couch next to Simon's knee, and abandoned all pretense of going slow anymore. Simon effectively muffled most of the ungodly moans that built up low in my chest, leaving the sound of flesh slapping against flesh to be the only competition for Jack's drawn-out groan when he came.

For a moment, our sandwich almost threatened to disassemble, but then Jack put his arms around me and pulled me back, giving Simon's hips enough range of motion to, well, move. Nerve endings that were already firing got even more stimulated as he grabbed my hips and started thrusting up into me, while Jack, the sneaky bastard, reached down to rub my clit.

I came again, and maybe a third time—I really couldn't say—before Simon stilled after two last hard jerks of his hips that reverberated through my entire body. My breathing was so irregular that I was seeing dark spots dance before my eyes, or maybe that was due to some weird brain damage because they'd literally fucked me silly.

Whatever it was, I didn't care because I'd never felt better in my entire life.

-5-

Jack let go to let me sag against Simon's chest just as Simon tried to shift some of my weight to the side, ending in a commotion of limbs and bodies that got me sprawling half onto Jack, half onto the floor. My elbow might have hit him in the ribs, but his pained groan got drowned out by my laughter.

"What the—" Simon started, then saw us two idiots trying to crawl off each other but not succeed, which got him joining in.

As amazing as everything else had been, being able to just lie there, gasping for breath, my face and stomach hurting from laughing so hard, was the best feeling in the world.

Eventually, Jack managed to push me off him enough to crawl out from under me, and when Simon slid off the couch to join us, I ended up wedged between them. That was a good thing because I wasn't sure if I could have remained sitting upright on my own. While Simon was busy unbuckling the cuffs, I leaned into Jack, and he planted a last, almost platonic kiss on my nose. I smiled up at him, then closed my eyes, happy to finally get control back over my arms.

The cuffs had been comfortable enough to leave my wrists completely unharmed, but the entire time my arms had remained pulled back, ending with protesting and slightly strained muscles in my upper arms that were in dire need of a massage right now. Watching me roll my shoulders and try to work the kinks out of my muscles for a moment, Simon nudged my knee.

"Come on, scoot over."

I skeptically eyed the offered place in front of him between his knees, then did what he suggested, because getting weirdly conscious about us both being naked and covered in sweat— among other things—felt like pure hypocrisy. His touch was gentle but deft, and I let out a truly unapologetic groan when his fingers found the right spots.

Jack snickered, which begged for physical retaliation, but that would have required me to get up or even open my eyes again, and that was not going to happen right now.

"You, shut up," I ground out, then tried to stifle another equally offensive sound when Simon increased the pressure. "That feels so fucking good."

"That's what she said," Jack continued to goad me, and when I did turn my head and sent him a veritable glare, he grinned and got to his feet slowly. "I'm calling dibs on the first shower. Besides, the way you both look, you're not going anywhere right now, anyway."

I tensed, ready to jump up and go after Jack, but Simon swept his hands up over my shoulders and onto my back, and any incentive I'd ever had to move again in my life dissipated. Letting my head loll forward, I relaxed again, keeping my arms braced on his knees.

Silence settled as he kept working my muscles, but it was a comfortable, companionable kind of silence without a trace of awkwardness. I couldn't remember if Simon and I had ever shared a moment like this, but doubted it. Almost dozing off contentedly was more something I did cozied up to Jack, when he wasn't getting under my skin for once. I definitely liked this new kind of intimacy.

"Feeling better now?" Simon eventually broke the silence as his fingers slid down my still aching arms again.

"Yup," I replied, because that was about the extent of my vocabulary right then.

I felt his soft laugh more through his touch than heard it.

"Still not quite back yet?"

"Hm," I hummed in agreement, a happy smile on my face. His hands started to wander back up to my shoulders, then down my sides, not quite coincidentally skimming the outsides of my breasts. That turned my smile into something different, but I was too lost in the haze to care about reacting. I felt him shift behind me, then he pulled me against his chest before his hands resumed their idle tours down to my partly spread thighs.

His cheek was warm where it pressed against mine as he put his chin up on my right shoulder, and I snuggled deeper into him, maximizing the contact. I wasn't quite sure what his hands were up to—mostly stroking my skin, too soft to dig into the muscles but also not in a terribly intimate way—but I didn't feel like protesting.

"I think we have something to talk about now," he eventually prompted, underlining his words with just a hint more pressure right above my knees.

Reluctantly I let my eyes drift open, but the ceiling above me didn't really yield any answers.

"You mean about where we'll go from here?"

"Obviously."

"Well, a shower would be nice," I joked, then tried to sit up, but my muscles were disinclined to obey.

"You know that's not what I mean," he chided me gently while his hands moved up my thighs again.

Oh, I did, but with a twinge of anticipation now peeking through the languid post-coital haze, I was reluctant to answer. Quite the tease, he stopped inches away from my pussy, then slid his hands toward my knees again. I let out a partly frustrated breath but really, I hadn't been that physically and emotionally satisfied in ages—it was hard to hold any sort of grudge right now. Besides, I wasn't even sure if my body would have responded favorably to stimulation, with a nice but distinct kind of soreness spreading from my genitalia.

"I can't deny that this has been fun," I agreed, then laughed softly. "More like amazing, but then you know that yourself. You don't need your ego stroked by me."

"Need, no, but stroking is always welcome," he murmured into my ear, making me shiver. Bastard wasn't playing fair, but then I didn't mind that much, either.

"Look who's talking," I huffed back when his hands—again!—stopped shy of truly interesting territory and wandered off once more.

He laughed softly, but the sound didn't hold the condescension I'd been waiting for, just genuine amusement.

"My offer still stands. You want more, you know where to get it."

I considered that for a moment, even though I felt like I'd already reached a decision somewhere between when he'd switched the flogger for his hands.

"And if I only want to be the filling in your sandwich again, without a spicy chaser?"

The analogy made him laugh, and my stomach rumbled embarrassingly.

"I'm sure that Jack wouldn't have anything against that. I certainly don't."

"But?"

Another chuckle.

"But I have a feeling that you won't be content with that alone."

I both hated and loved that he knew me so well. Hated because, well, the stubborn part of me still wasn't ready to accept that I might need something where I couldn't solely rely on myself—anything for that matter, even if sex was usually a two person minimum thing—and loved for the obvious reasons.

"I don't even know if I'll have the time," I offered, the next best excuse.

"Doesn't matter if you come over once a week, or once a month. You know that I have very few fixed appointments in my schedule, and when I know that there's a chance that you'll drop by later, I can work around my deadlines, too. The goal is to subtract from your workload, not add to it. Don't use that as a flimsy excuse just because you're getting cold feet."

Was that it? I really couldn't say.

"Exactly how much commitment to this would you require from me?"

Needing to see his reaction, I finally turned my head and got rewarded with a somewhat twisted but still pleasant smile.

"Not much, if you want to keep things casual, which seems the best option considering your time constraints. Vanity makes me want to ask you not to have sex with anyone else in the meantime, but if you keep your tests up to date, I can work with that, too. Besides that, nothing I can think of. You're new, and all things considered I would keep things mostly to the physical aspects, anyway, so there's not much else involved."

"What about you?"

Amusement flashed in his eyes, but he carefully kept it out of his tone.

"Besides what living in the same house with Jack might imply, I'm not really the guy to sleep around. I find it emotionally draining to have more than one sub at a time, and if you do show up a couple times a month, that more than covers my imminent sexual needs, so I wouldn't even be interested in getting some action elsewhere."

That was likely the weirdest—and best argued—statement of fidelity I'd ever heard in my life. Not that I had much experience with such things, but still. Very Simon.

"I wouldn't even know where to start," I pointed out, another obstacle occurring to me.

Now his grin could only be described as smug.

"Yeah, that's why I do the planning and you just show up to get fucked."

"Very funny."

"But quintessentially true."

I didn't know how to respond to that, so I remained silent, but Simon obviously wasn't done yet.

"Stop worrying about the fact that I have more experience under my belt than you do. Unless you're in a romantic relationship and explore together, it's always easier when one partner can lead the other. The only problem I see is that you're as stubborn as a mule, but I'm sure I'll find a way to whip that right out of you."

"Literally or figuratively?"

"That's entirely up to your pain tolerance."

It wasn't trepidation exactly that made me lick my lips.

"Okay, then let's see where this goes?"

"Let's. And I fully agree with what you said before. You really do need that shower now."

Laughing, I pushed his hands away, then got laboriously to my feet. Joints popped and muscles I'd forgotten I even had ached. The worst twinge came from where he'd pinched me, though, and when I absentmindedly rubbed that spot on my ass, Simon laughed softly.

"Next time, if you pull a stunt like that, you'll have more to show than a little ouchie," he pointed out.

"Is that a warning or a challenge?"

Now his laugh was anything but soft.

"Neither—just an observation. I'm well aware that you had no intention whatsoever to beg for anything, and if you keep that conviction up, things will get a lot harder for you than they have to be."

Maybe that should have scared me or made me laugh because it did sound kind of ridiculous, but fascination and excitement were what I felt welling up inside of me.

"We'll see. If anyone can make me beg, I'm sure it will be you."

The look he sent me let me know that, yes, he would, but he left it at that. The shower shut off at the other end of the house, giving me a good excuse not to linger, which was probably for the best. I really did need that shower, and with what Simon had just dangled in front of my nose, I wouldn't have to rely on my right hand to find a cure for that itch—and part of me wanted to jump him right then and there.

The shower was one of the best in my life, and without a doubt one of the most needed. I spent an unholy amount of time just standing under the hot spray, letting the water sluice away the evidence left by our recent activities.

As I'd expected, the general area of my genitals felt sore, but not in a bad way. My ass—inside and out—had definitely borne the brunt, but I felt kind of proud rather than grumpy. Nothing a little thoughtful application of lotion wouldn't take care of, and I'd keep the fond memories for the rest of my life.

After drying off, I spent a few futile moments wrestling with my hair, but between Simon's penchant for grabbing it and the lack of conditioner, it was a lost cause. Sweeping the long, black strands up into a messy bun was my only saving grace. I hesitated a moment in front of the mirror, staring at my own reflection. Somehow I felt different, but the woman staring back at me still looked the same. Same dirty hazel eyes that Brad

Champs had called weird in seventh grade, same even features that no one had yet composed any sonnets about, and hopefully never would. Maybe there was a slightly feverish glint in my eyes, but I was ready to chalk that up to my own perception. It made me wonder how many people I passed at work each day who spent their Saturday afternoons rutting around with their best friends.

Quite frankly, I really didn't care.

While Simon was the last to grab a shower, I joined Jack in the living room. As expected, he was busy cleaning up, his neat-freak OCD even overshadowing his need to get dressed. Then again, it was Jack we were talking about here, so I shouldn't have been surprised that he was busy scrubbing the floor in front of the sofa wearing just his boxers.

"You've decided to become a more permanent installment on Simon's cock, I hear?" he observed from his perch on the floor.

"Do you still wonder sometimes why I hit you when you say shit like that?" I retorted, and sat down on one of the high stools by the breakfast bar.

"Never," he laughed, then straightened, apparently finished with getting rid of the evidence of our debauchery.

I spent a moment admiring the results of all the hours of workout he did each week that Simon and I usually teased him about. For the first time in my life, I didn't feel remotely sleazy about doing so.

"See something you like?" Jack drawled, coming closer.

"Yeah, I could use someone to do just that to my kitchen, too," I shot back, a beatific smile on my face.

Snorting, he stored away his cleaning supplies, then took the seat beside me.

"Are you avoiding my question, or does all this ripped man-flesh distract you too much? I can get dressed if you need it."

"That was a question? I thought it was just another observation of yours that deserved a well-aimed punch."

"Oh, you wound me!"

"Not yet, but keep going and I will."

His shit-eating grin was too good to resist, and I felt myself smiling despite of myself.

"Things between us aren't going to turn weird now, right?" I asked, less because I was afraid they would, but mostly because I wanted to hear him say it.

"Just because I fucked you in the ass hard enough to come?"

He leaned close, as if I could have missed his leer otherwise. I pursed my lips and glared back at him, and after a second he looked away and started laughing, hard enough to almost fall off his chair.

"You're really not much fun when you get pissed off over nothing!"

"Jack, I'm serious."

Sighing, he straightened, although he didn't manage to wipe that stupid grin off his face.

"Will I make inappropriate comments when it's just the two of us? Hell, yeah. But apart from that, why should anything change? It's just sex."

From anyone else—well, maybe except for Simon—I wouldn't have believed that, but he sounded sincere.

"It's really that easy for you, isn't it?"

"Mostly," he agreed. "Besides, I'm not stupid enough to fuck up my chance of a repeat performance just because I have a little more ammo against you now."

"And you think that's going to happen?"

"I certainly hope so," he replied, then turned unfamiliarly serious. "Look, it's none of my business what you and Simon get up to, and I promise that I will never talk shit about what you do with him. I respect you too much, and, quite frankly, he'd give me so much shit if I said anything that would make you feel self-conscious or weird, so it's not worth trying to get under your skin. Besides, you know me and my fucked up sense of humor better than anyone else on this world. Sex is great, but not great enough to get between you and me."

Grinning, I reached over to hug him, which also put me in the perfect position to poke his ribs hard enough to make him wince.

"Argh! What did I do to deserve that?"

"Nothing. Yet. It's only a matter of time until you will."

"That's unfair!" he complained, but kept grinning amicably.

"What's unfair?" Simon asked from where he just entered the kitchen, wet hair dripping onto the shoulders of his T-shirt.

"She's poking me!" Jack complained, using his best whiny voice.

Simon sent us both a look that spoke plainly that we shouldn't involve him in our goofing around.

"So what, it's not like you didn't do anything to deserve it, I'm sure."

"Hey, what happened to 'bros before hoes'?"

Simon's smile was almost sweet, turning it creepy as hell.

"You two always side against me, so don't even try to play that card now."

"Ah, I see. So this has nothing to do with her now becoming your shiny new toy?"

That earned Jack a withering stare from Simon, so much so that it cracked me up.

"Sweet! All it takes for you to turn into my faithful watchdog now is for me to bend over and let you spank me?"

I could admit that I deserved the equally hostile glare directed at me now, making Jack share my grin.

"You two are so damn funny, you know that?" Simon retorted as he angled for the fridge.

"Of course we do. Do you think this comes effortlessly? We spend days plotting and planning each well-phrased joke to maximize the impact," Jack helpfully supplied.

"I hope neither of you ever lose your job, because if you decide to become comedians, you'll be broke for life."

"Oh, this reminds me of something," I said, using the worst segue ever. When I waited, the guys both turned to look at me. "Can you maybe not tell Kara about this? Not that I feel like being super stealthy about our thing here, but there are some things she really doesn't need to know."

Simon gave me a look that conveyed clearly that I needn't have asked, and Jack's shrug was rather nonchalant.

"Unless you tell anyone, I'm not going to. It's no one's business what we do or don't do when you're over."

I was surprised that none of them called me out on being a hypocrite, but then Kara and Jack had never made a secret of their random hookups. For a while I'd expected them to start dating and go steady, but the longer we were all out of college, the less that seemed likely.

"Don't worry—what happens in this house stays in this house," Jack remarked cryptically, then reached for his phone. "So who wants pizza? That stays in this house, too, just saying."

And, just like that, we fell back into old, well-established patterns, and all was right with the world.

-6-

It turned out, vigorous sex with two guys at the same time canceled out some of the benefits eight consecutive hours of sleep raked in. By the time I made it to the hospital, I felt mentally alert but physically drained, and working the usual rut took a worse toll on me than most days. I still couldn't bring myself to feel like it hadn't been worth it, even when I got up the following afternoon and felt a million years old.

Maybe there was a reason why most people went through their phase of sexual exploration in their twenties, but I had to admit that ten years ago I wouldn't have dared to just take the guys up on their offer, much less enter into an arrangement such as what Simon and I now had going.

That first night shift I was too out of it to care, but the following evening I dutifully trooped to the nurses' station to sign up for a routine blood test. It was just my luck that Nurse Dana was in evidence, but she'd already seen me approach, so it was too late to turn tail and run now.

"Dr. Slater, anything I can do for you?" she asked sweetly, baring her teeth in something that no one could mistake for a smile. Only the dumbest of interns would ever dare to approach her with work they could do themselves if they saw that smile.

Resigning myself to my fate, I put down the half-full urine cup in front of her.

"I'm here for my routine check. Blood panel and standard STIs."

She blinked in irritation, but as soon as she brought up my file on the computer, her eyes lit up with glee. I wondered how long it would take for half the hospital to know that I'd recently become some Colombian drug lord's mistress and carried his cocaine crack baby.

"You're not scheduled for another three weeks."

"I need the test now," I told her, trying to keep it as simple as possible not to give her any more munition for her gossip mongery.

"Would you like me to schedule an appointment with the OB/Gyn, too? Pregnancy tests are all the rage this week."

Her bright, fake smile made it hard to keep a similar one plastered onto my face, but I told myself that if I made it through this, I'd deserve some extra ice cream the second I got home.

"No, thank you, that won't be necessary. Just the blood panel and urine test."

"Of course," she simpered, then got up and reached for the gloves to get a syringe ready.

"When you leave, feel free to grab a couple of condoms from the bowl. Or will you require dental dams instead?"

"That's too sweet of you to ask, but no, I got that covered."

And some people were actually afraid of getting stuck with a needle when they needed their blood drawn. Who needed needles when they had Nurse Dana?

As usual at the beginning of a night float month, my circadian rhythm was fucked up enough that the moment I got home and felt ready to crash into my pillow, my body was wide awake. The sun was shining, the birds were singing, and just because I felt like a zombie didn't mean that I could actually catch some shut-eye. For a minute I considered calling Simon, mostly to talk but also because, well, I got terribly horny whenever I thought about Saturday, which happened a lot more than it should, yet then disbanded the idea. No one had ever died from sexual frustration, but lack of sleep could quickly become a problem, and with just a few weeks left to my rotation, I didn't want to endanger my performance by having to rely on chemicals to keep me up and functioning.

I gave up tossing and turning an hour later when I heard Marcy return home from a grocery run. Leaving my bed didn't sound very appealing, but it had been days since I'd seen my roommate, and since sleep was eluding me anyway, I might as well engage in some social interaction.

Marcy was her usual energetic self as I walked into the cubbyhole of a kitchen, busy unpacking what looked like half of the fresh produce aisle. She must have been on one of her clean eating binges again.

"Hey, girl, didn't think you'd be awake," she greeted me with a smile, her perfect white teeth shining brightly. She was the only one allowed to talk to me like that. Well, Marcy and Kara, but Kara was a different flavor altogether.

Maybe there was something to that nutrition thing. Her dark skin was practically glowing today, and she seemed to have energy in abundance. Or maybe she'd recently gotten laid. That just left the question why I was zombified, and she not.

"Can't sleep. Just started on night float."

She nodded sagely as she continued to unload a small country's needs for canned coconut milk onto the counter.

"Nancy from Pediatrics told me she'd heard that you've been bumping uglies with, who is that guy who's battling Tyne for Head of Trauma Surgery?"

"You mean Rigler? Ew! Besides, Zoe would skin me alive if I went behind her back. How do people even come up with shit like this?"

Marcy shrugged.

"Even under workaholics you're a zealot. I think the concept that you would spend enough time outside of the hospital to find someone else to do the horizontal tango with is beyond their comprehension." She stopped, then shot me a meaningful look. "Which reminds me—how was that party on Friday?"

My first impulse was to act like a deer caught in the headlights, but I forced myself to relax.

"The usual. I drank too much and some weirdo hit on me. The moment he found out I don't spend my days prancing around in a sexy nurse's outfit, he lost interest."

"You know, some people find scrubs sexy," she pointed out, grinning.

"Easily accessible maybe, but sexy? I'm not sure I would want to screw someone with a fetish like that."

"And that's why you'll never have a sex life worth bragging about."

Oh, if only she knew. For a moment, I considered dropping a few hints, but then kept my mouth firmly shut. Marcy and I were friends—good friends, but not "best, share your every secret with" kind of friends. We'd met in college, suffered through pre-med together, but while I'd gone off to Columbia then, she'd landed a spot at Johns Hopkins. It was a weird coincidence that had made us end up doing our respective residencies in the same hospital right across the country again, and moving in together had seemed like the natural next step. Our apartment was barely more than two tiny cupboards with beds and a bathroom only suitable for people who didn't suffer from claustrophobia, but it suited our hundred plus hours a week work schedules. She didn't really get along with Jack because she thought that he was a pig—

not quite unfounded—and Simon was dead to her because he was an arrogant prick—definitely justified. Somehow, telling her about the recent change in our friendship status seemed less like a good idea than a recipe for disaster.

"So why did you need an early check-up? Anything happen in the ER?"

I shrugged, trying to come up with a good excuse.

"Just got paranoid. You can tell sixteen-year-old girls only so many times that the clap isn't the worst they can catch from unprotected sex before you're sure that panty rash is genital herpes."

"You got a rash? Want me to check it for you?"

What I did have were light abrasions likely caused by the stubble on Jack's face, and just thinking about how I'd got them made me want to squirm in the best kind of way.

"No, thanks. Unless it involves broken bones, I don't need your expert opinion."

"Tease," Marcy accused, but let it slide. "Have you seen the duty roster for next week? I swear McGilles is trying to work us into the ground."

"No, haven't looked it over yet. Zoe roped me into signing up for the day shift on Saturday, though."

"Not just Saturday, but Friday and Sunday, too. You really need to stay ahead of your game if you want to survive in this jungle."

Doing a quick calculation, I realized that my plan to call Simon about me coming over next weekend had just gotten shot to hell.

"Are you even listening to me? I just told you that you'll be spending the entire weekend working, and still you grin like a fool? Should have scheduled an EEG with that blood panel," Marcy pointed out.

"What? No, I was just thinking about something else."

"Obviously," she snorted, but didn't say anything else. Some things are better left unquestioned, and the reason why Marcy and I were working out so well was that she always knew when ignorance was bliss.

I actually made it until Tuesday before I couldn't hold my curiosity in check any longer.

The deciding factor wasn't the horror weekend ahead of me, but the fact that I found myself horny at almost all times of the day—and nothing my own hands were capable of would do to relieve the tension. The solution was so simple, and just one phone call away.

I still stalled through the evening, until the ER hit the usual 11:00 p.m. lull. The accidents of the evening had all been taken care of, those of the night were only just occurring, all in-patients were looked after, and I found myself with a couple of minutes at my disposal. Habit had me hit the coffee machine on the way to the staircase, and I savored a few bitter sips as I made my way up onto the roof.

As the city lay in a sprawling sea of lights before me, I hit the second number on speed dial and waited for the call to connect. The phone rang a full nine times before Simon picked up; others might have been concerned about calling so late, but I knew that whenever he was working on a manuscript, he turned into a veritable night owl.

"Erin, so good of you to call," he greeted me, smugness heavy in his voice.

I took another sip of coffee, savoring it should it be the last. I wasn't known for hurling precious beverages away in a fit, but I was all about new experiences of late—who knew?

"So good of you to pick up, Simon," I replied, not even trying to hold back my light irritation.

He laughed, but it was a nice, warm laugh that somehow managed to appease me a little.

"I kept my phone on."

"Really?"

Simon was a great believer in shutting himself off from all forms of distraction when he was working, sometimes even going as far as unplugging their router. That routinely made Jack go ballistic, particularly if it happened when he was in the middle of a raid, but you had to expect something like that when you were bunking with an egomaniacal artist.

"Let's just say I was expecting your call."

"You were?"

Wasn't I Miss Eloquence tonight?

"Actually, I was expecting it yesterday already, but as you called today, I still won the bet."

"What bet?"

"Jack bet me that you'd either call within twenty-four hours, or not at all. Of course, I could be sorely mistaken and this is just a social call, but considering that you seldom do that and haven't bitten my head off yet, I think you want something from me, and we can both guess what that is."

Taking a cautious look around, I made sure that I was alone on the rooftop. It was bad enough that the rumors about my, ah, promotional work hadn't died down yet. I really didn't want to give them even a hint of credibility.

"We can?"

"Can't we?" he turned my stupid parroting around on me. I couldn't help a brief grin.

"I don't think I've ever been very good at guessing what goes on in your head."

I did feel like I should give myself a little more credit than that. At least I'd gotten their general sexual disposition somewhat right in my wank fantasies, but I wasn't about to admit that unless forced to do so under torture or a tickle attack.

Now his laugh was deliciously wry.

"Come on. I'm a guy—it's not that hard to guess what's going through my mind when the woman I had sex with three days ago calls."

"That easy, huh?" I teased, but felt things low in my body tighten in anticipation.

"Most things worth thinking about aren't that hard. Except if you're talking about my cock, but in all fairness I should disclose that that has only somewhat to do with the subject at hand."

I needed a moment to decipher that, and when I did, I felt my cheeks heat up a little.

"Why do you pick up the phone when you're in the middle of masturbating?"

"Closer to the end than the middle, I'd say. And it was your name on the display, so I figured I should pick up."

I wondered for a moment if he suffered from a similar problem as I did, but doubted it.

"I guess I should feel honored now?"

"Kind of," he admitted, then chuckled. "I wouldn't have picked up if it had been my mother."

"Well, good for you!" I laughed, then forced myself to quit joking around. "How are your deadlines shaping up this week?"

"Looming, but not threatening to kill me yet. Why?"

There was a clear note of teasing in that last word, but I couldn't hold that against him.

"Do you think you could make room for me, for maybe an hour or two?"

I really had no idea how long whatever he had in store for me would take, but I didn't expect that right afterward he would just throw me out and get straight back to work.

"I can definitely make room for you on Thursday," he offered. "You're on night shifts this week?"

"Until the end of the month," I confirmed. How he guessed I didn't ask; Simon had his ways of figuring things like that out. Or maybe he'd asked Jack. The idea that he kept track of my work hours was both endearing and disconcerting.

"My schedule is clear until mid-afternoon, so if you come over sometime after normal people eat breakfast, that should work for me."

"Thursday then," I confirmed, not quite capable of keeping a hint of disappointment out of my voice. Sure, it had been unreasonable to expect him to drop everything on the spot to make time for me, but going another one and a half days with pent-up tension driving me insane was not my definition of a good time.

"I have some homework for you in the meantime, if that helps tidy you over your burning desire."

That made me snort with laughter.

"Seriously?"

"On the homework or the burning desire?"

"Both, but the figure of speech is worse."

"Sorry, couldn't resist. My publicist is trying to foist a new project on me, and I've done my best to discourage him."

"And for that you need phrases like 'burning desire'?"

"Much worse. I guarantee you that you don't want to know."

"I'll take that at face value. Or whatever the verbal equivalent of that may be." I paused, then tried to get back on track. "So, homework?"

"Nothing too strenuous, don't worry. Just your standard lists of preferences and limits."

"You know that I don't really have much to fill out? We covered almost the entire range of my sexual experience on Saturday."

He made a sound that I thought was a grunt.

"I have to start somewhere, and I might as well begin with the things you feel familiar with or are mostly interested in. You got away last time without us having that conversation because I didn't plan on doing anything more elaborate than what most people do without considering it terribly kinky, but if we want to wade into deeper waters, I need to know what might get you going, and what sends up red flags when there's even a hint of it involved. Not that I expect that too many things really freak you out. This is your what, third rotation in the ER? I'm sure you've seen stranger things stuck in people's orifices than I can even think of."

As he'd likely expected, that made me laugh.

"Oh, I could tell you stories..."

"I'll email you the list, and we can talk about it over coffee. How does that sound?"

"Like you're trying to get rid of me right now."

His laugh sounded a little strained, and it suddenly occurred to me that I hadn't asked if he'd ever stopped jerking off. Just then my beeper went off, reminding me that I had another seven hours of shift ahead of me.

"Sorry, gotta run. See you on Thursday?"

I couldn't help but grin stupidly at that, because even if we were talking about sex and I was about to run off to save lives, I still had the humor of an immature ten-year-old.

"As bright and early as you make it over here."

"Well, good wank then."

"Thanks, you too."

Clearing my throat, I hung up. Really, did he always have to have the last word? Apparently, the smug bastard did.

It was 2:00 a.m. by the time things quieted down enough for me to sidle into the doctor's lounge and print out the list Simon had sent me. Medical knowledge, and, I could admit that at least to myself, years watching porn and lurking around online forums had given me a moderately good idea of what most of the terms meant that were mentioned, and the three that I had to look up were things I hadn't realized people could even fetishize.

Just to be sure, I also printed out an article from the Journal of *Advances in Neuroscience* just to make sure that the printer cache held something less incriminating should anyone check. I definitely felt stupid rather than sneaky, but Jack had told me too many hilarious stories from work for my paranoia not to run rampant.

I spent another thirty minutes I should have caught some sleep in poring over the list. I still didn't really know what to do with it, but if Simon insisted on this, I was game. I was also rather worked up once I was done but forced myself to keep away from the bathroom except for what it was strictly intended for. When that had become a Herculean effort, I couldn't say, but it was bothersome as hell.

The people of the day shift started trundling in just around six, but I still had some patient files to wrap up, so it was closer to eight in the morning when I finally hightailed it out of the hospital. At the small bakery right next to the train station, I hesitated, then went in, deciding on a whim that I really didn't want to have breakfast all by myself today. That had nothing whatsoever to do with my perpetual horniness.

Jack looked something between astonished and suspicious when he let me in, but welcomed the fresh croissants I foisted at him. He was ready for work, wearing the familiar T-shirt and jeans uniform of IT people everywhere, his bag ready by the door.

"Not that I'd look a gift horse bearing edible food in the mouth, but shouldn't you be comatose somewhere? Or saving the world one spurting artery at a time?"

"My body still hasn't adjusted to my recent switch to night shift, and I figured I'd rather hang out with you guys for a couple of minutes than spend my time tossing and turning in bed."

"Okay," he offered, still cautious, then preceded me into the kitchen, making for the coffee machine. "Coffee? Or not if you do plan on sleeping later, I guess."

"I'll take a cup. My body must have become resistant somewhere between undergrad and med school."

Simon looked up at the sound of my voice from where he sat hunched over the morning paper at the breakfast bar. Unlike Jack, it only took him a moment to assess the situation, and his wry grin made me kind of self-conscious about my decision to come over.

"You do know that it's Wednesday, right?"

"The morning after my Tuesday night shift is usually Wednesday, yeah," I agreed, maybe a little sharper than I had intended.

Jack looked from me to Simon, then handed me my coffee.

"I feel like I'm missing something here, and not just my train."

"Sorry, really didn't want to keep you," I offered, very unconvincingly.

"Don't worry, fresh food makes up for being a little late," he assured me, stuffing half a croissant into his mouth without bothering with a plate. Simon meanwhile started shredding his into a million pieces, his eyes never leaving my face. It shouldn't have been possible that anyone could unnerve me so much wearing a baggy tee, jogging shorts, and white socks.

"So why exactly are you here?" Jack asked when I didn't volunteer the information. "My coffee is great, I know, but it has never lured you into making a detour in the morning."

I opened my mouth, ready to spout the next bullshit that came to my mind, but Simon cut me off before I could get there.

"Because she's horny as fuck and can't wait for you to beat it."

My mouth snapped shut, all my excuses gone.

Jack's snort was exactly that kind of amused that usually made me want to slap him, while his smile was almost sweet. Almost.

"Ah, I see. Well, bring bagels with your next bootie call. I love the croissants, but the bagels are so much better."

Before I could protest, Jack swept by me, picked up his bag, and was out of the door in record time. That left me with Simon, his smirk, and his croissant genocide.

"I just dropped by to give you this."

Digging into my bag, I got out the list and handed it to him. If I ran now, I could likely catch up with Jack and ride the few stops back into the city. I hated leaving the coffee mostly untouched, but this had been a bad idea from the start and—

"Erin, sit your ass down right fucking now."

My ass hit the chair next to Simon's before my brain had even caught up with his command. My eyes narrowed at him, but the irritation coming up inside of me was more for myself than him. I really wasn't used to anyone ordering me around who wasn't wearing scrubs, and even then I usually took a moment to react.

He seemed to know what was going through my mind, forcing his smile to turn down a couple of notches until it was bordering on nice.

"Thank you for being so diligent about this, but you can stop lying now. No one's believing you, anyway."

"I really—"

"Stop."

Much to my surprise, my mouth shut, unbidden. Feeling stupid, I took a sip of coffee while I watched Simon pick up two more flakes of former croissant and nibble on them while his eyes scanned the print out. Twice I opened my mouth to just say something, but closed it again without a word coming over my lips. When he switched to the second page and hadn't said a peep yet, I treated myself to my own breakfast right out of the brown paper bag.

When he was done perusing the list, Simon got up. I made as if to follow him, and he held me back with a gesture in my general direction.

"Stay."

"If you say 'roll over' or 'heel' next, I'm going to bite you."

That got me a grin before he ducked into the back hallway. About half a minute later he returned with a stack of papers.

"My list," he needlessly explained as he handed it over and got himself another cup of coffee.

Interest flamed up inside of me, but I tried not to let my face betray any emotion. But, oh boy, he'd gotten around if the sheer amount of "done" checks was any indication. Some of it surprised me, a couple of the high "really dug that" marks kind of intimidated me, but it could have been worse. What the list underlined was just how inexperienced I was, and I couldn't help but feel like I'd really missed out on a lot over the past couple of years.

"Exactly how long have you been into this?" I asked, waving the list around as if that question needed clarification.

"Since I turned twenty, third year of college."

I tried to think back to that time, wondering if there'd been any change in his behavior or something—there should have been, right? But I honestly couldn't remember. I'd been under a lot of pressure back then to get my GPA perfect enough to land a scholarship on top of getting accepted into the med school of my choice, and I'd never been that observant when it came to people. I thought I remembered him appearing a little less awkward and somewhat more confident, but that could easily have been my memory playing tricks on me now that I wanted to see change.

"Any questions?"

I shook my head. That list was pretty self-explanatory, and while it was interesting to get a glimpse into his past and what I perceived where his interests, it didn't really pertain to me. I doubted that anything we'd do in the near future would range deeper into his comfort zone, let alone out of it.

"Not really."

"Why are you here? I think I can guess accurately, but it would be nice of you to say it."

Licking my lips, I hesitated, then put the list down and caught his gaze.

"I kind of hate to admit it, but I'm really fucking horny and excited about this, and waiting another day is the kind of torture I don't think I'm into."

He shared my grin and popped another piece of croissant into his mouth. That shouldn't have looked so damn sexy, but I got the feeling that my mind would have found toilet paper commercials sexually stimulating right now. My eyes must have lingered on his lips a little too long because they quirked up into a lopsided grin once he'd finished chewing, but for once he didn't use that against me.

"Trust me, I get it. I have a deadline at three today."

And just like that, my libido got a probably much-needed cold douse.

"Oh. Well, no problem—" I said, already sliding off my stool, but Simon's warm hand wrapping around my wrist stopped me.

"I'm done with writing and almost done editing, so I have some time. But for the future, I would welcome it if you called ahead without coming up with bullshit excuses instead."

The pressure of his fingers increased just a little before he let go, and I felt a hint of guilt and unease grip me. I normally didn't fib, but he'd never called me out on any of my white lies, even though I was sure that he'd seen through all of them.

"Okay. Sure."

"Good, because we can't do this without absolute disclosure and brutal honesty, like it or not. If that's too much of a bother for you, you can leave right now, no hard feelings."

His dismissive tone was like a hard slap in my face, but one I deserved.

"That's not going to be a problem. Promise."

His eyes remained on my face for a moment longer, then he nodded and gestured for me to follow him. I quickly finished my coffee, then skipped after him, a little surprised when he stopped in the middle of the back hallway and opened the door leading up to the attic. I couldn't remember when I'd been up there the last time, likely just after they'd moved in and we'd stored a last few unpacked boxes up there.

"What's up with that?"

"You'll see," he promised, sounding befittingly cryptic.

The steps groaned a little as we ascended, and without hesitation, Simon opened the door at the other end and stepped into the loft-like room upstairs, making room for me to follow. I stopped with one foot hovering over the threshold, air caught in my throat.

"I always thought dungeons were supposed to be in basements," I forced out when my voice box started working again.

"We don't have a basement," Simon pointed out, his voice dripping with sarcasm.

"That you don't," I agreed, my eyes still skipping from one piece of equipment to the next, disbelief and excitement warring inside my head. But a dungeon he definitely did have.

The room had changed a lot since I'd last seen it over half a decade ago. For one thing, it now had a hardwood floor, polished to an even shine, and huge picture windows set into the sloping ceiling, thick enough to make me guess that they were reinforced for soundproofing. Most of the walls were hidden by furniture, leaving the lavishly large space in the middle of the room unoccupied. But that was where the semblance to any other room I'd ever been in ended.

My hands felt a little bit clammy when I wiped them on my thighs, and then I took those last two steps to fully enter the room. Simon remained beside me, leaning against the wall with his arms casually crossed over his chest.

"Any questions?"

I sent him a sharp look, but I was, quite frankly, a little too intimidated to sass off to him right then.

"Want a quick tour?" he offered, taking pity on me after obviously loving how that revelation had managed to shut me up.

"Please."

"Oh, now you suddenly know that word," he muttered under his breath, but when I raised my brows, he shook his head and grinned. "Nothing."

I could have explained that I had understood, but kept that to myself.

Starting a counterclockwise circle right next to the door, Simon began pointing out things.

"Saint Andrew's cross, impact toy rack, supply closet where I keep most of my rope and other bondage gear, universal padded bench, supply cabinet for toys and miscellanea, pulley system for the suspension rack, swing. I've considered getting a bondage frame because I really like the one we have at the local dungeon, but I hardly use everything else to the point where I need it. Plus, it would limit the open space to the point where I'm unsure if I'd still have enough room for the bull whip."

"Room?"

"For swinging it?"

"Ah. Of course," I replied, trying to hide my gulp. Because that must have been vital. Hell, did I really know a first thing about whips? No.

He gave me an amused look, then turned so that he was facing me, standing just close enough to invade my personal space, but not too close.

"Not that that will concern you any time soon, if ever. Time will tell."

"I guess," I told him when he kept looking at me as if that required an answer.

"Just how much do you want to turn around and run off right now?"

That question surprised me, enough that it made me crack a smile. Somehow, that helped a lot to cut down on my anxiety.

"Not that bad. I'm more fascinated than scared. Only a little?" I raised my fingers maybe two inches apart.

Simon's grin widened.

"I think I have to work on my presentation next time."

"Why? Do people you normally bring up here have a habit of running off?"

"Not really, but most of them have played with me a couple of times before they come here and know their way around a dungeon." When I eyed him askance, he shrugged. "The internet has done a lot to get people curious, but I usually look for new play partners at the local community hangouts, munches, or play parties. Quite frankly, I don't have the patience to invest time in a girl who gets scared when she realizes that BDSM is more than a light slap on the ass and a little name calling."

"So you're taking a risk with me here?" I ventured a guess, feeling just a little smug.

"A very small, very calculated risk. You're a lot more intelligent than those women, not to say you're not a total fuckwit."

That made me snort.

"Have you ever considered that they're running away from you rather than your dungeon?"

Leaning closer, he crossed that distance he'd been keeping between us, but I didn't mind. Not really. And my libido definitely approved.

"Then I want to fuck them even less. I'm a package deal, winning personality included."

It was a little hard to swallow, but I managed.

"Considering I don't have a problem with that, I'm sure I won't have a problem with your equipment, either."

His smile widened.

"Isn't that the part where people say, 'that's what she said'?"

"About," I agreed, then took another look around, trying to relax again. "I guess you have a reason for showing me that now, besides full disclosure?"

"If things proceed as planned, we'll be spending quite some time up here, so I figured I'd give you a few moments to get comfortable before I set my mind to making you a hell of a lot more uncomfortable."

I really liked the sound of that, even if a very small part of myself started asking me if I had gone insane.

"Awesome."

"If you keep using language like that, I'm going to gag you."

"Is that a threat or a promise?" I quipped back, smiling brightly at him.

"Not sure, but either way I like the idea," he pointed out, making swallowing even harder than it had been moments ago.

"So we're doing this today?"

"Unless you got cold feet in the meantime?"

"Nope."

I shook my head, exhaling slowly. My heart was already beating a mile a minute, and I had a feeling that would get worse all too soon—but not soon enough.

"Do you want to go through what I have in mind, or just take it as I deal it out?"

Somehow this was all going a little fast, but I wasn't sure if my suddenly frayed nerves would have turned me into a very thoughtful negotiation partner.

"Honestly? I trust you to know what you're doing way more than what my mind could come up with. Surprise me."

"Will do," he agreed, only half as cryptic as I'd expected. Right then, Simon sounded more like he promised to get the right things from the grocery store than, well, drag me through the first stage of hell and back. "Anything you feel the need to stress, or that I should know? I know this might be a little overwhelming, but it will get better once we get things started."

"Well," I began, then forced my thoughts to get out of the gutter and that supply closet. Stapling my fingers, I thought about the few things I'd come up with since Saturday, trying to decide what to say and what was too stupid to mention.

"Anything that bothers you, I need to know. Remember what I just told you downstairs?"

"About brutal honesty?"

He nodded.

"Trust me, things will go wrong. If not today, then next time, or the time after. I will judge your reactions wrong, you will get cocky and get in over your head, or a knot slips, a flogger strand hits inches away from where it should have. There's no way of preventing that from happening, but scrapes heal, and mistakes are there to not be repeated. What is vital is that we can both trust each other to communicate well, and then we'll get through this without it all crashing down on us like a house of cards. I'm not telling you this to scare you, but simply because it's the truth. That can't be that different from your daily grind in the ER."

"Yeah, I hate it when patients don't tell us that they have a weird feeling in their chest, and ten minutes later we have to wheel them back into the OR because they collapse."

He nodded, then reached up to cradle my cheek in his hand. Even after Saturday, the gesture was strange, unfamiliar, and fucking intimate. I hesitated, then turned my face into his palm, letting it comfort me for a second.

"I'm here, and I will catch you when you fall, each and every time. And if I know that you're already teetering on the edge, I'll be extra careful to open my arms wide. But for that to work, I need to know of all the possible obstacles in the road, even if it sounds insignificant or stupid to you now."

Taking a deep breath, I inclined my head as air whooshed out of my lungs.

"My hands. The cuffs were fine last time, but I don't think I can stand any stronger restriction. You know that I freak out when there's anything wrong with my fingers, and having them fall asleep from restricted circulation will likely make me use that safeword before I can even think rationally about it."

"No problem. Pulling your arms back like last time was okay, or should I keep that to a minimum, too?"

I thought about that.

"I honestly don't know. I felt a little banged up Saturday night, but keeping my arms up wasn't a problem, really. Can I just, you know, let you know if it gets problematic?"

He nodded.

"Sure. Most bondage anchors here and here"—he lightly touched my sternum and lower stomach—"or at the center of your back. I can make sure not to stress your arms too much. If we get there, that is."

"I think I would like to get there, yes."

That got me a quick smile.

"Anything else?"

Making a face, I got to the point of my agenda I was less convinced about.

"I'm not sure the verbal component of this all works so well for me?"

"Like me calling you a slut?"

I wasn't surprised that he picked that. Pursing my lips, I shook my head.

"No, that part wasn't really a problem. Might sound weird, but it made me feel kind of empowered, you know? I don't have to tell you that under any other circumstances I wouldn't let anyone else refer to me like that, but in the heat of the moment, it kind of fit?"

The look in his eyes was a lot more knowing than I'd expected.

"Context can make a huge difference."

"It does," I agreed, strangely elated that he didn't make me explain any further. "No, I think I have a serious problem with calling you 'Sir.' And I'm not sure about that asking for permission to come part."

Now it was clear amusement that took over his face.

"Let's make a compromise here. You don't have to call me anything, but at least once I want to hear you beg. If things go according to plan, I should get you into the right mindset today. If not, we can change that up next time, but humor me?"

"Sure," I agreed, then frowned. "I thought that would be more of an issue for you."

The grin he flashed me showed a lot of teeth.

"Because I'm a pompous asshole and you can't fathom how I'd pass up a golden opportunity like that?"

"Well... yeah?"

For the first time, it occurred to me that this brutal honesty thing might be hard to swallow for someone other than me, but he didn't seem to have any issues with it.

"Ego doesn't have a place in the playroom. Maybe the role I slip into seems like an extension of what you usually refer to as my winning personality, but unlike outside of a scene, here I have the weight of responsibility solely on my shoulders. If anything goes wrong, it's my fault, even if it happened because you didn't tell me something I should have known. In that case, I should have made sure you're completely honest with me first. I get a lot out of what actually happens, but it's that responsibility and trust you place in me that gives me the greatest satisfaction. If you boil things down to the actual dynamics, the Dominant is always the submissive's bitch. Anything I do is to let you get the biggest kick out of it. A small detail like whether you pretend to be meek or not doesn't change a thing for me."

"Not really a big concession then?"

"Not for me," he agreed. "Someone else may very well think differently about this. I told you before that the biggest appeal for me is the physical side. Someone who's way more into the dominance and submission part will likely balk at the suggestion to keep protocol completely out of the scene. It's a wide playing field, and it works best if you find someone with similar interests."

"Okay." Then something else he'd said on Saturday flitted through my mind. "You warned me that if I mouthed off to you, you'd make me rue that—does that still apply?"

Now his smile turned evil, and I couldn't keep a shudder of excitement from running through my body.

"Let's phrase it this way. If you still have enough breath and energy to mouth off, then I can push you a lot harder, so I will. Does that answer your question?"

"Yes. Yes, I think it does."

My voice had lost most of its strength, and my knees might have gone just a little weak.

"Ready to start?"

"Very."

"Good. I need to get changed. You need to go use the bathroom and get rid of all these superfluous clothes. When you're done, wait for me here"—he pointed at a spot in the middle of the open space—"kneeling. You remember what I told you about position?"

"Legs apart, arms behind my back?"

"Perfect," he more purred than said, then gestured toward the door. "Shall we?"

-7-

Ten minutes later, my knees hit the floor, and I exhaled what felt like the hardest breath of my life.

So this was it. The moment of truth.

Saturday had been different—still nerve-wracking in a way, but not like this. For one thing, even with all the excitement, it had felt a lot more like fooling around. Jack had been there, adding a certain buffering layer to things. No doubt, I trusted Simon explicitly to keep me safe, but now things were more serious, starker somehow.

Intimidating.

Exhilarating.

I wondered how exactly I should keep my arms behind my back, then crossed them, my hands gripping the opposite forearms. Looking down my body, I quickly sucked in my stomach and tried to straighten my back into a perfect curve. The floor was hard and cold under my legs, and it took less than a minute for my knees to start aching. Damn, but I was getting old.

A sound somewhere behind me made me perk up, my entire body slamming into alert mode. Had that been a creaking stair? How long exactly was he going to let me wait here for him? Was this already part of the game? I didn't doubt it. And it was definitely working. Five more minutes of being alone with myself, and I'd be putty in his hands.

I really didn't know what to think of that.

The sound repeated itself, then the door swung shut, startling me. The impulse to crane my neck and look over my shoulder was strong, but I cut it short. I wasn't exactly a creature of grace, but I was sure that kneeling like this I gave a pretty picture, and I didn't want to destroy that by falling over because I shifted my balance wrong.

His footsteps were almost silent as he advanced on me, and I saw why when he walked by close enough to touch if I'd let go of my arms—Simon wasn't wearing any shoes, or socks, for that matter. I'd kind of expected him to wear a T-shirt and jeans like last time. The black tee was back in evidence, if hugging his torso tighter this time. I definitely approved of the leather pants he'd donned. They made his long legs look more buff and accentuated his ass perfectly.

I quickly looked away before I could start a hymn to praise his gluteus maximus. Then looked right back because he'd reached the cabinet he'd described as the storage place for his bondage equipment. Now he definitely had my attention. I couldn't exactly see what he was rummaging around for, but when he turned and came over to me, he carried several coils of rope, neatly rolled up and wound around themselves.

"Hard night at work?" he asked conversationally, which was about the last thing I'd expected.

"Not too bad," I replied cautiously.

Simon flashed me a grin, obviously amused about the fact that I didn't really know how to behave yet.

"Relax. I told you, if role playing and keeping to a strict protocol isn't your thing, I can do without that. Besides, it takes time to tie someone up. I don't want you to nod off in the meantime."

"I doubt that will happen," I snarked back before I could rein in the automatic impulse, gaining another smile for my effort.

"Would be quite the rude awakening, that I can tell you already."

As if anyone could nod off after that!

Still keeping with the laid back theme, Simon stopped behind me and let the rope drop to the floor. Leaning over me so that his head was upside down, he crouched until our faces were almost nose to nose when I leaned my head back.

"Does it distress you if I keep talking to you as if you were anything else but my wanton little slut?"

A second later his hand was in my hair, wrenching my head back hard enough to make me gasp, while the other grabbed my wrists just as they slid by each other when I tried to extend my arms to keep my balance. The look in his eyes was hard, but did oh so delicious things to me.

"Don't think for a second that you're anything else to me but a body to use, three holes to fuck for my pleasure only. Understand?"

"Yes!" I hissed, then sighed when he let go, almost missing the contact. How was it possible that a few words like that combined with a hint of being manhandled could make me so fucking aroused?

"Get up and follow me."

Curiosity let me do so without putting up a fight. I was a little disappointed when of all possible venues, he led me over to the padded bench, which he pulled away from the wall, the heavy wood needing his entire strength to be moved about. On closer inspection, it looked more like the box-like benches found at the foot of fancy beds than what I'd expected as dungeon furniture, but it was covered in black, padded leather, and a multitude of attachment points were distributed all over the sides, the purposes of which I felt only halfway qualified to guess. Once he had the bench positioned to his satisfaction, Simon told me to sit down, and dropped all but one coil of rope onto the bench next to me.

"Hand," he prompted, and when I extended both arms in front of me, he glanced from my wrists up to my face briefly. "I can use the cuffs, too, if you prefer, but let's try this once, okay?"

"Okay," I agreed, then watched as he wound the doubled-over rope around my right wrist, crossing and twisting it around itself several times. There was still a long tail left when he tied off the rope, and he held on to it as he nodded toward the newly created rope manacle.

"Yank."

I did, maybe a little harder than I'd intended to because of his single word orders, but besides putting tension on my upper arms, nothing much happened. The thick bands of rope didn't have much of a give, and also didn't tighten, making it obvious why he'd just told me to test his knots. I nodded mutely, and he set to creating a similar cuff around my other wrist, then also around each ankle.

I had to admit, I hadn't anticipated that just sitting around waiting was as much a part of bondage as everything else. I must have appeared a little bored because when he straightened, Simon grinned as he reached for the last remaining coil of rope.

"Bored already? The part they never show in porn is just how awkward and endless the rigging can get before you have your victim exactly where you need her to be."

"I haven't complained yet," I pointed out, slightly petulant.

"Probably because I haven't accidentally whipped you with a flying rope end yet," he remarked as he stretched my arms out in front of me, side by side, and started tying them together just below the elbows. "That will get better once you're in position," Simon went on when I rolled my shoulders a little to keep my arms from squishing my boobs.

"Has anyone ever told you that you're such a tease?"

He let his grin be the only answer while he threaded the rope ends into that last tie.

"Get on your hands and knees. Or elbows and knees, I should probably say, toes at the end of the bench," he instructed, then stepped up to wind a strong arm around my middle while I shimmied around, surprisingly constrained and unbalanced already. When he had me where he wanted me, Simon took the loose rope ends from the wrist cuffs and pulled them taught as he tied them to the front center of the bench. So far our light banter had kept me mostly calm, but when he moved to the foot end of the bench and ran his warm palms up the backs of my thighs, I felt my pulse pick up further.

"Spread your knees as far as it's comfortable."

With his fingers only inches away from my pussy it was hard not to get even more excited about his command than I already was, but in line with my former observation, he didn't make true on that unspoken promise but instead reached for my ankles and pulled them even farther apart. Then he tied the rope leading from those manacles to the sides of the bench at the very end, right next to where my toes hung off the thick padding.

"I expect you to keep your knees in exactly this position. You won't like it too much if you'll make me get more rope to restrain them."

Right then, that didn't really sound like much of a threat, but testing my bonds, I couldn't see how I would even be able to move them much. It certainly felt more comfortable to keep my thighs further apart than trying to close them, thus rotating my knees uncomfortably.

"A sign of acknowledgment would be nice, even if you can't swallow your stubbornness and do it in a courteous fashion," Simon remarked dryly, and gave my ass a whack that was hard enough to make me cry out and rock forward.

A part of me that I hadn't realized existed was about to offer a loud, "Yes, Sir!" but I nodded instead before I could paint myself a hypocrite.

Simon made a sound low in his throat that probably started out as a snort, and stepped away from me to admire his work.

"That should do nicely."

He returned to me then, squatting down in front of the bench so that we were at eye level. Glee filled his face, and it wasn't exactly the nice kind of glee that gave me a warm feeling in my heart.

"You realize just how helpless and vulnerable this position leaves you?" he asked, his voice sliding like velvet over my skin.

Holding his gaze, I swallowed but didn't reply. We both knew that was true.

"Maybe you want me to demonstrate?" he offered, still sounding so very pleasant.

I opened my mouth, ready to tell him that wasn't necessary, and he shamelessly used that to lean in and kiss me hungrily. Well, that wasn't so bad, even if there was a light strain on my neck from having to push my head up.

My eyes drifted shut, and for a few seconds everything was forgotten—my unease-laced excitement, the perpetual horniness. There was just his taste, so tantalizing on my tongue, his lips, insistent but gentle—until his fingers skimmed down my side, hitting all the ticklish spots over my ribs, making me shriek and try to wrench away. Yet the wrist ties made it impossible to do more than pull my shoulder to the side, shifting my balance slightly, and the wide spread of my knees guaranteed that my hips moved even less. My knees did slip a little, the position becoming painful immediately, and as soon as his fingers stopped tormenting me, I quickly moved them back to where they belonged. Simon must have noticed but he didn't call me out on it, just kept staring straight into my eyes.

"I can be nice. Much of what I'm going to do to you depends on your reactions. Your problem might be that I really don't want to be nice. You'll have to convince me."

He got up then and walked over to the impact toy rack, studying his tools for several endless moments before he picked up a heavy, many-stranded leather flogger and a leather paddle that was only about ten by three inches in length. Neither looked exactly threatening, but he'd already proved what he could do with his hands alone. I didn't doubt that he'd have me exactly where he wanted me in no time. That thought alone was enough to spike my pulse once more.

Simon walked by my side without touching me this time and put the paddle down onto the bench between my spread ankles. That way, it remained in plain view when I looked back down my body, somewhat self-consciously sucking in my stomach. Once he stepped away from the bench, I lost sight of him, except for when I craned my head hard enough to strain the muscles in my neck.

I'd kind of expected him to have a go at me with the flogger now, but instead of hitting me with it, he dragged the long strands over my calves, then up my legs and over my ass to my upper back. Tensed as I was, less from apprehension and mostly from excitement, the sensation was something between ticklish and sensual. It made me relax a little as he dragged the flogger back down my body, then up my thighs again, this time letting a few of the strands tease the insides of my thighs and my labia. That actually felt kind of nice.

Until the light teasing sensation disappeared, replaced by a whoosh of air and the sharp sting of leather hitting my skin as he brought the flogger down on the outside of my left ass cheek. I jumped, as much as my bonds let me, and grit my teeth, weirdly proud that this time he hadn't made me cry out.

Tense, I waited for the next swing, but now he was back to teasing me.

Up and down my legs the flogger went, making me go rigid whenever it disappeared, only to reappear on my other side after a second or two. I tried to keep up the tension, but my muscles refused to cooperate about a minute later, and that was when he hit the other side of my butt with equal force and precision.

The sting was minimal, and I made the mistake of relaxing right there, anticipating that he would resume teasing me now, which made the five consecutive strokes that came down in a descending path on the back of my thigh hurt just a little more. By the time he mirrored that on the other side, I was gritting my teeth, but only until he paused. The entire area of my ass and thighs felt warm, but except for the immediate discomfort of the impact, I felt fine.

Fine enough to be a cheeky bitch and wriggle my ass at him when I looked back and saw him watching me, a slight smile on his face. That made him grin, a deliciously wry twist coming to his mouth.

"Let me guess... you're bored?" he asked, the hand not holding the flogger catching the end of the strands, pulling the leather tight.

"I wouldn't call it—ouch!"

That next stroke landed squarely across my ass crack and with more force behind it, although he looked rather relaxed and casual about delivering it. I bit my lip, trying to keep from squealing, but when the flogger hit the exact same spot several times more in quick succession, I couldn't help the noises escaping me. Instinctively, I tried to move away from the pain, mainly forward as he was standing directly behind me, but the bonds only permitted me to lean more heavily onto my arms. Instead of stopping this time, he only changed course, hitting my stretched thighs instead.

I didn't count the strokes, but it must have been more than twenty when he halted, leaving me breathing heavily, my fingers clenched into fists. Now there was actual pain that faded quickly, but not as fast as before, leaving a stronger kind of warmth radiating from where the flogger had come down on my skin. With my mind not preoccupied with immediate evasion instincts, I felt a little stupid about cringing away like that and forced my body to assume its previous position. It hadn't really hurt that much, and with almost a minute passed now, the residual glow was actually kind of pleasant.

Looking back, I found Simon practically lounging behind me, again keeping the flogger ready but at ease. I wondered briefly if he was waiting for something from me, but apparently checking back with him like that had been enough because he moved into action the moment after, aiming for the fleshier parts of my upper back, well away from my spine. Immediately, I dropped my head, my back bowed, waiting for each stroke with a little more composure now.

This time I counted, and it was twenty hits, equally distributed between my left and right side before he moved to my ass, then thighs. He kept the force behind each swing steady, as far as I could tell, but brought the flogger down harder than on the pass before, and when I didn't do my evasion shuffle but only flinched a couple of times, he went back to my ass to deliver another twelve strokes with increasing intensity that had me jump with the last five of them. Those really hurt and were definitely on the side of what my mind was screaming to avoid, but I forced my muscles to lock in place and simply tough it out. I didn't care that I'd made a few unbecoming grunts and high whines, but was simply glad when he stopped.

My breath was still coming fast and ragged when he continued, giving barely half a minute of reprieve.

Now he was concentrating on my thighs directly underneath my ass, but it felt somewhat different. For one thing, he hit me a little lighter than before, back to what I could easily cope with, but also faster, alternating sides with every stroke. Chancing a glance over my shoulder, I realized that he'd switched from aiming each single stroke one after the other to sending the flogger strands flying from side to side, using the whole range of motion of his shoulder to gather momentum, if not force. That came after he caught me looking, and this time when he hit the line where the sensation dipped into torment, he didn't just stop after five more hits.

Clenching pretty much everything I had, including my facial muscles and teeth, I waited, but the pain kept coming and increased steadily. Temptation was strong to pull away and eventually I couldn't hold out any longer, but every inch that he made me try to crawl away from him I gave as grudgingly as possible.

Then the pain just got too much, making me jerk forward as far as the ropes would let me. Three agonizing strokes still lashed my ass and then it was over, leaving me sweaty, shaking, and feeling miles out of my league.

"Good girl," he murmured low enough that I could have ignored him, but I didn't. For some reason, what should have sounded like condescension in another situation was praise to me now, as was the gentle caress of his hand moving over what felt like fiery red patches on my ass. I might have flinched at the first contact, but quickly leaned into his touch, which got a whole lot more interesting when his hand eventually roamed from the tops of my thighs to between them.

Before, Simon had been a tease, but now he went straight for the bull's eye. Rotating his hand so that it briefly cupped my pubic mount, two of his fingers slid between my labia, spreading them. I inhaled sharply as he reached my clit, rubbing it deftly.

Within seconds, any and all discomfort was forgotten, and it was impossible not to rock into his hand. He didn't seem to mind. In fact, he increased both speed and pressure, making nerve endings all over my lower body light up.

I didn't pay attention to how long he went on like this, but it certainly wasn't long enough when he stepped away again and resumed tanning my ass with the flogger. My lust-addled mind was slow to catch up so that the first few strokes still hit me relaxed and unprepared, but unlike before, that didn't make me want to come out of my skin. For those first few seconds I wasn't even sure how hard he hit me as everything just seemed to be muddled into one conglomerate of sensations. Then the sting of the flogger strands won out, making muscles contract and my fight against my instinctive reactions begin anew, but it held a different edge to it. It wasn't exactly easier to bear than before, but somehow more rewarding.

Simon didn't escalate things quite as much as before, just to the point where the balance between enticing and uncomfortable tipped toward the latter before we went back to stimulating me with his fingers. Immediately I felt hot need spread through my body, which only increased when he switched to thumbing my clit so he could use his fingers to stroke up and down my slit, but without penetrating me yet.

That went on for another three cycles, and while the last stroke of the flogger had me cry out, my face pressed into my bound arms, the following treat fell far from the raging need that was building low in my abdomen. Seldom before in my life had I needed a cock in my pussy so badly, and it was insane how insufficient having my clit rubbed just the right way could feel.

"You know, if you want something, all you need to do is ask."

It was that remark that made me realize what he'd meant before about teaching me a lesson about begging. That realization made me bark out a quick laugh, although it sounded more like a frustrated sob to me.

Why I couldn't just do the sane thing and utter those few words he clearly wanted to hear was beyond me, but then I didn't feel too mentally stable right then as it was.

"Nothing? I'm not boring you, am I?"

Before I could reply, something hit my left ass cheek hard, and when my eyes flew open and I looked to the end of the bench between my ankles, the paddle was gone. Again he slapped me, never stopping driving me crazy with his other hand.

"Nope, not bored at all," I tried to reply evenly, but the last word cut off harshly when he hit me again. Damn, but that paddle packed more of a punch than I'd expected.

"Oh, I think you are bored, otherwise you wouldn't be so damn silent. Cat got your tongue?"

His fingers disappeared, and a moment later the flogger was back, although it was a half-assed stroke at best that came now where the paddle had hit me three times.

"Seriously? Worst pun ever."

Simon chuckled, then put both impact toys down—right in the middle of my lower back.

"Make sure those stay where they are, or I'll keep you right where you are for a lot longer than you'd like."

He lingered at my side, and after a moment of trying to figure out how I could relax without slumping enough to accidentally throw off the flogger and paddle, I craned my neck to the side, finding him looking down at me. He'd broken a bit of a sweat since the last time I'd gotten a good look at him, but considering that my breath was coming in labored gulps and my entire body was slick all over, I couldn't find it in me to care. Crouching down, he brought our faces to the same height, and I wondered why he was so nice. He had obviously been telling the truth before, that he had no intention of playing nice, and if the need and plethora of intense sensation that kept ebbing through my body was any indication, I really didn't want him to.

The look in his eyes softened as he reached out and pushed a sweaty strand of hair behind my ear, then leaned close, but not close enough for anything interesting.

"Exactly how sore did Saturday leave you?"

Considering that he'd upped the ante as far as anything hitting me was concerned within the first five minutes today, I realized that he didn't mean the fleshier parts of my body with his inquiry. Just thinking back made me grin rather stupidly.

"Somewhat, but only in the best of ways."

"Still sore?"

Reaching back and up, his hand touched down on my lower back, with one of his fingers circling my anus slowly. My pelvic floor muscles—among others—clenched, but I held his gaze easily.

"Not enough that it should deter you."

"Deter me?" he asked, the slight grin on his face dipping into darker registers just as his finger briefly dipped lower to gather some lubrication that was flowing in abundance from adjacent places, then returned to tease my rosette softly.

"Deter you from fucking my ass," I deadpanned, then grinned back at him simply because it was too hard not to.

"Who says that I intend to fuck your ass?"

That probing finger definitely did, but I really hoped that wasn't just my wishful thinking.

"Well, last time you got to fuck my mouth and my pussy, it seems logical that now you'd want to fuck my ass, particularly as you've had it wriggling right in front of you the entire time."

He snorted, a strangely endearing sound considering the situation.

"I don't know. Right now I'm pretty content with painting your ass a lovely shade of red, so why should I stop?"

My answer was momentarily delayed when his finger finally made it through my sphincter, not quite so pleasant a sensation with the lack of sufficient lube, but I swallowed my rising complaint when he withdrew immediately.

"Because sooner or later you'll drive me insane if you don't fuck me," I drawled, kind of hating the angle I was forced into which didn't let me catch any indication of whether that dirty talk affected him or not. Then again, tight as those pants were, they'd likely hide said evidence either way.

"As I said—ask me nicely, and you shall be rewarded."

He waited for my reply but I just stared back at him, my lips compressed into as tight a line as I could. After five seconds he shook his head and laughed softly, then got up.

"Good, have it your way. Or maybe you just need a little more of an incentive? Let's see if I can come up with something."

He left me with that rather ominous sounding statement, and I watched his every move as he went over to one of the supply cabinets. After the way the flogger had made me squirm, I would have expected to be glad to get a break now, but the more I calmed down, the more I started to wish all those sensations back. Only a very small part of me dreaded what said incentive might be. Right then I was, quite frankly, too horny to give a fuck as long as it would lead to more squirming and panting.

Simon returned with a box of wipes, of all things, in one hand and a butt plug and bottle of lube in the other. How that should have scared me, I couldn't say, and like before I wriggled my butt invitingly at him when he stopped behind me.

"I love how much of a slut you are," he told me as he sat his paraphernalia down between my legs, smiling.

Even if I'd wanted to, which I didn't, right then I couldn't have denied that I was acting rather wanton and loving every second of it. I still stopped what probably resembled a botched attempt at twerking, mostly because the muscles in my thighs started to ache. My position was, all in all, rather comfortable except for the strain it put on my neck when I didn't rest my head on my arms, but all that contracting gave my leg muscles a nice workout, something they weren't really used to.

Simon meanwhile busied himself with rolling a condom over the black butt plug, then squirted what felt like more than liberal amounts of lube onto my asshole. I didn't protest, though, even if it was a weird sensation to feel some of the lube dribble down to my pussy lips. Then he set to working the plug into my anus, while his free hand gathered up some of the escaped lube and resumed stroking my clit and everything else responsive down there, with the glaring exception of where I really, really needed to be touched.

As if he'd read my mind, which, I had to admit, couldn't have been difficult right then, Simon picked up our banter again.

"I'm aware that for whatever screwed-up reason you've decided that begging is beneath you, even if it drives you insane, but I have all the time in the world right now. And should worse come to worst, I can easily get off by fucking your ass only. You're the one who might need a cock in your cunt so badly that nothing else will suffice."

Gnashing my teeth, also because now there was no way to catch the look on his face, I glared at my arms instead of my intended target.

"You don't think I can come from anal alone?"

"Eventually, maybe, under the right circumstances, but I won't be rubbing your clit, either. If you continue to be a stubborn little whore, I'm ninety-five percent sure that my cock in your ass won't be enough."

The frustrating thing was that I silently agreed with him. As it was, feeling the plug push deeper inside me with every tiny, rhythmic thrust now felt divine, but then he was doing a great job working me into a frenzy with his other hand, too. Without that, getting spread open slowly might still have felt good, but not climax-worthy good.

Shit.

Simon clearly took my silence as acquiescence, and went on conversationally after stopping for a moment to squirt yet more lube onto the plug.

"This is really not about me getting a kick out of forcing you to debase yourself. That actually doesn't really do much for me. It's about power, and control. To know that I have it all and you don't is what makes this so special to me. The knowledge that whatever I decide, that what I do next will either make you come or pull you back from that ledge and keep you crazy with yearning. When you plead for mercy, you surrender to me, not just physically as you already do, but mentally. It's just a tiny, last step, but a tremendously important one. If you come then, it's because I let you, because I want you to, because I take that gift you offer me in exchange for your reward. And that reward isn't one measly orgasm, even if at that point you should be damn grateful for it. No—right at that point, I own you, and even if that sounds weird as fuck voiced like that, it's a damn powerful feeling."

Maybe it was that what he was doing right then made me perceptible to other related things, but what he said didn't sound so bad compared to my senseless resistance stunt. It actually made me feel a little stupid, although not in a "I should have seen this myself" kind of way, but I was starting to ask myself why I was deliberately raining on my own parade.

While I was still mulling that over, the plug slid in after a last, slightly uncomfortable push, settling quite nicely into me. It made me feel full and stretched, but in that enticing way that a large cock filling and stretching my pussy felt good. The pleasant sensation grew as he continued to rub my clit, making my muscles clench. For a little while, I thought that having my ass stuffed would help make up for the glaring absence elsewhere, but, no. It only took him lightly stroking one finger over my entrance, and I knew that I was still fucked, unless I got fucked, literally.

"Definitely an improvement, but I'm not sure that will be enough," Simon remarked as he withdrew his hands, then used more wipes to clean his fingers than seemed strictly necessary.

I wasn't sure if he wanted my input on that, but I couldn't really come up with anything until he walked to my side and hunkered down next to me again. Now he didn't focus on my face, but somewhere lower on my body. I got my answer to that question when he reached for my breast, getting a good grip and squeezing before his fingers found my nipple. I hadn't really missed being touched there until now, but as such things went, I immediately rued the loss of contact when he withdrew his hand.

"How sensitive are your nipples?"

I really didn't know how to respond to that.

"Kind of lacking comparison here, but not too sensitive, I guess. Why?"

Suspicion laced my voice, and Simon's grin was enough to make me want to wrap my arms protectively around my boobs. But that was, of course, entirely impossible with my arms tied down, leaving my breasts completely at his mercy.

"That needs to be remedied. Your lack of comparison, I mean, not your constant need to sass off."

Reaching into the pocket of his pants, he pulled out a chain, and when I saw what was attached to both ends of it, I tensed without intending to.

"Oh, don't worry. They don't hurt half as much going on as they do coming off," he tartly informed me as he reached for my breast, then fixed the clamp around my nipple.

Bracing for pain, I was almost disappointed when the actual result of the jaws of the clamp closing wasn't too bad, also not on my other nipple, either. The paddle was decidedly worse.

Stepping back, Simon eyed the result critically, then crouched down right in front of me, a terribly amused look on his face.

"I think part of what ruffles your feathers so much is that you're forced to be so passive. Maybe a more active role will spice things up for you?"

I wondered if I should point out that I still wasn't bored, but his statement made me frown for another reason.

"You tied me to a bench. How can I be anything but passive?"

"The devil is in the details," he observed, then picked up the chain that connected the nipple clamps, and using his other hand, pulled it between my upper arms. The sudden increase in tension that quickly turned to pain made me hiss, but that didn't seem to deter Simon one bit.

"Open your mouth."

I did, because with him yanking on my nipples like that, I felt disinclined to antagonize him. He pulled harder on the chain, which made me gasp, and carefully pushed it over my chin and into my mouth, making the sleek metal press into my cheeks. Immediately, I put my head down, trying to alleviate the pain, but that only resulted in the chain dropping from my mouth when the slack increased. My pulse spiked when I realized what had happened, but try as I might, I couldn't manage to pick it up with my teeth once more as the motion inevitably made my body move, and the chain slide back onto the bench between my arms.

"Don't do that again," Simon warned with gleeful malice in his voice as he retrieved the chain and put it back between my lips. He immediately grabbed my chin, forcing my head to remain bent back, the pain in my nipples a red hot flash that made thinking hard. I squirmed, but that only worsened my predicament, so I made damn sure to remain immobile while he kept staring into my eyes.

"Let's play a little game. You obviously like the flogger, and I think you'll enjoy the paddle, too, but as this is your first time getting worked over well with either, I think it's just fair that I give you a means to tell me exactly where that point is between pain that feels so damn good, and pain that doesn't. See, I'll even give you some of the power back that I've so sneakily acquired by tying you up like this."

Somehow I got the feeling that this had nothing to do with fairness, or mercy for that matter. He confirmed my guess as he went on, forcing my chin even higher.

"The rules are easy. As long as you can stand me hitting you with the flogger or paddle, you are allowed to keep your head down, thus keeping the strain on the clamps to a minimum. Once you grow tired of that, or it simply becomes too uncomfortable, you just need to raise your head, and I'll give you a break. When you've had enough of that, drop your head, and flogger or paddle it is again. Sounds like so much fun, doesn't it?"

I only took a moment to stare at him when he let go of my chin, then quickly dropped my forehead onto my arms, doing my best to maximize the slack in the chain, now securely between my teeth. Even then my nipples still hurt, but the sensation dimmed to the point of being the lesser of two evils when the flogger hit my back moments later. That wasn't so bad, particularly as Simon took it easy for a while, but that mostly served to make me suspicious. It felt too much like he was biding his time, and I already knew that there was no way in this that I could actually win.

His focus soon switched from my back to my ass, then thighs, then he exchanged the flogger for the paddle. Before, he'd just hit my ass with it, now he also brought it down on the top of my thighs, and that made me realize that I actually preferred that more compacted kind of contact, at least until he put more force behind it. I felt that balance he'd been referring to slide toward the uncomfortable part of pain, but still tried to hold out as long as possible—until the next slap hit me squarely between my spread legs, making me scream and jerk forward. The dull throb in my nipples increased to hot pain before I realized that I'd jerked my chin up, panting loudly around the chain that I thankfully still gripped between my teeth.

"Thought that would get your attention," Simon let me know way too sweetly as his fingers slid over my still-stinging flesh, finding my clit again.

Even with the pain in my nipples, I relaxed, then realized that it actually factored well into the heady lust spreading through me. It was a little too strong, too stark to fully enjoy, but it did something to me that I hadn't expected. Exhaling shakily, I closed my eyes and let myself fall deeper into the sensation.

A minute passed, then two, and for a little while I was getting a little concerned that I might have to resort to asking for that pesky permission to come, but then the discomfort in my nipples turned to agony and I reluctantly let my head droop again. Immediately Simon's fingers stilled, but his hand remained cupping my sex a little longer before he withdrew it with a not-quite gentle slap.

Oh, but he clearly had found himself a new favorite target.

I fully expected the paddle, and likely harsh enough to make me jump as much as my bonds would let me, but instead it was the many strands of the flogger that came down on my pussy, bringing a lot of weirdly enticing air and a contact that was soft enough to make some of the tension leak out of my weary legs. Of course he didn't keep it to such a low, comfortable, almost teasing level for long, but even when he increased the force with which he sent the flogger straight for my labia and sometimes even my lower stomach, it wasn't just easy to bear but made me yearn for more.

And then it was the paddle again, steady, fast and increasingly more forceful, but even with a different sensation, the result didn't change so much. It felt good, actually great, to the point where I did my best to push my ass farther into the air to give him better access. Everything except the paddle coming down on my pussy dissolved into the background static of my mind, with only my nipples remaining as two steady blips of awareness. Soon it was impossible to concentrate on anything else, and he just kept on going and going and going...

Until three successive hard smacks that came with enough force to rock my body tore me right out of that floating space, making my eyes go wide as I screamed, unable to give a shit about the chain any longer. Dumb luck let it remain between my lips, and once I could think past the blinding pain radiating from my pussy, I raised my chin jerkily enough to put some extra insult to the pain I inflicted on my poor nipples.

My mind was too addled to react properly, so I didn't shy away at all when his fingers cupped my still-aching flesh, massaging it slowly rather than doing something directly stimulating. Not that it wasn't stimulating now that agony had dulled to ache, feeling like a hyper aware second heartbeat between my legs.

"Good girl," he praised again, and I could hear the smile in his voice. "I think now you've earned yourself that reward."

And then two of his fingers slid into me while his thumb ground into my clit, and I could have wept with gratitude. Maybe I was actually weeping, I couldn't say, with sweat stinging in my eyes, and now drool leaking out of my mouth. Very appetizing, but I really didn't give a shit, because there were two fingers fucking me fast and hard, sensually rubbing against the plug that made everything so much more intense and tight that I felt my climax rolling over me as if it had slapped me in the face out of the blue. Tensing all over, my head dropped, more as a reaction to the wave of need sluicing through me than anything else, and his fingers slid out of me again.

Breathing heavily, I felt my pulse skyrocket as I waited for the inevitable—scolding, followed by more of that paddle, and I doubted that any kind of head jerking would bring relief now.

Instead, the telltale sound of a condom wrapper tearing was loud in the silence, then I felt Simon half-climb onto the bench behind me. I didn't react at first when I felt his cock slide up and down my slit, but then he thrust into me, making my breath catch in my throat for entirely different reasons than before. Shit, that felt so fucking good!

Getting finger fucked should maybe have been a clue, but feeling his cock in me now make me realize just how much my position and the butt plug tightened up my vagina. The sensation was somewhat reminiscent of last Saturday, but with everything else going on, mainly the dull aches coming from all over my body, it was hard to relate. And really, once he picked up his pace, I didn't care whether he was just lenient with me, or I'd actually managed to sneak that orgasm by him. Right now my body overruled my mind, forcing it to focus entirely on the sensation of getting fucked deep and hard.

Maybe it was because I'd only just come, but it didn't take long for tension to ratchet up again, and this time I felt almost obliged to do him that favor and beg. I still waited until I felt there was no way around my release any more, which was a good thing, because the moment the first "Please!" made it over my lips, he stopped and pulled out, making me scream in frustration.

"Not so fast, slut," he ground out, and slapped both of his palms flat down onto my ass cheeks. Compared to what had come before, that didn't even sting.

Grunting in frustration, I tried to move back to grind myself against his cock, even though I doubted that this way I could make him slide back into me. Simon quickly disabused me of that notion by grabbing my hips and holding me steady, and only let go with one hand when I finally stopped pushing against him.

I felt a brief tug and the plug slid out, leaving my ass with a weird sensation as air rushed in before my sphincter clenched shut again. There was certainly enough lube in evidence not to need a refill now—something I was really grateful for in hindsight—and he didn't hesitate, but grabbed his cock and aligned it with my anus before starting to work himself into me.

On Saturday, Jack had been very diligent in prepping and spreading me open, and I'd enjoyed that as much as I'd dug actually feeling his cock inside me. Now I think I would have gone insane if Simon had dragged things out, and, bless him, for once he didn't do everything possible to drive me up the walls. The shallow thrusts he used were slow if deliberate, but the moment he felt my body yield, he pushed harder while pulling me closer with both hands on my hips again.

There was some discomfort and maybe a little pain, but when he started fucking me in earnest, all that got swept away by one of the most incredible sensations I'd felt in my entire life.

"Keep that chain in your mouth," he warned, then grabbed my hair and wrenched my head back, making me yowl with pain and surprise both. Yet again that got swallowed quickly, paling compared to everything else.

And wouldn't you know it, as close as I'd been before he switched things up, I was rather quick to find myself in the very same predicament yet again—and this time, I didn't hesitate.

"Please let me come! Please! Let! Me! COME!"

The bastard actually slowed down a little, making me grunt in frustration until he let go of my hair, his chest partly leaning against my back while his hips were still doing most of the work.

"Wait," he warned, his voice raspy and hot against my neck.

"Please! I can't...! You have to...! I..."

"When the clamps come off, you may come."

He only left me with a split second to process that before his hands groped for my breasts, and another while my mind caught up to the fact that blood rushing into previously constricted tissue might come with some additional discomfort. Then the clamps were off, "additional discomfort" proved to be the understatement of the day, and I came so violently that I jerked up hard enough to drive my shoulder into something that didn't feel like muscle only. But Simon didn't falter, not for a second, and drew out my climax by continuing to fuck me steadily.

I felt like I came crashing down when the haze of lust cleared, my aching nipples like two clear pinpricks of centered attention, but then Simon's hand slid from where it had been back on my hip to between my legs, zeroing in on my clit with determination. And, just like that, the next wave started building, or maybe it was still an extension of my last orgasm—I really didn't care. With the chain now useless, I spat it out, buried my face in my arms, and started my litany anew.

"Let me come, please, let me come!"

"So soon again?" Simon taunted, or tried to, but almost out of breath as he was, it could have been a note of surprise, too. He certainly didn't slow down, but instead slid the fingers that had been busy worrying my clit down to thrust into me, and used the ball of his hand to keep friction going where I needed it the most.

"Please!"

"Hold it. Hold it, I said!" he shouted when he felt me start to shiver underneath him.

Biting the inside of my cheek hard, I tried to hang on, one more second, one more...

"You may come after I do," he ground out, already thrusting irregularly, and two jerks later he stilled deep inside of me, while his fingers fucked me frantically.

That third orgasm wasn't as hard as the one before but still sent me screaming, my entire body alive with need. Simon's fingers kept going until I sagged underneath him, spent and shivering and smiling wide enough to hurt my cheeks.

The very small part of me that was still checking in with the world and not soaring in the clouds noticed that Simon was rather quick to shake off his own post-orgasmic haze, and set to undoing the ties that kept me fixed to the table with the condom still hanging from his cock. I might have snarked about his priorities, but then he was done getting the ankle ropes untied and helped me to lie down and stretch out my legs, and that felt so fucking wonderful that any desire to give a speech dissipated into contented relaxation. The ties that held my wrists followed, and last came the rope that held my arms together, leaving me draped over the bench, half on my back, half on my side, unwilling to move a muscle except to maneuver myself into an even more relaxed position. Simon grinned down at me briefly before he took care of that condom, then returned to me and leaned against the bench in the vicinity of my hips.

"Congratulations! You survived," he offered, smiling.

"Are you sure? Because I'm not sure I can feel my legs," I joked, instantly ruing my words when he reached behind him and pinched the fleshy part of my thigh.

"Seems responsive to me."

He laughed, deflecting my feeble attempt of swatting him. I made a face, then let my eyes roll back to stare at the window above me, not really seeing the clouds streaming by. Simon caught my hand where it now rested idly on my thigh.

"Wrists are okay?"

"Perfect," I purred, then raised both arms to look at the already fading impressions the ropes had left. "Although I'm not sure I would have noticed if my fingers would have fallen asleep. You had me a bit preoccupied there."

Simon answered that with an even brighter smile.

"You're a tough cookie, you know that? I didn't really expect I'd get to use the paddle much except to scare you, but not protesting here."

I couldn't help crack a smile, feeling a little stupid how proud his words made me feel.

"Again, I'm missing data to compare it to, and this time there's no reason to help me out there right now, mind you, but at least to me it seemed as if you got some mileage out of my ass."

If I hadn't been quite so physically exhausted, I might have face-palmed myself then, but as it was, I got to see the full glory of his smirk.

"That I certainly did."

"You know what I mean," I accused.

"I do, but it's nevertheless the truth."

Scrunching up my nose, I pulled one of my legs up onto the bench, then shifted, trying to catch a glimpse of my ass.

"Just how bad does it look back there?"

"Nice and red," Simon confirmed, then put his palm almost proprietarily onto the aforementioned war zone. "A little warm still, but in an hour or two you won't see anything anymore. Maybe you'll feel it a little when you sit down later, but there's no deep tissue bruising and no marks."

That astonished me a little, because some of the fingerprint-shaped bruises from Saturday were still in evidence, if fading now, and what little manhandling the guys had done while they had me between them was laughable compared to what Simon had put me through today. Just thinking about it made me blush, although I wondered if that was even visible, with my face likely still red and blotchy from exertion.

"Surprised?"

"Kinda. A few of those strokes felt like they should leave marks."

"Floggers seldom do more than just redden the skin. Paddles, either, unless you really go to town on someone with a heavier paddle, like a wooden one. If you want welts and bruises, canes are your thing. Even if you try not to mark someone up, it often happens accidentally once you do more than just lightly tap their ass with them."

"Why would anyone want that?"

Simon's brows drew together, a sure hint of annoyance.

"Don't diss what you haven't tried. You were clearly into getting flogged and paddled today, and I wouldn't be surprised if you'd really dig a thorough caning."

The thought made me shudder, and not just because it scared the hell out of me, yet irritation made my tone sharper than I'd intended.

"Do you always have to be such a nitpicker? I meant why would anyone want welts on their asses?"

He gave a noncommittal grunt that might have been an apology. I sincerely doubted it, but at least his frown disappeared.

"Souvenir? As a badge of honor? That's at least how I've always felt about my own welts. There's something deeply satisfying to touch or see them later and think, 'damn, that was insane, and I did it anyway.'"

On second thought, that sounded a lot like the warmth radiating from my butt already felt to me. Grimacing, I brought my hands to my breasts, idly touching my still-aching nipples. By now they were the part of my body that was in the most acute pain, but I had to admit that even my own, light touch made me kind of horny.

"That was evil, just so you know," I tartly informed him.

"What, making you hurt yourself just so I'd stop hurting you?"

"Not telling me just how fucking much the clamps will hurt when they come off. But yeah, that, too."

Simon shrugged my accusation off.

"I did warn you, but I doubt you would have believed me otherwise. Some things you simply have to feel for yourself to believe."

It was kind of funny how he kept staring at my tits until I folded my hands over the affected areas, and he didn't look even the least bit guilty. For whatever reason, that was really reassuring.

"All in all, did you have a good time? The fact that you came twice makes it easy to guess that you did, but I still feel obliged to ask. You know that you can always veto anything you didn't like."

"Three times."

"Hm?"

Catching my lower lip between my teeth, I tried not to smile too openly.

"You said I came twice. It was three times. You missed the first, I guess."

Simon cocked his head as if he was considering where exactly he was going to pinch me now, and I stealthily started inching my butt away from him.

"When?"

That single word was a lot closer to a sharply barked order than an inquiry. I didn't know if that made me horny, or annoyed.

"Just when you stopped finger fucking me. I really didn't see it coming, and it wasn't that earth shattering. It kind of just happened?"

Pursing his lips, he was still considering, but then gave a brief jerk with his chin.

"Doesn't matter. At least now I know what I'll be doing the next time we're up here."

"That sounds rather ominous," I pointed out.

"Better if I tell you to be afraid, oh so very afraid?"

"Nope." I laughed, but couldn't feel a little intimidated nevertheless. "And can I veto whatever you're talking about? You just said I can veto anything."

Simon's sanguine grin left me none the wiser.

"Trust me, you don't want to veto that. You might hate me somewhat in the middle, but in the end you'll be quite satisfied. Unless, of course, you keep making a habit out of trying to sneak orgasms by me. This is your last warning. Next time, I will punish you, and that will go down with a lot more sobbing and howling than you did today."

I considered that, but there wasn't really much to consider— not really.

"I didn't mean to. I'm sorry. I'll try to do better next time."

"Oh, don't worry. You will."

And for whatever reason, that sounded like the real threat.

"Anything else you want to talk about, or are you ready to hit the shower now? I certainly wouldn't mind cleaning up, and I'm not the one who has snot, drool, and lube smeared all over my body."

"You say the sweetest things," I huffed, then straightened, making it off the bench on my third try. "Shit, I'm getting old!"

"That will be much worse when you get up in the morning, or, in your case, evening," he assured me.

Grinning back, I started making my way toward the door. Simon followed me after picking up his pants and T-shirt from where they'd ended up on the floor underneath the bench.

"Don't laugh too much at me now, but I only just noticed that you're naked."

I got a snort out of him, but he didn't look too surprised, and thankfully not hurt. I doubted that I could have said something similar to Jack without getting at least a pouty frown in return.

"You looked kind of out of it when I had the lengthy go at you with the paddle. I figured I should bring things to a close soon, so I used the time it took you to shake off your shock to undress. You know, the part before I finger fucked you and you came without permission. Again. And I don't really like to fuck wearing clothes. Feels kind of weird to me."

That reminded me of something.

"Yeah, about that. Did you have to tear me out of that trance so harshly? You could just have started fucking me there without giving me a heart attack and possible leather bottom."

Simon's grin could only be described as evil.

"Sadist, remember? If there's a chance that I can make you scream, I will always take it. You better get used to that quickly."

As strange as that still sounded to me, I really didn't think we would have any problems on that front, even if part of me wanted to protest. Instead, I gave him a private little smile, then turned back around and padded over to the door, a cozy feeling of accomplishment leaving goose bumps all over my body.

-8-

The last time I'd really needed a shower in this house, the guys had graciously let me take it on my own, but now Simon practically plastered himself to me as soon as we hit the bathroom. I raised my brows at him questioningly, but he just shrugged as he stepped into the admittedly large enough stall behind me.

"Be a dear and indulge me, will you?"

"Have you suddenly decided to be British?"

Instead of answering, he turned on the faucet, and any and all protest I might have harbored before died as soon as his fingers dug deftly into the knotted up muscles of my upper back. Who was I to protest when he was happy to throw in a massage on top of crazy, wild sex?

Things got a little weird when eventually his fingers started to stray—no surprise that they not so accidentally found my breasts, although I wasn't sure if he just intended to grope me, or tried to make me jump—and downright awkward when I turned around to confront him and found his face way too close to mine for any definition of friend zone on the planet.

I stared at his lips, almost mesmerized, then licked my own as I tried to decide what to do. That in itself was strange enough, but it got worse when he just kept waiting, studying my face.

"Okay, am I the only one who's kind of out of options here right now?"

"I don't think that a decided lack of options is the problem," he pointed out, then smiled. It was a really nice, cute smile, the kind that begged to be kissed away, and so at odds with what we'd been up to until a couple of minutes ago.

"What is, then?"

The urge to take a step back and cross my arms over my breasts—and maybe cradle them protectively, because my nipples were really fucking sensitive right now—was strong, but it was simply too nice to stand so close to him, almost touching but not quite.

"I think that you're desperately trying to return to a well-established comfort zone that isn't there anymore."

Cryptic as it sounded, it was fitting. Smiling slightly, I gave a hint of a nod in agreement.

"Honestly, I've never been in a situation where I just had sex with someone and didn't know whether it was okay to kiss him, or not."

Not surprisingly, his smile widened into a grin.

"Being a typical guy here, I'll never protest you trying to kiss me, particularly not after we've had sex."

It was an opening that my body yearned to take, but I knew that it wouldn't just stay at fooling around. For whatever reason, I really didn't feel up to that. Not physically, even with my posterior region still indecisive whether it should be declared a war zone or not I was sure that a quickie in the shower would be fun, but mentally.

"Do you ever feel a little lost after a scene?"

Now that smile turned knowing.

"Why do you think I'm here?"

His reply made a weight I hadn't known was there drop from my chest, but I had no intention of letting this conversation slip into too serious a territory.

"Because you're a gropy bastard?"

"That too," he admitted, chuckling softly, while his eyes never strayed from my face. "But I've been exactly where you are, on more than one occasion, and if I can help you get out of any possible funk before you drive head-first into a black hole of self-doubt, I will."

"Aren't you being a little melodramatic here?"

Simon shrugged.

"I'm making good money with melodrama. You can't expect me to drop that just because we're having a moment here."

"No? Too bad. But just for clarification, melodramatic expressions are not a requirement?"

"They might soon be if you keep sneaking orgasms by me," he pointed out.

"Ah, burn!" I cried, then did take that step back, but mostly to let the warm spray of the shower hit my back and hair. "But then I guess corporeal punishment doesn't really work well on someone who digs pain?"

I'd expected him to shrug, but his expression turned serious instead.

"I personally don't really believe in punishment. If you disappoint me, my disappointment should be what makes you want to do better next time, not some menial task I have you do, or getting a hard spanking. But then, I'm biased. Most people tackle the issue differently."

His words made me feel a little guilty, but then my mind latched onto what he'd actually said.

"Biased how?"

"Bad experience," he replied, then switched places with me as I reached for the shampoo bottle. "My first Mistress only ever hurt me when I screwed up. Not the best position to put a sub in, when on top of being frantic because they disappointed you they feel even worse because your punishment feels like the fucking best thing that ever happened to them."

"Sounds like a communication problem," I pointed out.

Simon nodded.

"A massive one. She wasn't exactly a bad Domme, but even after years of experience she was incapable of figuring out that we were a horrible match, almost polar opposites. Things got really bad, and we broke it off just in time before I could turn my back on all things devious forever. But I guess what I'm trying to say here is that if you need me in whatever capacity, I'm here. That's as much part of my job as the rest. And sometimes I need a couple of minutes to unwind myself. So, again, indulge me."

Lathering up my hair, I might have enjoyed watching water cascade down his naked body a little more than I probably should have, but I felt absolutely no remorse.

"So you had a rocky start," I noted, trying to bring the conversation back to the previous topic.

"In the end, it's probably Jack's fault that we're now standing here, with my left arm a little tired and your ass still a healthy, red glow."

I rolled my eyes at his moment of self-pity.

"What does Jack, of all people, have to do with that?"

Simon made an almost pensive face, although his grin ruined the effect.

"After a week, he got tired of my moping, so he went out, found another Domme, and dragged me to her, kicking and screaming. I don't think that without his incentive I'd have met Beth, or met her before my budding neurosis had bloomed into a full-blown chip on my shoulder."

"Are you being melodramatic again, or do you mean literally?"

"Psychology is full of figures of speech."

"I meant the kicking and screaming part. Sheesh."

His mouth twisted, faintly amused.

"There was dragging and loud arguing involved. I don't think I actually kicked him, but to my never-ending mortification I have to admit that a lot of sulking was involved on my part, as Beth never fails to remind me."

"The new Domme, I presume?"

He nodded.

"She's great. Very down to earth, no nonsense. I'm sure you'll get along well if you ever cross paths. I haven't decided yet if that aspect excites me or scares me to death."

"Why? Because she has dirt on you like few other people? Or are you afraid that I won't accept your authority if I meet the woman who made you kneel at her feet?"

"And lick them, too, if you're curious," he informed me, smirking. "And you already don't treat me with anything even close to respect, but I intend to keep working on that. She's great, but some people have problems with her 'in your face' approach to pretty much everything. But she wouldn't put up with your bullshit, so if you ever meet her, don't set yourself up to get your ass kicked."

"Duly noted." Bumping Simon out of the way with my hip, I reclaimed the spray of water, setting to the task of rinsing the suds out of my hair. "And, as usual, we got sidetracked. It's nice that you're here to lend comfort and a shoulder to cry on, but I'm not exactly plagued by second thoughts. We still haven't settled on where we draw the line between being friends and those extra spicy benefits."

"Never had to define that before," he mused, and shrugged. "That you even want to define it makes me guess that you're not comfortable with getting too casual, so I'd say that unless we actively set out to do anything, we'll keep our hands to ourselves? Although considering how touchy-feely you and Jack get sometimes, I'm not sure how well that will work."

"I don't think I'll have problems with Jack in that aspect."

At least I hoped that was the truth. I hadn't seen him for more than a couple of minutes since then, but the few texts we'd exchanged hadn't exactly made me want to jump his bones. Maybe that should have made me feel guilty now, but Jack was Jack, and what we had had always been special. Not that getting tied up, flogged, and fucked wasn't special, but it was definitely different, and just as it was typical for me and Simon that we had to hash things out first, I was sure that they would just flow harmoniously with Jack.

It seemed a little suspicious that Simon didn't reply, but once I reemerged from the spray, I found him leaning casually against the tiled wall, keeping his distance. Part of me wanted to kick myself for shoving that space between us that felt fake somehow, but going back on what I'd agreed to a minute later seemed too hypocritical even for my newly supercharged libido. It still would have been nice to have someone to soap up my back while I waited for the conditioner to do its magic, but asking now felt too much like a taunt.

"Anything about the scene you still want to talk about?"

He broke the silence before I could. Thinking about it for a second, I shook my head.

"Nope. But should that change, I'll let you know later."

"Anytime."

"Really anytime? You know that I don't believe in conventional work schedules." Or the hospital didn't.

"Anytime," he repeated, smiling. "I'll even pick up when I masturbate, as you very well know."

"Oh, how could I forget!"

With that, he left me to my own devices, which was probably for the best, else the temptation might have gotten too strong too soon.

Five hours of sleep had never felt so inadequate.

After Simon and I had both gotten dry and dressed again, I'd hung out another hour or so, idly chatting about stuff with him, but the extra dose of physical exhaustion I'd gotten had soon overcome what alertness the endorphin rush had lent me. Before long I'd been presented with the danger of dozing off mid-sentence, so I'd taken my leave before that could happen. Again.

Years of missing regular meals because of one more emergency surgery had taught me to be religious about eating breakfast, but today I barely had time to wolf down a bowl of leftovers that was bordering on possible health hazards before Marcy ushered me out the door, both of us running a little late for our shifts already. It was nice to get a chance to catch up with her, which didn't happen too often, but I instantly rued it when I plunked down onto a rare empty seat on the train and immediately shot up again when my ass reacted negatively to the contact. Marcy grinned but held her tongue, very paranoia-inducingly so. It became clear what she had in mind when we made it into the hospital via the ER entrance, and she asked me in front of the entire staff if she should bring me one of those donut pillows for my obviously sore ass.

"Slater, you're late," my boss cut through her giggling and grinning minions, and I'd seldom been that happy to get barked at. "I couldn't give less of a shit about your sex life, but I do give a shit about my patients, so you'd better be scrubbed in and ready in ten—we have three ambulances en route."

"Yes, ma'am," I shouted after her, already picking up speed to ditch my stuff in the locker room. For the first time, I was glad that I spent my working hours mostly on my feet than sitting down, though.

It took a couple of days for the rumors to die down, but I was too swamped with work to care. It would have been great to set up a repeat performance of last weekend that Saturday, but I had already let myself be talked into working those three shifts back to back instead; I simply couldn't say no to Zoe when she straight out told me that the ER was understaffed, and she expected me to pick up the slack everyone else had created. With anyone other than her I would have felt like a boot licker, but I doubted that working my ass off beyond the call of duty was what she saw as an attempt to gain her favor. I simply did what was necessary, as was my job, in her creed. Then the new week started with all the usual insanity, and it was Friday already by the time I could catch enough of a breather to call Simon.

I should have left the hospital at eight in the morning at the latest so I could catch a few hours of sleep before coming over, but as so often had happened over the last couple of months, reality gave me the middle finger. It was three in the afternoon when I finally staggered out of the ER, and it cost me a lot not to just call and cancel, including the plans for later that evening when Kara had roped the three of us into joining her for drinks. Apparently she had a new guy she was fucking whose friends bored the hell out of her, and some unwritten rules of friendship dictated that we had to act as backup small-talkers until she was ready to drag him off. Under different circumstances I would have looked forward to that as much as letting Simon do his thing, but just the idea of having to act somewhat civil and not fall asleep mid-sentence gave me hives.

It was a testament to just how horny I was, exhaustion notwithstanding, that I showed up at the guys' doorstep at all.

I was surprised to bump into Jack as soon as I opened the door, but judging from his running gear, he was about to engage in a different kind of physical activity than I was looking forward to. He flashed me his usual grin as he straightened from lacing his running shoes, and if his hug was a little more intimate than usual, it wasn't by much.

"You look like shit warmed over, do you know that?"

"You say the nicest things. Sometimes I really wonder how you manage to get laid at all," I shot back, silently agreeing with him. I'd had less than twenty-five hours of sleep this week, and it was starting to show.

His grin dipped into somewhat darker registers, but that was likely my imagination.

"If you're really concerned about that, I don't have to go for a run right now. I mean, you're a doctor—if you're concerned about my physical well-being, I should heed your advice."

"Get lost," I huffed, but couldn't keep the shit-eating grin from my face.

Jack snorted and did just that, but not without stopping inside the open door.

"He's kind of in a weird mood. Far be it from me to get between you and your choice of recreational activities, but I thought I should warn you. I've only been home for like fifteen minutes, and he bit my head off twice. You're always welcome to crash on the couch, you know that."

"Thanks, Dad."

"Oh, you wound me," he sing-songed, then ducked out of the door when I made a grab for him. "Have fun! Or not. Whatever floats your boat."

And with that he was gone, leaving me shaking my head and not knowing what to make of his warning. Simon could get moody at times, but I doubted that he would let that affect what happened in the playroom. He'd been quite adamant before when he'd stressed that ego had about as much place in BDSM as any kind of intoxicants had—none.

I found him lounging on the couch, feet up on the coffee table, laptop across his thighs. He didn't look up when I entered, although he must have heard our exchange at the door or at least been aware that I'd finally made it here. Not quite sure what to do with myself, I dropped the duffel bag containing my change of clothes and what I hoped might pass Kara's inspection later on the floor. Somehow I was starting to see a pattern here.

"You're late," Simon informed me about half a minute later, sounding distracted but also kind of pissed off.

"No shit, Sherlock," I grumbled, maybe a little angry myself because of the reason for my tardiness. "And wouldn't you have guessed it, it's not even because I overslept, but I haven't even hit the sack yet. Two of the interns called in sick and I got saddled with an extra eight hours of clinic duty." Which was bothersome in and of itself, because I could think of better ways to spend my time than get whined at by hypochondriacs with stellar self-diagnostic skills, with the odd coughing kid thrown in for extra fun.

Simon's eyes lifted from his screen to find mine, and as much as I tried, I couldn't read the look on his face. It was oddly bland, and I didn't know whether that was a good sign or not.

"You could have called."

"I sent you a text as soon as I left the hospital."

Truth be told, I could have sent that text hours earlier, but I'd clung to the hope that I could take off sooner than expected.

He kept staring at me, which made me kind of uncomfortable, but I was too tired for playing games right now.

"Look, I'm sorry. Yes, you're right, I should have called earlier. But I'm here now, and we've still got"—I checked my watch—"roughly two hours before Kara wants to drag us into the Friday early-evening madness. Do you really want to waste that with moping around?"

A muscle in his jaw jumped as he gnashed his teeth, or so I imagined, but blandness had seeped into his voice as he replied.

"As you wish. What do you have in mind?"

It would have been so much easier if he'd continued to be angry or started to pout—a first, but when he was like this, nothing was beyond him—and I felt like I was slowly maneuvering myself onto too-thin ice here.

"I don't know," I hedged, getting absolutely no reaction from him. "I'll leave the planning up to you?"

He held my gaze just long enough to make me wonder if I'd just thoroughly fucked myself, then looked away as he closed his laptop and got to his feet.

"You have five minutes. Do I have to repeat my instructions?"

I quickly shook my head.

"Me, naked, kneeling upstairs."

He nodded, then walked by me without saying another word, disappeared into his room, and shut the door behind him. I shook my head, too tired for more than a hint of annoyance to come up inside of me, then undressed and beat it to the bathroom. I was quick to finish my business, but barely made it upstairs into the attic before Simon arrived. He was wearing the same clothes as last time, which still had the same effect on me. Tired I might be, but not too tired to admire just how delectable he looked in those leather pants and tight T-shirt.

Unlike last time, he didn't make me wait but instead came to a halt facing me, his arms crossed over his chest.

"Before we begin, we have to decide on how to go from here."

That sounded ominous enough that it made me uneasy, but I quenched those feelings quickly, trying to remain calm.

"I guess this mostly depends on you. How much did you like our last session?" he asked.

I wondered if that was a loaded question, but decided that this was definitely one of those brutally honesty situations.

"I don't know. Honestly, 'like' is not what I'd qualify it as. I mean, it was awesome, and it completely blew me away, but there were times..."

I trailed off, letting that hang between us. Simon's mouth quirked into a brief smile of remembrance, and that smile was way too nice for what I knew must be lurking in his mind.

"Maybe I should have clarified. Our last session was very biased. Heavy on the physical side, light on the mental aspects. As I've told you before, I dig the physical stuff, and I get enough of a mental kick from this level that it satisfies me. The question is—does it satisfy you?"

"Wasn't that part of the problem?" I offered, not getting what he was leading up to.

Simon shrugged.

"Frankly, if you say that this is what you want, I'll drop the point of protocol altogether. You come over, you get your fix, you leave. There's no sense to me frustrating both of us with tedious lessons if I'm just annoying you with them. And before you start frowning at me as if I'd just offended you, there's nothing wrong with being a masochist without having stronger submissive tendencies. Frankly, my life is a lot easier and simpler if the only thing I have to worry about is your physical well-being. So, again, did what we did satisfy you to the point where you say yes, let's do this again?"

"As opposed to what?"

I was surprised at the amount of doubt that laced my voice. Simon picked right up on it.

"As opposed to shifting things more into mental territory. Do you just want me to simply fuck you, or also screw with your mind? I've told you before, submission comes wearing many faces. This is not about you being meek. I personally love to give you incentive enough to submit to me, but the question is—do you want to do it just on a physical level, or also mentally? Do you want to feel like on some level you belong to me? Do you want to please me? That comes with consequences if you screw up, and while I have no intention of intruding into your life outside of the playroom, sooner or later something might seep over that boundary. It's up to you whether that just sounds silly, or tantalizingly fascinating to you."

I licked my lips, a bit at a loss for how to respond. It did sound silly, but I also couldn't deny that the concept had a strong pull to it.

"When do you need my answer?"

"Right fucking now would be nice," he shot back, smirking.

I swallowed, also to gain a little more time, but mostly because thinking about that did terrible things to my mind. Part of me loathed that we had to have this conversation when it was hard enough to think, but then in my current state of mind it was easier to just go with what felt right rather than to overthink everything.

"If I agree to that, what would that make me, your collared slave? Because I'm not sure I'm exactly comfortable with that. And I doubt that I can call you 'Master' with a straight face."

My reply clearly annoyed him, and for a moment I thought that right there I had my answer.

"I don't give a shit about semantics. I told you before that I don't give a shit about protocol, either. This is about how you feel about me, about yourself, about us. It's about what you want me to do to you, and what you expect of me."

I thought about that, and when he realized that I was still biding my time, Simon sighed.

"Look, let's reduce that to the bare bones of it. I'm not going to expect you to be my meek little plaything. I'm not going to mentally mold you into a person you don't want to be. I love playing with you, and between the two times we've had sex, I felt like we matched pretty well, but there's potential for more. Maybe that's wishful thinking on my side—that's why I'm asking you now. With some women I'm more than happy to keep it physical only, but with you I feel like we both could get so much more out of this if you let me get a little further under your skin.

And it's not like you're cementing your fate with your reply right now. We will keep discussing this every step of the way, of course. I'm always open to negotiations."

Listening to him explain, I couldn't help but feel a little flattered. He made what we had sound like so much more. Realizing that I felt like what was developing between us was still pretty much just sex made me feel a little guilty, like I should confess that to him. But wasn't that exactly what we were talking about right now? That meant that on some level I already agreed with him, and if I was honest with myself, getting even more out of this than having that special itch scratched sounded too tantalizingly good to simply dismiss it.

"What exactly would happen if I did say that I'm interested in stepping up the game?"

The way his eyes lit up told me that he knew that he had me. Strangely enough, that didn't come with the expected knee-jerk reaction of me wanting to take a step back immediately.

"Baby steps. We'll see. Just think about it. Shall we begin?"

I nodded, a little miffed that he left it at that, but then realized that this would become a true uphill battle if I couldn't just let him take over and set the pace. Then again, if last session was any indication, Simon wouldn't leave me twiddling my thumbs for long if he could just throw me into the deep end of the pool instead.

"I've been thinking about how to tackle our little problem, if you remember," he went on, his previously relaxed pose becoming more authoritative. "That we're a little pressed for time and you're sleep deprived enough to fall asleep if I leave you like this for five minutes doesn't make my job any easier. With a less bratty sub, I would rely on her cooperation, but I'm afraid if I do that, you're going to leave with your ass too bruised up to sit for a week. This is why I've decided that we'll switch things up from last time. From now on, you will address me properly with 'Sir,' and I won't hear a single thing from you unless you are prompted. Any objections?"

It was then that I realized that my mouth was open, ready to snark back, but I quickly closed it. My body was running on autopilot, and there was no way of guessing into just how much trouble I could talk myself unwittingly if I didn't consciously shut up.

Simon's gaze kept boring into mine until I inclined my head, yet before I could look up again, he was crouching down in front of me, one hand catching my chin and holding it firmly, forcing our eyes to meet.

"I'm not trying to be a tyrannical asshole, although I easily could. This is my playroom, my rules. I don't owe you an explanation. Upholding a base level of protocol can help you ease yourself into the right mindset. In a way, a lot of what we do is conditioning. I don't expect you to be meek, just not to fight me every single step of the way. Be a good little slut, and you'll get your reward."

He didn't add any threats, but then he didn't need to. Last time had taught me that he didn't need to explicitly punish me to send tears into my eyes, and as much as I'd loved that part of the scene, I got that bad behavior would not be rewarded with leniency again. Now it was simply a matter of whether I wanted to play along or not.

He must have seen agreement on my face because he let go then and went over to his supplies, once more fetching rope and putting it down onto the bench. He really must like that combination. I didn't know whether that should have disappointed me—doing something new would have been fun, and there was so much we hadn't explored yet—but then I doubted that he'd just go for a repeat performance.

"Come over here."

Scrambling to my feet, I joined him, trying not to look too mutinous. Simon gave me a single, amused glance that told me that he knew that I was burning to give him a good tongue lashing, but I could see where he was coming from. And being ordered around like this also made me soaking wet, something I really hadn't expected.

"Sit down on the bench."

I followed suit, and he returned to the cupboard to get two sets of padded leather cuffs. While he buckled them around my ankles and wrists, I had a really hard time keeping silent, and judging from the way his eyes kept flitting to my face, his lips twitching, I guessed that he was highly amused by my likely not-well-hidden struggle.

Taking a deep breath, I let it out slowly, trying in vain to quiet myself.

"Sometimes I wonder how you make it through any long operation. At least I presume you're shutting up then, otherwise one of the nurses would have stabbed you long ago."

I didn't try to keep anger and challenge out of my gaze as I glared at him, but Simon completely ignored me.

"Lie down, ass right on the lower edge of the bench, as far down as you can manage before falling off."

I shimmied around until I was in position, keeping my knees tucked up to keep my balance. Weirdly enough, that made me feel exposed, as if having my ass almost in the air made me any more naked than standing around without clothes on. Simon connected my wrist cuffs to each other, then stretched my arms out behind my head as far as they would go and used a short length of rope to connect them to the head end of the bench. Lying with my torso prone like that made me glad that I'd shaved the last time I'd stumbled into my bathroom at home, or else my arm pits would have been glaringly stubbly right in front of my face.

Once he had my hands secured, Simon picked up one of the long coils of rope and unwound it, then set to tying it around my thigh, below my knee. He did the same to my other leg, then used the loose rope ends to connect my spread thighs to the bench also, with long enough leads that the strain on my hips wasn't too bad. The last two ropes went through the snap hooks on the ankle cuffs and were then connected to the same attachment point the wrist cuffs were tied to. Just for fun I tried kicking out, but while I could move the heels of my feet around, I wasn't exactly in a position that left me much room to move. With my legs raised over my body, that also put extra pressure onto my torso—not the best sensation in the world, but manageable.

And because he was such a caring bastard, Simon fetched a couple more coils of rope that he put under my neck and head, creating a surprisingly comfortable cushion that forced me to stare straight through the V of my tied legs. I tried to ignore what the position turned the lower half of my torso into, but then I doubted that a reed thin, perfectly toned body would have remained looking good like that. As usual, Simon didn't seem to give a shit. That playful smile that I saw ghosting around his lips likely came from seeing me helpless in front of him, and, well, quite exposed and available on the lower end. Just considering that made me forget all about being self-conscious.

His thoughts seemed to run along the same lines as mine as he stopped at the foot end of the bench, nicely framed by the V of my thighs, and used the back of his hand to casually stroke over my pussy. I didn't exactly jump at the contact, but need immediately spiked inside of me, my body screaming for more when he withdrew his fingers.

Looking up, he caught my gaze, and now he definitely looked like he was up to something.

"You know what always strikes me as peculiar?"

I wondered if this was a case of me being expected to reply, but he went on talking before I could.

"So many women make such a fuss about their personal hygiene, even if they pretend that they don't. They shave their legs," he went on, using his right hand to run up the back of my thigh, then up my thankfully smooth calf.

"They shave their armpits."

Leaning between my legs, his hands touched down over my rib cage, then stroked upwards over my breasts to my arms, thankfully only skimming the ticklish spots on my sides.

"They even go as far as to trim their pubic hair if they think they might get to fuck."

Straightening, his hand returned to between my legs, still not teasing enough for my liking.

"All apparently to please some cosmetic ideal that we guys supposedly notice, let alone subscribe to. But what you don't do is remove that last patch of hair that actually tickles in our noses and gets stuck in our teeth, and I think that's really inconsiderate, wouldn't you say?"

His fingers threaded through the short, curly hair while his grin widened. I was so tempted to bite his head off any moment now, but instead took another deep breath. He was baiting me so obviously, and I refused to dig my own grave over a stupid thing like this. His eyes remained on my face, taking my struggle in, and growing more amused by the second.

"You know, it should probably not cost you that much restraint to keep quiet," he observed, his fingers still drawing idle circles over my labia. "Let's see how long it takes to make you back down, shall we?"

Now that sounded ominous and promising in and of itself, and anticipation zinged through me as I watched him make another trip to his cupboard.

What he returned with made me frown and clench my teeth. My glare just made him crack up, his shoulders shaking briefly in silent laughter.

He set his paraphernalia down below the bench, then knelt down with his face right between my legs, which I might have appreciated under different circumstances. I still held my tongue when he used a washcloth to wet said offending remainder of pubic hair, then used gentle motions to spread the shaving foam evenly.

"If you hadn't been late by over an hour, the water would have been warm," he idly informed me, then picked up the razor, studying it for a moment. "Don't worry, I'll be very slow and deliberate with my work. And for every accidental nick, you get to come one more time."

Knowing Simon, that would likely mean that I got away from this frustrated as hell.

I had to hand it to him—he seemed to know what he was doing, but then I didn't doubt that it was easier to shave someone else than do it yourself, if the one time I'd gone to town on the vegetation downstairs was any indication. I had to admit that it felt incredibly frustrating to feel his touch, gentle and so fucking close to where I needed it, but not getting there any time soon. That the rope pillow underneath my head pretty much forced me to watch him work didn't help much, either. The way he kept sweeping the razor over my skin, his fingers slid between my labia, then pulled them apart to let him get even the most resilient hair, was so fucking intimate. Long before he was done, my pussy lips were puffy and swollen, and it wasn't the residual water from the washcloth that had me soaking wet. Frustration grew, every touch adding to it, and by the time he picked up the washcloth to clean up the remaining suds and shaved-off hair, I was ready to jump off that bench, if the ropes would have let me. Which they didn't. Which was clearly their purpose.

I really didn't know whether to hate or love this right now.

My resentment dimmed considerably when I felt the soft, wet fabric, even cold as it was, run over my pubic mound and over and between my labia. That felt different, and decidedly in a good way. I felt even more mollified when he repeated the process with his fingers. Well, there seemed to be one upside to having to run around looking like a pre-pubescent girl for the new few days.

Satisfied with his work, Simon picked up his utensils and put them away next to the door, then returned to me empty-handed.

"For what I have in mind today, I don't need any toys," he informed me, sounding that special kind of smug that made me want to jump up and slap him at the same time. Knowing what I did now about him, he'd likely get off on both. If not for the damn ropes...

"I've been thinking about that little problem the two of us seem to have," he said conversationally while he slid his hands up my thighs again. "Knowing you, my first instinct was to think that you sneak orgasms by me out of spite. But you've been very cooperative so far otherwise, like you keeping quiet today. You pushed yourself a lot in our last scene, and you had no reservations telling me that you're not comfortable with appellations. That got me thinking that maybe, just maybe it's less about your stubbornness, and more about you simply not having the required control over your body?"

That accusation made me tense up, and he seemed to have anticipated that reaction, judging from his jovial smile.

"And, just like that, I've incited the desire to prove me wrong. You know, it's so fucking easy to screw with you, almost makes me feel bad."

With that, he pushed away from me and I felt myself tense further, because last time that had been the only warning I'd gotten before he'd used the flogger or paddle on me. Not that I didn't want him to slap me—on the contrary—but physical reactions were much harder to reign in than emotional ones, and we both knew that I already had trouble enough controlling those.

Instead of slapping me, Simon let his fingers skip over my labia again, then turned his hand over and pushed two of his fingers into me, deep enough that the knuckles of the others bumped against my sex. A moan came over my lips before I could hold it in, and instinctively I tried to buck my hips against his hand to make him go deeper still. I knew that any second he would withdraw and do something else, but for the moment, I was hellbent on getting the most out of his attention.

Throwing me off-kilter, Simon did no such thing. Instead, he started fucking me with his fingers, and after a moment bent over my pussy and flicked his tongue over my clit. I hissed, loving the sensation but already dreading missing it in a few moments, but again he surprised me by closing his lips around it to suck, then went on licking with alacrity.

Holy fuck, but that felt amazing!

Last time, bondage had been restrictive in the way of preventing me from moving away. This time, it served as a kind of anchor. Tired as I was, I could never have remained in this position unaided for long, but the ropes supported my legs without actually straining my muscles. My bonds also left me enough room to roll my hips, if only somewhat, and the angle of penetration in context with the position seemed to make everything just that little bit more intense. And intense it sure was.

The circumstances alone would have been enough to have me worked up good, but between Simon's hand and mouth, he had me about to come in an embarrassingly short amount of time. Before long, keeping up the tension was impossible without my legs starting to shake, and I knew that if he kept this up much longer, there was no going back. Briefly I wondered if begging now would be against his order for me to keep quiet, but I figured that command overruled the new one easily.

I was just about to open my mouth when his fingers stilled and he moved his head away, then withdrew his hand altogether.

Breath spilled out of me in a shaky exhale, and frustration was back in the front of my mind. I tried to plead with my eyes for more, but the look I received from him was one of smug satisfaction.

That was when I realized why he had been looking like the cat that ate the cream the entire time until now, only the mental picture that brought up in my mind made my vaginal muscles clench even harder around nothing, yearning for more.

"You don't intend to let me come at all!" I accused, not giving a shit if I lost. Belatedly I realized that I'd forgotten that inane appellation, too, but I was beyond caring about that right then— as if I needed to prove him right even more.

Simon's answering smile was as nice as it was sadistic.

"Not until I feel like you've learned your lessons, no."

With that ominous threat he walked out of my field of vision, only to return with a red ball gag. I felt like protesting but swallowed that down as he pushed the rubber ball between my teeth, then grunted as he forced my head up uncomfortably high so he could buckle the leather straps behind it. The ball was large enough to force my jaws apart painfully, and the straps dug into my cheeks. Simon looking down at me for a moment, clearly liking what he saw, before he returned to his former place at the foot end of the bench.

"If you try hard enough, you can talk around the gag, at least one word sentences like your safeword, but you can also shake your head from side to side and utter a sequence of grunts that will serve the same purpose whenever you're gagged. I doubt we'll need that today, but I foresee more gags in your future."

He did slap me then, but it was a light slap on what was exposed of my right ass cheek, and barely hard enough to make me tense. Then his fingers ran up and down my slit a few times until he halted at my clit and started drawing circles around it, just slowly enough not to add to my arousal. That felt good, no doubt about it, but reaching my climax would have felt so much better.

I tried to remain patient but abandoned that after about a minute, bucking my hips in an attempt to either egg him on, or at least let his fingers slip into more fun territory. Simon snorted and just kept going, until I did it again, at which point he withdrew his hand.

"I can stop, too. Do you prefer that?"

I quickly shook my head. Not enough stimulation was still better than no stimulation at all.

He waited almost a full minute until he resumed, just as agonizingly slow as before.

That went on for a small eternity until he took pity on me again and went back to finger fucking me while rubbing my clit a little more insistently. Within minutes he had me writhing, getting ever so close—until he stopped again. His smile was taunting me, and all I could do was lay there, huff and puff around the gag, and ask myself what I'd done to deserve that.

The sad fact was, when he started the same spiel for the third time, I was ready to swear to never ever not ask for permission, but he'd cleverly—calculatedly!—rid me of that option.

By the forth time he stopped I felt like crying, and when his fingers returned to my pussy, I felt an actual tear slide over my cheek. This was just so fucking frustrating and a million times worse than anything I could think of! Not that my mental faculties were in evidence anymore by then as he'd successfully reduced me to a puddle of need and frustration. He had me at the point where I would have done anything if he'd just let me come, but of course the bastard slowed down rather than sped up once he had me shaking all over again. I kept pleading with my eyes, pathetic sounds coming from low in my throat, but while he seemed to enjoy both immensely, he still didn't budge. No, he just kept on smiling, the pad of his thumb stroking my clit in sync with his fingers thrusting into me.

"Wanna know what puzzles me?" he asked, and thankfully didn't wait for my reply, because really, I had no interest in hearing that at all. Unless it would lead to that orgasm that I really, really needed. Then he could tell me anything he wanted.

"People always associate sadism with the need to inflict pain. Which, I guess, in the strictest sense is the definition of the term. But they forget that there are so many other ways you can torment a person. Wouldn't you agree?"

Anger wanted to take over, but I forced it down, instead trying to stare at the ceiling above us instead of his face, but that only drew a laugh from him, and he leaned over me until I couldn't avoid him anymore. He added a third finger then, drawing something between a moan and a high-pitched whine from me, and that only added to his glee.

"I know you agree and that's why you keep trying to hold that temper of yours in check, in futile hope that this will somehow appease me. Well, good news for you, it doesn't, because you're a really shitty actress, but I love how you carry all your emotions on your sleeve. Have I made my point? Do you finally see that you have a very good reason to be fucking grateful for every orgasm I let you have? That you should be fucking grateful that I let you ask to come? I can continue this ad infinitum, but I doubt that you want me to."

I was nodding hard enough to twist the muscles in my neck, dislodging the ropes behind my head, before he had even finished his speech, and I meant it. I wished that damn gag was gone so I could tell him, or scream at him, that yes, I'd learned that fucking lesson, if he would just please let me come now!

"Good, because it would be a shame if we'd have to spend any more time doing something as boring as this. Although I guess it's less boring for you than it is for me, seeing how you're shaking and panting right now."

He did something with his fingers then, and suddenly the intensity of the stimulation was ten times worse. Or better, to be honest, but by now I was so afraid that he would just stop any moment now that I dreaded any increase in intensity more than was able to relish it.

"I guess this is the ideal moment to tell you what else I've been thinking about, seeing as I have your full attention right now."

No, it really wasn't, but far was it from me to protest!

"First, your cunt stays as hairless as it is right now. No discussion. I don't want to hear any of that 'so you want me to look like a little girl?' bullshit that I know is going through your head right now. You will shave as soon as any stubble appears, even if we don't have anything set up. I told you that I don't intend to screw with you in any way outside of the playroom, but those few minutes every other day belong to me. You're my submissive, so you will keep your cunt smooth for me. You can wax, too, but considering your inability to even show up here on schedule, I doubt that you'll find the time to make an appointment for that and keep it, so shaving will likely be the easiest option for now."

He sounded final enough on that not to need any acknowledgment, but I still nodded. To be fair, I'd kind of expected something similar last week already, and had to admit that as unfamiliar as the sensation of not having any pubic hair was, it felt really neat. It certainly wasn't anything I felt was worth objecting to. Right now, the only thing I wanted to veto was being teased mercilessly like this ever again!

"I love having you so cooperative. We should do this more often," Simon taunted.

I grunted loudly in response and shook my head, which made him chuckle. And then he removed his hand, and I felt like coming right off that bench. My frustration was so palpable that it seemed to have become a physical thing that was running through my veins, infusing my entire body. I screamed, the sound not muffled at all, which almost drowned out his laughter.

"You're such a drama queen sometimes," Simon pointed out, idly wiping his hand on my quivering thigh.

He looked as if he wanted to say something else, but at that moment the door of the playroom swung open, admitting Jack, his hair damp from a recent shower, his cheeks still flushed from his run. Or from wanking, what did I know? Or care?

He took in the situation with a bemused look on his face. Under different circumstances that might have turned awkward as hell, but I was too far gone to give a shit. His eyes skipped over me and went to Simon.

"Sorry to interrupt you guys, but this is kind of important."

"What is?" Simon asked, irritation lacing his voice, but less than I'd expected.

"Kara just called. She's annoyed that you don't pick up your phone."

"It's charging downstairs—of course I'm not picking up."

He got a snort for that.

"You can tell her that to her face soon. She'll be here in ten minutes."

And that, ladies and gents, was the last thing I wanted to hear right then.

What was equally worse was that Simon only seemed mildly surprised.

"Didn't she say she wouldn't be free until five?"

"Apparently she finished early because she's so eager to discuss the latest draft of your novel. Lucky you."

Simon snorted, and while he didn't exactly look pleased, he wasn't annoyed, either.

"Ah well, we were about finished, anyway. Can you keep Kara busy until I've wrapped things up here?"

"Sure. Need a hand?"

Now Simon's smile was sardonic, and the sidelong glance he shot me was enough to make me want to punch him in the jaw.

"No, I've got this."

Jack looked from Simon to me again, then shook his head as he muttered something under his breath and closed the door behind him. Which left me alone with Simon and the storm of need brewing inside of me.

"Looks like your time's up," he told me, sounding too chipper for his own good.

I grunted loudly in return and did my best to kill him with my glare. The only thing I got back was another of those asinine smiles before he turned his attention to the ropes.

It took him less than three minutes to set me free, most of which was taken up by undoing the ropes that had kept my thighs spread. The cuffs were ridiculously fast to unbuckle, as was the gag. That left me half sitting, half leaning against the bench, shaking with frustration and anger while I tried to work the kinks out of my aching jaw muscles so I could get into Simon's face.

He beat me to it, gripping my chin firmly and forcing me to look at him. It wasn't hard for him to loom over me on a good day, but the way he stared down at me now was downright intimidating.

"I don't want to hear a single word from you. You deserve this, and deep down you know it. I want you like this, and that should be enough to make you shut up and take it. You don't have to like it, but rather than glare at me, you should work on accepting that you bow to my will. I didn't plan on getting interrupted this soon, but karma can be a bitch. If you have learned this lesson, you will shut up and swallow that rage boiling inside of you. You don't have to thank me for teaching you this lesson, you just have to take it, even if it cuts you to the bone. It wouldn't be a real lesson if it didn't come with an impact. I know exactly how frustrated you are right now, how much you need to come. You will go downstairs to the bathroom now and take a shower, but you won't masturbate, and you won't touch yourself until I allow you to again. That might be later tonight, that might be tomorrow. If you piss me off and mope around like a small child, it will be next week. You don't have to like it one bit, but you will follow my order, just like the next time we play and you're about to come, you will ask for permission. Are we clear on that?"

I'd seldom before been this angry at anyone, angry enough to shake, and I hoped that he could see every bit of that in my eyes. But, once he let go of my jaw, my answer was still the one he wanted to hear.

"Yes, Sir."

I might have gritted my teeth and my voice might have been husky from how much this cost me, but that didn't change the fact that my acquiescence was still the honest truth. Even if I felt like I would instantly combust, I would tough this out.

Simon held my gaze for another moment, his own face stern, then gave the briefest of nods.

"Now go clean yourself. It won't really subtract from your stellar mood if you run into Kara, sweaty, buck naked, and shaking with frustration."

Swallowing thickly, I eased myself off the bench and started for the door, my legs shaky enough to make me stumble a little, hating every single step I took.

-9-

Of the showers I'd taken here over the last two weeks, this was the worst, but also the longest. Not knowing just how literally Simon wanted me to take that command not to touch myself, I only focused on any receptive part of my anatomy long enough to clean it, then kept my hands at my sides as I remained standing under the lukewarm spray, hoping that the water would sluice away more than just sweat and suds.

Not surprisingly, that didn't work at all. By the time I finally vacated the shower and toweled myself dry, I was just as horny as I'd been when I'd slinked down the stairs, if a little less afraid that Kara was already waiting downstairs to uncover and dissect every despicable detail of my sex life.

Glaring at my reflection in the mirror, I couldn't help but crack up. I not only felt as if every fiber of my being was vibrating with frustration, I also looked the part, eyes too bright and red splotches all over my face.

The worst part about it? As much as I resented Simon right now, and there was a lot of resentment bordering on boiling rage going on, I had to hand it to him; he knew exactly how to get under my skin. That frightened me a little. It also excited me a lot.

I'd spent years lurking on blogs and message boards, reading firsthand accounts of submissives and how they felt about their place in the relationship. Some of that had sounded strange, and I'd had problems relating to all of it. Right now, as angry, frustrated, and painfully aroused as I was, I was feeling the first stirrings of all those emotions, though. And thinking about the directions he had sent me off with, that point became even more glaringly obvious. I felt like he did own me, strange as that sounded—at least a small part of me, the part that wanted to be owned, that wanted to please him, that yearned for all this and so much more.

And on that same level I felt weirdly happy about it all, even if it came with me wanting to scream like never before.

Realizing all that instantly made me feel better about the need to get back at him—however I could.

Hey, just because I was embracing my inner submissive slut didn't mean that I was ready to leave my vindictive, self-righteous streak behind. And knowing him, he'd take whatever I'd dish out in stride and just push me right on to the next level.

Someone, likely Simon himself, had deposited my bag in the corner of the bathroom, letting me get dressed without the joys of a towel-wrapped dash of shame in my near future. Even with that tiny bit of mental satisfaction and reassurance that I desperately clung onto, I still almost started to cry when I put on my panties and felt the soft cotton brush over the swollen flesh of my pussy. The fact that the skin felt wonderfully smooth, begging to be explored and touched in its altered state now, just made it ten times worse. And the soft material of my too-hideous-to-show cotton bra was abrasive on my erect nipples, then pinched the entirety of my breasts in all the right ways as I adjusted myself. The tee and yoga pants were only a small degree less painful to put on.

In short, I had a shit ton of reasons to scowl as I made my way into the front of the house, my hair dripping cold and wet onto my upper back.

The picture I was presented with looked so harmonic that I wanted to scream.

While I'd been busy moping around in the shower, Simon had managed to change into his previous clothes and looked like he hadn't been up to any nefarious deeds in his entire life. Maybe his hair was a bit more mussed than before, and I thought I detected a hint of residual tension in his shoulders as he sat on the couch, one leg curled under him, a sea of paper spread out all around him, but that might have been my imagination.

Or not. It took me seeing him to wonder just how much sending me off like that had cut into his own flesh. Those damn leather pants were tight in all the right places but did a stellar job hiding his actual state of arousal, but if his words had been any indication, he'd gotten off by tormenting me like that—without actually getting off himself.

Maybe that should have been some small consolation for me, but it really wasn't. Not one bit.

Jack had retreated to the huge beanbag on the floor and was intent on his console game, his fingers manipulating the black controller in his hands in a way that made muscles all over my body clench with yet more unwelcome need. Oh, wonderful—now the most sexy thing in the world—watching a guy play a video game—was enough to send me salivating. I was truly and utterly fucked.

The opposite side of the couch from where Simon had staked his claim was occupied by the third possible victim for my latent hostility, and it took her exactly five seconds from the moment I entered to attract said attention.

"What are you doing here, bitch? Shouldn't you be working or something?"

I gave Kara the bland, toothy smile those questions deserved.

Unlike the rest of us, she was already in her evening clothes, but then I'd never seen her in anything that wasn't suited for a catwalk. Even her bikinis were stylish. Her long, blonde hair was always perfect, as was her flawless makeup, and she'd rather be caught dead than wear anything that didn't accentuate her tall, thin body. On more than one occasion I had called her superficial and fake, but truth be told, Kara had one of the sharpest minds I'd come across, which likely explained why she was still Simon's close friend, even after their lives had taken separate lanes. Her intellect had nothing on her tongue.

I opened my mouth, ready to spew vitriol, but my mind ground to a halt. I was awake now, there was no doubt about that, but between the mental drag of sleep deprivation and the sexual tension that was still infusing my every fiber, I found myself weirdly dumbstruck.

Instead of reaming me good, Kara frowned, then turned from me to Simon.

"Are you two banging?"

Jack uttered a sound low in his throat that made me guess that his headphones weren't turned on, but Simon didn't bat an eyelash as he held Kara's inquisitive gaze steadily.

"What makes you think that's even a possibility?"

There wasn't a note of doubt in his voice, but the way he said it made me get angry for a wholly new reason.

My irritation seemed to be infectious as if, her obvious incredulity aside, for once Kara chose to get offended on my account. Considering that she was, hands down, the person who got in my face the most often, that was hilarious on so many levels, but also appreciated.

"Last time I checked she had an overabundance of tits and ass going on and that's what you guys go for, isn't it? It's kind of conspicuous, seeing as she's all wet and dripping, and you're sitting here smelling all weird."

That made me realize that there hadn't been any time for Simon to shower, and I'd been alone in the bathroom the entire time I'd fumed in there, so unless he'd washed his hands in the kitchen sink, he still had my juices all over them. And his mouth. Just thinking about that kicked off a new avalanche of toe-curling memories, kicking my frustration up yet another notch. I wouldn't have thought it impossible right then if my entire body had started to vibrate with tension.

Simon seemed completely unfazed by Kara's observation, but he glanced at me briefly. That was enough for me to realize that he was acutely aware of what he'd done to me, and it was obviously still going on.

"With that sort of combinatory skills, I'm surprised you haven't started working as a script writer for a second rate crime show yet," he noted, then looked pointedly at the stack of papers spread out between them, as if casual banter was beneath him.

I wasn't sure whether that pissed me off or not, but Kara wasn't satisfied yet. Turning back to me, she looked me up and down, as if that would make me spill all my secrets. I was well aware that of the four of us, I had the worst poker face, but Simon wasn't the only one who could pretend to be obtuse.

"I got off my shift late and figured it would be nice to grab a real shower after more than thirty hours wearing the same clothes, instead of reveling in the prison shower room glamor of the locker room stalls." She didn't look convinced yet, but it wasn't the first time that exactly that had happened. Realizing that I would have to pull a better stunt, I snorted derisively, and there was a lot more emotion in that sound than I had intended. "Besides, do I look like I just had sex?"

"I don't even want to guess what your 'freshly fucked' face looks like. Quite frankly, you look like the cross of death warmed over and a drowned rat," she remarked, but she was already relaxing, a bloodhound thrown off its trail. "The usual, you know?"

Smiling blithely, I wrapped my arms around myself, focusing on her mainly because looking at anything that had a cock attached was downright painful.

"Not that it's any of your business, but on a scale of one to ten on the sexual frustration scale, I'm right now bottoming out on a fifteen. Does that satisfy your curiosity?"

Jack gave another one of those suppressed cackle-snorts, and Kara rolled her eyes, mostly for his benefit.

"As if I give a shit? But, really, as a doctor you should know how to take care of that yourself. Or are you too holier than thou to rub one out?"

It was so hard not to glare at Simon, but Kara likely took the set of my jaw as anger at her baiting. Not quite trusting myself with an answer, I ignored her and stalked over to the fridge instead. Before I'd even made it halfway across the kitchen, Kara and Simon had resumed what I figured was that animated discussion they'd planned well ahead of time—and I doubted that he'd forgotten about that.

My knuckles stood out white from how hard I grabbed the fridge door handle.

"Do I even want to know what this is about?"

I jumped, then forced myself to relax as I turned my head and stared at Jack.

"Leave me alone."

Unlike Kara, he wasn't so easily dissuaded from keeping the conversation going, even when I reached into the fridge for the OJ and started guzzling it straight from the bottle. A muscle in his cheek jumped, the only indication that my behavior ticked him off, but when it became clear that I didn't intend to put the bottle back, he relaxed. How I could be the medical professional and he the germophobe of the two of us where food was concerned was beyond me.

"There are some leftovers in there if you're hungry," he pointed out, but still didn't return to his chosen method of wasting time.

Instead of thanking him for pointing out the obvious, I grabbed the container, cautiously sniffed the contents, then decided that projectile vomiting caused by food poisoning would at least take care of my unchecked libido. The silence between us got strained as I waited for the microwave to do its thing, and Jack was the one who finally broke it.

"Look, if you're pissed at me for interrupting you, I'm sorry, but I've seen you naked before. That shouldn't be cause for giving me the silent treatment."

I quickly cast a glance toward the couch, but between the distance, the hum of the microwave, and their animated discussion, Kara was oblivious to what Jack had just said. Then again, he had seen me naked, or close enough to count, before that Saturday—it was just my frayed nerves that had me so on edge.

Forcing air out of my lungs, I tried to get my temper in check, then did my best to appear calm even if I still felt the need to slap Jack for not leaving me be. He was standing decidedly too close to me even for our usual casualness around each other, and the fact that he didn't seem to have a clue what he was doing to me just made my awful situation that much worse.

"I'm not angry with you," I offered, then exhaled loudly again, screwing my eyes shut. "I'm not angry with anyone. Just... give me some space, okay?"

Jack studied me for a moment longer, then backed down and returned to his console, leaving me to my own devices. I thought about eating at the breakfast bar, but that seemed considerably close to moping, and the last thing I wanted to do was give Simon any ideas. So what I did was sit down next to him, both because it was the part of the couch that wasn't littered with papers or fashionably dressed girls, and because he was sitting in my usual spot, so it was only fair to take his—only that until now I'd never felt weird about sitting so close to anyone.

I didn't really pay attention to Simon and Kara's to and fro as I shoveled warm pasta into my mouth. My body was still on high alert, but fogginess already started seeping back into my thoughts, and bailing on our night out started to sound good again. But then, my half-assed explanation might get more scrutiny, and I doubted that I could throw Kara off track that easily again. When I was done, I got out my phone and started scrolling through my inbox, doing my best not to notice that Simon sat just an enticing couple of inches away from me.

After what felt like hours, they finally reached the end of their debate—or so it seemed when Kara got up to call someone on her phone, while pointing at me, then at the back hallway. I got to my feet, resigning myself to my fate, when Simon suddenly grabbed my hand and pulled me down toward him, almost making me end up in his lap. I stared at him, momentarily paralyzed from not knowing what to make of that, and his smile was exactly that kind of pleasant that led to unpleasant things happening to me.

"Do something different tonight."

"Different how?"

Maybe I should have protested that he even thought he could give me any instructions outside of the playroom, but that idea was quickly quenched by the hope that if I followed along, he wouldn't make me suffer that much longer.

Cocking his head, he let his eyes roam over the bunched-up expanse of my tee and pants before they returned to my face.

"You decide, but you do it for me. That should give you some ideas."

I held his gaze for another moment, then moved away. To myself I could admit that yes, it was stubbornness that made me not acknowledge his order, but when he only looked pleased as punch, I realized that he'd chosen to see my silence as acquiescence. Perfect. Not only was he leaving me hanging—no, he had to do it in a way that made me see just how at his mercy

I'd set myself up to be. Like before, that knowledge came with a wave of lust, sending me right back to the point where the urge to touch myself was strong enough to need actual willpower to keep my hands still.

Still chittering away on the phone, Kara followed me into the bathroom. Picking my bag up from the floor, I studied my options, not sure what to wear. I never wasted any time on choosing outfits, a fact that Kara bemoaned every single time we got ready to go out together. For once, though, I would have appreciated her input.

Do something different. How the fuck could I do something different with just two sets of spare clothes, all packed for their casual comfort?

Pulling the bottom-most item out of the bag, I studied the soft jersey dress critically. I'd worn it before over a pair of jeans like a tunic, but now I wondered if the hem went low enough to go without.

"Do you think I can pull that off?" I asked, holding the slate gray garment out to her.

Kara rolled her eyes and hung up, not quite ending her conversation mid sentence, but close.

"You already wore that like five times before. Is your sleep deprivation dementia that bad already?"

"I meant without pants."

She looked at the dress again, then much more critical at me, ending with a shrug.

"Only one way to find out, right?"

Someone else might have left the room, or at least turned away, but Kara kept swiping away on her phone while I shed the outer layer of my clothes. She seemed occupied enough to lend some comfort, but not too occupied not to notice my underwear.

"No wonder you aren't getting laid if you dress like that."

"Not getting laid isn't the issue here," I shot back as I pulled the dress over my head. It came to mid-thigh, a little too high up for my comfort, but not too bad. And it was different, damn him!

Kara motioned me to turn around, and when I'd dutifully shuffled my feet, she smacked her lips.

"Panty lines. No way I'm going to let you hang out with me looking like that."

"Better now?" I retorted, not even trying to keep my annoyance out of my voice as I reached up underneath the dress to yank my panties down. Uh, bad idea, I realized when air hit my still overly sensitive pussy, and feeling the soft material of the dress slither against my now naked ass wasn't exactly helping the entire situation.

"That's one solution," Kara remarked dryly, and when I shot her a dirty look over my shoulder, she returned it blandly. In that moment she looked so eerily like Simon when he didn't let me see into his cards that it freaked me out a little. I'd never realized that, until now, I'd missed what felt like half of what he was capable of. Before I could, she looked away, then pursed her lips.

"The dress still looks a little wonky. I presume you don't happen to have a different bra in that bag of yours?"

I shook my head.

"Just the same one in another color."

"See, this is what I have to work with. How do people expect me to make you presentable!"

"They don't."

Ignoring me, she dove into her handbag and resurfaced with two elongated, small gel pads.

"Here, put that into your bra. Much as I hate to admit it, you have the tits to make them work."

I took the proffered pieces from her, then examined them suspiciously.

"I don't think I need anything that will put even more emphasis on my boobs."

"And that's why you don't get laid!" she repeated, then forestalled me when I tried to object. "Just try them. For me, pretty please? Because I'm not envious enough of your rack as it is."

"You could try eating something once in a while. Maybe you'd grow your own then," I shot back, but turned back around to start the long and enduring process of shimming around underneath the dress. Probably should have thought twice about dropping my panties just like that, but I was sure that she would have called me out for putting them on again now, and I was too strung out to have that conversation again. That woman simply had no shame when it came to fashion, which probably was the case for any girl Jack banged. Which now also included me. Not helping, either!

When I finally had the stupid things where Kara claimed they belonged, I presented myself again, fake grin in place.

"Better?"

"Not half bad," she agreed, then kicked a pair of terribly high heels toward me. Where she'd hidden those, I had no clue, but it was just my luck that we had the same size feet. Grumbling, I took off my socks, then slipped the shoes on. They instantly made me feel like a colt minutes after birth, but after taking two steps I found my balance. There was the usual discomfort of having my whole weight on the balls of my feet after being on them for way too many hours during the past two days, but it could have been worse. Studying myself critically in the mirror over the sink as best as possible, I had to admit that I liked the result.

"Makeup next!" Kara ordered, and I was surprised when she only got busy with her trusty eyeliner and mascara wand. That woman could spend insane hours thrusting things into my face that I didn't even know existed, let alone for what purpose, but today she was satisfied with what she referred to as the basics.

Washing my face sounded basic enough, but she ignored me when I pointed that out.

"You have such a healthy glow to your cheeks today, I don't think you'll need any foundation or blush," she remarked casually as she stabbed the mascara wand toward my eye. At least to me it felt like stabbing.

"It's called being healthy."

"Yeah, like as if what you stuff inside your body is considered food," she retorted, then narrowed her eyes critically. "I can do more but we're already late, and I'm not in the mood for one of your diatribes about how makeup is clogging your pores. You'd need cement to even those out."

"Guess we can't all be as pretty as you are! Gosh, that would make you look so drab and normal, you'd have to kill yourself if that ever happened!"

Kara snorted.

"Whatever. You know Dan, the guy I'm seeing right now, he has a couple of friends who aren't half bad, either. Just say the word and I'll set you up with one of them."

"Gee, thanks. I can do without your pity."

A frown stole onto her face, and she stopped checking her work and instead looked at me directly.

"That's odd."

"What is? That I'm not in the mood for you to pawn me off on one of your guy's buddies so you can claim you're the best matchmaker there is?"

"No. Just the fact that whenever we've had this conversation, you always get in my face about being an emancipated woman and not needing a man in her life to feel fulfilled. You really are having sex with someone, only right now he's not doing a good enough job making you scream."

"That's not the problem," I replied, maybe a little too fervently. Her eyes narrowed, and for a moment I wondered just how much she knew about what Simon liked to do for recreational activities, but then her features evened out again.

"Suit yourself. If you don't want to dish, I'm not going to pry. But why are you making such a secret out of this? Just call him—he can tag along. Unless it's someone from the hospital... I don't need another stuck up doctor raining on my parade. Plus then all anyone would talk about are horrible infectious diseases, and I've listened to you lecture Jack one time too many on that topic."

Shrugging, I got up and reached for the small handbag I'd brought along, but before I got to the door, Kara was at it again.

"Ha, you didn't even bat an eyelash on that! Is it Jack? I'm totally fine with you screwing him. I mean, I'm lending you my shoes, I have no issues with sharing my fuck buddy. Just not when I'm in the room—that would be too weird."

As if on cue, Jack stepped out of his room just as we were leaving the bathroom, crowding us all into the hallway. I had no clue how much of that he'd heard, but he had one of those shit-eating grins going on, so I had to do damage control before this could get out of hand.

"Do you really think that such a prime example of the male species like Jack here would leave me almost insane with unfulfilled sexual need? No need to guess, just speak from experience."

Kara laughed, then pushed me toward the front room, almost unbalancing me on those fucking heels.

"Nah, it can't be him. He's pretty good with the ladies."

"Only pretty good? You offend me! Deeply wound me!" Jack protested. "I think I need to refresh your memory. Care to step outside with me for a moment?"

"You two are disgusting!" I huffed, then fled into the front room, happy that Jack had thrown Kara off my trail. That put me right in front of Simon who was waiting, leaning against the kitchen counter, delectable in dress slacks, shirt, and a sports jacket. He normally didn't dress up like that, but he looked good in it. I might have been biased. He'd have looked even better naked, screwing me silly upstairs.

Stomping down hard on those thoughts, I did my best to appear calm and confident, or lacking the former, I thrust my chest out, hoping those stupid pads really did something else than feel weird. Simon's eyes roamed over my body, and I had a moment where all I wanted to do was race back into the bathroom and put on pants. The dress was too short, and considering that I could walk in heels but not too well, that sounded like a recipe for disaster—or at least flashing someone.

"Does this meet your approval?" I said, aiming for haughty, but my voice sounded a little too strangled to pull it off.

"It will do," he shot back, adding just enough condescension to make me mad, saving me from glowing with pride.

Yep, I was truly and utterly fucked.

Kara and Jack spilling out of the hall saved me from having to come up with a reply, as did the timely arrival of the taxi. As usual, Jack took the seat in the front thanks to carrying the most physical bulk with him, while Simon had to make do with folding his long legs into the middle seat in the back. Kara squeezed in on his right, I on his left, and off we went.

After giving directions, Kara continued the discussion with Simon until her phone rang, distracting her. I was surprised when my own phone chirped in my bag, signaling an incoming text message. It was from Simon.

I approve.

Thank you, I sent back, then, after a moment's pause, I added, *Sir*.

I got a grin for my effort that was both devious and strangely enticing.

Good girl.

That mollified me a little, but not enough to smooth my ruffled feathers.

Just so you know, not wearing any panties, either, I texted back.

He sent me a sidelong glance after skimming his phone's display.

Definitely approving of that.

Because I never knew when to let things be, I had to have the last word.

And how does it feel that you know, and can't do a thing with that knowledge?

I might have gloated a little as I watched him read my message, but that look froze on my face when he shifted and suddenly his hand was high up on my thigh, barely hidden underneath where I'd folded my jacket over my arm. Not enough that his warm fingers on my skin felt good, no, he had to slide his hand further up my leg, inch by enticing inch, until the heel of his hand bumped against my pussy. I sucked air in noisily as his little finger found my clit. Even squeezing my thighs together didn't stop him.

Then my phone chirped again, both a welcome distraction and a true annoyance. This time the text was from Jack.

What the fuck are you guys doing back there? You just went beet red in the face?!

Just breathing without letting out the moan building inside my chest was a feat, and I kept my eyes trained ahead in my attempt not to let distraction get the better of me.

"None of your damn business," I hissed under my breath, sure that the words would find the right recipient.

Simon heard, of course, and besides grinning like a fool, he twisted his hand further so that now his middle and ring finger could join the party.

Tension ratcheted up inside of me beyond what I could take, and my fingers closed around Simon's knee, pretty much the only part I could reach with his arm now wedged in between our bodies. That was exactly the moment Kara ended her phone call, making me want to shy away before she could notice, but I simply couldn't as it was the only lifeline I had left. The only thing I could do was nudge my jacket forward to try to hide it, but it felt like the most glaringly obvious thing, impossible to ignore.

As if nothing had happened, Simon resumed his former conversation with Kara, all the while continuing to stroke me in that maddeningly steady, slow rhythm—and we were still several blocks away from our destination.

I tried to clear my head of anything, and when that didn't help, I tried to focus on something, but my phone chirping with yet another message sent that all to hell. It took me almost twenty seconds to swipe the screen saver away so that I could blink owlishly at the new text from Simon. How he could talk, text, and drive me insane all at the same time was beyond me.

Just a little reminder, you're still not allowed to come without permission. And I'm not granting you permission until you beg.

For a moment, the messages seemed like my salvation, but then I realized that they truly weren't. The interior of a car was not the space where I could hide a climax just like that, and one that felt like it had been building for two hours now no less. And judging from the glint in his eyes when he glanced at me briefly, I doubted that he'd even give his permission if I pleaded for it at the top of my lungs.

"Are you even listening to me?" Kara complained, sounding annoyed.

"I'm hanging on every single word you say," Simon assured her, turning toward her as much as his position would let him. And oh, wonder of wonders, that finally dislodged his hand from where it had been tormenting me.

I could have cried with gratitude, then again because the need to come was overwhelming.

The rest of the drive went by in a haze, and my legs were still kind of unsteady when it was time to exit the car. As he followed me to the entrance of the bar we were aiming for, Simon rested his hand at my lower back in passing, making me even more conscious of just how I craved his touch.

The people we were meeting here were already in evidence, evenly distributed around a couple of low tables. Smiles, greetings, and names were exchanged, washing in a wave over me that didn't leave an impression in my mind. There was a free space at the end of one of the low benches that I fled to, happy to be off my feet quickly, only to find Simon taking the freshly vacated seat next to me. Jack took the single chair across from us, while Kara disappeared into the mass of well-dressed people on the other end of the group.

At first I was afraid that Simon would keep up his game from the car, but he remained relaxed—and at a comfortable distance— beside me, soon letting himself get drawn into a conversation with two bankers sitting across from him. Jack oozed his charm all over the waitress until the impressionable git fled with a giggle and bright eyes, and I resigned myself to the fate of light conversation and equally light drinks. As much as the war zone between my legs called for tequila, I was scheduled for work at six sharp in the morning. No rest for the wicked.

As the evening went on, I felt myself relax, even though the need to either wring Simon's neck or drag him into the next half-hidden corner remained. Kara's friends were less annoying than I'd feared, but more vapid than I'd hoped. Two of the guys made a move on me, but I needn't have bothered trying to deter them. Between them, Jack and Simon took care of discouraging my would-be suitors, and with enough ease to make me wonder just how often they'd played that very hand in the past but I'd remained oblivious to it. I didn't dwell on those thoughts, though, because they would have complicated matters that didn't need complication right then.

It was a couple of minutes after 9:30 p.m. when my phone rang. I knew the time because I'd checked repeatedly during the past hour, and decided that any moment now I could start excusing myself and claim my need for rest for my exit strategy. The number flashing on the display made my heart sink as I got to my feet, stepping around Simon to extricate myself from our merry round.

"Hospital," I explained, my voice sounding terribly dejected even to my own ears, and angled for the terrace just outside our sitting area.

I picked up as soon as I was out of the perpetual noise pollution of the bar, my tone now hard and clipped. They knew I'd just come off a shift—if they called me in now, I was going to rip McGilles a new one... ignoring the fact that I was lightly intoxicated, and thus in no state to come in, anyway.

"Slater."

"Erin? I'm so glad I got a hold of you," Eliza piped up. I felt myself stiffen instinctively. We weren't exactly friends, more like rivals from the day we'd both started our internships and then transitioned to our respective residencies, and as far as I knew, she'd ended her ER rotation the week before.

"What's up?" I asked, sounding as wary as I felt. If this had been a social call, she would have used her own phone, not one of the hospital lines.

"You're scheduled for day shift tomorrow, right? Would you mind... I mean, I still need a couple of..."

Already I felt my heart sink, but before I could speak up, I heard a commotion on the other end of the line, then Zoe Tyne's voice barked harshly at me.

"Slater, you're delegated to night shift tomorrow. Little crybaby Eliza here wants more practice, and whoever she's blowing right now penciled her in for half the OR plan tomorrow. Besides, with only two nights until the next full moon, I'm sure that the ER will be flooded with lunatics again, and I need my best soldiers manning the stations. Any objections?"

"No, ma'am," I piped up, only marginally amused by the sound of her grumbling under her breath.

"Make the best of it. Catch up on sleep. Eat. Read. Fuck whoever had you hightailing it out of this shithole this afternoon, I don't give a shit. I'll see you at six sharp tomorrow night."

"Yes, boss," I pressed out between gritted teeth, not sure what I was annoyed at the most—that my bootie call routine was that obvious, that Eliza was stealing the few scheduled ORs I'd already had my eye on, or that chances were slim to none that Simon would even let me take care of that peskiest of businesses. Thankfully Zoe hung up before I could say anything else, leaving me fuming about her and the unfathomable unfairness of the world in general.

In fact, I was so busy moping, if stealthily so, that I didn't notice Jack stepping up to me until he touched my upper arm lightly.

"Whatever that phone did to you, I doubt it deserves that death glare," he remarked, beaming his best charming smile at me.

"Guess not," I admitted, then turned the screen off, casting us both into momentary darkness.

We were alone on the terrace, but still close enough to the sitting area that there was enough light to illuminate his features. He was standing decidedly too close, but then being in the vicinity of anything fuckable would have qualified as such for me right then.

Why the fuck did I let Simon do this to me?

Ah, right—because it was as fascinating as it was frustrating.

Either I had a worse poker face than I'd guessed, or Jack had picked up a few hints along the way, because the look he regarded me with turned shrewd.

"Trouble at the hospital?"

I shrugged.

"Sneaky resident stole my day shift and all the ORs I've been penciled in to assist with."

"Do you still need any? You only have a few more weeks to go, right?"

"Eight weeks on this rotation," I agreed, then gave a noncommittal grunt. "Any hour in the OR that I can log is vital, but she definitely needs them more than I do. I got the night shift instead, boss told me so herself."

His eyes narrowed.

"Let me get this straight. You're complaining because you get an extra half day of free time and your boss calls you personally because she wants to make sure that she has her star pupil exactly where she wants her to be? Remind me again why you're complaining?"

Looking at it like that, I was left with remaining silent. Jack laughed softly but took his small victory in stride.

"Seriously, why are you gnashing your teeth like that? And it's not just the phone call. You've been terribly irritable tonight."

"Maybe because you and Simon have joined forces in your League of Extraordinary Cockblockers?"

I got a snort for my troubles, but if that was even possible, he leaned closer without actually moving.

"Just weeding out the sub-par offerings you would have rejected yourself. Last time I pulled Barry out of the equation, you didn't complain that much."

"Not to you, maybe. I still remember complaining to Simon."

"And I remember that that ultimately ended with you writhing between us, which you seemed to enjoy a lot, so remind me again why you're protesting now?"

I blinked, anger slowly fading into even more of that horrible burn in the back of my mind. And between my thighs. Irritation about people screwing with my schedule wasn't enough to take care of that, and Jack's mere presence made me fidgety all over again—not that I'd ever admit that.

"You're evil, you know that?" I asked, trying hard to sound put off, but I might as well have started rubbing myself all over him from the husky tones my voice picked up.

Jack didn't bat an eyelash, but his grin turned a little darker.

"If that turns you on, I have nothing to protest about that. But you're evading my questions, and that's not usually your style."

"What questions? You can't seriously expect me to be happy that you and Simon team up and decide who is good enough to make a move on me and who isn't."

Jack snorted, but the look on his face was suspiciously bland.

"Trust me—if we really did that, you'd likely spend your days in isolation right now."

"What's that supposed to mean?"

He blinked as if he was surprised by my reply, which in turn made me wonder if his last statement had been supposed to be voiced aloud. Another issue I didn't want to think about right fucking now.

"Whatever," I deflected, and the way I crossed my arms over my chest might have been only slightly defensive. "I'm a little on edge right now as you can very easily tell, so if you don't want me to bite your head off, leave me alone."

"Just because I walked in on you? You can't be mad at me for that!"

"And I'm not."

He opened his mouth in protest, but then closed it again abruptly.

"You're mad at him."

Not a question but a statement, yet I still replied.

"I'm not."

"Oh, yes, you are, but for some unfathomable reason you're trying to hide it, and... shit."

My glare certainly wasn't friendly, but it didn't warrant the way he cut himself off. He looked downright apologetic, and if Jack was one thing, it was straightforward. He never backtracked.

"This thing between you is getting more serious than just the occasional ill-timed bootie call, isn't it?" he asked, a lot more cautious. Caution didn't work well with my sunny disposition right now.

"That's none of your business," I pointed out, maybe a little more harshly than warranted, and with a note of defensiveness that I really hated hearing in my voice.

"Right, it isn't," he agreed, and seemed to mean it. "I just didn't figure that you're the type who, you know, doesn't punch a guy in the face when he's, well..."

"Well what?"

Jack's eyes zeroed in on my face, and after a second or two he broke out into a stupidly wide grin.

"Who works you into a frenzy and then doesn't let you come."

I seriously considered punching him now, and while that might have been rewarding, violence by proxy certainly wasn't the answer. His statement also made me wonder just how much in cahoots the two of them were.

"How much did he tell you?" Then something else occurred to me. "Did he send you out here after me?"

Jack's beginning smile strengthened, and that did ungodly things to my body.

"Nothing and nope, but you just confirmed it. And it's the only reason I could think of for why you're acting like a bristling cat ever since you stomped out of the bathroom." He pursed his lips, and suddenly he was really standing too close to me, close enough that I could feel the heat radiating from his body, which made me shiver for reasons other than leaving my jacket inside.

"You know, even if he's acting like a prick and stringing you along, that doesn't mean I have to. I'd be more than happy to lend you a hand there. Or tongue, or dick, or all three. I could fuck you right here, if you want to, with no one the wiser. Well, no one but Simon. He's been watching us the entire time, but I doubt that he'd object."

Somewhere during that declaration, my eyes had latched onto Jack's lips, and it was almost impossible for me to drag them back to his eyes now. Fuck, but this situation was starting to become impossible! Just listening to him talk like that fanned those now again-raging flames, and I'd never been known for my self-restraint.

Taking a shaky breath, I forced myself to look away and shook my head.

"Jack, I can't."

"Why not? You're not exactly bundled up for an arctic expedition here. Let me demonstrate."

Then he was standing behind me, his body pressing into my back, soft, warm fingers ghosting down my arms, then to my hips. One hand stayed, the other slid down to my thigh, then underneath the soft fabric of my dress, and I let out a harsh breath when skin met skin. Through his jeans it was easy to feel his erection pressing against my ass, and it was impossible not to grind myself back against him as that hand started its quick trail up my leg.

"Jack!" I more groaned than said, the words I wanted to utter getting stuck in my throat when I looked toward the seating area inside, and, true enough, found Simon studying us over his bottle of beer.

"Shit, you're not wearing any panties," Jack ground out when his hand confirmed as much, the need in his voice whipping my own pulse up further. Jerking his hips forward, maybe even in an involuntary motion, made my dress ride up enough that the denim of his jeans was now pressed directly against my ass. I'd just have to reach back, undo that zipper, and I was sure that a minute or two later I'd be one very happy puddle of goo. I knew that he wouldn't take longer, and he wouldn't tease me or let me hang, and suddenly the fact that I'd only had his cock in my ass but not in my pussy before turned to a glaring need that was impossible to ignore. I shuddered all over, which only grew worse when his lips appeared on the nape of my neck, pressing a series of light, hot kisses onto my skin.

But I couldn't. It was killing me right now, but I just couldn't give in like that.

"Jack, stop."

I made my voice as harsh and cold as possible, which still sounded like a husky whisper, but he stilled immediately, which left him pressed against me, his fingers about to discover that my underwear wasn't the only thing that was gone.

I felt him relax, then let out a long-drawn exhale, but that only ended up sending my nerve endings screaming from where his breath ghosted over the sensitive side of my neck.

"Why?" he asked, sounding not a hint annoyed, but there was something in his voice that made my heart ache weirdly deep down.

"Because I can't. Because he told me not to touch myself, and I'm not allowed to come until he gives me permission, and there's no way you won't have me screaming in under ten seconds flat if we keep going."

I hoped that alluding to his sexual prowess would patch up whatever caused that weird tone in his voice, and when he started to chuckle low under his breath, I felt tension leave me. Not much, because I was still impossibly high strung on the physical level, but my mind quieted down. Had that been jealousy in his voice? No, couldn't be, because if anyone had no cause for that, it was him.

"He's really pulling a number on you, eh? Simon, you cocky rat bastard."

His chuckle turned into a full-blown laugh, and I wasn't exactly content when he stepped back enough to let the fabric of my dress settle between us again, although he was a little more reluctant to let go of me. I might have lingered a moment too long before I turned around, making sure that we weren't touching but unable to put more of a distance between us than that. Looking up, I found his face slightly flushed, his eyes bright, but it was his smile that almost did the trick of making me abandon every single thing I'd vowed to myself just this afternoon. That he obviously respected my choices so didn't help right then.

"Wanna know what's the worst about this? He's been such a tease tonight that I'm sure he won't change his mind until I go home. And instead of being able to work my frustration off tomorrow, I'll spend the entire day at home, too worked up to get some rest, unable to take care of it, and just because that sneaky little bitch stole my OR time."

Jack grinned, clearly amused by my mental roundhouse kick, and, infuriatingly enough, got out his phone.

"What, my plight concerns you so little that now you have to check your texts? And send some?"

I was ready to sock him a good one but he just kept grinning as he typed away, leaving me fuming in silence. His phone vibrated twice when replies came in, and I'd resorted to a pissed-off glower by the time he turned his attention back to me.

"I don't think that's going to be a problem," he remarked, sounding way too self-satisfied.

"I agree—you don't think. Period."

That made him laugh, and when he swept his arm across my shoulders and started steering me back toward the others, I had to fight a grin on my own. But shit, this was slowly going to kill me!

Simon looked decidedly too smug upon our return, but I did my best not to give away just how much pushing Jack away had cost me. At least now enough time had passed so I could make an exit, or so I figured, until Kara put her scrawny ass down on the armrest of Jack's chair.

"What are you guys doing this weekend? Any grand plans for world domination?"

"Why, do you need my moral support for yet another lazy Sunday at the country club?" Jack egged her on.

"Nope, unless you'd otherwise sit home, alone, and wallow in your misery?"

I wondered if that was the worst pick-up line in existence, but judging from how the guy she was apparently seeing had his hand on her knee, I figured it had to be genuine interest. It was so tempting to complain about my own situation, but I stopped myself short, lest Simon could accuse me of that moping he'd expressly told me not to do. That in turn made me wonder again just how much of Jack's uncharacteristic show of affection was due to our recent activities, and how much it was Simon's doing in the end.

My train of thought was quickly derailed when Simon answered Kara's question.

"Sorry to disappoint you, but we already have plans. The three of us are going hiking tomorrow."

Now that was not what I'd expected to hear.

"We are?" I inquired, turning to him, which, for whatever reason, gave him the excuse to smirk right in my face.

"Unless you'd rather stay home and mope around the entire day?"

My mouth was already open, about to ask him how he knew about my very recent change of schedule, but I cut myself short when I realized that it must have been the content of Jack's infuriating slew of texts. It wasn't hard to extrapolate from there where this was going, and I fervently hoped that it wasn't just wishful thinking on my part.

"I don't mope," I pointed out, although I sounded petulant enough to make myself wince. "But hiking sounds fun."

Kara stared at us for a second, and I was sure that she was checking her inner radar for possible euphemisms for said physical activity, but then shook her head.

"I'll never get why you think that outdoors stuff is fun. I mean, I get it with those two hillbillies." She nodded at Jack and me. "But you? Didn't we vote you 'least likely to do non artsy stuff' in high school?"

Simon answered that accusation with a jovial grin.

"People change. And the great outdoors has been inspiration for many lyrical masterpieces."

"I'm not bringing you cake if you lock yourself away in a cabin next," she warned, then laughed. "Anyway, should your plans fall short, call me. Dan's sister keeps reminding me that she wouldn't mind me setting her up with some eligible bachelors, and they have an open bar up there. Not interested? Spoilsports."

I waited exactly long enough for her to sashay out of earshot before rounding on Simon, who looked completely nonplussed by my glare.

"Hiking? Seriously?"

"Remember that lake we were having a few beach parties at over the last couple of years?"

I frowned, and Jack was only too happy to help, leaning across the table so he could join our little whisper session.

"The one where you kept either excusing yourself or ended up falling asleep in one of the cars less than ten minutes after joining us?"

"It was at least twenty that one time," I pointed out.

"That lake," Simon confirmed. "Weather forecast is good, and most people barely make it ten yards away from the parking spaces. There are a couple of trails leading around the lake. Back there, we'll be pretty much undisturbed and can spend the entire day doing whatever we want."

Now that did sound promising, if for one little detail. It rankled that a part of me even thought about objecting.

"I'm not sure I can do this with the two of you."

That sounded rather obtuse, and Simon's frown let me know that, so I was quick to lean closer and pitch my voice even lower.

"I'm quite happy to accept you as my Dom, but I can't do this with Jack. It was weird enough the first time, but after today I'm a hundred percent sure that I'm going to end up rolling on the floor, laughing, rather than play along. You understand what I'm saying, right?"

His features evened out, and one of those almost sweet smiles returned.

"We don't always have to play just because we fuck." Just hearing him say that gave me the best kind of goose bumps, but he wasn't finished yet. "So far it looks like you're really trying to hold your temper in check, and it must have cost you not to let Jack fuck you out on that terrace over there. Antagonizing me comes with punishment, but if you obey, you deserve a reward. If you can make it to that lake without succumbing to your baser nature, you deserve such a reward, and I think I can speak for Jack, too, when I say that we'll make up for all that pent-up frustration you're positively humming with. As equals, on common ground, no rules, no regulations. Sounds good?"

I nodded, unable to keep myself from responding as quickly as possible. Who in their right mind would have been opposed to that?

Jack's laugh cut through the haze my mind was quickly getting lost in, pulling me back to the here and now. He'd leaned back during our quick conversation, giving us privacy, but now he was once again moving closer.

"Don't forget to pack some sunscreen and bug spray. But if you ask me, you can forget your panties any day of the week."

That got the sneer from me that it deserved, and I really hoped that Simon wasn't filing that away for later use. Then again, if he planned on always rewarding obedience like this, he might find me very agreeable.

-10-

In accordance with Simon's plan to drive me insane by means of instant combustion, the guys had shared a cab with me on the way home. There hadn't been any touching or even dirty talking involved, but more than once I had asked myself why I hadn't just joined them right fucking then instead of agreeing to sleep at my own place. I'd been out cold as soon as my head hit the pillow, but still, waking up wedged between them would have been all kinds of neat.

I woke up an hour early in the morning, uncharacteristically so, which left me too much time with my own thoughts as I showered, dressed, and ate breakfast alone. Marcy wasn't home, and I'd forgotten to ask about her schedule. I was too excited about today to read, so no wonder that my inner monologue resembled a porn flick. By the time Jack called to let me know that they were waiting for me downstairs, I was ready on so many levels and couldn't leave the house quickly enough.

It didn't come as much of a surprise to find the passenger seat of the car that was idling at the curb unoccupied, but it wasn't like Simon to be sleeping in the back while Jack was driving. At my raised brows, Jack grinned and gunned the engine as he swerved back into the light morning traffic.

"He was up until the early hours of the morning, writing. Said he was so inspired after last night."

I didn't know whether that made me frown or laugh harder.

"So glad that my plight gets his creative juices flowing."

"Not just the creative ones," Simon grumbled from the back, not even opening his eyes as he curled up more tightly against the window. Jack shook his head, grinning, while I was seriously considering reaching back and hitting Simon with something, but only for a moment. Instead, I filched Jack's coffee from the cup holder and busied myself with staring at the city streaking by the windows.

"You're really serious about taking things to the next level with him, eh?" Jack broke the silence a little while later.

"Kinda," I admitted, then passed him the coffee as he held a hand out to me. Glancing at him, I saw that he was trying hard not to grin. "Why? Is it that obvious that I'm a little worked up still?"

"You look like a bristling cat, just so you know," he informed me. "I really don't get why you let him put you into a situation like that."

I shrugged, not quite sure how to reply.

"Because it's fun, even if it's terribly frustrating? And if you're bothered on my behalf, you know how to make things right later."

"Counting on it, actually," he replied, and the playful leer he sent in my direction made me laugh.

"Why did we never have sex before two weeks ago?" I asked, surprising not only Jack but myself with the question.

"Well," he started, then shut his mouth again as a light frown crept across his forehead. "Do you want the honest answer, or the reply you expect me to give?"

"How do you know what I expect you to say?"

"Because I know you like no one else does. Except maybe him, if you keep this up for more than a couple of weeks."

Had he just sounded a little annoyed? He didn't look it, but there was a certain tension in the line of Jack's jaw that made me wonder.

"Hit me with both. I mean, you're self-centered enough to believe that I've always been pining for you, so it's only fair that you give me something to laugh at, too."

I got a snort for that.

"Pining, eh? You could have just said something and spared yourself decades of longing."

"I wouldn't go that far," I pointed out.

"With the longing?"

"With the decades."

"It's been more than ten years since we graduated high school—you can't tell me that you've been oblivious to my charms before that."

This time shaking my head came with a weird pang of regret.

"You know, for a while I really thought you'd be the one to pop my cherry. Teen girl fantasies... I know, I had them, too."

Changing lanes kept his eyes focused on the road for a couple of seconds, but once the car was steady again, Jack turned to me, a strange look on his face.

"You're serious? I thought you were joking when you made me promise to be your first if you made it through high school without getting laid at least once. You know, that thing about not being a naive girl from a hick town freshly moved to the city, and a virgin to boot."

"Oh how could I have forgotten about that?" I snarked back, hoping that my sarcasm sounded less defensive to him than it did to me. "But yeah, I was kind of serious."

"Then why did you fool around with Bobbie Miller? It was in the backseat of his mom's car, right?"

"Why do you know where I checked in my v-card?"

Jack gave a sound between a snort and a grunt.

"Because the fucktard bragged about it in the gym locker room. Or why do you think I socked him a good one that landed me in detention for a week?"

"Because he was a fucktard?" I pointed out, but couldn't help feel strangely satisfied about that little morsel. Bobbie hadn't been the only guy who'd ever pissed me off who ended up on the wrong side of Jack's attention, but I'd never made the connection between him dumping me and the shiner he'd been sporting for weeks. It also made me feel better, if just a little, about letting him grope me.

"Then why didn't you say something to me? I doubt that you just let Bobbie molest you. You were pretty blunt even back then."

"Because you screwed half of the cheer squad, and I wasn't really into being associated with that lot in any way?"

That was only part of the truth, but it sounded better than admitting that back then I'd been sure that I couldn't quite live up to his standards, his weird promise aside. That would have been a pity fuck, and while even as a horny seventeen-year-old I had been sure he would have made me feel good about it, I'd been happy not to depend on him in that way.

"Well, there's that. Although it was only three of them, not half. I had a lot less game going than people thought."

"You were still a manwhore back in high school. Not that you've changed that much."

He didn't deny my accusation, only smiled that small smile that made me forget all about being pissed at him for his promiscuity. At least he owned it.

"Why didn't you say something to me?" I asked. "You know, as an impressionable seventeen-year-old, I would have been unable to resist your charm."

"You're still as defenseless now as you ever were," he said, letting me know.

"Yeah, because I totally didn't shoot you down last night."

"Only because you and Simon have your mindfuck stuff going on. Without that, you would have been all for me bending you over the next available hard surface."

It annoyed me a little that it was true, but not enough to keep a stupid grin off my face.

"And you wouldn't have made a move on me otherwise."

"Are you accusing me of being in cahoots with him? You offend me, woman!"

Both of us laughed at that, but I shook my head.

"Seriously, he didn't set you up for that? Not even a little? And it was his fault that I wasn't wearing any panties."

"He told you to go commando?"

The incredulity in his voice rubbed me the wrong way. It sounded too much like an accusation of me being a pushover.

"Well, he told me to change something up, and it seemed like the logical thing to do."

"Yeah, swaying around in a dress that's tight in all the right places without panties is my kind of logic."

I considered slapping him for that resurfacing leer, but decided that our safety was more important than my pride.

"It certainly felt interesting," I pointed out.

"You've never gone commando before? You've got to be shitting me."

I shrugged.

"Not wearing a short dress, horny as fuck, after someone shaved off my pubic hair."

Jack's face went comically slack, making me grin brightly. Ah, so he hadn't been aware of that.

"He did what?" he asked, looking at me out of the corner of his eye.

I blinked innocently, donning my sweetest smile.

"Shaved me, you mean?"

Jack forced his attention back to the road, but it was hilarious to see him swallow twice.

"Simon, you're such a rat bastard!"

Something that sounded like a vaguely affirmative murmur came from the back seat, making me grin even more brightly.

"Now how do feel about getting cockblocked last night again?" I teased, feeling wonderfully vindictive about my own horniness just then.

Jack uttered something low under his breath while his knuckles stood out white on the steering wheel, but after a few more seconds he relaxed with a lazy smile spreading on his face.

"Why are you telling me this now?"

"Because you've added substantially to my own plight, and it's only fair if I spread the misery."

"Huh."

"And because he said I just have to hold it until we get to the lake, not hike halfway around it, and while I don't hold it beyond him to enjoy dragging me along a little further, I think I have a good chance making you hard enough to just drag me behind the next tree and have your wicked way with me."

He laughed, and it was a deep, rich sound.

"See, that's why I would have been defenseless to you if you'd come on to me like that in high school."

That remark reminded me that he still owed me a reply.

"Then why didn't we end up screwing?"

Jack was silent, and for a moment I thought he was trying to come up with the answer that would annoy me the most, but when he replied, he sounded sincere and also a little self-conscious.

"Trust me, the thought kept me awake more than one night. And not just because you were sleeping something like a twenty-second dash across the backyard away from me. I guess I never came on strongly to you because I was afraid you'd just leave me behind like everything else from back home as soon as you saw that there was so much more out there in the big, wide world."

That was the last thing I'd expected him to say.

"Seriously?"

He shrugged, clearly uncomfortable.

"Kinda. Not that I was insecure or some shit, but I was well aware that if we hooked up, you'd always see me as your goofy best friend and high school sweetheart. And then you would have gone off to college and realized that I'd never be more than that, while on the other hand you'd have all those smart college seniors who never laughed about fart jokes and who could finally match your wits and stuff. It was easier to just remain your trusty fall-back guy from the get-go and not give you an extra incentive to leave me behind."

I didn't know what was worse—the wave of sadness that swept through me as I realized what I could have had back then and what was lost forever to us now, or the biting knowledge that he was likely damn right in his assessment.

"Or, you know, we could have stuck together through it all. Hell, we could have been married for over ten years already."

I didn't know why I said that, most likely to make myself feel better, and the dark smile he sent me told me clearly that he was aware of that.

"I doubt that you'd have been so happy about me and the legions of women I've screwed since then. Not quite hundreds, but, you know."

"Yes, I know. I've walked in on more than one. Or five," I enthused, not quite enthusiastically. "Do you have a thing about others walking in on you, because if I think about it now, it seems like an awful coincidence."

Jack's shrug was rather noncommittal.

"Habit, I guess. You can only double-team so many girls with your roommate before you stop really giving a shit whether he knows or not. And you kind of got between us by accident. Before you got between us literally, I mean."

"So nice of you for pointing out the obvious, again and again. My memory's not that scattered yet."

He was back to grinning widely now, of course.

"Eh, whatever. But seriously, I doubt that married us would have been that liberal about adding Simon to the equation. And I certainly wouldn't be okay with some guy shaving my wife's pussy and not letting me reap the benefits of that immediately afterward."

That made me laugh, but also weirded me out a little.

"Can we please stop with that train of thought now? I don't quite feel very matrimonious things for you, exactly. And don't even think about referring to me as your wife ever again."

"Not your kind of kink, eh?" he teased, then braced himself when he saw my slap coming from the side. It was barely more than a pat on the upper arm, but he still grunted as if I'd socked him a good one. "Okay, okay, disbanding all thoughts about fucking you in your wedding dress... Ouch!"

"Don't be such a crybaby."

That thankfully concluded that conversation, and it was a couple of miles later that Jack picked up the threads.

"Speaking of our plans for the day, I have a question."

"Just because my pussy is bare, I doubt that it functions any other way than before," I let him know.

"Very funny," he grunted, but the careful look on his face had me perking up instantly.

"So what has you in such a tizzy?"

"Nothing," he replied way too quickly, then made a face as he realized it. "Just promise me you won't hit me right away once you hear this."

"No such promises will ever be made."

He opened his mouth, and for a moment I thought he was going to ask Simon to make me not hit him, but he refrained from it and instead started anew.

"Just how much do you need to be the absolute center of attention the entire time?"

For a moment that question made me frown, mostly because it was hard to think with anything else than my overly excited sexual organs that wanted to be very much the center of all attention possible for the maximum amount of time, but then what he actually said filtered through that satisfaction-starved haze.

"I'm completely okay with you fucking Simon as long as I get to watch and take care of my own needs."

The deer caught in the headlights look he gave me made me want to laugh, but I quickly staunched that to avoid turning a casual moment into an awkward one.

"How the fuck do you do that?"

"Do what? Oh, you mean because I'm not obtuse enough not to get where you're going with that question? Seriously, you're not that dumb. That thing between us is a two-way street. You know me, and I know you. Sure, I've been kind of in the dark about what you do between the sheets for the past years, but I'm not blind. Besides, it can't have been that much of a surprise for you that I like it rough, so why should it come as a surprise that I can guess that you like to get a little curious yourself?"

"It was that insistence that we've never had anything with each other while we tag team girls, right?"

I shook my head, now unable to contain that laugh, but at least it came out as a soft chuckle.

"I really don't care, okay? But I have been wondering why you never did anything before. I mean, you haven't, right?"

Jack made a face, then shrugged.

"Nothing beyond accidental touches. You can't do a DP without getting really comfy with the other guy, obviously, but it's easy to shrug that off. At least it was always easy for me, with Simon. Never did it with another guy."

Thankfully, that made him laugh himself, so it drowned out my own mirth.

"Never did it with another guy, huh?" I echoed, unable not to rub that in.

"It's not like I've never looked at anyone else. But everyone does that, right? Don't you girls get all comfy in the locker rooms at the gym? Soap each other up and stuff?"

"No, the extent of physical contact I usually have with other members of my sex is to push their stuff away if the bitch was too inconsiderate not to put it all over the bench right in front of my own locker. Female interaction is usually a far shot from porn. But then I'm personally not really interested in girls," I pointed out when I realized that my dismissive comment might have made him self-conscious. "I can appreciate the female form, but it really doesn't do it for me. Sorry, I'm completely boring when it comes to what gets me going."

"And you can still say that with a straight face after what I walked in on yesterday?"

"There wasn't even a flogger or cane in sight," I offered.

I got another snort for that, but a good-natured one.

"So no objections from you."

"As long as I can watch and wank," I amended.

"What is it with women and gay porn?"

"Why do you love to watch girl on girl?"

"True," he admitted, not the least bit chagrined.

"I presume you and Simon talked about this already?"

He nodded.

"Last night. He said he was fine with it, as long as I asked you and you didn't throw a hissy fit."

"He really expected me to throw a fit?"

"No, that was me paraphrasing his much less animated expression. I added that just for kicks and giggles."

"Are you sure you're not gay? Giggles, really?"

Before Jack could reply, Simon interjected, sounding surprisingly awake.

"What I actually said was he should ask you himself if he was afraid that if I asked you, you would feel obliged to go along for whatever fucked up reason."

"Hey, that's not—"

"It is," Simon said right over Jack's feeble protest. Finally opening his eyes, he looked at me, a hint of a grin ghosting over his lips. "He was especially concerned about your unfamiliar recent receptiveness concerning suggestions coming from me."

"Not getting myself off until you allow me to was not a suggestion," I ground out.

"See what I mean?" Jack pointed out. "I'm totally fine with whatever you crazy kids do when I'm not around, but I'm not happy with stirring up a hornet's nest by inadvertently acting as his proxy."

"But you were fine with grinding yourself against me and offering to fuck me last night."

"You were doing at least as much grinding as I did," he defended himself. "And besides, that was different. But same point. You're confusing me!"

"Welcome to my world," I jeered back, but then got serious again. "But I do see your point. Let it be said that you have my uninfluenced consent to do whatever you want in front of me, as long as I get to—"

Jack sighed.

"Yes, we got it. You want to get off while watching us."

"Hey, I'm going out of my way here not laughing at your behavior, and you don't take my very pressing concern seriously?"

"Simon, stop being such a bastard and let her rub one out right here and now so we can go on and enjoy the day without her being all cranky."

"No!" I shouted, a little surprised myself, just as Simon gave a way more succinct, "No way in hell." That made me glare at him, but he just settled back against the window and closed his eyes.

"Wake me when we get there. As much fun as listening to you two bicker is, I really need some more sleep."

Jack and I traded glances, and after a second he flashed me a broad grin that I was only too happy to return. Oh, this was going to be so much fun! And if the look on Jack's face was any indication, I would get my payback only too soon.

The lake was just as I remembered—large enough not to see the other end from the parking area where most people remained who got here, and away from the hiking trails so it was not that frequented in the first place. Except for a few stretches of beachy shoreline, trees grew right up to the water, making the entire area a tranquil oasis only an hour or two away from the city.

Much to my dismay, Jack didn't drag me off to fuck me right behind the next tree when we arrived, even when I hinted that I wasn't wearing anything underneath my shorts today, either. However, with the fresh air in my nostrils and the sun shining warmly on my face, it was hard to hold a grudge for long as we picked up our backpacks and made our way around the lake. Simon still seemed half-asleep or otherwise lost in thought, and Jack regaled me with spoiling every single TV show I hadn't yet caught up on. More than once I was tempted to try to push him into the water whenever the small trail we followed got close to the lake, but considering that he was strong enough to pick me up and throw me in, I refrained until we'd arrived at our destination, a small peninsula reaching out from the wooded shoreline, a single, huge oak lending shade on the otherwise vegetation-free beach.

Simon and I took our time putting our stuff away and getting blankets and towels ready, but Jack dropped his things right there, wrenched his clothes from his body, and ran straight into the lake, his lily white ass in fascinating contrast to his otherwise tanned body and the black tattoo snaking up his right biceps and shoulder. I shot Simon a pointed look from where he was watching the spectacle beside me.

"I shouldn't have bothered bringing a bathing suit, right?"

"It's always nice to unwrap presents," he pointed out, but forewent donning trunks himself as he followed Jack.

Then it was just me, still partly clothed on the beach, feeling ridiculous about the amount of time I'd wasted this morning trying to puzzle out whether I could dare wear that bikini that made my boobs look great but left my mid-section obviously exposed, or rather take the swim suit that pushed everything into lines sleeker than gravity had left me with, but also squashed what didn't need squashing away. Shrugging, I left my clothes in a heap as I made my way into the water myself.

It was still early in the season and the water would have been cool otherwise, but the brief hike had let me work up a bit of a sweat, and if the guys went in, I couldn't very well not follow. Kara would have stayed outside, staging herself into the best sunbathing position that still let her look fashionable and sexy, but that wasn't my style. I was actually surprised that Simon had beaten me to the cool water because normally he was the one who avoided such things, while Jack and I raced each other, trying to outdo one another with creating the hugest splash. Simon did look rather cold and uncomfortable while he swam out into the deeper water, while Jack only let me catch up to him so he could try to dunk me under while I was throwing my entire weight into my grip on his shoulders, attempting the same.

Then there was cold water caressing me everywhere while his body was incredibly warm and strong as it pressed against my own, and familiarity fled to let something else take over. Jack seemed just as aware of it as I was, only twisting on my grip so he was facing me, rather than pulling me under, and we stared at each other from way too close—or not close enough.

I blinked, and the moment passed, at least for me. Jack was a little too slow to shake it off, thus giving me the perfect opportunity to dunk him under and flee before his flailing arms could catch me underwater. By the time he resurfaced, sputtering, I was halfway to Simon, and Jack didn't catch up until I'd managed to put Simon as a somewhat insufficient buffer between us. He stopped his assault but his eyes remained narrowed as he stared at me, waiting for me to either make a move first or come out of hiding.

"Sometimes I wonder why I bother associating with that infantile lot of you," Simon remarked dryly, looking from one of us to the other.

"No one's forcing you to get in between us," Jack pointed out.

"Unless, of course, that's exactly where you want to be," I agreed, letting my smile add to my suggestive tone.

Simon pursed his lips, then looked back to Jack.

"I catch her, you dunk her. Deal?"

"What, no!" I screeched, then kicked away, not waiting for the affirmative response I knew was about to come.

I almost made it into shallow waters where my feet could have touched the bottom and helped propel me forward before strong fingers closed around my thigh and pulled me to a sudden halt. I made the mistake of not kicking hard enough to make Simon let go, and then Jack was on me, throwing himself physically onto me so that he pushed me under easily. He was about to let go when I felt more weight coming down on us, and when I made it back around him and to the surface, Simon was grinning at me while Jack was still under water.

"Oh, you got this coming!" I shouted and threw myself at him, but unlike me he already had gained sure footing underneath, and all I accomplished by heaving myself up and trying to push him down with my hands on his shoulders was push my boobs into his face.

Gravity pulled me back down and Simon closed his arms around my torso, both to pull me close and keep me from trying again. And then Jack was behind me, molding himself to my body, his arms circling me just above Simon's. The water was cold enough by then to make physical contact a comfortable excuse, but the way Jack briefly kissed the soft skin below my ear was a different kind of intimate. Relaxing against his chest, I let them both hold me up so I could comfortably wrap my legs around Simon's hips and pull him closer, smirking up at him. His hold on my sides tightened, but Jack slid his hands up, cupping my half-submerged breasts. I sighed contently when his fingers stroked over my hard nipples, and ground my hips against Simon, even though the cold water kept that maneuver from being really effective.

"I think it's about time we take this out of the water, before I freeze off something more vital than my toes," Jack murmured into my ear, his hands telling a very different tale entirely.

"You think? I'm rather comfortable here, wedged between the two of you."

"Yes, I really do think so," Jack said, then abruptly moved away from me—only to push my head and shoulders under again.

By the time I came up sputtering and snorting water, he and Simon were already halfway to the shore, and it was way too cold to linger and sulk. The upside of being last out of the water was that Jack already held my towel open for me, happy to enfold me with it and give me a weird back rub to warm me up faster. Tired from our splashing in the lake, I sat down on the remaining free spot on the spread-out towels on top of the blanket, conveniently placed between the other two.

I closed my eyes, and for a few minutes I was very happy to let the towel dry the rest of me while the sun quickly warmed my cold skin. I couldn't even remember when I'd last spent a day lazing outdoors with not a care in the world. But with warmth and comfort obtained, other needs returned, and before long I opened my eyes and found both guys propped up on their sides, watching me. I still had my towel and arms folded around me, but the desire to just throw them to the side was very appealing.

"How are we going to do this now?" I wanted to know, trying hard not to rub my thighs together to create the kind of friction I needed so badly all over.

"How starved for attention are you?" Simon said, his voice in itself a caress.

I pursed my lips and considered, and might just have let the towel slip away accidentally as I stretched. Feeling their eyes on my naked body between them felt all kinds of good.

"You always have such a fancy way of phrasing questions like that," I teased him.

"Then let me rephrase that," he offered and leaned close enough that a droplet of water fell from his hair onto my shoulder, his eyes intent on mine. "How badly do you need to be fucked?"

Breath caught in my throat, but I forced it out with a bright smile.

"Badly. But considering the options on the table, I wouldn't mind waiting just a little longer. I'm feeling generous today."

Simon's eyes flitted toward Jack for a moment, then returned to me.

"As long as you get to watch and touch yourself, eh?"

"Does that thought turn you on?" I shot back. "Watching me make myself come while he fucks you, hard and fast?"

"I could think of worse ways to start the day," he offered, then leaned so close and whispered so softly that I could barely make out his words. "I'm convinced that he's sure that he wants to give this a try, but I think it would be a tremendous relief to him if you just happened to jump in should something not work out exactly to his expectations. What he avoided admitting to you in the car is the part where he still thinks there's a chance he's not at least curious. With the other girls, he always had the excuse of saying he doesn't want to frighten them away or lose faith, but since you so eloquently stripped him of that option, he might feel a little intimidated flying blind now."

I nodded, getting what he meant, then turned away so I could grin at Jack, who seemed to wonder if he should be suspicious about our whispering, or concerned.

"I certainly don't mind lazing around here while you two do all the work. Do me a favor and put on a nice show for me, will you?"

Simon snorted, and Jack looked ready to throw something at me—or lacking that, maybe pick me up and throw me into the lake—but he shrugged it off after a second.

"Your wish is my command. At least then you can't complain that you feel neglected."

"Don't give me a reason to be bored, and I won't complain at all."

It took us another ten minutes to shuffle around and get everything ready. Unlike in porn where people just happened to roll over and fuck, reality was a long shot from that. Porn actors also never got nervous, and Jack was definitely not as cool as I was used to seeing from him. Simon picked up on that, too, and while I'd half expected him to rub it in Jack's face, instead he caught his upper arm with a strong hand and made him still from where Jack had been fidgeting with the blanket to kick away random pieces of wood from underneath. They looked at each other for a moment, Simon smiling, Jack a little wide-eyed.

"You set the pace, and we do what you want to do. I already told you that. And if all I get to do is touch and kiss you, I'm okay with that, too. I'm not going to push you into doing anything you don't want to."

I wondered if I should have felt miffed at how different Simon treated Jack and me—he got all the consideration while for me it was "do this" and "take that," but if I was honest, I wouldn't have wanted to start a scene in Simon's playroom with him not taking charge and letting me second-guess anything. Besides, he'd proved that once we were done, he could be caring and gentle, provided I even wanted that. Our shared shower after our first scene seemed like something he needed just as much as I did, maybe even more. If he suddenly came on to me like that, I would have laughed in his face, not rolled over, ready to be fucked.

But the same wasn't true for Jack, judging from how he relaxed, then gave a somewhat shaky laugh.

"Honestly, I think I could use a little nudge right now."

Simon's smile widened as he moved closer, then reached up with his other hand to touch the side of Jack's face.

"Like this?"

Instead of giving him time to reply, he closed the distance and kissed him, first just lightly pressing his lips against Jack's, then deepening the kiss as Jack responded.

As supportive as I'd been about the two of them getting it on, I'd still expected to feel left out, but while I definitely felt something low in my stomach knot up, it was with arousal, not envy. Watching Jack relax further, then reach up to touch Simon's shoulders before he pulled him closer was kind of sweet, and in no way something I felt like I had to get in between.

They started slow, but things quickly heated up when Simon stroked a hand down Jack's ripped stomach until he drew a sharp breath from him, then wrapped a sure hand around his hardening cock. Jack didn't hesitate to grind his hips forward, then let go of Simon's arm in favor of reciprocating. Their kisses got more needy fast, and before long Simon broke away, directing a veritable leer at Jack.

"I really want to suck your cock," he said, his hand speeding up in turn where he was stroking him. "I want to wrap my lips around it and suck, then take you in as far as I can. Do you want that? Do you want to fuck my face?"

Jack let out a low moan and nodded, then Simon gave him a gentle yet insistent push so that he sprawled back on the blanket. Grinning, Simon hunched over him and stole a last kiss, then working his way down his body in a trail of kisses and light nips. Jack shuddered as Simon reached his goal and licked slowly over the head of his cock, then took him in, one inch deeper with every time he bobbed up and down. The look on Jack's face was pure bliss as he relaxed, then tensed when Simon must have done something that felt even better. His previously closed eyes shot open and he propped himself up on his elbows so he could watch, absent-mindedly licking his lips while one of his hands ran up and down Simon's upper arm where he could reach it.

I was well aware of the fact that giving head was not my strong suit, but watching Simon, I wondered if I should take notes. Without a doubt he was very effective about it and massively enjoyed himself, while he continued to idly stroke his own cock. When I looked from him to Jack, I found Jack watching me, slightly flushed but more alert than I'd expected.

"You do look a little bored," he ground out, his voice heavy with need.

"Nope, that's my slacked-jawed 'fascinated by porn' face, not my 'oh would you finally get it on?' face."

"You could still lend a hand—or two," he offered, then his eyes rolled back when Simon sucked a little harder. "Shit, I don't know how long I can do this, and I'd rather come in your ass than your mouth."

Neither of us seemed to have issues sorting out what was meant for whom, and Jack gave a loud hiss when Simon went even lower.

Considering for a moment, I finally rolled onto my side, then crawled over until I was hunkered behind Simon. Not exactly the best position to get the right view, but a chance to touch still beat just remaining on the sidelines. And when I leaned close enough to stage whisper into Simon's ear, I got a wonderful look of his lips wrapped around Jack's cock.

"I think he wants me to lend you a hand there," I said, and reached from behind between Simon's legs. At my insistence, he withdrew his hand so I could wrap mine around his cock. He thrust appreciatively into my fist, then used his now free hand to start playing with Jack's balls.

"Fuck!" came Jack's exclamation, which turned into a whine when Simon switched to pumping him with his hand, and licked and sucked on his scrotum instead. Jack tensed further, which did wonderful things to the already prominent muscles in his abdomen and chest, but before long his hand clawed for Simon's head, then nudged him back toward his cock.

"Want something else?" Simon teased and caught one of his fingers between his lips, only to suck on it greedily.

"I want you to... fuck!" Jack groaned, then tried again. "To suck me off!"

Simon responded immediately, letting that finger trail from between his lips before he bent his head again, and after a teasing kiss took Jack's cock back into his mouth, while keeping up the stroking motion with his hand. Jack shivered, then sagged down onto the blanket, his hand remaining on Simon's head to guide him. Simon definitely liked that, judging from how his own dick jumped in my hand, but he was much less emphatic with reacting to my stimulation.

Looking around, I found the bottle of lube I was looking for right next to Simon's hip, but then something else occurred to me. Glancing back up at Jack, I grinned, then cleared my throat loudly until his head lolled to the side and he looked at me.

"Do you want to prep his ass for fucking, or should I do the honors? I know you're quite proficient with the job from my own experience, but you seem a little preoccupied right now."

Jack's eyes glazed over a moment, then snapped back to focus on my face.

"If you don't mind?"

"Certainly not. I'm glad to help," I said, and withdrew from Simon to get the gloves from my first aid kit.

When he heard me snap them on, maybe a little theatrically, Simon stopped, then let Jack's painfully hard cock slip from between his lips to smirk at me.

"What?" I asked. "It's much quicker to take them off so I can finger fuck myself rather than get soap and wash them clean. Besides, some habits are hard to break."

"Did you hear me complain?"

"No, but you were clearly judging me," I accused, then reached for the lube. "And maybe you should think twice about talking back to the woman who is about to ram her fingers up your ass."

Instead of a verbal answer, he had the audacity of wriggling the posterior in question at me and went back to driving Jack insane with his lips and tongue.

I was rather liberal with drizzling lube onto Simon's anus, then added some more to my hands to make any kind of manual stimulation more enjoyable for him. Moving in closer, I gently rubbed two fingers over his anus, then started penetration with one slowly, while I reached for his cock with the other hand.

Let it be noted that it was a lot easier to open him up than the better part of the patients I'd had the joy of subjecting to rectal exams as part of my clinic hours, and he was a lot more responsive. He also had a healthy prostate, which I couldn't help notice as I worked a second finger in and remained there, stroking gently while drawing the most delicious sounds from him.

Jack suddenly sat up and pushed Simon away, and for a second we both went still, confused and a little wary, but instead of bolting, Jack knelt down and moved closer until he could nudge Simon into a more upright crouching position himself. I quickly pulled away when I felt Jack's fingers brush against mine, and he briefly flashed me a sweaty grin over Simon's shoulder before leaning in to catch Simon's lips with his own. Now his former reservation was only a ghost of itself, and it was deliberate teasing that made his motions slow, not hesitation.

"Told you I want to come deep in your ass," he murmured into Simon's mouth, then started stroking him harder.

Simon gave a low groan as he rocked back onto my fingers, then thrust forward into Jack's hand. My, but wasn't he a happy puppy, about to get happier soon, too.

I could probably have kept this up longer, but being so close, watching, touching, made my own need unbearable, and with a somewhat jerky motion I moved back, then pulled the gloves off. I couldn't quite resist slapping Simon's ass.

"You're as ready as you get. Continuing now would just be greedy."

Instead of withdrawing completely, I simply sagged down onto the blanket and spread my legs, then started rubbing my clit without further ado. My pussy was still as smooth as the evening before, my labia already puffy with arousal and quite wet with need, and it felt incredible to finally be able to explore, appreciate, and alleviate what dearly needed doing.

In a brief tousle, Jack grabbed Simon and flung him onto his back, making him end up right beside me. I grinned at his flushed face, his lips a deeper red from first sucking Jack off, then kissing him until they both were breathless. On impulse I rolled partly onto my side so I could crane my neck, and flicked my tongue over his bottom lip. Simon responded immediately, moving close enough to thrust his tongue into my mouth, while his hand touched down on my thigh and swept upward in a hot trail. I moaned into his mouth, then laughed when he had to pull back because Jack was gripping his legs and pushed them toward his chest. Simon rolled his eyes, then closed them with a satisfied sigh as he felt the head of Jack's condom-covered cock push into him.

Fascination overcame my own need, making me push myself into a half-sitting position so I could look down Simon's body. Jack went slow, then a little faster when he realized that he wasn't met with as much resistance as with me before. Simon gave a satisfied little grunt when Jack was fully inside him, making Jack laugh as he shifted so that he could lean forward and capture Simon's lips in a hungry, sloppy kiss. He withdrew, then thrust forward, making them both moan low in their throats.

I tried to inch away to give them some space, but Simon's hand wrapped around my wrist, pulling me back with unmistakable intent. With nothing better to do, I flopped back down, then cozied up to Simon as much as I could, with the hand Jack was supporting himself with between us. Feeling me there, Jack looked up and flashed me a grin, then lowered his lips to the right side of Simon's neck. Taking his pointer, I leaned over Simon and raked my teeth over the other side of his throat, then turned that into a kiss of hickey-producing strength. Simon gave a long, drawn-out groan that got cut off when first Jack, then I leaned in to kiss his mouth deeply. All the while Jack was rolling his hips forward and back, setting a slow rhythm, but before long I could tell that he had trouble pacing himself.

"Flip over?" Simon suggested, and before I knew what was going on, he was over me on all fours, grinning down at me while Jack thrust into him from behind. His mouth crashed down on my lips, his tongue twining around mine while his hard cock rubbed uselessly over the outside of my left hip with each of Jack's motions. I reached down to grab it, but Simon caught my hand before I could do more than touch and brought it back to beside my head. He did the same with my other wrist, then stared down at where he had me pinned underneath him. The intensity of his gaze was almost enough to make me come right there, and no part of me felt like protesting that we weren't in his playroom right now.

He leaned down to lick a hot line from my jaw to my neck, making me shiver until he reached my ear.

"I want to feel you come underneath me while he's fucking me," he rasped into my hair, making me positively writhe with need. My hips bucked up almost on their own volition, and right then I couldn't have cared less about finding a condom in all this fray, but Simon wasn't done yet. "I want to make you come with my lips. My tongue. My teeth."

There wasn't a fiber of me that was ashamed of the needy moan his words pulled from me, and there was no question of what to do as soon as he let go of my wrists. He barely left me time enough to shimmy up, then he was on me, pulling my thighs apart and burying his face between them. And unlike yesterday, he went straight for the kill.

The orgasm that slammed into me was hard enough to make me rear up, but that didn't deter Simon in the least. The only thing he did was wrap his arms around my legs to keep me from moving away further, and he kept going, sending nerve endings all over my body reeling. Jack grinned at me over Simon's back, then I lost sight of him when I sagged back down, but I felt him pick up his pace because it translated into an added rocking motion to whatever Simon did. Sinking my fingers into the towels and blanket underneath me, I let go, feeling a second climax sweep through me that wiped my mind clear of coherent thought.

I barely noticed when Jack came with a shout that had him sag down onto Simon's back, panting. Only when Jack pushed him over onto his back beside me did Simon stop, and I was too out of it to protest, and too sensitive to care much. Simon pulled me close so he could kiss me once more, his mouth tasting of me. Jack joined him on his other side, his hand working frantically on Simon's cock. I considered lending a hand or mouth myself, but satisfaction spreading through me made me sluggish, so I contented myself with kissing the side of Simon's neck while my hand ran all over his torso.

He was much less loud than Jack or I had been when he finally succumbed to his need, jizz spurting out of his cock to coat both Jack's hand and stomach, and my arm. Grinning, I ran my fingers through it, then wiped them on Simon's thigh, not quite coincidentally in imitation of what he'd done to me the day before. Simon smiled up at me and then pulled me on top of him, right through the sticky mess, making me laugh until his mouth silenced me momentarily.

We ended up in a sweaty heap and remained like that a good ten minutes before anyone found the will to complain. I was more than unwilling to go back into the cold water, but my protests didn't help me one bit when Jack simply threw me over his shoulder and waded into the lake, Simon following behind me. My shrieks of protest echoed across the lake but there was no one around to hear them, which was a very good thing.

And, of course, Jack dunked me under yet again, and there was nothing I could do about it.

After the exertion of the morning, we spent the next hours sleeping, eating, and lazing around. Our romp without sunscreen had made my chest, face, and Simon's upper back and shoulders go a little red, but we caught it before it could get uncomfortable. Still, retreating into the shade of the oak tree was a good idea, and I only left my feet in the sun to keep myself from cooling down too much.

There was some casual touching going on, but no one seemed ready to initiate round two for a while yet, and when Simon's phone went off around noon, I was only a little annoyed. Checking the display, he murmured something about his editor, then picked up and made his way to the other side of the peninsula as if not to disturb us. Strangely considerate of him, but after coming twice thanks to his oral skills, I felt a lot more forgiving toward Simon than the night before.

Rolling over onto my stomach, I looked for the paper I'd just been reading, only to find that Jack was holding it out of my reach.

"If you want that, you'll have to come get it."

I glared at him for a second, but then cocked my head to the side.

"You know, if you want me on top of you, there's an easier way for that."

Jack kept grinning, but there was definite interest in his eyes, and the way his cock stirred spoke for itself. Instead of going on like that, he shoved the paper down underneath my backpack, then rolled over so that he ended up pressed against my side, his face above mine. I just looked back at him, but might have kicked the leg on the opposite side of him a little farther to the side. The motion drew his gaze from my face down my body, and on the way back up he let his hand settle almost unassumingly onto my hip. Almost.

"Shouldn't we wait until he's done?" I asked, not very inclined to do so myself.

Jack shrugged, and just how that motion got his hand to slide down instead of up was beyond me, but I certainly didn't mind that it now rested just above where my panties would have ended if I'd worn any.

"You know Simon—if he gets into a fight with his editor, that call could take hours. I'd much rather do something else than sleep in the meantime."

He looked slightly alarmed when I pulled his hand from almost between my legs but moved closer, one hand reaching up to stroke his cheek, the blond stubble scratching my hand. Even if I'd tried, I couldn't have looked away from his light eyes, and I really didn't want to. His hand wrapped around my lower back, pulling me closer, a smile playing around his mouth before he turned his head so he could press a tender kiss against my palm.

Our conversation from the car flashed through my mind, stirring up feelings that I hadn't expected. Had he really held back because he thought I would reject him? It was true; on some level I'd always regarded him as just my friend, but most of that had fallen into place because he'd never made a move on me—but neither had I on him. He'd always been there for me, the time before that long forgotten, a comfortable constant at my side, a safety net that would catch me should I ever stumble and fall. The thought that complacency might have killed the spark between us and pulled us apart rankled, but being so close to him right now didn't make me feel like I'd given up anything or missed out on much. We'd been different people back then, both of us.

His head turned back so he faced me and I moved in, kissing him gently. He shifted until he could push one arm underneath me, then pulled me closer still with both hands, molding my body to his. What started out slow and languid soon turned heated and full of passion, and before long I needed more. Twining my legs with his, I tried to seek friction, and it only took him a moment to catch on. He smiled at me, still looking deep into my eyes as his hand ghosted from my back down to my thigh, then around and between my slightly spread legs. I moaned when I felt him rub over my clit and reared up, pressing my mouth against his, my lips already parting. His tongue stroked into my mouth exactly in sync with his finger sliding into me, slow and deliciously stoking glowing embers into flames again.

He shifted, now more over than beside me to give him better access. Things… changed, for lack of a better word. Intimacy receded while passion took over.

I wrapped my arms around his neck to pull him close, breathing in his scent, full of fresh air, sunshine, and water. A second finger joined the first and his thumb returned to my clit, soon working me into a frenzy. It occurred to me that I probably should have stroked his cock, but the way he was leaning over me, I couldn't reach it, and I figured he wouldn't be shy about telling me to stop being so selfish if it bothered him.

It was less a testament to his skill and more the residues of Simon's cumulative efforts that had me shudder and clench around Jack's fingers in no time, but he just kept on going, kissing me deeply until I relaxed again. Only then did he withdraw his hand.

While he was busy looking around for a tissue to wipe his hand off, I caught his wrist, then set to licking and sucking each of his fingers clean. I loved how his eyes never strayed from my face—or mouth, rather, but that still gave enough chance for eye contact. Once I was satisfied, I nudged him over onto his back, which revealed his cock, hard and ready for me. I thought about giving him a blow job then, but honestly didn't want to lose to Simon's skills. Instead I grabbed a condom and rolled it down Jack's cock, then crawled over him so I could straddle him. Taking his cock into my hand, I stroked it a few times, then lowered myself until I could rub it over my clit and up and down between my pussy lips before I finally sank down on it. Feeling him penetrate was so fucking good, particularly after coming three times already without that amazing full sensation.

Leaning forward, I stole a kiss from Jack, then started rolling my hips above him while his hands wrapped around my waist. That made me grin and straighten, and he picked up immediately when I pulled his fingers away from there and up to my breasts.

Like in the water before, he handled them deftly but gently, massaging rather than digging in, rolling my nipples instead of twisting them. As much as I loved the other, it was nice to be treated like a lady for once.

Looking up from Jack's face, I found Simon pacing up and down the beach a short distance from us. The motion of me sitting up must have drawn his attention because he stopped for a moment and stared at me, but rather than doing the normal thing and hanging up, he just grabbed his cock and started stroking himself. If not for the general annoyance of the interruption, I could have almost felt sorry for the caller.

Leaning back so I could support myself with my hands on Jack's thighs, I pushed my chest into his caresses, moaning unapologetically whenever he did something that felt particularly good. And there was a lot of that going on. Not enough to make me come with no one paying attention to my clit, but it was nice. Definitely nice.

Only that nice wasn't enough.

"You don't have to be that gentle with me. I'm not made of porcelain, I won't break."

Jack chuckled under his breath, and his hands slid down to grab my hips. The next time I came down, he thrust his hips up hard, making me yip with the sudden deeper penetration. That was better, but still not quite it.

Putting a hand on his chest, I stopped moving, slightly out of breath as I gazed down at him. There was something about the way he looked up at me that made me feel like the only woman in the world, but I could tell that neither of us was getting exactly what we wanted out of this. Leaning forward, I let my hair fall around my face to tickle his, a black curtain to hide us from the world.

"Is this what you want to do with me? Have me ride you like this?"

"Well, it's nice," he echoed my thoughts, then laughed when I made a face. "Isn't not what you want? You just climbed up onto me after molesting my fingers."

"I thought it would be a nice way to switch things up," I admitted, then looked over to where Simon was still busy jerking off on his own before my eyes returned to Jack. "Guess I don't want to become a one-trick pony."

"I wouldn't be afraid of that if I were you."

With that, he pulled me off him, down onto the ground and flipped me over onto my stomach before he crouched over me. I tried to draw my knees up to get into a kneeling position, but he pushed my ass down again before he moved over me, his legs outside of mine, most of his weight settled onto his left forearm and elbow. That put his chest close enough for me to push against it as I arched up when he guided himself into me, spreading me easily before he slid deeper slowly. His mouth was so close to my ear that I could hear him moan softly, the sound incredibly arousing. I couldn't suppress a shudder, feeling his entire body pressed against mine, so much closer than when we'd been side by side before, both physically comforting and dominating.

He set a slow pace at first until I eased back down onto my stomach, laying flat except for my raised behind, giving me time to figure out how to move with him and what would deepen his angle of penetration. There was something entirely decadent about the position, maybe because I could just lay there, relaxed, while he did all the work, although besides keeping himself suspended above me it didn't seem that strenuous. I certainly felt his every move with my entire body, the way he raised himself slightly as he thrust into me, then came back down as he withdrew. He could have easily shifted the balance to take complete control, to hold me down and just drive into me, but he left me that degree of freedom instead. His lips ghosted over my shoulder, then on to my ear, nibbling a little until he made me laugh. And all that while he hit exactly the right spots, creating a deep-seated kind of need churning low in my stomach.

"Better now?" he asked, then bit my shoulder playfully before peppering it with kisses.

All I could do in reply was nod, sigh, and clench my pelvic floor muscles a little more to make him speed up. Which he did, unlike what I would have expected from Simon, and I couldn't help but get a small kick out of that, too.

Speaking of Simon, he chose that moment to return, sauntering over to us after putting his phone away. Sitting down next to us, he watched for a moment before he cleared his throat.

"Need any help?"

"No, we're good," Jack ground out, then thrust in harder and faster than before, making me gasp, and realize that there was more to get out of this still.

"Want help?" Simon amended, grinning.

"Well, if you ask me like this—" Jack started, and shut me up with another hard thrust before I could open my mouth to object. Not that I intended to, but as much as I loved feeling him above me, my fickle libido was already salivating for more, if more was so very close at hand.

"Don't switch things up on my account. I love watching the two of you get it on, too."

That was evident from how hard his cock was, standing up at an angle from his body.

Jack seemed to contemplate that with his next two thrusts that made me moan loudly, but then stopped and reached underneath my hips, helping me bring up my knees underneath me. Simon moved in as soon as I was upright, his mouth hungrily fastening round my left nipple while his hand cupped my pussy. I closed my eyes, relishing the extra stimulation when Jack picked up rocking his hips into me, but even with Simon's fingers circling my clit, it still wasn't enough.

"C'mon, haven't you teased me enough already?" I complained, only to be shut up by Simon's tongue in my mouth when he switched targets.

But it was only a brief kiss, barely more than a nip, and thankfully he didn't stop rubbing me when he leaned back far enough to look me squarely in the eyes.

"How do you want us?"

There wasn't really much to think about.

"Jack underneath me, in my pussy, and you from behind."

It was only logical to switch things up from last time, and neither of the guys protested.

I got a moment to catch my breath when Jack moved away from behind me, making me feel empty as soon as his cock slipped out of my vagina, but it barely took me a minute to climb back into him once he lay stretched out before me. We shared a grin as I got back into the same position from before, only that now I set a faster pace, partly urged on by Simon's fingers on my clit, while those of his other hand started working their way through my sphincter.

Just feeling the friction of Jack's cock along with one of Simon's fingers was enough to make me want to buck my hips uncontrollably, but Jack's hands continued to guide me in a steady, maddening rhythm. Then, it was time for Simon to climb on behind me, and reason fled my mind.

Last time we'd gotten this far, I'd been terribly strung out and kind of overwhelmed by sensations and new experiences. Now, I was just as ready, but the different pace, and likely the fact that all of us had come at least once before, let us approach this at a somewhat relaxed level. Not having to give a shit about anything else but my own satisfaction was liberating, although a small part of me remained that wouldn't have minded a little hair pulling and growling from Simon behind me. What made a true difference was that, besides having their hands all over me, the guys were also more open about touching each other, a stroke of a thigh here, a gripped arm there that only added to the wonderful familiarity and closeness building between us.

Of course they were once again fucking me silly and made me scream between them, until first Jack, then Simon reached his climax. And when I still wasn't about to collapse after that, Simon pushed me down onto Jack's sweaty chest and finger fucked me to one last, final release that curled my toes even minutes after I'd come down from my high.

This time it took us a lot longer to find the energy and will to clean up, and I so didn't mind just laying there, my head cushioned on Jack's shoulder, Simon's cheek pressed into my hip. The sun shone in patches through the canopy of leaves above us, and before long I was drifting off, content on so many levels, not just the physical one.

Due to my work schedule, we had to leave hours before I was ready to return to the real world. A strange kind of nostalgia spread through me and seemed to be catching, judging from the fact that neither of the guys was very chatty on the way back to the car. I didn't say so out loud, but I was sure that we were all sharing the sentiment—life would be perfect if things could always be like this.

Almost at the car, Simon pulled me to the side and nodded for Jack to go on. I eyed him askance, not quite sure what this was about, and for a second there, he seemed almost hesitant.

"I know that this is likely a redundant question, and for once, do me the favor of not taking everything too personal, okay?"

"What is it with you guys and asking me not to hit you today?" I tried to diffuse the sudden tension between us, but Simon's deadpan look made me shut up instantly.

"I'm going to ask you this only one last time, because by now you've likely made up your mind either way. Do you want to be my submissive, including everything that entails?"

The question hit me kind of out of the left field.

"Why wouldn't I want to?"

He shrugged, and it wasn't exactly comfortable.

"If I consider your reactions today and compare them to how you act when there's something limiting you, I'm not entirely sure what to make of it."

I didn't know what to make of that, either, but tried not to get offended on the spot, and not just because he'd asked me not to.

"Simon, I love having sex with you and Jack. If what you're trying to say is that today felt a lot more natural than our first threesome, I agree, but I think that's because today neither I nor Jack were second-guessing everything we did, but just let go and enjoyed ourselves. But that doesn't mean I like this more than being in the playroom with you. We're just getting started, and while you're kind of a pro at this, it's damn fucking new to me, and I feel like I'm suddenly caught out on a sheet of ice, scrambling to get my footing while trying not to fuck things up every which way possible."

He nodded and offered me a small smile.

"It's okay, and while I think you perform best if I make you push yourself the hardest, I'm always willing to take it a bit slower."

"I don't think that will be necessary. Or good for my sanity, if it means more lessons like the one yesterday."

That made him snort, but he didn't say anything about that likely not happening again.

"Good. I'm not saying that I didn't thoroughly enjoy myself today, but I can't deny that I can't wait to have you kneeling at my feet again."

I remained silent, not sure if he'd appreciate a snarky comeback right there, or if that would just doom me all over again. Simon seemed a little befuddled, but then shrugged it off.

"I intend to step up the game a little bit. I know, at the beginning of our arrangement I promised not to interfere with your life, but I think that you will benefit from being a little shaken up sometimes, so let's give this a try. I expect you to tell me the moment this gets too overwhelming, or our schedule doesn't work out for you anymore."

I nodded, feeling a jitter of excitement come alive inside of me.

"Good. The general idea is that you come over twice a week, with several days in between for you to catch up on other things. I'll share my schedule with you and let you pick the days for now, but I expect you to hold yourself to that rhythm. If you can't make it because something comes up, no problem. I'm happy to give you some homework instead if it's no more than every third time or so. You can always crash at my place, day or night, so just running late won't be cause to flunk on me. I'll keep any activities outside of the playroom to a minimum unless you provoke me, and unless you protest, I don't mind switching a few of our sessions for hanging out with Jack, if either of you starts to feel lonely."

"That's a euphemism, right?"

"It is," he agreed, grinning.

"I'm so not opposed to that idea."

"Thought so. Back to what only concerns us. When you get home tomorrow, I want you to make a few lists for me. I'm not necessarily going to use them, but I value your input, and no one can set you up for failure as well as you yourself."

Now that sounded ominous.

"What lists?"

"First, one list of possible rewards and punishments. Those should be self-explanatory. Be honest, and don't hold back. I'll soon know if you pick something that's not really fitting."

"Like what?"

He shrugged.

"Rewards should be easy. Being allowed to come, for instance. But it doesn't have to be pleasant things only. I would more regard it as a list of strong preferences. Something that gets you off, something that you'd rather take than something else, something that makes you feel like you're getting a treat when I feel like you've earned it. Punishments, the opposite, and obviously your truthfulness is even more important here. Mind your limits, but don't be afraid to think of something that might even end up pushing you over that boundary. Think about it as your extended least-favorites list. Remember when I told you that a lot about BDSM is like conditioning? Those are the things you'll try to avoid at all costs, but they should be reasonable things. If I feel like none of them hit even close to the mark, our next session will consist of me going through that list, and once we're done, I'm sure you can think of better items."

Even though his sadistic smile scared me a little, it also did a lot to make me look forward to being at his mercy again, if not necessarily provoke that scenario.

"Okay. What else?"

"I also want you to think about what we've done and what you want to do, and write down a list of about five points you want to work on or improve. Your obedience comes to mind when I think about that, but it can be something completely different, too. Things we haven't tried, things where you feel I stopped well before pushing your comfort zone, or if you feel agreeable, something you think I might enjoy doing to you. Just don't make it about that altogether, or this will throw off our dynamic."

"Is that even a possibility? This makes me sound really selfish, but if it's my wish list, why should it be all about you?"

He gave me a look that made me consider putting "be less selfish" on that list, but he sounded more amused than annoyed as he replied.

"There are subs like you who don't have a problem with that. Adrenaline junkies, pain sluts, bondage whores, also in for the mental kick, but usually reaching for physical limits when prompted. And then there are the subs who above all aim to please their Masters, completely forgetting that in all their selflessness they overcomplicate things because none of us are mind readers. Try to hit the balance between the two extremes, and you should be in the green. I want you to keep that list updated whenever you think of something new. I don't have to factor it into my plans, but I might, if I feel generous."

"Generous like you felt yesterday?" I asked, half-teasing, half-afraid.

Simon snorted.

"What's a few hours spent squirming in exchange for feeling a lot more secure about what you want to do and what you can take? And correct me if I'm wrong, but you reaped the benefits of holding out so long more than once today."

I had to admit that he was right, and after a moment of petulance did so, too.

"Good. One last point now that that's settled." He looked at me intently until I stopped fidgeting, holding my attention completely. "Starting right now, I don't want you to wank at all. Any orgasm you have will be sanctioned by me. If you really can't stand it anymore, feel free to call or text me, but I won't let you come just because you get impatient. If you make it to our two sessions a week, you should walk away satisfied enough to tide you over until the next, and if not, homework will usually entail one orgasm at the end. Of course, you can always ask for some kind of bargain. If you prove to me that you deserve to come more often, I might feel like granting you that release."

"Prove it how?"

"Small tasks, or giving up part of your freedom. For instance, if you chose not to wear panties for a week, I might reward that with an orgasm or two on the side, taking into consideration that you'll likely feel like you're under my thumb a lot more often than if you didn't change anything about your routine. Or you do some chores, say, like cleaning your apartment with a butt plug firmly lodged in your ass, and every ten minutes you kneel down and rub yourself almost to a climax before you continue cleaning, until the work is done. I don't have to be in the same room for you to curse me into the next century inside your head."

That did not deserve a reply so it didn't get one, but it made me realize that this could range a lot farther than I'd calculated. Considering how fucking horny I'd been last night, it was only a matter of time until I would have to resort to something like that.

"Nothing that will jeopardize my attention at work."

"All those extra tasks are for you to decide, or pick and veto if you can't come up with a good suggestion for a bargain yourself. I have no intention of making you do any of that. It all comes down to your willpower versus your eagerness."

I wondered if this was more than I had bargained for, but the way my muscles clenched at just considering this, I didn't think I could tell him to go fuck himself with a straight face. So there was nothing left for me but to agree.

"I'll email you my schedule for the next month and expect your reply no later than Sunday midnight."

With that sorted out, we followed Jack to the car, but I held Simon back just before we got there.

"So no wanking at all? I don't even get tonight as a kind of transitional period?"

His smile was barely more than a humorless showing of teeth.

"You can get into the car completely naked and spend the entire way back to the city making yourself come over and over again, if you really need to."

I considered that option for only a moment.

"Nah, I think I'm good with coming a crazy five times or so today."

"Thought so," he snorted, then gave me a push toward the passenger seat.

Jack looked from one of us to the other but didn't say anything, just shook his head. Considering I did none of this to please him, I really didn't give a shit about his opinion. With luck, none of that would ever become a problem.

-11-

After the changes Simon had introduced on Saturday, I expected life to get, if not difficult, at least annoying, but it was Monday by the time I felt the first sting of that no-wank rule, and then it was only eighteen hours until our next planned session. Work kept me busy, and between other social obligations and trying to catch up on quality sleep, there wasn't much time for me to grow overly frustrated.

The sessions in the playroom itself went down without much ado for the most part, and with fewer hiccups than either of us seemed to have expected. I managed to mess up a few times but never enough to do more than annoy Simon, and while he picked up the pace, he did so slowly enough that I didn't even think about my safeword once. I did have to take two rain checks over the course of the next month, though, and when the third happened in the same week as the second, things got a little frustrating on my part. Bargaining really wasn't my thing, and the lives we kept outside of the playroom didn't really lend themselves to reliable real-time communication, so the following week Simon proposed a change.

By then, things had picked up a lot on the physical side, and more than once I'd needed a couple of minutes to stretch aching muscles back into cooperation after restrictive bondage. This time he suggested that, whatever else we'd do in that scene, some form of impact toy should round up the end. For every set of fifty hits I took without begging for mercy, he'd grant me one orgasm, stackable up to five orgasms per session, for a week to use up on my own discretion outside of our scenes. If we made it to two scenes a week, the countdown would reset, but for every unused orgasm he'd give me the chance to earn one extra for another fifty hits.

The first time he went at me with a light flogger, and I hit the mark easily. The second time he used a heavy flogger, but I still made it to seven times. Two weeks later my ass ended up with actual dark bruises that hadn't faded until the next session, but ten freebies were added to my list, and that was when he declared that my scoreboard would get reduced to zero if I didn't make it to at least the count of the previous session.

That day was the first time he got out one of the canes, a sturdy, heavy thing at that, and I left the attic humbled, my score reduced to zero until the week after.

One might have guessed that an experience like that would have left me scared of that most elegant of impact toys, but the opposite was the case. Sure, my respect for all things that came with a thud rather than a sting was renewed, but by then I'd accepted that Simon made a game out of confronting me with obstacles that my competitiveness could handle with ease. The next time he got out the exact same cane, I finally made it back to my five freebies, two of which I spent that very evening after dragging my sore and sorry ass back home. It was also the day the cane got its first mention on both my reward and goals lists.

As the weeks went by, Simon and I fell into an easy pattern, but things didn't really change for us outside of the playroom. Right after a scene I sometimes had problems acclimating for a while, but those were usually the days when he stuck to me like glue, soaped up my back in the shower, and once even tried to cook me dinner, a catastrophe thankfully averted when Jack got home early and called the pizza delivery service. Those days were also when I noticed that Jack was a little at a loss for how to behave around me, but usually curling up on the couch between the guys as we watched a movie together did the trick.

We didn't manage to stage a third instance of a threesome, mostly because I was working the entire weekend blocks to have breathing space during the week, and those were the only days when Jack had time himself. He didn't seem too annoyed about it, though, and on some level I was quite happy that I wasn't confronted with regarding Simon as something else than my Dom in a sexual setting. What had been strange the first two times until that lesson, and a little tedious in the following weeks, soon became second nature, at least for the set time span we spent in the play room. I still fought him tooth and nail whenever he pushed me—and push me he did with almost every session— but giving in never felt like defeat anymore and was usually rewarding on a deeper level.

Unfamiliar as it felt at first, I liked that sensation of being at his mercy, and while I didn't exactly crave it yet, there were times when it was like a buffer of comfort at the back of my mind. It helped that he never overstepped my limits, and while he never passed up a chance to one-up himself and get that extra bit of yielding from me out of a scene, he always rewarded my cooperation. More weeks than not, earning my freebies was more about proving to him that I could rather than needing that little bit of freedom, and more than once I considered giving up that option altogether.

I felt good in my role as his sub, not only physically fulfilled, but mentally strengthened, and I felt like it was starting to show, judging from people's reactions. More than one nurse remarked that I seemed a little less strung out although I worked extra hours whenever possible, and when I didn't bite off the head of one of my interns when he completely botched a diagnosis, even Zoe showed herself impressed, which, for her, meant she didn't bite my head off in turn. Kara stopped needling me about the mystery guy I was obviously screwing, but I had a feeling that she hadn't given up the hunt for him yet. Jack I kept happy with a constant supply from the bakery next to the hospital, earning his goodwill and cooperation whenever he had to field calls—mostly from Kara, some from Simon's work-related contacts—while we were at it.

In short, life was awesome, if a little extra painful at times. I would have been so happy if that streak of luck could have gone on forever.

Then the inevitable happened, and things started to go bad in the worst kind of ways.

It was a typical Monday for me, which, unlike most people in the country who suffered greatly under their first day of work after the free weekend, meant I was fielding the fifth shift in the space of time where three would have been the sane maximum allowed. I'd been feeling a little off before the weekend already and had taken a rain check on our usual Thursday session, and when I hit the bathroom at noon after fighting for a little boy's life for six hours straight, I realized that the reason I'd felt like shit since morning was that my period had set in, a comfy five days ahead of schedule but packing some extra punch, just for fun. With any other guy, I would have canceled, but the way everything was coming down at me at once, I felt like I needed that session tonight more than I needed oxygen to breathe. So I checked back with Simon, explaining the situation as much as it was possible in a sequence of 140 characters, and he told me to just come over after my shift, and he would work something out.

During the afternoon, info came down from Intensive Care, letting me know that my patient hadn't made it, and I was ready to just curl into a fetal position and rock in the corner until exhaustion would pull me under.

Coincidence had it that Jack hopped onto the same train I was riding in, and by the time we made it to their front door, he had convinced himself that the sane thing was to just grab some food and spend a comfortable evening in front of the TV. One look at me, and Simon agreed with him.

I did not.

Ten minutes later my knees hit the floor of the playroom, and for the first time, my mind didn't clear, and also didn't shut up when Simon bound my arms behind my body, tied my calves to my thighs in a spread kneeling position, shoved a vibrator into my vagina and put it on high before he strapped it in with yet more rope, and got the cane from its rack.

It didn't shut up when Simon threatened to beat me until I stopped glowering at him, it didn't shut up when he gagged me and went to town on my quivering thighs and tits, "until I gave him reason to stop," meaning I'd just have to clap my hands behind my back, signaling that I'd had enough and we could finally end this farce.

But it did quiet down when he finally realized that I really needed an outlet tonight, and nothing short of maxing me out would do. For the sake of hitting that spot exactly and not pushing me too far, he re-tied my hands so that they were by my sides and I could give him signals—up for more, and down for slowing things a little. And because he took pity on me, he told me to just go ahead and come if I could, but for each orgasm he would hit me harder and more frequently.

I made it through five rounds of that, although I sobbed through the fourth and pretty much screamed myself raw at the escalation after that last climax hit, but that was also the point where that dam inside of me broke that I'd shoved all my misery and grievances behind, and suddenly I was free.

And it wasn't just that I didn't feel like any of that wasn't suffocating me any longer. No, it was an almost physical high that swept through me, made me feel as if I was floating— soaring toward the sun. I was free, and everything was great, and even though the cane coming down on my inner thigh hurt like a motherfucking red hot poker, it felt so fucking amazing that I could have remained right there until the end of my life, happy forever.

That high lasted maybe two minutes, and then it was suddenly over. I crashed right down onto the bottom of reality, and if Simon hadn't been there to catch me, I might also have physically tumbled off the bench I had been kneeling on when my entire body went slack from one second to the next. And then it was all too much and I started crying uncontrollably, confused about my reaction and unable to stop myself or even tell him that I was really feeling okay, but this was just happening and I didn't know how or why. Simon just held me, rocking me in his arms, cooing all kinds of soothing endearments to me that I barely heard over the sounds coming out of my own body. Unlike me, he seemed better equipped for handling this, whatever it was, and when I finally accepted that and just let go, I eventually quieted down again.

I had no idea how late it was by the time I slid off his lap and landed, quite painfully so, on my ass, but outside the sky was pitch black, and the sun had still been up when Jack and I had made it to the house. I tried to ignore the mess I undoubtedly was, my eyes sore from crying, my muscles hurting from exertion that had nothing to do with the cane. Simon smiled at me gently and reached up to push a wet strand of hair off my face, and that gesture alone was enough to make me sniffle all over again. As much as I longed for basic human contact, I suddenly couldn't stand his touch, drawing in on myself, but he didn't look surprised about that, either.

"I don't feel comfortable leaving you alone like this, but if you need some time on your own, I can go downstairs and leave the door open. Just call if you need me, okay?"

I nodded, insanely grateful that he seemed to pluck my desires right out of my brain before I could even become fully aware of them myself, then curled up in the middle of the floor while he left me to myself. I just continued to lie there, hugging myself, and waited for the world to fall back into place, which it did, one little piece after the other.

Simon returned after a while but didn't approach me when I didn't react, instead cleaned up around me except for the spot I still occupied. When he was done, I was ready to join the world again, at least as far as hitting the showers. He was reluctant to leave me alone in the bathroom, but when I told him that I really needed a few extra minutes to gather myself, my voice hoarse but calm now, he nodded and promised to wait for me in the kitchen.

I spent an obscenely long time just standing under the hot spray of the shower, waiting for my misery to return, but it was gone now, swept away in that overwhelming tide. Slowly but surely, my mind ground into gears, and by the time I toweled myself dry, I felt vaguely like myself again. My body was aching all over, and I had to admit that I looked kind of beat up. I spent a few minutes with a small hand mirror, counting the welts the cane had left on my legs, ass, chest, upper arms, and even one on the sole of my right foot. I counted thirty-seven distinctive marks, three of which had actually broken the skin and where scabbed over now, and I was sure I would feel all of them keenly by tomorrow morning.

If I hadn't been so fucking tired, I would have glowed with pride and maybe high-fived myself. True, it all was a little insane, but considering how bad I'd felt before coming over and how relieved and at ease I was now, I would have gladly taken it all over again. And I would hardly have come, hard, a complete five times if I hadn't gotten a massive physical whammy out of it.

As I found out as soon as I shuffled into the front of the house, stupidly only wearing a tee and shorts that left half of the welts on my thighs uncovered, Jack begged to differ.

While I'd procrastinated in the bathroom, I'd already heard the low murmur of voices, but I hadn't paid attention to them, too concerned with myself. And now my mind was on autopilot as soon as I smelled food, suddenly realizing that I hadn't had anything to eat since breakfast, and microwaved pasta was exactly what the doctor prescribed. So I didn't really notice that Simon was hovering in the kitchen, looking pissed off while trying hard to hide it from me, while Jack was leaning against the back of the sofa, obviously waiting for my reappearance so he could finally get the comforting on that he felt was the solution to everything, and what I should have gotten all along.

One good look at the welts crisscrossing my thighs, next to a weirdly shaped bruise developing on my upper arm just below the end of the sleeve of my tee, and he went ballistic, reigniting the fight I'd clearly been oblivious about the entire time.

"What the fuck is this?" Jack called out as he came after me, and when I didn't react, still zeroing in on my food, he grabbed my arm, if gently, and pulled me around so that he could see the back of my thigh better where the light hit it directly. Pivoting on my foot made me put too much weight on the welt down there, making me hop ungracefully and curse under my breath, which didn't help de-escalate the situation. And because I still hadn't gotten that pasta and Jack was the only thing standing in my way, it was the obvious thing to pull out of his grasp and tell him to go fuck himself so I could finally get food into my rumbling stomach.

What followed wasn't pretty, and about two minutes in I'd all but forgotten about the steaming pile of junk food on the counter.

"What the fuck did you do?" Jack shouted, gesturing in the general vicinity of my exposed legs while glaring at Simon.

"I did exactly what she wanted me to do. What she needed me to do," Simon tried to explain, his voice pressed with frustration, but Jack would have none of that.

"Are you fucking insane? Those are fucking welts! Welts! That's what, like, second-degree assault?"

Simon was too stunned by that accusation to find a quick reply. He was staring at Jack, and that was about the time my mind finally rerouted brain power from foraging to actual higher brain functions. Turning slowly, if a bit gingerly, I looked at Jack, maybe still a little slow on the uptake.

"Just look at you! You're completely traumatized! Who the fuck does this to someone they supposedly care about?"

Simon did another eloquent fish impersonation, so I decided that it was about time to tear Jack off his high horse.

"The only one who's traumatizing me is you with the shit you're spewing right now," I spat, and after a last, longing glance at the cooling pasta I rounded on him, full force. "I'm hungry, I'm fucking tired, and the last thing I need right now is your idiotic, misguided sense of chivalry. Fuck off, and take your sanctimonious bullshit right out the door with you!"

I don't know what made me say that. In all fairness, I really wasn't up to running my thoughts through any kind of filter, but that wasn't the whole of it. I didn't like him going after Simon in the first place, but Jack's accusation didn't just hit him squarely in the nuts, but socked me a good one on the return. Anything that went down in the playroom was consensual, and with this scene in particular, I could have stopped it at any single second. Simon had hit that mark perfectly, and if my addled mind hadn't completely flunked out on me during the scene, he hadn't derived any sort of pleasure from it himself. He'd done it all because I wanted him to, he'd let me take charge and had just delivered what I'd, quite loudly, begged of him. So if Jack thought this was assault, it wasn't Simon's doing but at least partly my own.

And, even worse, if by whatever upside-down logic it was still all his fault alone, that simply meant that Jack had so little faith in me that he saw me as the victim who was too stupid to even see what was going on when it hit her in the face and kept defending her abuser to her last breath. That made me feel dirty and weird, and suddenly a hell of a lot more insecure than ever in my life before, and I hated Jack for being the cause of all that.

I was too out of it to voice all that, but I think he could read it right off my face as I stared at him, quivering with rage. If I hadn't cried myself into exhaustion, I might have started bawling right there again, but somehow I managed to hold myself together.

Maybe if it had just been me and Jack, we could have hashed this out right there, but Simon took that moment to regain his voice, and everything went to hell.

Shouting ensued. I think we all said some things that we didn't really mean, but reason went flying out the door pretty fast. Jack clearly hadn't expected to be met with any resistance, let alone me and Simon joining forces—something that never happened in the few fights we'd had over the years—and it only took another couple of minutes before he turned around and stormed out of the house, shouting over his shoulder that if anyone stopped being so fucked in the head and would care to see reason, he was bunking over at Kara's, because there at least he wouldn't have to watch firsthand how I let Simon beat me to a bloody pulp.

After that, I really didn't need that pasta anymore, and the very thought of it was enough to make me want to hurl. At least that was a convenient excuse for the dark mass churning in the pit of my stomach.

Simon did his very best to run interference now that he could and do some damage control, but he looked shell-shocked himself, and I knew that I wasn't helping when I kept insisting that I was fine, while inside I felt like a huge part of me was dying a slow, painful death. He tried to insist that I stay over for the night, but now more than ever, I needed to be by myself and left half an hour after Jack had vacated the premises. As I made my slow and painful way over to the train station, I had the sinking feeling that somehow, things would never be the same.

-12-

I was too exhausted to remain awake for long that evening, but that didn't mean that I slept through the night or that my rest actually left me feeling rested. I was almost happy when my alarm blared me into wakefulness, if not alertness, and I quickly dressed before hitting the bathroom, trying to avoid a repetition of last night should Marcy, for whatever reason, pass me in the hallway.

By the time I left the house, I felt marginally more like myself, but that wasn't an improvement. All that tossing and turning at night, the least cause for which had been physical discomfort, had given me time aplenty to think things over. I still wasn't ready to take any crap from Jack, but doubt had firmly settled in my thoughts, making me second-guess pretty much everything about my relationship with Simon.

Who in their right mind let another human being do something like this to themselves? Who in their right mind wanted to do that in the first place?

Rationally, it was only too easy to reduce everything to endorphins and physical reaction, and what before had fascinated me about the mental side of it now scared the living shit out of me. It had only been a few weeks, and already people noticed a change in me? I didn't want to change, and what kind of good could come out of driving a wedge between me and my oldest, closest friend?

It was hard to focus on work that morning, which just added another item to my ever-growing list of reasons why I should at least break this off, if not have myself checked into a mental facility—if I ever ran out of shifts that I could slave away in the ER, which would hopefully be never. With less than two weeks remaining in my rotation, I really had to keep up working at top performance, and nothing would get between me and snatching up that fellowship I'd applied for. With just one more rotation at another hospital left to my residency, I needed it as much as I wanted it. I was, all my sudden insecurities aside, the best trauma surgeon for the job, and any day now someone would be approaching me with that contract to sign—I just knew it. With that new level to my career, I wouldn't have time for idle fancies like my dysfunctional sex life, anyway, so I might as well cut all ties to that right fucking now.

My resolve wavered when I returned to my locker after my shift, only to find five missed calls and a whole slew of texts from Simon. There wasn't much of his usual arrogance remaining in any of them, and the last couple sounded downright anxious, washing away my conviction to tell him to go fuck himself like a sand castle in the rising tide. I barely had the energy left to text back that I was okay, and then I went home to another night of barely dozing off, followed by hours spent staring at my ceiling, scared and alone in the dark.

The next day it was seven missed calls and even more texts, which I fended off the same way.

On Thursday I finally made myself return his calls, not just because part of me felt sorry for Simon, but also because there was that annoyingly ingrained need now to cancel our session. Simon sounded cautious throughout the entire conversation and accepted my rain check without a hint of surprise or annoyance, but I hung up as soon as he tried to actually talk to me. I asked him to give me a little more space, though, and Friday came with just two texts and no call.

None of which were from Jack.

With each day that passed that I didn't hear from him, the iron grip around my heart tightened a little more. Thanks to the wonders of modern social networks, it was easy to verify that he was, indeed, still alive, and when I made up an excuse to call Kara to stealthily find out if he was still crashing at her place, she happily divulged that she and Jack had pretty much screwed the entire night after our fight. She was still seeing that Dan guy, but things were winding down, and it really was so convenient that she didn't have to rely on him to get her rocks off. In short, everyone should have a Jack.

Only that I felt like I'd somehow lost mine.

I made it through the weekend somehow, thanks to coffee and a couple of supplements that probably would have screwed up my next drug test had anyone forced me to piss into a cup that day, and Monday rolled in much to my rising dread. A week had passed and that should have made a difference, but I still felt as raw inside as before, even though my skin had healed completely.

And then it was Tuesday, and when I opened my eyes that morning, a full hour before my alarm would go off, I felt like crying for an entirely different reason.

There was no sense in putting this off any longer, so I got up, showered, dressed, and made breakfast. My cereal tasted like cardboard, but I forced myself to empty the entire bowl. Only twenty minutes had passed, but I still got ready and left, figuring that maybe someone else might be happy to get off work a little early and spend the day actually enjoying themselves.

A couple of years ago I'd tried taking the day off, but that had been worse. Routine was the only thing that helped, and today I was glad for every second I could be on my feet, occupied even though I felt like a zombie. I knew that somehow I would make it through the day, and then everything would be okay for another year.

My plan was working all right, until when at 3:27 p.m. an ambulance came screeching up to the ER, carrying the victim of a car crash. She was in her late twenties, long, dark hair, light skin where it was even visible between all the blood, and because the universe was out to get me, her husband arrived just in time, their little girl crying in his arms, to shout after us that someone had to save her mommy.

I barely managed to step back from the OR table and wrench off my face mask before I started to hurl, and it happened twice more on the way over to the locker room, where I dragged myself into the last shower stall at the end of the row, still in my scrubs and cap, and turned the cold water on full.

Zoe found me there an undefined, endless time later, my knees drawn to my chest, staring at nothing. I looked up when I heard the door fall shut behind her, just as she was rounding on me.

"What the fucking fuck just happened in there? Are you sick? Knocked up? Because you better have a damn good explanation for not only running out of the OR, but threatening a patient's life with almost puking your guts all over her!" Then my state registered and her blonde brows drew together, anger slowly turning into concern. "What the fuck is wrong with you, Slater?"

And wasn't that the question of the month?

Yet for this time only, I had an explanation. One I hated to give, but I knew my boss well enough not to feed her any bullshit, even though I'd avoided talking about this with anyone here in the hospital so far.

"My mother died today, twenty-six years ago. She was twenty-nine, and she had terminal-stage brain cancer. She committed suicide, drove her car straight into a tree. She looked exactly like that woman did. I was five."

A little more tension leaked out of Zoe's posture, but she didn't go, nor kick me out of the hospital straight away, but just shut off the shower before she hunkered down in front of me.

"You need to tell me shit like that so I can be prepared. Why didn't you take the day off? You have enough free days on your tab to force the hospital to close down if you demand to be paid for them."

Closing my eyes, I turned my head away, hating that look of pity mixed with understanding I saw in hers.

"It's easier when I don't have time to think about it. And it's never been a problem. Last year I was doing a rotation in pediatrics, and I was fine. Had a patient in the cancer ward die on me the year before that, still not worse than the usual. I don't know what triggered it this year. I'm sorry. I know my behavior is inexcusable—"

"Shut up and get out of here," she told me, chiding but gently. "Do you have somewhere to go? Family, friends?"

I nodded, peeking cautiously at her. The pity was gone, at least, but she still looked slightly pissed.

"I promise it won't happen again. Next year, I'll stay home."

Hearing that made her deflate somehow, and when I frowned, Zoe sighed.

"Might as well tell you now. Your day can't really get any worse."

"Tell me what?"

She didn't even shrug or try to beat around the bush.

"The hospital's not renewing my contract, and I'm only here until the end of the month. And because they needed something to lure in my replacement, he gets to choose who he wants for the trauma surgery fellowship. Prick of course selected one of the residents he's currently working with at his old hospital, and there's simply no money for a second position. I know, I should have told you weeks ago because I know how much you were gunning for that job. Fact is, you're not going to get it."

I waited for the tears to come, and the disappointment, but I felt cold inside and out, the news likely not penetrating through that haze yet.

"There's no chance at all for me to return here after I've finished my residency," I summarized.

She sighed and inclined her head.

"You and me both. And it's entirely my fault. I'm sorry."

"How is it your fault?"

Zoe hesitated, but after a moment she exhaled loudly, steeling herself.

"I'm sure that gossip has made the rounds already that I'm going through a nasty divorce right now. The good news is, since last Friday I'm a free woman again and only have to pay that bastard of an ex-husband way more money than he ever was worth. The bad news is, his lawyer dug up every single bit of dirt, and as it so happens, that includes the reason for said divorce. My girlfriend, Rhea. The hospital of course has more anti-discrimination clauses than any sane person can actually remember, but that doesn't mean that the board members aren't a bunch of homophobic pricks. It so happens that someone handed around a paper including the details of the divorce settlement, and, lo and behold, only a day later there's that bullshit excuse that I overstepped my limits because I reamed one of the Intensive Care nurses for being a dumb twit. My contract doesn't get renewed, and they only need an hour to hire my replacement. Sure, I could sue, but that likely means not working for the entire time of the lawsuit because no one wants to burn their fingers or get dragged into this. They bent me over and fucked me good, and I'm afraid the same's happening to you by proxy."

I took that in with the same kind of stoic calm, then forced my mind to function for a few moments.

"I haven't applied anywhere else. Guess I should do that now. I still have five more months of residency left, so I'm not yet standing with my back against the wall."

"Should be enough time to find a new position," she agreed. "You're a capable, dependable surgeon with absolutely no dark spots to your record. And even if you have to wait another year for a fellowship, you can always moonlight at a couple of clinics. They always need good people."

If she meant that in a comforting way, it didn't really work.

"I'm still not done learning as much as I can. I need that trauma and critical care fellowship. Without that qualification, I might as well move back into my dad's basement and start as a general practitioner."

"Hey, don't diss the grunts. You're not a good enough clinician yet to diagnose anything that doesn't need a scalpel to fix." She let that sink in before her gaze turned shrewd. "Just how determined are you to stick with that idea?"

"Very."

"Maybe I have a proposition for you, although I can't say anything more detailed yet. When I moved to the city a couple of years ago, another hospital was in the grabs for offering me a job. I declined because I didn't get along with their chief of staff, but he recently retired, and they might take me on now if a position opens up. I can't promise you anything, but I might get you in somewhere. Might not be a fellowship, and you definitely have to figure in pay cuts."

That was actually the best thing I'd heard all day.

"I don't care about the money as long as it pays my loans on a regular basis. I'd hate having to wait another year, but if it means I'll get the fellowship then, I'll wait."

"I'll keep you in the loop if I hear anything new," she promised, then got up. "And you're going home now. Call in sick if you're not feeling better tomorrow. You've been working yourself to the bone the last couple of weeks, and there's no sense to overdoing it if you end up killing someone just because your ego won't let you back down."

"Yes, ma'am."

"And stop with that bullshit. You make me feel older than I am."

"Yes, boss."

She grumbled something under her breath, then she was gone, leaving me sitting there, dripping wet, feeling only marginally better than before.

It took me longer than it should have to get dressed, and anxiety was gripping me hard as I made my way out of the hospital. I'd been avoiding this call for over a week now, but there was no sense to it now. Deep down I knew that what had happened aside, today of all days he would be there for me, because he had always been there for me on that day, ever since we'd waited in that damn hospital waiting room and he hadn't let go of my hand, even when his mother brought us ice cream and fries.

Only that when I called him, Jack didn't pick up, and the call went straight to voice mail.

I was so perplexed that I hung up, then tried again, only to be met with the same result.

"Jack? It's me. Call me, okay? I need you."

I hung up, then called him again immediately after when dread settled in the pit of my stomach.

"Look, can we just forget about last week? I'm sorry. We need to talk. Please. Okay? Call me."

The urge to keep apologizing, not because I meant it but because I needed him to be there for me right then was so strong that I almost left another message, but I forced myself to calm down and put my phone in my pocket instead while I waited for the train to arrive. There must be a good reason for why he hadn't picked up—maybe he was on the phone right now, or taking a dump—and as soon as he saw that I'd called, he would get back to me. And that second message should do the trick.

The train arrived and I got in, and still my phone didn't ring. I counted down the stops, then got off, and still, silence. I was already halfway down the street when it started to ring, making me smile despite the tears clogging the back of my throat.

"Jack?" I asked stupidly. It was his number calling, after all.

Silence greeted me, then a loud sigh.

"What do you want?"

That was not the answer I'd expected.

"Did you get my messages?"

There was no way he could have forgotten what day it was today.

"I did. I don't care. You didn't need or want my help last week, and you were very emphatic about that. Why should I take time off now just because you're in the mood for it? Find someone else who you can treat like a dog you play with and pet one day, then discard like a wet rag the other. I'm done with this shit."

With that, he hung up, leaving me staring at my phone, unable to even form a coherent thought while my heart seized up.

I wanted to cry. I wanted to scream. Most of all, I wanted someone to hug me, hold me close and tell me that it would all blow over soon and be okay, and tomorrow would be a better day.

But that was Jack's line, parroted after what his mother had told me while she held me after the doctors had told my dad that Mom was gone, and he'd been too out of it to comfort me.

And now I'd lost Jack, too, and I was all alone in the world.

Well, almost.

I blinked away the tears, then started walking again, setting one foot in front of the other. It was only a little farther, less than two blocks, but every step leeched energy I didn't have from me, and I wasn't sure what would happen if I was met with rejection yet again. My hand shook as I raised it toward the door, then stopped and instead rang the bell, feeling like I had no right to just walk into the house anymore.

It took thirty-seven slow, painful heartbeats, then the door opened and Simon blinked rather owlishly at me. His shirt was rumpled and looked slept in, and he was wearing his glasses, a sure sign that he hadn't been out of the house today or he would have switched to his contacts. He was clearly surprised to see me standing there, and considering how my day had gone down so far, I half expected him to kick me out, but instead he stepped aside to let me in as soon as he recognized me. I turned to him, my bottom lip quivering, and a moment later his arms were around me and he pulled me close.

Breathing in the scent of cotton laced with the musk that was purely Simon opened the flood gates I'd tried to keep shut for the past hours, grief and pain pouring over me.

"He doesn't want to see me," I sobbed into his shirt, not giving a shit about making sense right now, but then Simon had been around long enough to be at least aware of the rituals Jack and I went through each year. "First he didn't pick up, and then he told me to fuck off, and I don't know where else to go. And I almost threw up all over a patient and I'm not getting that fellowship, and what the fuck is wrong with me that everyone in my life has to fucking leave me?!"

I doubted that Simon caught more than a word or two of that, but just the fact that he was there, holding me, hugging me, not shoving me away or discarding me was enough. I started to cry, then cried all the harder when I realized that part of why I'd been so damn miserable over the past couple of days had been because I'd missed him, too, and desperately needed him, now more than ever.

I don't know how long we remained standing there before he started walking us into the living room so he could pull me down on top of him on the couch, grabbing a blanket on the way to bundle me up. He kept his arms around me the entire time I cried and didn't let go when I stopped, still clinging to him while he stroked my back soothingly. Dusk settled over us, casting everything into a perpetual gloom, but neither of us seemed ready to reach for the lights. Even with my heart hurting in my chest, I couldn't help but feel incredibly warm and comforted by his mere presence, letting his strength slowly seep into me.

Grief ebbed away, letting me catch my breath and calm down in earnest, then snuggle closer when the need for something else than just comfort welled up inside of me.

"Have I ever told you how it happened?"

I more felt than saw him shake his head.

"No. Do you want me to know?"

"I don't normally tell people. Jack knows. Of course he does, he was there. His mom knows. I'm not even sure my dad knows, or wants to know."

Did I want Simon to know? Thinking about it, I realized that yes, I did. Not just because he was here now, but because over the last couple of weeks he had become such a vital part of my life that I felt like there was nothing I couldn't —or shouldn't—share with him.

"I'm not sure I can do this twice. How much do you know?"

"Only that your mom died in a car accident."

Taking a deep breath, I tried to steel myself, but that was as useless as always when I thought about it. But pressed against Simon, listening to his steady heartbeat under my ear, it was just a little easier to revisit the darkest hours of my life. His fingers, soothing, stroking my hair gently, stilled for a moment, then resumed as I started talking.

"I don't really remember much of it. Some days I think I even start to forget how she looked, although I have pictures. What I do remember was her holding me while she was crying. And I was crying, too, because I was only five and I didn't know why my mommy was crying and wouldn't stop. And then she told me that I had to be a good girl and do what Jack's mom told me to, and then she was gone, and I never saw her again."

Exhaling slowly, I caught a single tear that rolled down my cheek with my tongue.

"Years later, Malory told me some of the details. I think I was sixteen and rocking the whole emo teenage angst pretty hard. The rest I got from her medical file. Sometimes it does pay off to go into medicine." I knew I was just stalling, so I forced myself to go on. "She had terminal-stage cancer. Brain tumor, malign. They couldn't operate, and she knew that she was dying, but she chose to fight for every day that was still left to her. For me. She should have died when I was three, but she was still around two years later yet was getting worse. Chemo stopped working, and her headaches grew worse and worse. She started having blackouts, only for a few minutes, but then for hours. And on that morning she came to, lying on the bathroom floor, pills strewn around her, and I was sitting there, crying, begging her to wake up. She was horrified just because of the situation, but then she counted the pills and was missing some, and didn't know if I'd accidentally taken them. I was too young to understand and could have mistaken them for candy. So she bundled me up, ran over to Jack's mom, and with both of them along for the ride we went to the ER to have me checked out. The doctors assured her that I was fine and would have started showing symptoms by then, but she just couldn't calm down."

I had to pause for a moment, blinking hard to disband the feelings those old memories dragged up inside of me. When I was able to continue, my voice was flat, most of the emotion in it gone.

"She called my father, but he was away on a conference, not even available for a quick call. So she decided that she had to take matters into her own hands. She flushed all her pills down the toilet, left me with Malory, then got into her car and drove away. She even picked the perfect spot, a winding road where accidents happen almost every year. The tree she crashed into isn't there anymore, the force of impact strong enough to uproot it. The coroner ruled her dead right at the crash. All the drugs in her system made a drug test inconclusive, which was enough for the insurance not to pay anything, but that didn't matter. She killed herself because she couldn't take care of me anymore, and she couldn't stand the chance that her blackouts would endanger me even more. Rationally, I understand why she did it, but she will always be my mommy who cried and wouldn't stop as she said goodbye. And then she left me. And I'm still here."

I fell silent then. There wasn't anything else to say. Simon didn't say anything, either, just held me as we sat there in the gathering darkness. I felt so emotionally drained that I didn't even have the energy left to be ashamed of my breakdown, either one of them. This so wasn't like me, and right now I was ill equipped to handle any of it. But at least my tears had dried, and by the time it was too dark to see anything around us clearly anymore, I knew that the worst was over, and life would go on.

"Feeling a little better now?" Simon asked when I extricated myself from him and got up, muscles all over my body complaining as I stretched. I nodded although I still felt raw inside and out, but it was better, even if the sinking feeling in my stomach remained.

I turned away from him, not sure what to say or do now. Raiding the fridge sounded like a good point to start, but Simon reached for my hand, his fingers entwining with mine gently, and he tugged me back toward him. I looked down at him, my eyebrows raised in askance, and he returned my gaze with a pleading one of his own, a different kind of pain plain on his face.

"Don't go. Please. It kills me to see you like this, when I'm helpless and can't do anything for you."

"You're already doing something. You're here."

He kept pulling on my hand so I let him reel me in, and I ended up half straddling him, half sitting on his lap. His face was partially hidden by the lack of light, but there was still enough illumination to see the hurt in his eyes. Reaching up, I ran a finger along his temple, then over his jaw, ending up hovering near his mouth. His lips moved, and for a moment I thought he was going to say something, but he planted the softest of kisses onto my fingers instead.

Something inside of me gave a start, but then was swallowed by the wave of grief all over again. The entire last week I'd spent moping and hiding like a child, and he had reasons aplenty to demand an explanation at the very least, but he didn't. Instead he was just there for me, to listen to me, to lend what comfort he could, and it was more than anyone else in the entire world was offering.

Why that was still beyond my expectations, I couldn't say, but it wasn't the kind of offering I would ever refuse.

His hands touched my sides, then slid up my back, slow and warm, making me want to melt into his touch. Part of me tried to hold back—over the past couple of weeks, what we had between us had changed, had grown into so much more than just random kinky sex, but it had also created a different kind of distance between us. He was my Dom, and in so many ways that made him the person closest to me, but there were things I felt I shouldn't see in him, feelings I shouldn't have. If he'd just been here for me to lend a shoulder to cry on and comfort me, that would have been the same, but seeing him look at me like this, touch me like this, everything shifted. Maybe I should have stopped it, gotten up and left, but I was too wounded, too raw, and just a little too selfish for that. I wanted what he was silently offering me so fucking much that it hurt, and I'd used up all my willpower just to pull myself together. Even if it was just for now, just for a night, I couldn't walk away from him, even if this, whatever it might be, would complicate everything so much more.

And looking into his eyes, seeing unspoken emotions roiling in them, I saw that I wasn't the only one acutely aware of how things were shifting between us, but try as I might be hunting for it, doubt wasn't what I recognized in his gaze.

Like so often of late, I chose to let him lead me along and quenched my own need to second-guess what was going on, and just act.

Leaning into him, one hand at his shoulder, the other at his side, was all the invitation he needed. Simon pulled me close, his touch still light and gentle, one hand cradling the side of my face. My eyes closed as he brushed his lips to mine in a slow kiss that deepened as I let him in, then molded myself more firmly against him. There was so much familiarity there that it was easy to ignore the war slowly subsiding inside my mind, to push it all away, let sensation take over. And judging from the way he pressed feather-light kisses onto my skin before his hands tightened on me almost reverently, it made me realize that I wasn't the only one feeling this, either.

Stopping for a moment, I smiled down at him, not sure how much of the warm feeling spreading throughout me showed with my eyes puffy and not quite dry yet, but Simon was quick to grin back, letting his forehead touch mine lightly. My smile widened, and then I was kissing him again, a little less tentatively than before, a little more demanding. His hands tightened on me, then ran up my back to pull me closer, his tongue giving way reluctantly until he felt me explore his mouth with new eagerness.

We spent more time on the couch just kissing and touching than some of our scenes had lasted, locked in a game of stop and go, give and take, tease and withdraw. I still felt vulnerable, fragile even, but whenever I was about to falter, he picked up the slack, coaxing me back from the still-threatening abyss of grief. Then it was me who pushed him deeper into the cushions, taking what he so freely offered, always demanding more.

Time passed, but I didn't really notice beyond my lips becoming puffy and swollen from kissing him as if my life depended on it. I knew every line of his body by now, the same as he was intimately familiar with mine, but exploring now with tentative touches and languid strokes was different. And for whatever stupid reason, running a hand across his lower abdomen underneath his shirt, feeling warm skin and taut muscle, was tantalizing, different somehow.

And then it simply wasn't enough anymore, and it only took a brief exchange of looks before he got up and pulled me along, back to his room, into his bed. I'd slept in that very bed a couple of times, but we'd never had sex in it, and when I lay back and he started to push my shirt up my stomach, I realized that we'd never undressed each other, either. That thought must have made me frown because Simon stopped in mid-motion, hovering beside me.

"Something wrong?"

I shook my head and reached up to pull him close, letting my own fingers skim over the waistband of his pants.

"Not at all."

Whatever he saw on my face made him smile, then lean in to steal my breath with his lips. That was the last we spoke for a long, long time, and neither of us seemed to miss words.

Once he had me naked next to him, Simon made as if to kiss a trail down my body, starting at my collarbones, but I stopped him before he'd even gotten to my breasts. I knew well enough what he was capable of, and as much as I normally would have loved to feel his mouth on me, that just wasn't what I needed right now. Nudging his chin up, I shimmied alongside him until we were face to face again, and when I wrapped myself pretty much around his body and kissed him, he was eager to reciprocate, one strong hand pulling me flush against him.

Before long, both of us were moving against each other, slow at first, more frantic later, but always touching, maximizing contact. My lips were tingling from kissing him, and I felt like the skin on my entire body was on fire from being so close to him. We barely made any sounds besides the occasional moan that was really more of a sigh, and while I felt warmth and need spread throughout me, it was so different from the usually highly coordinated moves. There was a little teasing, and stopping and readjusting, but most of all I felt like we were slowly melting into each other until it was hard to tell where I began and he ended.

When I eventually succumbed to my need, it wasn't just a physical release, but also an emotional one. Instinct had my eyes want to flutter closed, but all the time spent in the attic together made me keep them wide open so I could watch him drink in every second of me writhing in abandonment, then follow along with an almost peaceful look on his face.

Both panting now, our mouths found each other, and I felt something inside of my chest soar. His eyes were still wide, shining from exertion and satisfaction, but something was different about the way he gazed at me. Deep down I knew I could have pointed a finger at it, but that would have meant another level of complication, and right now I was simply glad to be here with him, closer than ever before, and not have to think about anything.

So I smiled, and Simon smiled back, and then he rolled us over so that I was mostly lying on him, positioning me just so that I could continue to kiss him without having to crane my neck, and that was exactly what I did.

Much later, my eyes drifted shut and I relaxed, wrapped in a cocoon of Simon, his body spooning mine, his scent all over me, both of us sweaty and spent, and, most of all, content. Happy.

After the day I'd had, I hadn't expected to find any rest, but a few moments later I drifted off, and slept straight through the night, that smile still on my face.

-13-

I woke up... alone.

Soft light was filtering through the half-drawn curtains, early morning light that I was terribly familiar with. Too early for decent people to be up, too late for anyone to still be on their feet. The bed was not my own but still familiar, and not for a second did I doubt where I was.

Turning my head, I looked over to the other side, finding it empty and cold. For a moment I listened, wondering if Simon had just gotten up to use the bathroom, but the house was completely silent.

I didn't want to get up, but as I lay there, a spark of restlessness flared up inside of me that soon had me checking the alarm on the nightstand. My estimate had been correct; I still had about half an hour until I had to get up and leave if I wanted to be on time for my shift.

Exhaling slowly, I considered not getting up at all. What was the sense of working myself to the bone for a job I now knew I wouldn't get? And Zoe had told me to call in sick if I wasn't feeling up to par yet. I could just stay here, wait for Simon to return, and ignore the world at large until the next best thing sucker punched me again.

Suddenly disgusted with myself, I got up, not bothering with clothes except for my panties and shirt. The door to the hallway was not quite closed, but the entire house was dark, so I made a brief detour to the bathroom before I hit the kitchen. In passing, I noticed that the door to Jack's room was open, and I could see that his bed was still made and clearly hadn't been slept in.

As I turned on the coffee machine, I considered what I should do next.

One thing was obvious. For the past months, or even years, I'd been single-mindedly focused on just one thing—my career. It was my life, was what I got up for in the morning, what defined me. Almost everyone else my age that I knew had long finished school, built a life, family, home. All I had was the certainty that in nine days from now I would be out of the hospital I'd hoped to return to after my last rotation, because it was the best opportunity for me. And now that option was barred to me. Not because I'd made any mistakes or been bad at what I did, but I'd set all my expectations on that one single goal and ignored that there were other options out there.

What was even worse was that I felt like I could suddenly see a pattern there. In many ways, my reaction yesterday had been the same. Each and every year I dreaded that anniversary to come, and I always used Jack as my fall-back guy. I had been so sure that this would go on forever that I hadn't even considered the possibility that some day in the future he wouldn't be there for me, for whatever reason.

But my thoughts stuttered to a halt when it came to Simon. How did what we had going on fit into that? Was it just one more crutch I used as an excuse not to be completely self-reliant? Or was it those very experiences and changes that finally opened my eyes and let me see, if not quite react, to what was going wrong in my life? It was so easy to doubt, to let what Jack had said in that fight drag me down and question every single thing about it. But it stood in stark contrast to last night. How could I demonize the man who had never, not for a single moment, made me second-guess myself or put me down, not even once? Who was caring and sweet, and underneath that all remained the same egotistical bastard that I'd been close with for ages? But when it counted, he was there, and unlike every other person in my life who felt like they had the right to tell me what I should do, he respected my wishes, gave me privacy when I needed it, and caught me when I stumbled.

And it was fucking four in the morning and I still hadn't had my coffee, which was way too soon to ramble on like that inside my own head.

Watching coffee drip into the pot was only so entertaining, so I went over to the fridge to get some milk, and grabbed the bottle of OJ when I saw it sitting, half empty, in the door. Defiance made me drink right from the bottle, because whatever decisions might plague me, deep down I was still a petulant little girl, and the least I could do was spread my girl cooties all over Jack's groceries.

I stopped in mid-drink when I heard the door open and close, admitting Simon as he tried to sneak into the kitchen. He stopped in his tracks as he saw me next to the fridge, then straightened and brandished the tote bag he'd been carrying at me.

"I hope I didn't wake you. I thought I might as well make myself useful seeing as I couldn't sleep anymore."

I knew the logo of the bakery on the bag, not quite as good as the one by the hospital, but a wonderful upgrade from what I'd seen sitting in the fridge.

"No, I guess I just got enough sleep. I rarely make it through more than five or six hours at a time."

We stared at each other across the kitchen, neither of us knowing what to do. The coffee machine gave a few last gurgling sounds, then silence settled over us, turning the moment even more awkward.

Simon was the one to break the tension, shaking his head as he laughed softly and put the bag up onto the counter. I relaxed and looked away, then reached up to get two mugs for the coffee. When I turned back around, he was standing right next to me, close but not uncomfortably so. I was still hogging the space right between the fridge and the coffee machine, after all.

"Hm, orange juice," he murmured, but instead of reaching for the bottle, he touched the side of my face and kissed me, long, slow, his tongue swirling against mine before he playfully sucked on my bottom lip.

My mind went blank, but thankfully my body was a little harder to stun, and I wrapped my arms around his neck to keep him right where I wanted him to be. Simon pressed his body into mine, definitely not a casual move, and I was only too happy to trail my hands up his back to divest him of his shirt. Clothes were so overrated.

And just when we were both light-headed from stealing each other's breath and about to get to the good stuff, the front door opened again, spilling high, feminine laughter followed by a lower masculine rumble into the kitchen.

I tensed, but there was warm skin and delicious muscle under my palms while rough denim rubbed over my bare thigh, and the last thing I wanted was to let go. The feeling seemed to be mutual, because Simon's grip on me tightened, and just when Kara's laugh cut off as she must have stepped into the kitchen, Simon let out the most delectable moan.

Someone cleared their throat noisily, Jack most likely, and Kara let out a very pointed snort.

"Now look into my face and tell me that you're not screwing. I dare you to lie to me again."

Simon stilled, then sighed as he moved away, but only enough to look deep into my eyes and share a small smile with me. It was so easy to grin, even though my hackles were already up.

Then Simon let go and turned to face Kara, looking terribly at ease, as if they hadn't just caught us, me without pants and Simon decidedly shirtless.

"I never actually denied that we were having sex. You were just jumping to the wrong conclusions."

Kara narrowed her eyes at him, then glared at me, but she was already fighting a smile of her own.

"I just don't get why you were making a secret out of it. You're not quite what I'd call compatible, but that's between the two of you and absolutely none of my business." She then shot a sidelong glance at Jack, who hadn't said anything yet, and also looked as if he was not concerned by anything happening in front of him. My stomach seized as bile climbed up into my throat, but I quickly put a lid on my resurfacing anger. At least it wasn't tears I had to fight.

"Do I even need to bother asking whether you knew about this? I doubt they could even hide it from you if they'd tried."

"Hardly," was all he said, making Kara frown for a second, but she shook it off, clearly satisfied that finally she had uncovered the mystery of who was getting into my pants on a semi-regular basis.

"Wonderful. This is the perfect opportunity I've been waiting for. There's this new restaurant I've been dying to make reservations for, and it just so happens that they have a spot open tonight. Guess we can't really call it a double date, seeing that we are certainly not dating." She indicated Jack and herself, then gave Simon and me a shrewd look. "Are you two? Official, I mean. Because if this ends up with some lovey-dovey shit going down, I'm not subjecting myself to that."

I looked at Simon questioningly and was surprised that I got a rather guarded look back from him. Jack snorted in the background, which pissed me off even more, and it was strangely satisfying to see Simon's eyes narrow with annoyance. Petty games, maybe, but it was still a hell of a good feeling to know that I had him firmly in my corner, should this drama unfold as I was afraid it would very soon.

"We are what we are," I replied, trying to sound neutral. "Why complicate things by affixing a label to it?"

Jack didn't look pleased by how I'd scampered around that possible pothole in the road, but Kara seemed satisfied.

"Good. The fact that you're here means you're working day shift right now? How anyone can ever keep up with that is beyond me. 8 sounds reasonable?"

I nodded, and she got out her phone, likely to set herself a reminder, but then stilled in mid-motion. When she gazed up, the look on her face was unreadable, and the sidelong glance at Jack wasn't the friendliest.

"Why are you even here? With Simon, I mean, and don't tell me that you've been screwing all night. I don't need to hear that. But yesterday..."

"Was the anniversary of my mom's death, yes."

It was impossible not to stare a hole into Jack's skull, and at least he had the decency to look embarrassed. Kara picked up on that, of course, but she only made a face and didn't ask, which was likely the reason why I managed to remain on my side of the kitchen without feeling the need to get physical.

"Anyway, I guess that means we'll see each other tonight? Do you want to share a cab back into the city?"

I shook my head.

"Thanks, but I still need to grab a shower and load up on coffee. The train's fine."

Kara shook her head as if I was the crazy one in this, but her eyes lit up at the mention of coffee.

"I've been up all night. Doesn't change a thing if I'll add another hour to the tab. Shoo, I'll fix you a travel mug while you get ready. But, you," she said, pointing a finger at

Simon as she stalked toward the coffee maker, pretending to be annoyed for a second. "You stay here and answer a few questions, mister."

I was only too happy to escape the inquisition, grinning at the way Simon winced, and not even Jack's glower could change anything about that.

I kind of hated washing Simon's scent off my body, but I couldn't very well go to work distracted like this. I wouldn't have minded him joining me in the shower, either, although the idea of fooling around while Kara and Jack waited in the kitchen creeped me the fuck out. I couldn't say what was different—it wasn't just Kara's presence, and we'd had more than one session in the playroom while Jack was around—but it was probably for the better that they left me to my own devices.

I half expected the kitchen to still be a cesspool of awkwardness upon my return, but Jack had apparently gone to sleep in the meantime, and Kara pretty much assaulted me with my coffee before she shooed me out the door. I just had time for a slightly bewildered, halfway terrified smile to share with Simon, then we were in the taxi, and I knew that my time was up.

"You and Simon, huh?" Kara poked the elephant in the room.

I just stared back at her blankly, then took a sip of my coffee that was hot enough to make me wince.

"Is that so hard to grasp?"

"I'm just wondering," she pointed out, and took a drink from her own mug. Of course she didn't even smear her lipstick. Typical. "You're not really the type to just screw around, and he's not exactly a commitment kind of guy."

"But apparently we've found a way to make uncomplicated sex work—eureka!"

The cab driver gave me a look that I ignored.

"If you say so," Kara muttered, but it was obvious that she was trying to hide a grin. "At least now I can tell Linda the good news when she asks."

That almost made me scald myself with my coffee.

"Why the fuck would you tell his mother that we're having sex?"

Kara's smile brightened.

"Oh, don't worry, it's not like that. But she worries sometimes. You know, the whole, 'I raised a beautiful, bright son who has money—why are women not throwing themselves at his feet!?' spiel. It will be hilarious to watch you try to field the 'when will you finally make me a happy *abuela*!' question."

It took me a moment for my mind to overcome the imminent terror that idea brought up inside of me.

"Stop that, you insufferable hag! I'm aware that you know Linda better than I do, but she'd never call Simon anything but an insufferable brat, and last year at the garden party she got offended because someone said she looked good for a woman who has an adult son. I doubt she's secretly waiting for grandchildren!"

Kara snorted, very unladylike, and finally succumbed to the laughter she had been trying to hide so desperately.

"But you should have seen the look on your face just now! Golden! I should have taken a picture of that. Oh, look, we still can. Selfie, hashtag 'if looks could kill!'"

I gave her exactly such a look, making her crack up anew, but at least she didn't brandish her phone in my face.

"Annoying you aside, what's up with you and Jack?" Kara went on, making me go still for a second. Just how much of my dirty laundry would she make me air in front of her today?

"What do you mean?"

Her brows drew together at my cautious tone, but when I gave her my best innocent look, she shrugged.

"He's been intolerable the entire last week, needy and irritable at the same time. I don't mind it when he's broody as that usually translates into pretty intense sex, but I don't really need all that huffing and chuffing whenever we're not screwing. And don't look at me like that. You're fucking my best friend—it's about time you accept that Jack and I have our on-again, off-again thing."

I hastily did my best to wipe my expression clean. Had I really been frowning?

"Trust me, everyone is aware of your arrangement. Don't you think I would have spoken up like ten years ago if that bothered me?"

Kara struck a thinking pose, but her bright grin wasn't terribly friendly.

"Like I'd give a shit about it if you did. But yeah, we haven't been exactly stealthy about it. Unlike you and Simon. This still sounds so weird, thinking of the two of you getting it on."

"I can't speak for Simon, but I personally don't need you picturing that too clearly."

She snorted and took another sip of coffee.

"Don't worry, I won't. But really, are you his girlfriend now, or what?"

"I seriously don't know," I admitted somewhat absentmindedly. So Jack's moping reached beyond avoiding me? It was only then that I realized that I hadn't had a chance to ask Simon how things were between them. He hadn't seemed overly tense when Kara and Jack walked in on us, but then it took a lot to unnerve him, and I knew him well enough to know that he'd suppress his own reaction if he thought it would upset me in my not quite settled state.

"Well, it must be getting serious if you break your pattern and hunker down with Simon instead of spending the evening curled up with Jack." She hesitated, then opened her mouth but closed it after a second. It didn't happen very often that she was censoring herself.

"Simon wasn't my first choice," I admitted, hating how vulnerable and sad that came out.

Kara's cautious mood changed immediately.

"What? Are you trying to say that Jack deliberately blew you off?"

I shrugged, a lot more uncomfortable with the topic than I'd expected.

"Kinda. We had a fight last week, and he's been weird since then."

That was one way to describe it, and as it did fit into Kara's observation, I figured it was the way to go.

"Weird how?"

"I haven't talked to him since then," I admitted. "Except for calling him last night. And when he hung up on me, I went to Simon instead."

Although it was the truth, that statement rubbed me the wrong way. Sure, I'd been completely out of it, running on autopilot rather than acting on intent, but still. Thankfully, Kara ignored that part completely.

"What an ass! I swear, if I'd known that he'd done that, I would have kicked him out the moment he showed up on my doorstep. I was surprised when he did show up, but I figured you'd decided to hunker down on your own this time, or something."

"So your immediate reaction was to think I'd drink myself into a stupor, alone, rather than jump some guy to distract myself?"

"You're not exactly the jumpy type," she pointed out, her smile doing nothing to cushion the blow. "Besides, you've obviously been seeing that mystery guy on the side. I guess I half expected you'd end up there. As you did. See, I'm omniscient."

"That was very apparent just half an hour ago," I pointed out.

"I was on your tail the entire time. I just let Simon's obtuse answers distract me. Really, why did you two asshats think you had to keep this from me?"

"Maybe to avoid getting roped into double dates?"

She considered that for a moment.

"Whatever. You're not getting out of tonight. But, for the record, I always keep that day clear in my schedule, so if next year you decide you want to get stupidly drunk without any mopey guys getting in the way, just call me, okay? That's what friends are for."

I nodded a quiet thanks, but couldn't diffuse the feeling of guilt rising inside of me. The last twenty-four hours had made me realize that I'd been kind of an ass to my friends, or more so than usual, and having everyone but Jack fall in line didn't actually make me feel better.

"What was that fight about? Must have been big if you're still on thin ice."

She really had a talent for dragging up exactly those topics I didn't want to talk about.

"Nothing, really." I wasn't sure I could even have explained, but certainly didn't want to. "He doesn't agree with some of my choices, and having Simon get in the middle of that didn't help."

Kara pursed her lips, considering.

"I guess it makes sense that he's jealous."

"Who, Jack?!"

The idea was so incredulous that it was hard to wrap my mind around it.

"I doubt Simon would get jealous of himself." She laughed. "Of course I'm talking about Jack."

"What would he be jealous of?"

There was one answer to that in my mind, but it wasn't an option I would offer up unless she next walked in on Jack and me, which seemed even more unlikely now than two weeks ago.

"Maybe jealous is the wrong term," she agreed, as if the very idea of Jack having sex with me was impossible. I didn't know if

I should have been offended or not. "It's probably more like two little boys fighting over a shiny new toy."

"Wow, good job making me feel good about myself."

"Oh, shut up!" she interrupted my comeback. "Do I really have to spell it out to you? You've always been Jack's exit strategy, should everything else fail. Or rather you, the girl who went to prom with some other guy, was. And then, wham, more than ten years later you start something with his roommate who's never really shown any interest in you. Guess to the whacked-out way guys think, it makes sense that suddenly he starts seeing you as an option again, and, correct me if I'm wrong, but you and Simon don't necessarily harmonize each other in a way that you get less blunt and 'in your face!' with things. I don't know the details, but that alone makes for a wonderful setup for that fight you had last week. And, of course, now Jack's feeling rejected by both of you, and my vag is reaping the benefits. Although, I admit, he has been kind of a pain in the ass over the last couple of days."

"Then use more lube," I proposed, hoping that this once my poker face would not betray me.

Kara gave me a wink, and thankfully moved on now that she had imparted her never ending wisdom on me.

"What are you going to wear tonight? Not this, I hope?"

She indicated my shirt and jeans.

"Probably not—I already wore that yesterday. I have a change of clothes in my locker."

Huffing, she shook her head.

"You're hopeless, you know that?"

"Deep down I care a lot about fashion, but it's so much more fun to annoy you that I can't help myself."

"Bitch, please. Don't flatter yourself! But I guess as it's just the four of us, I can let you get away with it once. It will be much more fun to watch both you and Simon squirm! And you deserve to do some squirming for keeping this under lock and key for over two months!"

I tried to protest, but already knew it was useless. Just one more thing to look forward to, besides having Jack glare at me the entire time.

When had friendships started to become so complicated?

-14-

I was running a little late, so we switched plans to meet at the restaurant. The moment the hostess walked me up to the table, I knew that this was not going to be one of those evenings that would leave me happy and mellow. Not because of the scenery—that was perfect; the table was the very last in a row of tables that was separated from the main part of the restaurant, downright cozy, and unless anyone actually shouted, animated conversations wouldn't be overheard by half the diners. The decor was simple but elegant, and I doubted that it was coincidence that Kara fit right in. The table was just large enough to comfortably seat four people, and the remaining free spot was the one next to Simon, which didn't come as much of a surprise but was still unfamiliar. Kara was busy explaining something or other but finished as she saw me approach, leaving way too much attention from all sides resting on me.

I murmured something about being sorry for being late and sat down, just as Simon kicked his chair back in what I belatedly realized was a last-second attempt to get up to hold my chair out for me. We stared at each other for a moment until he shrugged and I rolled my eyes, but when I focused back on the others, I found Jack veritably glowering at me. An entire shift on my feet with all the usual annoyances and stress had already set my nerves on edge, and the last thing I needed was for him to keep adding to that.

Kara was watching the spectacle with one eyebrow cocked, her eyes skipping between the three of us momentarily before she glanced down at the menu in front of her.

"Oh, please, don't act like strangers just on my account. A little PDA won't kill me. Or you."

That made me frown, until I glanced at Simon and found him smiling back, clearly amused.

"I think what she actually wants to say is that she grants us permission for a kiss hello."

I opened my mouth, ready to explain that I never kissed him when I came over, but the words got stuck in my throat. It occurred to me then that even with the casual sex excuse that wasn't really an excuse, just not the whole truth, Kara probably still expected us to act like, well, lovers. Only now the moment for that had already passed, and acting on it would have felt twice as weird.

"This is priceless," Jack muttered under his breath, and when I looked at him sharply, I got a jovial smile in return that sent my bullshit radar into overdrive. "This reminds me of when you brought that one girl to the garden party a few summers ago— what was her name? Melinda?"

The name didn't tell me anything, but Simon went rigid next to me. Jack's grin grew just a hint more feral.

"Or what was that other chick's name, the one who wouldn't even let you grab a beer without her trailing behind you? Suzy? And let's not forget about Erica, who crashed not one but two parties after you dumped her because you got bored with her and who bitched you out in front of everybody."

Kara looked more bemused than alarmed, but the tension that came off Simon in veritable waves irritated me. None of those names rang a bell, but I could take an educated guess of what the nature of their relationship to Simon had been. A tiny part of me might have felt a little jealous, but all that was in the past, and there was a good reason for that, and none for me to act up. What made me angry was the implication in Jack's words.

"Want me to list all the whores you've been screwing over the years? Present company excluded, of course."

Likely not the best thing I might have said, but it certainly made Kara crack up and Simon swallow whatever he had been about to say. Jack cocked his head and regarded me levelly, and I felt my cheeks heat up a little when I realized that I'd not only implicated Kara with that statement.

"Didn't know they'd serve comedy with the meals," Kara interjected before I could put my foot into my mouth again. Following her example, I was only too happy to open the menu, my stomach growling on command.

Scrolling through the options, I tried hard to get a better grip on my temper. The last thing I needed tonight was to escalate the situation in front of an audience. Just between the three of us had been bad enough already.

"Any suggestions on what's good here?" I asked, more to break the silence that at least to me seemed uncomfortable than to really ask for anyone's opinion.

"Why, aren't you allowed to choose your own food anymore?"

This time it wasn't just Simon who tensed, and Kara gave Jack a look that was bordering on hostile.

"Is it 'bring your favorite asshole to dinner' day and I missed the announcement?" she chuffed.

Jack murmured something that might have been vaguely apologetic, then continued to stare a hole into me. I chose to ignore him and went back to browsing the menu, glad that Simon held his tongue. That in itself was a red flag, but one I was ill-equipped to make sense of.

Our waiter returned with our drinks and took down our meal choices, and conversation leveled out when Kara and Simon started chatting about a movie they'd both seen recently. Jack didn't seem interested in anything except glowering at either me or Simon, and I hadn't even heard of the film, so it left me itchy on the sidelines. Things got marginally better as the food arrived, but by the time I'd polished off my salmon, I could have really used a drink. I'd seldom been so uncomfortable sitting at a table with people who I'd known for almost longer than not, and I couldn't fault Simon for bailing when his phone rang. Then Kara got up herself to use the bathroom, leaving me and Jack to our less than amicable selves.

"Do I even want to know why you've been behaving like an asshole the entire evening?" I hissed at him, wishing I'd kept my dessert fork so I could stab him if he kept this up.

Jack didn't react for a full ten seconds, and just continued to stare at me.

"How are things as his doormat working out for you? Not too well, judging from the fact that you've pretty much shut him out for an entire week, and this morning you didn't look like you'd just made it out of the attic, either."

It was hard to keep my irritation in check, but not having to censor myself anymore helped.

"Not that it's any of your business, but this is none of your business."

"He's certainly not screwing you for your eloquence, but then I don't think you get to do much talking, anyway."

The temptation to go into full-frontal assault was strong, but I tried to take the high road this once.

"It's not like he's asking me to marry him and spend the rest of our lives together. Why are you making such a huge deal out of this? It doesn't even concern you."

He opened his mouth to deliver what likely would have been another acerbic comeback, but instead thought of something else.

"How are your thighs? Arms? Pretty much the rest of your body, too, I presume. Are you still all black and blue? Did he leave scars?"

Unease spread up my spine, but I did my best to keep my composure.

"What you saw last week probably looked worse than it was. I'm all healed up, completely. No scarring."

"If you're feeling so chipper, why didn't you just ask him to beat you into oblivion last night? Would have been one way to deal with shit."

"Shit I wouldn't have needed help dealing with if you weren't acting like a petulant five-year-old!" I hissed, then took a deep breath to calm myself again. "But on one thing I have to agree with you—it was about time that I learned to deal with my own shit without relying on you to help me through it. Turns out, I don't really need you."

It was a low blow, and I was kind of sorry for delivering it when I saw his eyes harden, but there was no taking it back.

"True, instead of letting your friends be there for you when you need them, you run to the guy who's physically abusing you so he can pull a mental number on you, too. Very mature, Erin, very mature."

Like the last time he'd flung that accusation around, it cut deep into me, but this time I'd at least had a chance to brace myself for it. Not that it helped take away the sting.

"It's not abuse when it's consensual," I pointed out.

"It's still abuse if you just think it's consensual," he shot back, and when I wanted to reply, he forestalled me with a raised hand. "But for the sake of this argument, let's pretend you're really fucked up enough that you actually, physically need this. Why did you shut him out of your life for the past week? And I presume you really didn't play last night?"

I'd thought the worst he could do was victimize me, but this was worse. I hated how he was able to just pull my own doubts from the depths of my mind and fling them right in my face. I briefly considered just ignoring Jack and forcing an end to the conversation that way, but the hint of triumph on his face made it impossible for me to shut up.

"Just for your information, we sat on the couch and he held me while I cried my eyes out. And after that, we had sex because I was so starved for basic human contact that I couldn't stand the idea of being alone. He was there for me while you apparently had nothing better to do than mope around and screw Kara!"

That didn't sit well with him, but didn't make him drop the point, either.

"Don't you see what's wrong with this picture? You wanted comfort, and what he did was fuck you. Don't deny it. You know I'm right. That's all he ever does, because that's all he's capable of."

I didn't know why that even hit home.

"You weren't even there last night, you have no idea—"

"Do you think you're the first of his subs who cracks and ends up falling for him? I've seen this exact thing happen more than once. Don't believe me? Ask him. Ask him what made those girls lose it in front of a room full of strangers, or what turned moderately confident women into clingy, weepy shadows of their former selves. And while we're at it, ask yourself why you give me those wide eyes whenever I mention the attic. Is what you have right now really a strong, healthy relationship? You did call me first."

For several seconds flat, all I could do was stare at him, and just as I found my voice again, he suddenly reached across the table and caught my hand, his fingers warm and gentle. From one moment to the next his face crumbled, clearly visible pain replacing his arrogant jeering from before.

"I'm sorry if I hurt you with what I said. I know, I acted like a stupid prick last week, but you should have seen yourself. You were completely out of it—shell shocked, your eyes all red and blotchy. And then I saw the marks, and I pretty much lost it. I've been along for a few of his sessions and I know what it takes to leave bruises like that. Seeing you like that scared the shit out of me. I don't know why I said what I did yesterday. I guess I was still pissed at you for being so dense. You're not like this normally, and you wouldn't even hear me out, so I figured maybe giving you some of your own medicine might finally wake you up, make you see him for what he is and what he isn't. I know that Simon is a good guy at heart, but that side of him turns him into a misguided—"

He stopped himself there, and the sigh he added was almost a hint too theatrical, yet the pain in his eyes was real.

"I just can't stand the thought of you becoming like any one of those girls. I get that after years of sexual frustration, everything you do with him is exciting to you, but in the long run, do you really need that? Wouldn't you rather be with someone who's here for you any hour of the day, any day of the week, without any rules or reservations?"

With my thoughts reeling, and not just from confusion, it was hard to find an answer, particularly when he was still turning those puppy dog eyes on me.

"You mean someone like you?"

My voice was hoarse and unfamiliar in my ears, and sounded strangely hollow. Jack's answering smile warmed something deep inside of me that had been in turmoil for the past days, but it also made me want to pull my hand out of his and wipe it on my pants leg.

"For instance," he offered, but it came out with enough satisfaction to leave no room for guessing.

In more ways than one I felt like someone had sucked all of the air out of the room, leaving me gasping for breath without being able to draw any oxygen into my lungs.

"Jack, I..." I started, but trailed off when words just didn't want to come.

His smile turned a little sad, but there was still a hint of satisfaction to his face that was so at odds with everything else.

"I don't need an answer right now. I don't need an answer, stat. Just some food for thought. Maybe now that you understand where I'm coming from, you can see things a little more clearly."

I understood nothing, but I didn't say that. I was both relieved and sad when he let go and settled back more firmly into his chair. Feeling like things weren't right between us had upset me, but listening to his reasoning now didn't help me sort things out. That he had dropped a few bombs in there that I absolutely didn't want to think about only made it worse.

"Are you going to keep this up now? Voicing your misgivings, I mean, whether anyone wants to hear them or not?"

He made a face, but didn't look away.

"Would it make a difference if I did? Trust me, I'm not particularly fond of pissing you off, or Simon. You're my friends, but that's why I care. And I have nothing against you getting your rocks off in whatever way, but I don't want you to get hurt. Do you really get that much out of being his plaything? You weren't quite so out of it when you kept things on a more random basis, like when you started out."

"That I'm a little under the weather has nothing whatsoever to do with Simon, or what we do in the attic. And you haven't exactly helped yourself."

"You certainly weren't this strung out when we were fooling around on the lake."

"I didn't know back then that I was losing that fellowship I've been working toward for years without having any idea of how I'll provide for myself once my residency is over!"

Jack's mouth snapped shut, and for a moment, he looked genuinely guilty.

"Seriously? That's the fellowship you've been talking about for ages? Hasn't your boss told you on various occasions that you're her first choice?"

"Doesn't really matter when they're booting my boss, too, now, does it?"

"Shit," he agreed. "And if you apply for a fellowship at another hospital? Or skip a year?"

"If they change half the staff, they won't be happy to have anyone they want to be rid of hanging around. I called a couple of hospitals today, some still take applications, but I'm late. I can maybe, temporarily, moonlight in their ERs, particularly on weekends and for the night shifts, but like any temp job, that's hell. And I really need that fellowship to finish my trauma care specialization, or I might as well throw in the towel."

"Did you tell Simon?"

That question surprised me, and I shook my head after only a moment's hesitation.

"Not yet. It's my job, my life, and I'm not obliged to tell him about every single detail of it."

Jack didn't react for a second, then offered me a concerned if warming smile.

"If you need anything, you know that you can always count on me. I don't really have much cash stashed away, but I can help you if you need some to cover the rent. Or, you can always move in with us for a couple of months—it's not like we actually need all that space in the house."

"Count on you to be there for me like I could count on you yesterday?"

On some level I was grateful for his offer, but the simple fact that I might even have to consider it made me desperately defensive.

"If you would have called me a second time, I wouldn't have acted like such an ass."

That irritated me even more.

"Like what, first you let me down, then you count on Simon to let me down, too, so you can swoop in and collect the shattered bits and pieces? And you still have the gall to accuse him of pulling a number on me?"

Some of his previous arrogance resurfaced, but Kara chose the very best moment to return, with Simon trailing behind her. That made me wonder if they'd had a conversation of their own, but as long as this evening would be ending soon, I didn't care. Thankfully, Kara had had about enough of awkward interactions for the night, and less than twenty minutes later, we left the venue. I half expected Jack to go home with her, but she informed me with a wink that she was dropping in on Dan for a surprise visit. Apparently his country club membership still trumped broody sex, or maybe she'd had enough of Jack for the week.

Simon looked at me expectantly then, and I couldn't help but feel a little unnerved by his uncommonly uncommunicative behavior. I was used to sifting through possible insults from him; silence wasn't anything I was familiar with.

"Look, I know we still have to talk—" I started, just as he said, "Are you going home, or do you want to come back with me?"

I blinked, not sure if I'd actually heard right, or if this was just another case of him meaning something completely different than the rest of the world understood. I considered for a moment, but shook my head.

"I'm tired, and it's a lot closer from my apartment to the hospital than from your house. Rain check?"

He didn't look particularly disappointed, which made me guess that he'd intended it as a jovial offer of companionship rather than anything more intimate. So much for wishful thinking.

"You'll call me?" he asked. "Or just come over so we can sit down and talk."

That sounded kind of ominous, but then I had been a little flaky on my replies the past couple of days.

"I will."

I wondered if I should have added that after next Friday I would have more time, but it was bad enough that I'd already lamented to Jack. Simon nodded and looked away for a moment, as if trying to remember something.

"About next Friday," he began and scratched his head. I felt something in my stomach knot. Did he know? I was sure that I hadn't randomly babbled about it last night, and he'd been away from the table when I blurted it out earlier.

"What about it?"

He seemed a tad irritated, probably at my tone, but then offered me a cute, boyish smile.

"You remember—my book launch party is in the evening? I asked you a couple of weeks ago if you'd come, but you didn't have your schedule yet. So, can I count on you, or do I have to fend off the spitting critics all on my own? The official launch may be four days later, but I'm sure that my publisher has been giving away review copies like candy."

That rang a bell, and made me feel guilty for completely forgetting about it in the first place.

"Of course I'll be there. I'm on for night shift that entire week, so it should be no problem."

"It's in the evening," he pointed out, sounding a little as if he was explaining something to a small child.

"And I don't work Friday night, just the night before that. I might even be moderately awake for it. I hope you don't mind."

He chuckled and shook his head, suddenly standing a little too close. Not that I felt like protesting, but with Kara and Jack only a few yards away, talking quietly between themselves, it was strange somehow.

"So I guess I'll walk you to your train, then?"

"I'll take the bus from here—it's faster. And I'm not that tired yet, so I think I can find my connection," I huffed. "I might look like a zombie, but I'm actually still moderately alert."

Why that gave him pause, I didn't know, but the moment passed and he shrugged.

"As you wish. Guess this is goodbye, then."

Now he was really starting to freak me out.

"Is something wrong? Did I do something?"

That I had the urge to ask that unnerved me, and Simon seemed perplexed himself, which in turn made me relax a little.

"Why are you asking?"

I was probably just paranoid, and the way Jack kept gloating from behind Simon's back made it worse.

"Forget I said anything. I'll call. Promise."

"Sleep tight."

I nodded, then wished both Kara and Jack a good night. I didn't miss the look on Simon's face, but as I really didn't know what to make of it, I had no intention of obsessing over it. Likely, this was all just in my head, anyway.

But, try as I might, and I did try, the entire way home I couldn't shake off the feeling that I'd somehow missed something incredibly important.

-15-

As my last morning in the hospital rolled in, I had to admit that I was somewhat underwhelmed. Not that I'd expected anything spectacular to happen—or for anyone to organize some kind of "we'll miss you, the time together was awesome!" bash—but something should have been different. Not just the same routine of checking one last time on my patients, of making sure that the day shift people knew what to do with the patients that had come in during the night, and topping up the coffee depot as a small thank you to the nurses. Sure, I got a smile or two and had to promise to come visit in the future, but by 7:30 a.m. I found myself holding a box containing the meager belongings I'd kept stashed in my locker, and not even a T-shirt saying, "all I got for my trouble is this lousy T-shirt."

Besides the typical fatigue after spending most of the night on my feet with only two half-hour breaks to catch some shut-eye in between, it could have been any other morning. My bed certainly sang its usual siren song, but I decided that instead of heeding its call, I went to a coffee shop, ordered the largest foamy atrocity on the menu, and sat down to browse the emails Kara had been flooding my inbox with during the night. The first critiques of Simon's book were online, and what better way to start the day than by amusing myself with someone else's shit-shoveling?

About half an hour in I had to stop, mostly because I'd spilled coffee over my hand and shirt twice, laughing so hard it wasn't funny anymore. I hadn't read the final version of the book but spent enough time around Kara and Simon's near endless discussions of the different drafts, so I thought I had a pretty good grasp on both the story and the utter lack of a message Simon had intended to impart with it. As he'd claimed on more than one occasion, it was simply a story he wanted to tell, full of sordid details and characters who excelled at making the wrong decisions. Half of the reviewers now lauded it because it supposedly settled the score with society in a most acerbic way. Others called it pretentious bullshit. Knowing Simon, he would roll his eyes at the former, get angry at the latter, and not let any of that actually affect him. I knew I would have been pissed if I were him as one of the reviews actually made me want to email the critic and ask him what had crawled up his butt and died there. Guess there was a reason why I had a job where my work was judged by the patients' survival rates, not whether I'd made an artistically valuable incision.

It had been three days since I'd last had a chance to touch base with Zoe, and things hadn't looked particularly good back then. She'd promised again to get back to me as soon as she had something for me, but that was all I got. One of the hospital admins from across town had gotten back to me about moonlighting in their ER or clinic, but their budget cuts had boarded up that possibility for the time being, and there wasn't much hope for that to change by the time I finished my residency. They'd need someone to draw blood and change bedpans, but would prefer a qualified nurse instead of an uppity surgeon for that. Not that she'd told me this in so many words, but it had rang true. The worst thing about it was that three times already I'd gotten the same reply—if I'd applied three months ago like every other soon-to-be-finished resident, they could have easily found a place for me. I'd gambled without even realizing just how high the stakes were, and I now found myself sorely wanting to kick my own ass.

Eventually my coffee was finished and all the reviews were perused, and I found myself with nothing but time on my hands. I couldn't remember the last time I'd had no clue what to do with myself.

I considered hitting up Kara, but the last social media update from her was only hours old, so she was likely asleep, and unlike me she didn't perform particularly well running on caffeine alone. Besides, I had a certain feeling that I'd need booze to get through the book party tonight, and Kara was the kind of woman who thought last days at work warranted mimosas for breakfast, and I couldn't do that to my liver right now.

Marcy was at work, and I didn't particularly feel like calling Jack. We'd sent a few texts to and fro over the past couple of days, but I couldn't just swallow my misgivings about him like that. He was enough like a brother to me that I'd already forgiven him his brief, misguided stunt as wannabe knight in shining armor, but that didn't mean that I felt like being around him so he could continue harassing me.

It was kind of sad to admit, but that left Simon as my last remaining social contact, provided I didn't want to ring up family, which I certainly didn't. It bothered me that calling him felt like a last resort, but we still had that outstanding talk to get behind us, and even if he was busy, I could always catch up on sleep on the couch while he was working. If I was physically around, I was sure that eventually, temptation would become stronger than his need to hit his daily word count, and maybe that would make me feel a little less like I was floating in a vacuum.

I wasn't overly concerned when he didn't pick up and decided to just try the house. I knew where the spare key was should no one be at home, and the guys had never complained about me crashing there—on the contrary. I still grabbed a box of bagels, just to make sure that my welcome would be a warm one.

Half an hour later, I strolled up to the front door and found it unlocked, a very promising prospect.

I was surprised when I heard voices in the kitchen, but then it was late morning only, and sometimes Jack worked from home, thanks to his company's dedication to always abuse their employees wherever they may roam. It made me doubly glad that I'd brought my offering of food with me.

That was, until I walked into the kitchen and felt as if I'd been sucked into an alternate reality.

At first glance, everything was harmonious and nice. Jack and Simon were both busy preparing breakfast, chatting amicably while cutting this or fetching that. As befitted what could have been a lazy morning, they were both dressed casually in shorts and T-shirts, with Jack, as usual, having to show off while Simon seemed to have grabbed the next best clothes that weren't in too dire a need of washing. In short, your typical bachelor roommate situation.

Except that it was not. Something felt way off, and before I'd even kicked off my shoes and set down my bag and box, my mind started collecting clues.

The first thing that tipped me off was that they both looked fresh out of the shower, hair still damp. For Jack, that wasn't exactly out of the ordinary, but Simon was not a morning person, and unless Jack had somehow forced him into joining him for a run, I doubted that anything could have made him shower just because most people thought it part of their morning routine. The only exception to this that I knew was a session up in the attic, as apparently sex trumped morning grumpiness any morning. I sincerely doubted that Jack would go anywhere near the playroom, though, and the idea that Simon had somehow pulled a new sub out of his imaginary hat wasn't even anything I considered.

Clue two was that neither of them seemed particularly wary around the other, which was definitely an improvement from the dinner of awkwardness Wednesday before last. I had to admit that they'd had more than a week to patch things up between them, and while Jack had proved that he could be a first-class asshole, I doubted it was his goal to drive a wedge between him and Simon over something that I denied was even an issue.

That led me to clue number three—the almost affectionate way they were talking with each other, stealing glances and pausing to offer a smile or wink. Over the years, I'd had plenty of opportunity to observe them in their native habitat—this very house—and while they were usually friendly around each other, they didn't really interact a lot unless they had something to talk about. Jack often complained that Simon barely got out five words before midday on a bad day, and more than one of our morning sessions had been preceded by him and me both reading in silence while I waited for him to finish his coffee.

Maybe I should have been glad about that change, but what it did was make my internal alarm bells go off. That only grew worse as I stepped farther into the room so the guys noticed me. Simon looked positively guilty before a smile spread on his face. Jack looked smug.

"Hi, guys," I said in what must have been the lamest greeting ever.

"Not that I'm complaining, but what are you doing here?" Simon replied, while Jack left it at a nod before he came around the breakfast bar to investigate the contents of the box I was only too ready to foist at him.

"I thought I'd drop by, see if anybody's home. And I did come bearing gifts."

The whole thing reminded me of the day Simon and I had had our first session together. I half expected Jack to start reaming me for this being my routine bootie call performance, but he didn't. Maybe that should have been a pointer, too, but right then I was caught up in trying to decide what to make of Simon's behavior. He didn't act exactly withdrawn, but he wasn't as open as I'd gotten used to, and for once that wasn't due to any kind of distraction that I could tell.

Free of my burden, I made a beeline for the coffee pot that had only just finished collecting liquid ambrosia. My hand shook slightly as I poured myself a cup, and I tried to tell myself that I was just being paranoid. That didn't help, though, when I turned around and found both guys still watching me, a hint of awkward caution in the air.

"Do you mind if I use your bathroom?" I asked, already feeling stupid about it. Asking, and needing to go back there, because it wasn't actually nature's call that made me run for the back hallway.

There were no exercise clothes anywhere, not in the washing machine, nor the health hazard that Simon used as a hamper.

My heart sank as I traipsed back into the kitchen, and for a moment I contemplated just tucking my tail between my legs and fleeing.

Whatever was going on, I didn't need to find out right now. It could wait another day. Or at least until tonight, when we were in public at the stupid book party, and I couldn't very well make a scene in front of a room of strangers.

Immediately, what Jack had said about Simon's previous subs echoed through my mind.

Shit.

By then it must have become apparent that I was behaving like a cat in a room full of rocking chairs, but I tried to play it cool as I returned. Tried, but likely failed, because I couldn't even keep my arms by my sides but felt the need to hug myself, and crossing them over my chest seemed like the only viable compromise. Jack followed my every move with his eyes while he kept munching his yogurt, but Simon had assumed a much less blasé attitude in the meantime. There was tension in the lines of his body, and he fidgeted uselessly with a towel resting on the counter in front of him, his half-eaten sandwich forgotten.

There was no way to breach the subject carefully, and considering the buildup that had been happening over the past two weeks, bluntness was likely not the worst option out there.

"Are you two screwing each other?"

I already had my answer when Jack snorted and held my gaze, challenge in his eyes, but it was Simon's reaction that surprised me—and not in a good way.

"Do you care? Because, quite frankly, you don't seem to give a shit about anything lately."

I wasn't so far into hypocrisy territory that I got really upset about the fact that the guys I'd had two threesomes with had narrowed things down to activities between them, but the hostility in his voice was like a slap in my face.

"Of course I care!" I bit out, definitely on the defensive, but of a mind to get pissed off myself. "I do understand that we didn't exactly set up a contract or agree on exclusivity, but how can you accuse me of not caring? After all, I'm your—"

I hesitated for a moment, not sure how to end that sentence, and Simon used that mercilessly to keep driving that verbal blade he was wielding home.

"What exactly are you to me? Ever since our last scene, you've been avoiding me like the plague, and it was rather obvious just how deep Jack's accusation cut you. Are you still my sub? I don't know! It should be easy to answer if you were. And should I even dare use the term 'girlfriend,' when you can't even bring yourself to kiss me in front of our closest friends, and act as if we never even had sex when we're in public? I don't think so, either. So what exactly are you to me, Erin?"

He kept glaring at me, not even blinking once, and his words left me speechless. Not just because they made me feel like he'd just cut out my heart, but because they were true. Not in the sense that I agreed with his conclusions, but he perfectly described my actions, and if I knew anyone who judged people by that, then it was Simon.

"Don't be too hard on her. You know she just pretty much lost her job," Jack helpfully supplied. If I hadn't been stunned by Simon's words, I might have felt like punching him for it, but right now, just sorting my emotions out in my head was hard enough.

Simon didn't leave me any time to do so, anyway.

"Yeah, right. How could I forget about that? Your residency ends in a couple of months and you're left without any follow-up employment, and you don't even see the need to tell me? Are we even still friends?"

That left my mind reeling even more, but this time Simon didn't go on steam-rolling over me, but waited every painful second it took me to find my voice again.

"It's not like that," I started, but then had to stop, because I really didn't know how to explain the turmoil that had been going on inside of me for the past weeks.

"Then how is it?"

The tension between us was thick enough to cut, and when I didn't reply, he pushed away from the counter to walk around it, coming face to face with me. From up close, it was even more obvious how angry he was, but that wasn't what made me grow cold inside. No, it was the utter disappointment in his eyes that slayed me.

"I get that our agreement was basically set up as a means for both of us to satisfy our urges. And for the most part, I did get my rocks off while it lasted, but that last scene? I did that just for you and got nothing out of it myself. It wasn't a selfless act on my part, we both know that, but I thought I was doing you a favor in obliging you. In letting you push yourself past the brink, because I thought you'd gathered enough experience to handle a scene like that. To pretty much let you use me to satisfy your needs. And how did you repay me? You shut me out, completely, on all levels. You don't want to talk about what happened, fine. Maybe you have doubts, maybe you're a little afraid of yourself, maybe even of me—it happens. That's to be expected, and while I hate that it happened, it's part of the process, sometimes. But that's not why you've broken off contact, is it? It's because for whatever fucked-up reason you believed his bullshit, and suddenly you're the poor girl and I'm some kind of despicable, violent Neanderthal that you only deal with if you absolutely have to. Did our last time together really disappoint you so much that you couldn't even call afterward, although you promised? Didn't I fuck you hard enough, or did the fact that I let you cry on my shoulder twice in one week emasculate me?"

If his voice had been laced with venom, his words might have been bearable, but he sounded calm and mostly composed, with only a note of pain coming through here and there. The only hint I had that he was really upset was the fact that halfway through he'd started to ramble, but that didn't take away from the fact that I could understand how he jumped to all those conclusions, wrong as they were.

Still I didn't know how to respond, and for a moment, his composure cracked.

"Fucking say something, Erin!"

I felt him slip away, mentally withdraw, and I realized that if I didn't turn this ship around right now, it would sail off without me and likely never return, so I said the only thing that I could.

"I love you."

I had no clue what he had expected, but that wasn't it. Simon looked as if I'd slapped him or maybe kicked him in the junk. For just a moment, hope flickered alive inside of me. It was the truth, and it was the explanation to all the wrong decisions I'd taken over the past weeks, and for a few seconds I hoped that it was enough.

But then Simon blinked and took a step back, and something died inside of me.

"You love me."

Simon said the words as if he was testing them, and the utter lack of enthusiasm in his voice made my throat tighten up.

"I told you that this wasn't going to end any other way," Jack pointed out, and in that moment, something clicked inside of my mind.

Turning my head slowly, I looked at him, really looked at him, and for the first time in my life I wondered if I even still knew the guy who had been my best friend growing up. What was his agenda? Was he actively working against me? Because that was the only conclusion I could draw from the pieces that were all falling into place now.

Jack held my gaze for a second but then had to look away, making him at least human.

Life slowly returned to my limbs, and I swept my gaze back to Simon, finding him still looking at me with a borderline quizzical expression on his face.

"That can't be that much of a surprise to you?" I asked, still feeling like my life was bleeding out through the ruin of my heart, but somehow managed to keep my voice level. "And even if it is, I don't see what the big issue is about it? I don't expect you to feel the same way about me."

Maybe that had been a little nasty, but keeping my calm when I was this upset with someone had never been my forte.

"It's not—" Simon started, but Jack interrupted him, drawing our collective attention back to him.

"That's all it takes for you to back down? Sheesh, you're hopeless."

Simon ducked his head, and I didn't know what to expect, but it wasn't the anger in his eyes when he turned to face Jack rather than me.

"Remind me again where what is going on between Erin and me is any of your business? You expressly told me you wanted to keep out of it, so shut the fuck up and let me think."

Now it was Jack's turn to be irritated.

"I don't give a fuck about what you do up there, but it does concern me when you two go toe to toe with each other and start driving each other insane. Remember what we talked about?"

I really would have loved to know what exactly Jack had told him, but it didn't really matter. I guessed this was what I got for not dealing with shit—it bit me in the ass at the worst possible moment. Before Simon could reply, I got right in his face.

"Why do you even listen to him? He's the one who called you an abusive asshole, and now you act as if he's your external conscience?"

"At least he is still talking to me," Simon started, but I didn't let him go on.

"Yeah, I get that. It's all my fault that shit turned sour. Boo hoo. The last couple of weeks haven't been easy for me, or fun. Sure, now it's obvious that I should have opened up to you from the start, but have you never been insecure about something that was incredibly overwhelming, and you tried so hard not to jeopardize or ruin it?"

I really didn't like the sidelong glance he shot at Jack, but before I could lose him, I went into the offense.

"Seeing as Jack has been so chatty, has he also told you that he came on to me at the restaurant last week? No? So he didn't share that he thinks he's a better and more reliable match for me than you are? Wake up, Simon. He's using the fact that we're both emotionally stunted asshats sometimes, and he's playing us against each other. Don't ask me for whatever fucked up reason, but don't you see that?"

If I hadn't been so fucking hurt by his rejection, I could have felt pity for the look of doubt and pain that settled on Simon's face, but right now that was not in the narrowing range of emotions my mind was capable of. At least my revelation shut him up for the moment, leaving me free to deal with what I started to see as the real problem.

Turning to fully face Jack, I fixed him with the coldest glare I was capable of.

"Exactly what do you hope to gain by ruining what we have going on? I know that you think this will just blow over like any other fight we've had in the past, but you fucking disgust me with all this lying and scheming."

"I'm not lying," he started, but shut up when I took a couple of steps toward him, halving the distance between us.

"Oh, yes, you are. You're a sneaky, conniving piece of shit, that's what you are! First you try to demonize Simon so I run, then you play my insecurities against me when you try to convince him of, I don't know, my impending insanity? What's the matter with you? Can't you stand us not being totally codependent on you?"

It was barely more than a wild guess, and half-assed at that, but when I saw Jack's jaw tremble as his eyes got just a little wild, I realized that I'd hit straight on. Simon's ignorance might hurt, but this—this was far worse.

"You've got to be fucking kidding me!" I screamed, my voice breaking when it went up an entire octave at the end. "Are you fucking insane? Are you seriously telling me that you've started tearing apart our friendship just because there is someone else in my life that I'm close to? You put me through hell because you're fucking jealous?"

Maybe that was a little melodramatic, but with the stress of the past weeks bearing down on me, I didn't have it in me to be diplomatic anymore.

"I am not jealous!" Jack ground out, the anger in his tone laced with just enough petulance to turn that claim into a lie.

I shot a glance at Simon, but he didn't seem ready to stand with me in this. In fact, he looked downright shell-shocked—or like someone had just wrenched his heart out of his chest and was shredding it to pieces.

Oh, this was just getting better and better.

The realization that I wasn't the only one who was ready to curl up in a corner and die doused some of my rage, but the mix of desperation and just plain old pain that was left made me feel like shit. Turning back to Jack, I found him still breathing heavily with anger, but there was something in his eyes that made me look away.

"I'm not jealous," he repeated more evenly, the words grating along my soul. "But how do you think it makes me feel when the two people I care about the most, the two people who define me, suddenly don't need me anymore? And don't look so fucking surprised. You wouldn't even be screwing each other if not for me—you wouldn't even know each other! For fucking forever you've always run to me with every single stupid thing that went wrong in your lives, begging me to fix it. Did Simon ever tell you that he's been wanting to fuck you for years but never quite worked up the courage to have that talk with you? That he needed you drunk and blundering about, and, most of all, he needed my help to set things in motion? Guess it must really suck for you that now that he finally got you, he's much more into another shiny new toy he picked up along the way."

The satisfaction in Jack's tone was enough to make anger flare through the uneasy guilt that his words had brought up inside of me, but he only paused long enough to let what I'd already realized settle in as confirmed before he went on, his voice hardening.

"You two both do nothing but look down at me, day in, day out. I'm your eternally funny, slow-witted sidekick, because, guess what, not everyone can have a genius-level intellect! But you're both so fucking stupid and naive in your own ways, it almost feels like beating a child when I give you that overdue, well-deserved shove that makes you stumble! You two are so fucking pathetic, it's laughable. And it didn't take more than two conversations of telling you exactly what you already know to make you fall flat on your own face."

His malice shut me up, leaving me gulping like a fish caught on land, but now it was Simon's turn to regain his composure—and lose it within the first few words that came out of his mouth.

"You make me doubt myself, you make her, your oldest, closest friend, break down because you cut her off from her support net, and for what? For your own vanity? No one fucking thinks that they're superior to you! I don't, and I doubt that Erin does, either!"

I nodded, even though neither of them was more than glancing at me.

"But you sure know how to act like superior assholes for people who are supposedly so humble!" Jack cried, still not calming down. "Do you ever stop for a second and think what you're doing to me? You moan and bitch and complain about how things are so bad when I would die to share with you what you find insufficient in others, and, obviously, me too? I was the driving force that got you together, first as friends, then as lovers. I set this up, and what do you do? First chance you get, you cut me out completely, and then get in my face when I do what you always have depended on me to do and tell you that you're idiots?"

His eyes were frantic as they shifted between us, and suddenly he was on his feet, coming toward us, fast enough that I almost cringed away from him. Glaring at me first, then at Simon, he pulled himself up to his not unimpressive height and glared at us.

"You know what? I'm done. With both of you. It's just like you to band together against me now. Just look how you do without me. Have fun picking up the pieces of the relationship you both were incapable of building. I'm out."

With that, he turned around and stormed back into his room to change into street clothes and grab his laptop, which made his subsequent exit a lot less dramatic than he'd probably intended. It didn't matter, because both Simon and I watched him leave in silence, incapable of doing anything until the front door was shoved shut with a booming sound. Seconds later Jack's motorcycle roared to life, and then silence fell.

Deafening silence.

One thing I'd always been proud of was that I rarely started to cry when I got emotional, but suddenly the lump in the back of my throat was making breathing hard, and I felt tears burn in my eyes. Angry pants turned to shallow breaths, and my fingers trembled when I stretched them out from the fists they'd been in for what felt like forever.

Turning slowly, I looked at Simon, but he was ignoring me, his eyes still fixed on where he'd last seen Jack.

I should have probably said something. Anything, really, but I simply couldn't. I knew that I would start bawling like a child the moment I opened my mouth, and if Simon had ever been completely incapable of acting like a functioning human being, it dwarfed how he looked now. Lost, devastated, guilty, all alone in the world—exactly how I felt.

So I did the only thing I could, and left.

-16-

I wasn't exactly sure how I made it home. I might have hit the wrong train, gotten off at the wrong stop, but it was early afternoon when I finally shut the door to my apartment, sagged against it, and started to cry. Marcy was thankfully out and about, or working, or screwing some reckless intern silly, I really didn't care. I was alone, and I wanted to be alone, because no single person could have helped with the deep-rooted feeling of utter loneliness that spread through my heart.

How could I have been so blind? And on so many levels?

What bothered me the least was still the actual physical hookup between the guys. Sure, it rankled that I hadn't been along, and if everything else had been okay I would have given them both shit for it, but it paled in comparison to how much everything else hurt. Like me taking forever to sort out my feelings for Simon. How he had been oblivious of them, and how quick he was to reject me. How he clearly was head over heels in love with Jack, which I figured had been the chink in Simon's armor that Jack had used to turn our combined world upside down. What I didn't know was whether Jack felt the same way about Simon, but while that idea hurt on a different level than his betrayal, it didn't really matter. In the end, Jack had pulled the exact same move on me, only I hadn't been stupid enough to fall for it.

Maybe things would have turned out differently if I had. My vanity insisted on it, made it easy to believe that Jack had just used Simon to get back at me for rejecting him.

And it was likely that same vanity that had caused this shit-storm of epic proportions, and what hurt the most—more than rejection, more than betrayal—was the guilt that slowly ate me up from the inside.

The game Jack had played was one thing, and it was easy to hate him for doing this to me, but that didn't change the fact that the more I thought about his accusations, the more I tended to agree with him. And when I started looking for clues, I found them, enough to stop the tears and make me miserable for simply being a fucked up, egotistical bitch.

I'd always known that I was likely a little too dismissive of Jack to be healthy for our friendship, but it had never been a problem. Things had always been like this, from the first day on. I guess I'd always figured he knew that I didn't mean it, that I was simply a little too blunt for my own good. I'd always been the intelligent one, while he'd been the smart one. Some kids who lost a parent had a hard time in school because they couldn't concentrate. For me, excelling at everything I did had been my way of dealing with that bleeding wound in my soul that could never fully heal. Meanwhile, Jack had always been the one who had friends who covered for him or helped him cheat, and it wasn't like he was too dumb to study on his own, he was just lazy. Being the son of a single mother who was working herself to the bone on minimum wage jobs to support herself and him, while half raising me along with Jack had left a certain parental freedom that just begged to be abused by the charming little git he'd been.

But never, not once in my life, had I ever felt like I was better than Jack, just different.

Thinking back to our conversation in the car en route to the lake, his words cut even deeper. It had been right there, his insecurity, his feelings like he thought that he just wasn't good enough for me. And what had I done? I'd brushed it off as teenage stupidity and never wasted another thought on him.

The truth was, if we'd been born a couple of decades earlier or hadn't gotten the scholarships that allowed us to go to college, we likely would have ended up getting married before we were twenty, with a bunch of kids to follow soon after. That thought had always amused me, and more than just alienated me—I loved my job, and for nothing in the world had I ever wanted to give it up—but sitting here, knowing that I'd not just lost but shoved my friend away one stupid remark at a time, I asked myself if that wouldn't have been a better life. At the very least we would have been equals, and maybe then I could have shown him just how deeply I cherished and appreciated him.

Not that it mattered now, and I was aware that I was wallowing in self-pity more than anything else. If we'd never gone to college, we would never have met Simon, and life without him would just not have been the same.

Thinking of Simon made me hurt even more, but I tried to put a lid on that can of worms. It was easy to jump to conclusions, but in the end, we hadn't exactly ended things between us. Not mended them, either, but maybe with time, we could probably find a new balance. I felt vaguely ashamed for gushing about my feelings for him like that, but his rejection hadn't been painful enough to make me give up on us completely. Maybe turning thirty last year had left me cynical, but even if he wasn't about to confess his sudden, undying love for me in turn, I wasn't ready to give up on being his sub. Unless that was a deal breaker for him, which I didn't know as we'd never even broached the topic of what would happen if feelings got involved.

Guess it all came back down to one fact: we really needed to talk.

But not now. What I really needed now was ice cream.

I was halfway through the carton of creamy deliciousness when my phone went off. I ignored it, mostly because there was an instant flare of hope deep in my chest that it would be Simon, and I couldn't let reality whip that right out of me again.

Five minutes later, the doorbell rang, making me go still, the last scoop of ice cream melting on my tongue.

The bell chimed again, then kept going when whoever was pressing the button downstairs didn't stop.

Holding my breath, I walked over to the intercom, cutting the annoying sound short when I activated it.

"Who's there?"

My voice was so hoarse from crying that I could barely understand myself, making me hope that it would be enough to fend off whichever idiot was interrupting my pity party.

Idiot was right, I realized, when Jack's voice came on, distorted by static.

"Erin? Can we talk?"

I considered just walking away without even giving an answer, but something in his tone made me pause.

"Why?"

"Please, can I come up?"

I considered for a moment. Ignoring him was still an option, but frankly, after his tantrum it was surprising that he showed up here, and although I felt even worse than during the fight, the vindictive part of me wanted another chance to tear into him.

Taking a deep breath, I buzzed him in, then waited until I heard his steps in the corridor. Making sure that the chain was on, I opened the door as far as it would go, peeking outside.

Quite frankly, Jack looked like shit. His eyes were red and swollen, his posture barely better than a slouch, and if the sight of him hadn't rekindled the anger simmering inside of me, I might have even felt pity for him. The fact that he still looked better than I felt negated that, though.

"What do you want?" I bit out as soon as he looked at me, although it came out a lot more petulant than angry.

"Can I come in? Please, just for a few minutes. Just hear me out, okay?"

Right then my neighbor's door opened next to mine, and the last thing I needed was for the old gossip to harangue me over "young men loitering outside my door" the next time we crossed paths. Sighing, I closed the door, unhooked the chain, and opened it again, just long enough to let Jack squeeze through.

I'd never seen him look so damn uncomfortable standing in the small space that was supposed to be my hallway. Suddenly tired of this, I turned and walked back into the kitchen, on the way dumping the empty ice cream tub in the trash. Sitting down, I looked at Jack again, who had remained standing just inside the door.

"You want to talk? Well, talk."

Instead of opening his mouth, he just looked at me, and it took me kicking out a chair and shoving it in his direction for him to take a seat.

"You've been crying," he said, his voice cracking and thin when he finally managed to speak up.

"What did you think, that I'd dance around, whooping?" I shot back, then let out my breath slowly. "Just say what you're here to say. I've had enough of your games for a lifetime." Not the nicest thing to say, but he'd hurt me too much that I couldn't resist taking a jab at him.

He made a face but didn't protest. When he did start speaking, his voice was a little less thin, but still didn't sound normal.

"I came here to apologize."

I waited for more but he'd fallen silent, studying his hands where they rested, twined around each other on the table top in front of him.

"So far you're doing a shit job of it," I told him, my voice holding less anger than I wanted it to.

"I know." More silence followed before he looked up, the skin around his eyes crinkling from the obvious pain he felt. "I fucked up. I know that. I never wanted to hurt you. Not like this. Please, you have to—"

"I don't have to do anything!"

He stared at me, wide-eyed, then let his head fall onto his hands, effectively hiding his expression from me. Even though there was still rage churning in the pit of my stomach, it hurt to see him like this, but I had no intention of easing his torment.

"I lied," was what I think he said next, muffled until he raised his head and looked at me directly, tears threatening to fall from his eyes. "When I said I'd done it all because you both deserved it."

I didn't even try to keep a frown from showing on my face, but didn't say anything. He sighed, then looked away, but his eyes returned to my face when he started anew.

"Not that you two don't deserve to be pulled down a few notches, but if I couldn't handle the finer points of your casual conduct with the world at large, I wouldn't have put up with it for so long. But it wasn't the reason why I did what I did."

He stopped there, and the temptation to just shake him to get him talking again was strong. His words made the ache in my chest swell to its previous height, but this time I let it. I knew that he could see it on my face, in my eyes, and somehow it still hurt him, too, and I had no intention of sparing him that.

"Then why did you act like an even bigger asshole than usual? Just so you know, Simon and I might not be without fault, but you're not an angel yourself."

"I know." More hesitation, then he visibly pulled himself together, his voice gaining a little more strength. "I did it because it was the only way I could think of to pull you two apart. And I'm not even sure I managed that much."

That wasn't exactly news, and I opened my mouth to tell him so, but he forestalled me.

"Not because I think he's not good enough for you, or hurting you besides what you obviously get off on. Because I want you, and as long as he's in the game you don't even see me."

That was news to me, and not the kind that made my heart beat faster with excitement.

"Jack, what the fuck?"

He gave me a blithe smile back.

"See? Exactly what I'm saying."

"You're not making any sense here! What do you mean by you want me?"

Probably not the best way to phrase it, because that part was obvious, but thankfully he didn't take me literally.

"I wouldn't mind it that much if you two were just screwing around, but ever since things got more serious between you and him, you've been completely ignoring me, and you have no idea just how much that hurts."

"But you never said anything!"

He opened his mouth to reply, anger now seeping into his pose, but after a few seconds he closed it again and visibly deflated, then put his elbows up onto the table and hid his face in his hands.

"I know. And that's not making anything easier."

That he was confusing the hell out of me didn't help, but I forced myself not to tear into him right there, but waited until he looked at me again. I couldn't tell for sure, but it seemed as if he'd tried to hide a few tears spilling from his eyes.

"I love you, Erin. Not just some random infatuation—I'm not just 'in love' with you. I've always loved you. And you don't even know."

The panic and frustration in his tone cut into me and made it even harder to keep up the hard, unforgiving exterior. Sure, I was still mad as never before at him, but that didn't mean that I'd burned all the bridges between us. Reaching out, I hooked a finger around one of his so I could pull his hand toward me. Twining my fingers with his, I brushed my lips softly over his knuckles, then caught his gaze again.

"I do know."

"No, you don't," he chuffed and blinked, tears spilling from his eyes now unhindered. "You think I like you, like my sister, but that's—"

I shook my head and pressed my mouth against his hand again.

"Why did you never say anything?"

He exhaled slowly, his eyes now fixed at where our fingers were knitted together.

"It wasn't that obvious. There's no one who can look inside your heart and qualify what you feel for another person. Guess I've simply known you for too long, know what I mean?"

I nodded, because I did know, and that made his entire confession so much worse.

"And it's not something that suddenly changed," he went on. "I didn't just wake up one morning and, bam! And it wasn't really... acute, for lack of another word, until a while ago. Guess turning thirty pulled a number on me, or something." He looked away, then back to my face. "I feel old sometimes, you know? Not geriatric, pensioner kind of old, but when I hang out at a club and there are all these perky twenty-somethings rubbing themselves all over me—"

"A truly horrific fate, I'm sure," I interjected with a small smile, simply because I had to.

Jack barked a brief, harsh laugh, but it seemed to lighten his mood a little.

"Hey, I'm not gonna change just because I'm getting a little weird in the head, okay? You know me better than that."

"I do."

"Anyway. Makes me realize that I'm no longer the guy who just wants to pick up some chick, have a good time, and then move on. I know that you probably think that's as deep as I go, but—"

"Hey, give me some credit here, asshole!"

Now his smile held a little longer, but it disappeared as he had to blink away tears again.

"Shit. Can you please stop interrupting me? I'm trying to pour my heart out here, and all you do is try to make me laugh."

"I'm a terrible person, I know."

He stared back for another second, then shook his head.

"Whatever. It's not that I want to settle down and have a bunch of kids, but there are days when I just want to stay home, curl up on the couch with pizza and a beer, you know? Snuggle up, maybe fool around a little bit—"

I just couldn't resist that one.

"Only fool around? You're disappointing me."

He rolled his eyes, but seeing him not about to sink back to the bottom of depression lifted some of the weight off my chest.

"There might be some bending you over the couch and fucking you silly involved, too, but that's not the primary thing anymore. Five years ago I would have laughed about this notion, but now..." He paused. "Remember when I flung that tidbit into Simon's face that he's been lusting after you for a while?"

"You really think I could forget that?"

He shook his head.

"Truth it... it was less like stupid puppy dog love that I tried to make it out as, and more basic carnal interest. He brought up the idea a couple of times but I always ignored it, and for whatever reason he didn't feel like making a move on you on his own. Guess because sometimes he can be one hell of an insecure fucker, even if he doesn't show it often."

"Which you exploited, shamelessly."

Just because it made me feel better to make him smile, I wasn't above putting him down again where he deserved it. Jack looked away and sighed.

"Guess I deserved that one. Yes, I did. But back to before that. At that party, you made it so fucking difficult to resist you, and then those girls kept rubbing themselves all over me and all it did was annoy me because what I really wanted was to fuck you. By now I guess you've realized that Simon can be one observant fucker, and he got wind of that even before I could make up my mind. I think I don't need to recount the outcome of that?"

I shook my head, although like always, thinking back to our first threesome gave me the best kind of tingles in all the right places. It was muted by my general dark mood right now, but not much.

"Anyway, that was fun. And not much different than anything else. Sorry if it bothers you to hear that—"

"It doesn't."

It did, a little, but in the light of what else he'd coughed up already, I could very well live without instant love at first fuck confessions. Jack gave me a look that told me that he knew I was lying, but let it slide.

"What I want to say is that it didn't bother me when Simon and you started your thing. Sure, it was strange to reconcile you with the picture of his usual playthings, but just because that's not what gets my rocks off, I can still accept it. And do. It was nice to have you around more, and the promise of fresh bagels didn't hurt. What was different to any other time I've shared a chick with him was that it was a lot more comfortable for me, because with you, I didn't have to worry about the usual shit."

I couldn't resist that.

"Like what? What exactly do you worry about when you tag team a girl?"

I got a ghost of a smile for my effort.

"For one, there was not the usual guessing of how we should balance things. You know, if she's a chick I've been banging who was curious for more cock, I'd usually take the lead and Simon kept his other interests on the back burner. If she was one of his subs, he'd take charge and I'd just do support. It was a little weird at first with you when we started out like that, but he let me take the stage completely after he fucked your face. He never did that before, but you didn't mind, and neither did I. And there's always that thing about either of us getting a bit too comfy with each other and then the girl freaks out. Not the best way to end it."

He looked at me with something akin to challenge, but I just held his gaze evenly.

"Of all the things you've done today, fucking Simon is what least upsets me."

Jack snorted, and for a moment I couldn't quite make sense of the expression on his face.

"Or let him fuck you?"

Just because I was pissed and felt betrayed didn't mean that I couldn't still be curious.

"Gotta try everything at least once before you diss it, right?"

He probably tried to make that sound light, but that was not what I clearly heard in his voice. And, just like that, the elephant in the room turned into a dinosaur.

For several seconds neither one of us said something, until Jack straightened in his chair, his fingers squeezing mine gently.

"Then we had our second threesome at the lake, and that was about when things got complicated." He paused briefly, but when no witty comeback from me followed, he went on. "I don't know how it was for you, but for me it felt like coming home. Not just because I finally got to put an end to years worth of guessing, but because everything, with you, with Simon, with both of you at the same time just felt like it should be. No need to pretend, no need to hide, just do whatever I wanted, be myself, one hundred percent. Don't tell me you didn't feel it."

A deep-set melancholy made me hesitate for a few heartbeats, but in the end I nodded.

"I felt it, too."

"And after that, everything went straight to hell."

It only took those few words for his voice to break, and seeing the tears return to his eyes was like an iron fist clenching around my heart. I squeezed his fingers, but wasn't even sure he noticed. When he looked at me again, his gaze was filled with sadness.

"I get why Simon and you stepped up your game. I really do. But did you have to completely ignore me just because he was giving you what I can't? I was so sure that we had a moment there at the lake, that you felt exactly the same about me as I did about you, and suddenly I'm invisible to you?"

"I didn't—"

"Yes, you did!" he ground out, then glared at the ceiling when looking at me became too painful. "It was as if you'd used that as a way of saying goodbye to everything we've ever had. You rarely talked to me again, you had no time to just hang out, and whenever I could pull you away from him, all you gushed about was him. Simon this, Simon that, and oh, he makes me come like nobody else!"

"I never—"

"You didn't need to!" he cut me off before I could get more than two words in edgewise. "The attic might be soundproof, but it doesn't help when the door's not shut tight. I have no idea if he did that on purpose or if it was an accident, but I heard you. Scream from pain, scream with lust, you name it. And I couldn't help myself—I was stupid enough to walk up those fucking stairs and take a look. Kind of horrified me that I could get such a boner from watching him do all that to you, but I didn't really care. And the next time I didn't even wait until you were halfway into the scene, but jerked off as soon as you were out of the room, then followed you. And came again, way before you, if you're wondering. And then was that fucking day I met you in the train, and I thought that with all three of us around and you obviously needing some distraction, we could have some fun together again. But you didn't even listen to me, and Simon almost kicked me out of the house before he went to town on you."

I didn't know what to make of the fact that he'd watched us, but that last bit made me decidedly uncomfortable. It explained his reaction to some point, but also made it even less understandable.

"Did you watch that one, too?"

He nodded, still not looking at me.

"I did."

"Then why..." I trailed off, unable to finish the sentence.

Jack let his head fall onto his free hand before he turned it, his eyes seeking mine.

"Because I realized just how far you'd withdrawn from me. I never had a problem with anything you did up there. The only thing that made me uncomfortable was my own reaction to seeing you hurt like that, but I guess it's because I knew you wanted it, and my cock's too stupid to make a difference between what gets me going and what doesn't. It was obvious that what he did, he did because you urged him on, and he stopped as soon as you had enough. And then you broke down and all I wanted was to run in and be there for you, but you clearly just wanted him, or else you would have come downstairs and curled up with me."

He stopped and let out a harsh breath.

"Wanna know what's the worst? Ever since Simon got his kinky shit on, I've known the one thing that can throw him completely off balance. Don't know how much he told you about that, but the shit he went through with that cunt who got him into this wasn't pretty. I don't always get along with Beth, but I'll always be grateful to her for the fact that she took him in and set his head straight again. I don't know if he even realized how much being with her changed him. It's as if she somehow reached inside his head, kicked out all the stupid, defensive shit he'd built up over the years, all his doubts and insecurities, and turned him from a somewhat awkward boy into a man. And that was long before she told him to stop wussing out and pick up the whip himself. I'm not saying that he wouldn't have eventually gotten his shit together on his own, but she set him on the fast track to get that done in record time. And he's good at what he does, even if things don't always work out with his subs."

His eyes fell back onto our still joined hands.

"Wanna know my guess? Same as I've been screwing around with random girls for years, I think he never really got in too deep with any of his subs. Just wasn't the right match that he was biding his time for."

He let that hang between us for a moment before he went on, his voice hardening now.

"I knew that the one thing he's always been scared shitless of is that he'll make the same mistakes as that cunt did with him. He never said it to me, but Beth more than once ranted that, his given consent aside, the bitch pretty much abused him. If there's one thing you kinksters are adamant about, it's respect and consent. Guess it makes sense with the stunts you pull on each other, but I've seen how it shaped him, and it's obvious that what you two do is good for you, too."

That admission surprised me, also because it wasn't exactly what I felt sometimes.

"You think? I completely lost it on my mom's death day, and it hasn't been that bad in years."

"Because you never really let yourself grieve? Don't you dare deny it—I've been there every single year. I'm not putting the blame on anyone, but I've watched, helpless and frustrated, how your father just couldn't handle it and you had to support him, rather than the other way round. You've always had to be strong, and eventually that became second nature to you. But it's not healthy if you can never just let go and let someone else be there to comfort you, you know?"

He bit his lip while I considered that, and went on before I reached any kind of conclusion.

"The rest was easy. Accusing him of abusing you worked in both directions. It scared the shit out of you and made him insecure as hell, and I thought it would be easy pickings then. What I didn't count on was that he could actually pull his head out of his ass and act like a normal human being for once, and my plan backfired. I thought that if I rejected you, you'd either go home and call me later, or you'd go to him and he would be helpless and just make everything worse. Either way, I could then swoop in and pick up the pieces. Then I'd have my in, and you'd finally see what you have in me and..."

He wasn't able to finish, and my grip on his hand was loose enough that when he pulled away, I was too slow to stop him. Getting up, he started pacing, and stopped with his back turned to me.

"I understand if you never want to have anything to do with me ever again. Or just for now. I know that I screwed up. Massively. In pretty much every way possible. I don't deserve your forgiveness—hell, I don't think I even have the guts to ask for it, but the idea of living without you just kills me. I know... I can't..."

Whatever else he might have wanted to say got drowned out by a loud sob, his entire body heaving with it. Seeing him in so much pain hurt a lot more than anything that had transpired today, and

I was on my feet before the conscious thought of going over to him even formed in my mind. Stepping up to him, I wrapped my arms around him and pressed myself against him, hugging him for all I was worth. He let out another soul-wrenching sob before he turned around, enfolding me in an embrace that was so warm and familiar that it hurt on a different level.

Yes, he'd screwed up. He'd betrayed me, he'd hurt me like no one had ever in my life, maybe even more than anyone could ever hurt me. But just listening to him say those words, thinking of a world without him in it, hurt even more.

I felt myself start to cry, and without the will to fight it, the tears streamed down my face and soaked into his T-shirt. When he noticed, his arms tightened around me and I think he cried harder, too, until we were one pathetic, shaking heap of misery. That seemed to have become a thing for me lately, but even the irony of that couldn't stop the tears from coming.

Then I realized what would, and from there, taking action was a surprisingly small step.

Reaching up, I touched my hands to the sides of his face, forcing him to look at me, strands of blond hair partly obscuring his eyes. I tried brushing them away, but that only made Jack turn his head so he could nuzzle my hand, effectively hiding from my gaze. That wouldn't do for another reason, so I shifted my grip on him to pull his head down to me and pressed my lips against his.

I felt him startle and actually heard his next sob because he tried to pull away, but I didn't let him, and it only took the sensation of my tongue sneaking into his mouth for him to stop protesting and deepen the kiss. His arms around me shifted, now not just hugging me but holding me close, his palms hot through the fabric of my shirt.

It was a slow kiss at first, and we both had to break away too soon because snot and tears had led to some disgusting buildup, but as soon as I could breathe again, my mouth found his, and there was nothing left of his previous tentativeness anymore. One of his hands stoked up to cradle the back of my head while the other settled firmly at my lower back, making sure that I couldn't get away so easily again—not that I wanted to. Things heated up quickly then, and before long, just kissing him and bunching his T-shirt up in my hands wasn't enough.

Pulling away, panting heavily, I grabbed his hand instead and started tugging him toward my room, while trying to clean up the mess on my face on my right shoulder. Jack took a step, then stopped, bringing me to a sudden halt. Turning around, I gave him a glare that made him bring up his other hand defensively, which looked kind of weird because he still seemed only a step or two away from starting to bawl all over again.

"I'm not protesting. I just want to know what this is."

Instead of answering, I jerked him along with me, but once we'd stumbled into my room, I let go of him and shut the door, leaning against it while I tried to sort out the chaos inside my head. Jack waited patiently, looking a little lost.

"I'm not over this yet," I started, then felt like kicking myself in the teeth when I saw his shoulders sag with defeat. "Your betrayal, I mean. And I mean it when I say that I fully intend to make you suffer until it gets ridiculous, and for that I need you to stick around, right? And knowing you, you'll keep finding excuses to keep me pissed off, so I might as well give up on the idea of getting rid of you altogether. Life would be too boring."

He took that with a stoic look on his face, not giving me the smile I hoped my teasing would bring back. Well, no one had ever accused me of being a smooth talker. I'd always been better with bluntness, anyway, so I walked up to him and shoved my hands under his T-shirt, feeling his skin so tantalizingly warm and smooth until I managed to nudge him into taking the stupid garment off. It fell to the floor beside us and I ignored it, reaching up to link my fingers behind his head after pulling it down far enough to touch my forehead to his.

"I'm not kicking you out, Jack. I'm not letting you go, I'm not giving up on you. On us. Okay? But I'm raw inside, and I feel like we've done all the talking we can right now, and I need this. I need you right now."

He didn't reply, but then that wasn't necessary. His lips found mine eagerly while his arms came around me, but unlike I'd expected, he didn't get right to divesting me of my clothes.

We ended up on the bed, still unmade from when I'd rolled out of it half-awake yesterday, in a tangle of limbs, our lips barely separating for more than a second. Then he was leaning over me, deepening his kisses further, but before I could reach for the zipper of his pants, he stopped, his face buried in the side of my neck. For a moment I thought he was going to tickle me or something, but then I realized that he was crying again, giving my heart another painful stab.

"Oh, Jack," I mumbled into his hair and just held him.

"I don't deserve you. Neither of you, but you even less than him."

He didn't have to explain that he was talking about Simon, and with a hint of surprise I realized that it didn't even rub me the wrong way to hear him acknowledge so much. Coming first still felt good, even though it dragged a different kind of unease back up in my mind.

"Shhh, it's okay," I tried to assuage him, stroking his hair slowly.

"It's not. I know that it's not, and I have no fucking clue how to make it right again, if I can even—"

A finger to his lips made him stop, and he looked at me with so much longing and desperation that it might have swayed my heart had I not already forgiven him.

"We'll find a way. Together. You weren't alone in dragging us down, and you won't have to be the one to make it all work again, either."

"But—"

"No buts," I said, hoping that the small smile I managed didn't look forced. "If we want to find a way, there will be a way, and I really want to. And I want you. Not just now, and not just until I feel I've badgered you enough for being such an idiot. You're my idiot, and you will always remain that unless you don't want to anymore."

"Never," he breathed against my lips, then closed the distance between us, and for a blissful time, neither of us felt the need to talk, or even think.

At first I'd expected things to feel similar to my tumble with Simon the last time I'd cried my heart out, but of course it wasn't. Being with Jack never felt like being with Simon, or vice versa. I couldn't even put a finger on what exactly was different, it just was. The way he looked at me, touched me, how he felt under my palms, how he moved—how he made love to me. Because that's what we did, and although I felt like I was the last one to actually realize it, that's what it had been with Simon, too. And on some level I hated myself because even when slow and tender turned to needy and passionate, I couldn't stop thinking about another guy than the one who was very successfully making me forget about everything else in the world. But only a little.

That sentiment grew exponentially when I looked at the alarm clock on my nightstand a while later and realized that although what I wanted to do was remain cuddled up with Jack, I'd have to leave here soon if I didn't want to be too late.

I hadn't even started to extract myself from his arms—and leg—when I heard Jack sigh, his hold on me tightening for a moment.

"You're going to see him now, aren't you?"

I told the pang of guilt his words ignited in the back of my mind to shove it.

"Someone has to. Might as well be me."

He tensed, but instead of keeping me locked in his arms, he let go, flopping onto his back beside me. Rolling over, I looked at his face carefully, but he didn't look half as upset as I'd expected, but mostly defeated.

"I'm not going to run off with Simon to leave you here, alone."

"And what if he asks you to do exactly that? What's your answer then?"

A question I didn't even want to think about, so I didn't.

"The entire mess we're in right now happened because none of us said even half of what we should have said, so avoiding each other won't help at all. Have a little faith in me. Besides, how could I leave all this behind?"

I pointedly poked a finger into his obliques, making him grunt but also look a little mollified.

"Promise?"

"The only promise that you'll get out of me is the promise that I will kick your ass if you don't stop moping around soon."

With that, I got up, fetching my panties and shirt from the floor before I went into the bathroom. I splashed some water in my face, but there was nothing I could do about my puffy, red eyes, or the hickey high on my neck, just below my ear. A shower would have been nice, but I wanted to get this behind me before the book party started, and I was already running late for that.

My urgency went up a notch when I picked up my phone from the kitchen table and saw that I had a text from Kara.

Just as I was perusing the few words that had landed in my inbox, the door opened, spilling Marcy in. I only gave her a cursory nod of greeting, but before I could duck back into my room, she made a beeline for the fridge, accidentally cutting off my exit.

"You really missed out by leaving early in the morning today," she pointed out, but ignored my state of undress. "You know that I always laugh at people when they ask us if the hospital is like these overdone TV shows, but today that was pure comedy. Almost missed it myself, but I thought I'd hit the ER before going to get some grub because I wanted to ask you if you'd join me, but you weren't there anymore."

"Yeah, I left right after my night shift was over."

"So the wrong decision, girl!" She laughed. "Anyway, where was I? Right, so I'm in the ER, looking for some hapless intern who likely knows where you are at all times so he can avoid you, when Tyne comes barreling down the hallway, screaming at some guy who's trying not to look like he's running away from her. I know, you keep telling me that she's a spitfire, but none of your anecdotes had anything on this! She's all red in the face, spitting mad, flinging expletives around, half of which I swear I haven't even heard before. So I ask a nurse who's standing beside me with a grim yet satisfied look on her face who the dude is. Turns out, he's her ex-husband who's taking over the ER as of tomorrow, and there's no need to guess who of them has been wearing the trousers all through their marriage. By the way, did you know that the reason she divorced him was that she was cheating on him with a woman?"

"Her girlfriend," I helpfully supplied.

"Of course you know," she huffed, but wouldn't let me get a word in edgewise. "And you would have loved watching this. When she ran out of insults, she tried to slap him, but the guy's like a full head or more taller than she is, so she starts jumping up and down like a blonde gummy ball, still screaming at the top of her lungs. And everyone is just staring—the nurses, the doctors, the patients, the EMTs—and no one makes a move to help him."

As much as I tried to get away, I couldn't resist being curious.

"Do you know what had her in such a tizzy?"

"Everyone knows! That's the best part about it. Apparently the board kicked her out because someone filed a lawsuit against her, some weird shit of improper conduct and stuff. Made it out as if she'd hooked up with one of her patients, on duty no less. But now it turns out that the P.I. has come forward and claimed that he'd tampered with the 'evidence,' and all has been in the then-still-husband's name. Apparently he knew about the affair, then set it up that an actress he paid and the P.I. both got admitted into the ER. The girl did some touching and leaning in so the P.I. could take the supposedly compromising pictures. The whole thing came up when he broke his arm for real and one of the nurses not only recognized him from before but from an ad she's seen online, and then it was only a matter of some arm twisting, know what I mean?"

I hoped for the guy's sake that she didn't mean literally, but knowing Zoe, I didn't get my hopes up. Marcy took my noncommital grunt as affirmation and went on.

"Now the thing's out in the open and the hospital has already suspended our new head of the ER the day before he starts the job, investigation pending. Seriously, I have to ask around if someone filmed this with their phone. You had to be there, sure, but as you missed out, you deserve to see at least some of it."

I opened my mouth, about to tell Marcy that her recount already served as comedy enough, when I heard Jack clear his throat behind Marcy's back.

"Does that mean they'll consider giving her the job back? Would at least make it easier to get back in if you're chummy with the boss, Erin."

I winced just hearing Jack's voice, but he being, well, him, he could easily top that.

Marcy whipped around with a small yelp, then her eyes went wide as she took Jack in.

"Hey there, Jack. Hey there, Jack's underpants!"

And there wasn't anything else he was wearing, and no way to do damage control now. Marcy turned back to me, a calculating look on her face.

"At least you did something worthwhile in that absence! Or, should I say, someone?" she jeered, showing way too many teeth for that grimace to still count as a smile.

Now both Jack and I made a face, but there wasn't really any sense in denying it. Didn't mean I couldn't put my foot into my mouth, though, as it turned out.

"It's not what it looks like."

That got me a weird look from Jack, which Marcy of course didn't miss.

"It isn't?" she asked.

"Yeah, am I wearing too many clothes? I thought you'd be less comfortable with me wearing your panties instead," Jack supplied, helpful as always.

"It's complicated," I deadpanned at them both before brushing past Marcy and trying to get back to my room. Jack didn't even make an attempt to move aside, and trying to stare him down wasn't yielding any results.

"I must be missing something vital here, because there's only so much complication two people can rack up," Marcy informed us both.

"Move it, damn you!" I hissed at Jack, then shot Marcy a look over my shoulder. "Two people, maybe, but if you throw in a third, you get a real mess."

I probably shouldn't have said that, but it made Jack flinch, giving me a chance to shove him aside and squeeze into my room. I hastily put on a less-torn pair of jeans than I had worn to work and started sniffing bras until I found one that hadn't suffered through several shifts in a row, giving Marcy plenty of time to consider. Once all clothes were in their appropriate place and I'd put on enough deodorant to hide what my brief wash-up hadn't removed, I ducked back under Jack's arm.

Marcy was looking at him with shrewd consideration, as if that alone would let her work out all the details. Jack busied himself with returning her scrutiny with a slight smile that held just enough smugness to make me want to wipe it off his face.

"That explains a lot," she surmised, likely trying to make me spill more details that way. "So who was it who didn't use enough lube and left her sore for an entire day—you or Simon?"

It shouldn't have surprised me too much that she jumped to the obvious conclusion, but it still pissed me off that Jack was only too happy to confirm it.

"When was that, during the week or on a weekend?"

"You worked out a schedule?" She chuckled, shaking her head. "Week, I think."

"Then it was likely Simon's fault. Some of us do keep normal working hours, so I likely missed out on that one."

Glaring at both of them, I made my way to the hallway to hunt down some shoes.

"It was Simon, and there was some lube involved, but that wasn't the reason I couldn't sit for a whole day." Then it occurred to me what else I'd just dished out, and cursed under my breath. "Damn it!"

"Hey, I don't judge," Marcy replied, raising both hands, but her grin was of the shit-eating kind. "We're all one big, happy family where everyone knows everyone's sex stories! Or it's just the moon phase. Whatever. Guess in the light of full disclosure I should probably tell you something now."

That made me halt in the middle of putting my jacket on.

"You're pregnant?"

Not that I thought she was, but it would have fit the bill. Marcy scowled for a moment but shook her head.

"Nope, but remember Luke, my on-again, off-again boyfriend? Turns out, he proposed last weekend, and I said yes!"

I was too stunned to react for a moment, but Jack thankfully jumped in to deliver the hug that I was obliged to. Marcy didn't seem to mind, engagement nonwithstanding.

"That's great—congratulations!" I finally got out once she was free of half-naked hunk again.

Her smile clearly showed that she thought so, too, but then it dimmed a little.

"I didn't know when to tell you, with all the shit you've been going through lately. Thing is, he also asked me to move in with him, and I said yes to that, too!" Which meant that I was quickly running out of options of how not to get evicted end of next month. Marcy must have expected my less than frenetic reaction, because she was quick to raise her hands. "Not right now, unless, you know, you're of a mind to move out yourself." She sent a fake conspiratorial look in Jack's direction, then frowned when he just stared back at her blankly. "Luke's starting a tour with Doctors Without Borders in a couple of weeks, and we decided to make things official once he's back. But you know that I've been thinking about going myself for years, and that would be the perfect opportunity."

I didn't have to think about what to reply, even if it made me even more uneasy.

"Of course—you go. Don't worry about me."

"We'll find a way to make things work," Jack offered me my own words from earlier back.

The fact that now he seemed to believe them made me feel just a little better myself.

"I won't be long. You can stay here if you'd like. I'm halfway sure Marcy won't kick you out if you don't wear a shirt."

"Gotta make the best of my last months as a free woman!" Marcy crooned, then looked at Jack sideways. "Something wrong, because you're looking like a lost puppy who just got abandoned. I promise I won't make you look at bridal magazines."

"Nah, I'm good," he replied, but his voice was hoarse.

Sighing, I rubbed my eyes.

"Wanna come with me? But, quite frankly, I doubt it will be smooth sailing either way, and as much as a sensitive man who can show emotions is nice sometimes, I don't see how this will work better if you start crying in the thick of it."

So maybe I was an insensitive bitch, but Jack looked a step away from needing a box of tissues, and Kara's message made me guess that she was going to chew both of us out if we made the mistake of showing up together. Or at all, and in Jack's case I wasn't sure he'd survive that right now. Her, *Bitch, I'm going to cut you for this!* was clear enough.

"You're probably right, but that still makes me feel like a damn coward."

Exhaling loudly, I tried to offer him a smile, if a shaky one.

"You don't have to fight my battles for me. Besides, if this works out even half as well as I hope, there'll be plenty of discussions that you can join later."

He nodded but lingered as if he wanted to say—or do—something else, but if I didn't leave now, I'd never make it out of that door.

"I'll let you know as soon as I know more. Promise."

With that I turned around and left, feeling like half of my heart and the better part of my courage remained behind with Jack.

-17-

As such things go, I was running exceedingly late. First, I missed the train, then the bus took forever to pull up to the curb, and finally I got stuck in the heavy Friday evening traffic. When I ran out of patience, I decided to walk the last couple of blocks, but although that was without a doubt faster, it also made me show up at the venue of the book party annoyed, winded, and with way too many jumbled thoughts lodged inside my head.

I knew I was out of luck the moment I walked inside and checked my watch. With only five minutes until the bash started, there was no way I could track Simon down and have any sort of civil conversation with him. I had only a moment to gather myself before someone called my name behind me, making me jump.

Flight was no longer an option, I realized, when Linda Chalks, also known as Simon's mother, waved at me, already herding her husband before her in my direction. Any other day I would have welcomed meeting them, particularly somewhere I didn't really know anyone, but right then they were at the top of my list of people I'd hoped to avoid like the plague.

No one in their right mind would have accused Simon's mother of being old enough to have a son his age, but for the first time, I could actually see him in her. Temperament-wise he was more like his father, but I'd never noticed that he had her smile. Or maybe I was just projecting, which was entirely possible.

And over her shoulder, off to the side of the foyer next to a small bar area, I caught a glimpse of Simon and Kara. They were both sitting on a low bench, him sunk over with his elbows on his knees, face in his hands, while she sat next to him, prim and proper and obviously bristling like a cat while she kept talking to him nonstop, not even pausing to draw breath. My heart ached just seeing him like that, but before I could move in their direction, Linda had caught up with me, and there was no evading her.

"So good to see you again, Erin! Simon wasn't sure if you'd have time when I asked him last week. Come, let me look at you— you are such a beautiful girl!"

I wondered briefly if that was an improvement. Most days she said I had a beautiful soul, and once she'd even used the term "aura." I was half convinced she'd been high that evening. It happened.

It was surprisingly easy to return her smile with one of my own, likely because I'd always gotten along great with her, even if she scared and confused me half of the time. Lacking my own biological role-model for comparison, Jack's mom had always been my point of reference, and the two women couldn't be more different. Linda was loud, foul-mouthed, got offended when anyone addressed her as anyone's mother, and was more likely to offer me a joint than a tray of cookies. I didn't even know if she could cook. What she could do was throw parties and paint pictures that held more emotions than other people's movies. Like her son, she could rock that whole "not of this world artist" thing, and as she looked me over critically, I got the sense that, also like Simon, nothing escaped her if she just set her mind to finding it.

Simon's father was the polar opposite to her—quiet, laid back, and often prone to accidentally offending people by asking them inappropriate things. There was a reason for why we got along great. Dinner conversations with him were always hilarious, at least for me, although Jack had told me on more than one occasion that if I explained one more time how a vaginoplasty was performed, he would run out screaming. Today I wished for that to happen for another reason than simply to annoy him. Having dinner again at Simon's parents' home implied that by the end of the day the three of us would still be talking to each other, which sounded like a huge improvement from what ate at my soul right now.

I got through the usual greetings—and Thomas's question about whether I'd performed any interesting surgeries lately—with a straight face, but by the time I hoped I could extract myself from them, Kara suddenly appeared at my side, with no hint of Simon anywhere. Her focus was on Simon's parents as she greeted Thomas cheerfully, then did that weird French air-kissing thing with Linda. Very European, very not me. Another day I might have said something snarky, but I couldn't even run away now, as a minute later the microphone-enhanced voice of a woman, presumably Simon's publicist, announced that everyone should please join her in the main room, and refreshments would be served presently. Before I knew what was happening, Kara had looped her arm around mine and started dragging me through the open doors, then quickly took a left that made us end up at the back wall of the room where we had a good view of the stage and were as out of earshot of anyone as we could get and still be in the same room.

Kara's eyes remained fixed on the busty platinum blonde on the stage who was now prattling on about Simon's many accomplishments, a fake smile on her face that showed enough teeth to make a shark turn green with envy.

"Didn't think you'd show up here today," she started, her grip on my arm tightening slightly as if she was afraid I'd try to run.

The thought might have occurred to me.

"Because of your heart-warming message?"

For a second, her smile turned real, but quickly flipped back into a grimace.

"As if that could deter you. No, because of what apparently happened today. I figured you'd hole up somewhere and throw yourself a pity party." She leaned closer then, and it was too late to pull away when I realized that she was sniffing me. How she pulled that off without actually looking at me was beyond me. "Ah, the smell of cheap deodorant and desperation."

"You should know. You've rolled around in it way more often than I."

Kara opened her mouth, doubtlessly to deliver some scathing remark, then paused as she sniffed again.

"So that's where Jack ended up. I was wondering when he didn't pick up his phone. Guess it makes sense that you reek like him when you've been literally rolling around in his sweat. Classy as always."

"At least I don't blabber about other people's private lives to just anyone," I remarked dryly.

Now her eyes flitted to me and remained on my face for a couple of seconds before returning to the stage.

"I might have heard more about your sex life today than I ever wanted to know, but Simon's been surprisingly constrained regarding details. It's kind of hard to keep up with the proceedings when half of what you're listening to gets redacted." She paused, and her real smile re-appeared, this time to stay. "Guess I never told him about the time Linda called me when she renovated his old room and accidentally stumbled over his porn stash. We had quite a lot of fun researching the implications together. I think by the end of that neither of us could sit upright from how much we'd drunk. If you were ever wondering about the cryptic remarks she keeps dropping sometimes that make him look at her cross-eyed, now you know what's going on."

I'd never really noticed that, but then I'd been rather oblivious about that side of Simon until it directly involved me.

Not knowing what to reply to that, I held my tongue, and Kara gave me a brief, disappointed pout for it.

"Oh, come on, like I give a shit about what you two are up to in the bedroom. Or elsewhere. Just thought I should let you know that I know how that implicates you. You know, ho code and the like."

That made me snort.

"Ho code? Seriously?"

"So you haven't forgotten how to speak!" she cheered, then turned serious again. "I have to admit, I've underestimated you. The worst I thought I'd ever hear about your sex life is the lack thereof, but you've been quite the busy bee, now, haven't you?"

"No more so than anyone else involved," I pointed out succinctly.

That made her chuckle.

"I expect shit like that from Jack," she replied. "On a good day I could maybe admit that Simon's not a completely asexual being. But you? Didn't they vote you 'least likely to end up in a threesome' in high school? Seriously, what the fuck got into you? Everyone knows that you don't fuck where you sleep. Or was that shit where you eat? I can never remember."

"Just for your information, it wasn't my idea, and I didn't instigate it. Not that it's any of your business."

"Don't be such a spoilsport. Simon already left out all the good stuff, so it's your obligation to fill in the blanks now," she continued to needle me.

I hadn't expected her not to tear me a new one within the first five minutes, but with Kara, I never could tell when that might happen.

"What did he tell you? Not to sound cruel, but his version might be somewhat different than mine. Or the truth."

She heaved a theatrical sigh as if I'd asked her to do something incredibly hard and laborious.

"The Cliff Notes version? The three of you were screwing each other while Simon and you had your thing going on the side. Jack got jealous because he realized that he'd somehow become the third wheel, so he seduced Simon to try to wrench you apart to have you to himself, which kind of worked because deep down you're an insecure scaredy cat."

I blinked, surprised how close to my version of the events that was. Kara noticed but held her tongue, clearly waiting for me to reply. Then I realized the reason for that grin.

"Are you smug because you got one part of it right?" I asked.

"Not just part of it, the main catalyst, please! That's something to be proud of," she jeered back.

"It's not. It's pathetic and petty."

"Potato, potahto." She waved me off. "The real question is, what are you going to do now?"

Just then a waiter approached us, offering us champagne flutes on a tray, and I took that opportunity to extricate myself from Kara's grasp and take two glasses. The waiter didn't even blink when I drained the first and handed it back to him straight away, while Kara shook her head in silent reproach.

"I don't know. Talk, I guess," I offered once we were on our own again.

"Is that what you and Jack did today? Talk, until you were both sweaty and panting?"

Her tone held just a hint of scorn, but it was too much to ignore.

"You're aware that I didn't start this? Any of it. I almost walked in on them doing it. Why am I to blame now if I don't turn into the paragon of celibacy?" I bit out.

Kara looked playfully aghast for a moment, then shrugged.

"It's so typical that you and Jack gang up against the world. Just saying."

"That wasn't my idea, either," I informed her. "Jack turned up on my doorstep this afternoon. What should I have done, kick him out? You were likely next on his list. Would you have preferred that?" She held my gaze evenly but sipped her champagne a little too fast, making me realize that for once I'd hit the bull's eye right on. "That's it, isn't it? You're pissed because he came to me, not to you!"

Her shrug was less than convincing, and when I kept staring at her, she eventually caved.

"Okay, maybe a little. I just hate being excluded," Kara admitted.

"Are you aware that you're just as childish as he is sometimes?"

That made her consider her reply for a moment.

"Maybe I am, but then, don't I have reason aplenty? Inside of a few weeks, you've managed to have not one, but two insanely bright and handsome guys panting after you, while I'm left at the sidelines to watch this whole spectacle unfold."

"Trust me, it's less amusing when you're caught in the thick of it. And what about Dan? There's still the country club," I pointed out.

Her answering laugh was loud and brash, making a few heads turn in our direction.

"That's true. Too bad I can't go there tomorrow. They're having their yearly bake sale."

"Other plans?"

"Well, there's Linda's garden party. You know, the one I keep reminding you of, and which you've obviously forgotten about again?"

"Ah, that one," I confirmed her guess. As if I didn't have enough to keep track of right now that gave me hives, a garden party was exactly what I needed.

"That one." She laughed, and, much to my surprise, a rather insipid smile crept onto her face. "I might be bringing someone. You don't know him yet. His name's Andy."

"Let me guess... a banker? Broker? CEO of a start-up turned billion-dollar corporation?" I proposed.

She didn't even frown at me calling her superficial.

"Actually, he's working as a barista at my favorite coffee shop. Nice guy, really. So not my type, but with the peanut gallery all up in your business, I might stand a chance of actually introducing him to people before he gets scared and runs off, never to be seen again."

That gave me pause, but then neither Jack, Simon, nor I had ever exactly bonded with any of the guys Kara kept dragging along. Not our fault, if anyone asked me, but I was careful not to point that out.

"Nice way to get back on topic, by the way." I had to give her that.

"I know." She grinned. "So what are you going to do now? Just talk?"

"Why is it any of your business?" I asked, a little suspicious.

"It isn't," she agreed, surprising me. "But Simon's my friend, and so are you and Jack. As much as I love teasing you, I don't like seeing any of you in any real emotional pain, and if Simon's any indication, the three of you managed to really fuck each other up. Besides, you can't very well be interested in hearing about all my most interesting conquests and undertakings when you're all busy getting your collective shit together. I'm just looking out for myself here."

It gave me the strangest kind of warm feeling to realize that she really cared, in her own way.

"How bad is he?" I asked, chewing on my lip as unease continued to creep up my spine.

Kara made a face, her eyes back in front where the blonde had finally beat it and removed her abundantly displayed goods from the podium to give Simon the stage. I hadn't had a good chance to look at him before, and watching him now, I had a hard time at first seeing any signs that anything had happened today. He was wearing that sports jacket again from the night we'd been out with Kara and Jack, combined with dark jeans and a form-fitting black T-shirt underneath. It took me a moment to realize that it was one of those he usually wore in the attic. As he looked out over the crowd, his face was calm and composed, and his voice was steady and strong as he started thanking everyone for coming here tonight.

Then his eyes skipped to where we were standing, and for a moment our gazes met. He glanced away quickly, and a look of pain crossed his face, but was gone before it really registered. If I hadn't known him so well or hadn't been looking for something, I would likely have missed it.

"That depends." Kara cut my observation short. "I think he's taking the entire getting his heart ripped out by those he feels closest to thing rather well, considering the circumstances. He sounded defeated rather than angry when we had our little chat right before you showed up. It could be a brave front he's showing to the world, though. It's been a while since we had a talk like that, and he's grown a lot harder and colder since he was seventeen." She considered something for a moment, then looked at me with concern shining in her eyes. "It really isn't my business, and even if it was, you should know best what you're going to do, but if you care about him, don't screw this up. I'm not saying that it all rests on your shoulders, and he's old enough that no single person can truly screw him up for life anymore, but this goes a lot deeper than any relationship that only lasted a couple of weeks should go. If you don't want to continue what you've had going on, try to at least save your friendship. I think he could deal with a clean cut now, even if you and Jack hook up. What he can't deal with is being led along."

I had to blink several times to keep myself from looking at her cross-eyed.

"Did he mention the part where I told him that I loved him, and he looked back at me as if I'd just told him this was all a joke?"

Her smile was rueful as she nodded.

"He mentioned that. Not one of his brighter moments, I might add."

"Then why would you think that I'd end up with Jack?"

Now her smile turned condescending, until she realized that it wasn't a rhetorical question.

"Seriously? The way you two have always behaved, it's a wonder that I don't accidentally call you Cersei on a regular basis! You do lack the awesome hair, which makes it easier, I guess."

"And there's the lack of psychotic offspring," I pointed out.

"And that. Have you finally caught up on this season?" she asked.

"Not even started it," I had to admit. "Between working and trying to juggle two guys, something had to fall short."

Kara heaved a theatrical sigh.

"See, that would be a deal breaker for me. You're so lucky that we're not screwing each other."

"Be still my heart. The very idea has my stomach all aflutter," I stage-whispered.

"Oh, shut up. You know that I'm irresistible. And I give the best advice."

"I don't know about that."

She raised her brows at my retort, then pointedly jerked her chin toward the front of the room.

"You. Him. Talk. Either be blunt and forward, or let him down gently, but don't string him along. Maybe pad out your bra beforehand—shoving your tits into a guy's face seems to get you everywhere. Now, shoo! There are a couple of lit critics here that I need to work over for the shit they've been writing about the book this week. That they even dare show their faces here is inexcusable."

"Really, the gall!" I huffed.

Kara muttered something under her breath, then leaned close. "Good luck. You'll need it."

And then she left me standing at the back of the room, all by myself, with only my dark thoughts for company.

I must have been scowling quite a lot because no one dared approach me over the next couple of hours, which turned them into their very own ordeal. The first thing I did after Kara left me to my own devices was text Jack that I would be later than expected as I hadn't gotten the chance to talk to Simon yet. He replied with a one letter acknowledgment that made me wonder if he was really too down to write more, or so busy regaling Marcy with tales of our explicit adventures that he had no time. I didn't know what I would have preferred, but the latter sounded healthier.

The party took forever to wind down. I had no idea how long they usually took, but even with a quick pass by the open bar and a few canapés, I felt like I was dying from boredom while anxiety ate away at me. Kara's words left me hopeful but also scared the shit out of me. I certainly had time aplenty to watch Simon from afar, and from what I could tell, he didn't look at me again once. He was busy talking with people, but even when they left him some breathing space, he didn't look even remotely approachable to me. I couldn't help that sickening feeling of jealousy creep up whenever another easily excitable woman did her best to throw herself at him, even though I tried telling myself that likely none of them could offer him anything he'd want. I'd never noticed how many guys made goo-goo eyes at him, too.

My only saving grace was that he didn't seem to be aware of any of that happening.

It was well after 11:00 p.m. when the party started winding down, likely because people were either flocking to other venues or leaving for home. And suddenly Simon was gone, leaving me with panic rising inside of me. I was ready to freak out when my phone chimed with a text from Kara.

Check the hallway by the bathrooms. You're welcome.

I didn't hesitate but left the room immediately, familiar with the venue thanks to the five cups of coffee I'd chugged once my lack of sleep had started catching up to me. I could only worry myself into ulcer territory so long before my body started clamoring for its due.

I'd barely made it around a corner when I almost collided with a solid, tall body, and it took me a second to realize that I knew every line of it all too well. For a moment, all I could do was gawk up at Simon, and he looked actually startled to find me here. Then I saw him shut me out, his face becoming a calm, composed, but cold mask. I'd seen that happen a few times, particularly when someone annoyed him, but I'd never expected him to look at me like that.

Remembering Kara's words, I decided to cut right to the chase.

"Can we talk? I know this is weeks overdue, but, please?"

The way he looked down at me—at least physically, and the sudden guilty feeling rising inside of me made it a mental thing, too—made me lick my lips, but that didn't seem to sway him one bit.

"Kind of ironic that now you finally know how to beg?"

My first impulse was to keep a tight lid on my temper, but after a moment I tore it right off.

"I can play nice if I want to, but you're at least consistent in acting like an asshole to me. What does that do for you, Simon? Does that keep you warm and happy when you're all alone?"

Maybe I should have stopped after the first part, but my words, if not my tone, did the job and wiped that arrogant, cold look off his face. What lurked underneath wasn't exactly better because seeing anguish in his eyes made me feel like the lowest kind of shit immediately, but at least it made him seem a little more open to my suggestion.

"Talk, please? Just hear me out, and if you don't like what I have to say, you can leave and I won't bother you again."

That made him look even sadder, but after a moment he nodded.

"Sure. Talk."

It was then that I realized that while I'd spent hours agonizing over what I wanted to say to him, I was all out of words now.

Taking a deep breath, I tried to come up with something smart, but ended up blurting out the first thing I could think of.

"I had sex with Jack. Not to get back at you, exactly, but the thought crossed my mind. For all intents and purposes, we're even now."

He took that in calmly, his utter lack of reaction angering me a little. He could have looked a little annoyed at least, if not because of me, then for Jack's sake.

"I wasn't aware that we were keeping score, but if you want to then yes, that makes us even."

I hated that he didn't give me any point I could latch on to, but at least the block in my mind was dwindling now.

"Does it make any sense that I'm trying to save what we have?"

"Are you? Trying, I mean. Because that must be the worst possible way to start a reconciliation. I fucked the guy you were stupid enough to fall for. Great start."

That point definitely went to him.

"At least I'm being honest. And it's not like I can't relate to the feeling."

Simon winced, but I got absolutely no satisfaction from his reaction—quite disappointing.

"I'm sorry that I hurt you. I really didn't know," he began, then looked away, using one of his hands to comb through his short hair, making the dark strands stick up. "That's not true. The part about being sorry is, but the rest is not. I didn't want to see it. I guess on some level I knew, but it was easier to ignore it. You see, you're not the only one who can set herself up for disappointment."

I didn't know what to make of that, but the fact that we were both talking now had to count for something.

"I didn't tell you to put any pressure on you. It was kind of my last resort. Couldn't think of much else to say, kind of like now."

That made him smile, even if it was a sad smile.

"You're not alone with that, either. Exactly when did just talking become such a fundamentally hard task?"

"No idea, but it is ridiculous." Sighing loudly, I tried to think of something else, but my mind was strangely blank. "Why don't we take this somewhere a little more private where we don't have a good chance that your mom barges in on us any minute now? If I can avoid clueing her in to what we've been up to, I'd be much obliged."

"Sounds good," he replied, but I didn't miss the hesitation in his voice.

"And I should probably call Jack to join us for that talk," I added cautiously.

A muscle jumped in Simon's jaw when he gnashed his teeth, but before he could protest, I raised my hands placatingly.

"He's an idiot, I'm not going to protest that, but he's still our friend, and he's in this as much as either of us, whether we like it or not. Unless you want to break off all contact, we should do this with him present. Maybe he has a few things to cough up that will make your decision easier."

Simon looked away, and when he caught my gaze again, a strange kind of tension had seeped into his shoulders.

"I knew what he was doing, or trying to. Get you away from me and choose him, I mean. I've known for weeks, and I didn't do a single thing to stop it. I realized that something was going on when he started getting cranky and felt neglected, I knew that it was likely to blow up in our faces, and chances were good that you'd get hurt in the fallout, and still I did nothing. On some level I realized that he was just using me to set up the next stage of his plan, but I let it happen, because right then it was all the same to me if I could just get what I wanted out of it. Does that change your view of me? Can you still trust someone who does that to you?"

What surprised me about it was just how honest he was, and while hearing all that hurt, it could have been worse. At least it was the truth.

"Why didn't you do anything?"

It was the obvious question to ask, and I knew him well enough to realize that he wanted to tell me the answer.

"Because as much as I hate that I've become a pawn in his game, it didn't mean I wasn't petty enough to play my own. You have no idea how gratifying it was to have a piece of you that he couldn't have and keep dangling it in front of his nose, just out of his reach. And if I'm honest, giving in to him when he made a move on me felt like I was turning those exact same tables on you."

I thought about that for a moment, and while it pissed me off, it didn't make me change my mind.

"One thing is for sure. If we don't make this work, we might as well check ourselves into therapy, because this shit can't be healthy."

"Agreed. And, as I said, I'm sorry, however pathetic and superfluous that sounds."

I nodded, and he motioned for me to precede him on the way back into the main room.

It didn't take long to wrap things up, and not ten minutes later we were standing at the curb waiting for a taxi, only inches between us, but it could have been miles. I'd texted Jack to meet us at the house, and while his reply hadn't sounded enthusiastic, I was sure that he'd be there by the time we arrived. The few tidbits Simon had revealed kept zooming through my head, making it hard not to sink back into a bleak state of frustration and anger.

Then his fingers brushed against mine, making me jump but not withdraw my hand. He hesitated, looking down at our hands, then wrapped his around mine.

"I won't lie to you. I can't tell you that I love you, because that would be a lie. But it means the world to me that you do, and I could really get used to waking up next to you, each and every day."

He offered me a smile then, small and weak, but it was a smile, and as the taxi finally pulled over, I managed to return it with one of my own.

Coming from anyone else, those words would have hurt me deeply, but while they still grated, they also warmed something inside of me that had been frozen since I walked out of that damn bathroom this morning.

And it got better still when we filed into the back of the cab and Simon leaned close so he could murmur a single word, just to me.

"Yet."

-18-

By the time we got home, Jack was already there, sitting on the front steps. The lights were on, so I presumed that he'd been inside before, but for whatever reason had chosen to wait for us. Simon just shot him a quick glance before he strode by him, so I stopped long enough to offer Jack a hand and pulled him along with me. When I realized that I was stalling, I let go of his hand quickly, though, trying not to upset the fragile balance by doing something stupid.

Once inside, I fired up the coffee maker, although the way my pulse was racing, I doubted that I could have fallen asleep if I'd tried.

"Anyone else want a cup? But only if you trust yourself not to turn it into a projectile. The last thing I need tonight is a trip to the burn ward."

The guys both declined, making me wonder if they just didn't want any, or whether I would have to play referee. The thought wasn't as hilarious as it should have been, considering that the last time I'd grabbed a coffee here—and completely forgotten about it—they'd pretty much ganged up on me, and not in the way I liked.

Right then the kitchen held too many bad memories for me to want to have any conversation there, let alone one that would likely take up the better part of the night, so I shooed them on into the living room. Simon fell onto his usual seat on one side of the couch, Jack taking his a little more gingerly. Settling between them felt weird, so I opted for pushing stuff aside on the coffee table and sitting down there. It was hard and uncomfortable, and perfectly suited my mood.

Both of them were looking at me now, avoiding more than glances at each other, making me pinch the bridge of my nose in frustration. This had all sounded way simpler inside my head. Taking a deep breath, I forced myself to relax, not that it helped.

"Before we start this—one question. Has anyone said or done something to you that you feel is unforgivable, and consequently you've got no interest in working things out and are simply here because there hasn't been enough shit flinging happening today yet?"

Simon's lips started twisting into a smile but it never came to bloom, while Jack just stared at me with a jaded look on his face. Apparently that was as good as I'd get.

"Okay. Return question—do you want to work out some kind of compromise right now? Because I'm not doing this to myself if all we do is fight, and in the end postpone things to an infinite day later. I haven't slept in over forty hours, and you can tear into each other without me, unless your intent is to blame me for something, and then you can just go fuck yourself straight away."

Now they did exchange glances, making my brows shoot up.

"What?"

"If this wasn't such a fucked up, miserable situation, I'd say that you're damn hot when you're angry."

I glared at Jack until the smirk disappeared from his face.

"I'm serious. I've put up with too much bullshit from all of us, myself included, to let that go on any longer."

Simon seemed surprised at my admission, making me sigh with frustration as I leaned forward, elbows on my knees.

"Look, I'm not stupid, or not that stupid. I know that I did my fair share to contribute to this mess. The way I see it, the main catalyst of this was lack of communication. And while I didn't actively plot to play anyone's insecurities against someone else's, I internalized my doubts and shut anyone down who tried to get through to me. If I'd done what I always do and gotten right in your faces, none of this would have happened, or at least not escalated so fast."

Jack looked less pleased than Simon with my conclusion, but apparently neither of them had any intention of doing any talking, so I forced myself to take the next step.

"There are two possible resolutions to this. Well, I guess in detail there are more, but two categories. Either we get our shit together and manage a kind of restart of what we've had going on for a while now, including all three of us in one way or another, or we reduce this to any possible kind of platonic friendships that at least I feel we've never had, not for a long time." Looking first at Simon, then at Jack, I went on. "My own choice would be the former, but then I spend the least time available for any kind of social interaction, and I'm not living here." Turning back to Simon, I hesitated for a moment, but then added the last part I still felt like cringing over. "Marcy told me today that she's going to move in with her boyfriend, and I can't support myself and the apartment alone. I could look for a new roommate, but it was hard enough to hash things out with Marcy in the first place."

Simon nodded, pensive.

"How bad are you off?"

I shrugged.

"You know how much my student loans are because your education didn't cost much less than mine?" He nodded. "Well, then add a hefty addition to that for my malpractice insurance, and I haven't been able to pay back much more than interest in my loans over the last couple of years. I make enough to support myself, but not enough for more than a cubbyhole."

I felt a little ticked off that he made me explain that, but Simon didn't bat an eyelash.

"Move in with us. Whatever we end up making of this, we have room, and you don't have to help with the rent if things get tight."

"Just promise you won't even try to cook!" Jack interjected, making Simon nod in agreement immediately.

"I guess... thank you for insulting my finer feminine qualities?"

Jack snorted.

"We both know that between the two of us, I'm the girl. You know how to operate machinery so coffee and microwave meals are options, but I think I remember you burning water. Water! And I told you this would happen back in high school."

"You only took home ec because of all the girls there!" I accused, remembering that conversation all too well.

"Yeah, well, that, too. Obviously."

I rolled my eyes but had to fight the tears welling up in them immediately.

"Thanks, guys. I know you don't have to do this, but it's good to know that you have my back."

Jack nodded, but Simon was biting his lower lip, and when I eyed him askance, he snorted.

"There might be ulterior motives involved. Do I really need to spell this out?"

That at least helped me get over my sappiness.

"Then we should get back to discussing that?" I proposed.

"Guess so," Simon agreed.

I fell silent, trying to gather my thoughts.

"I don't know what else to say," I offered. "I hate this whole fucked up situation, and if there's a way to clear it up, I'm all for it. Ball's in your court now."

Both guys focused on something between the floor and my knees, before Simon sent Jack a long glance that made Jack grimace. I couldn't read the look on Simon's face, but Jack seemed to have no such problem, and he didn't sound happy as he picked up the thread from me.

"I get that I'm the black sheep in this. I deserve it, I know, yada yada. I know you both well enough to know that you both, in your own ways, will make me pay for this. Which is fair, I guess. I just have to be around for that to happen, and I'm not exactly sure how I can make up for instigating this. And it's not like you both didn't need a good slap in the face to get your own issues cleared up."

It would have been so much easier to just brand him as the scapegoat and be done with it, but in true Jack fashion he managed to twist it all around just enough to spread the blame. That I agreed with him helped only so much.

Simon didn't take his statement much better than I had.

"You could have done that by just telling us to stop being idiots, too. And neither of us set anyone up for disappointment, while you actively played us against each other."

"And you were aware of that and didn't lift a finger to stop me," he pointed out.

Apparently, I'd been the only one completely in the dark of what had been going on, and that didn't exactly help improve my mood. Simon glared back at Jack, but then looked away, clearly uncomfortable.

"So I'm human. Don't act so surprised. It's not like you've never lost your wits over anyone."

That prompted Jack to look cross-eyed at him, as if he hadn't really taken Simon's previous statement seriously.

"I would say I sympathize, but really, I don't," I said to no one in particular, and the fact that now both of them were looking guilty was at least a little amusing.

"How exactly did we slide into this mess?" Jack mused, but neither of us had an answer for him.

"We should perhaps start with clearing up what exactly we want, and what we can compromise on?" Simon proposed. "Short and long term options, if you want to, but I highly doubt that any big plans we come up with now will hold much longer than the weekend."

"Shall I go first?"

Jack's offer surprised me, and when both Simon and I nodded, he sagged deeper into the cushions of the couch, as if he had to force himself to go on, which wasn't that unlikely, come to think of it.

"I think we've established that I'm an idiot."

"Nothing new there," I interrupted, incapable of keeping my nasty streak in check. Jack grunted, but otherwise ignored me.

"I guess I can live with reducing everything to a minimum if it means that you both don't completely shut me out. Never thought I'd say this, but even after the stunt I've pulled, your friendship is worth a lot more to me than sex. Took being afraid that I'd lost you both for me to see that. I'm ready to promise you to change, but realistically speaking, neither of you will even buy that bullshit, and I'm not sure you'd still like me if I changed."

"A little less conniving backstabbing might be nice," Simon offered.

"And cut that pseudo possessive crap. It was kind of fun when you threatened a couple of guys who rubbed me the wrong way, but we're not in high school anymore. Besides, I can take care of myself," I added.

Jack listened to both of us in silence, and while I could tell that he burned to contradict me at the very least, he only inclined his head in agreement.

"Just let me know when I'm overstepping my limits. I will let you run face first into the wall next time without trying to stop you. Or shove you."

"Much obliged," Simon grumbled, then took over from Jack. "I honestly don't know what to say. What I want mostly depends on what the two of you want to do with me."

That created some obvious confusion, and he turned to Jack first.

"Just how much of this morning was real, and how much were you just screwing with me?"

Jack considered that for a moment, and he looked more guilty than uncomfortable.

"A lot more than I'm happy to admit. Not because I'm insecure about my sexuality or some shit, but it was easier to plan when I thought I was just manipulating you. It's a lot harder to pull that off when shit suddenly gets real."

Simon took that with a simple nod and a lack of emotion that would have driven me crazy if it was directed at me.

"I think that's something we need to discuss between the two of us once I'm not itching to do the next best, most hurtful thing I can come up with to you, and I'm not talking about anything physical."

For only a few words venom leaked into his voice, but it was enough to make Jack fidget. Simon turned to me then, and I got the feeling he'd started with the part that was easier for him when I realized that he was now internalizing that very spite.

"You seem to be mostly mad at Jack, but I deserve at least as much of your scorn as he does. Maybe not as a person, but as your Dom. I clearly let you down. I should never have let you withdraw like that, and I shouldn't have used that insecurity of yours to ignore what else was going on. I don't have any valid excuse. Like I just said, emotions can fuck you up and make you do weird things, but it was my responsibility to hold myself above that. Not because of some bullshit like emotions, feelings, or love have no place in the playroom, but simply because it was dishonest of me, and I have to put your safety and sanity over my own, which

I didn't. It's more than enough that I'd understand it if you'd say that you don't want to continue that part of our relationship, although I'd really miss it. I hope that you still want to be with me otherwise, because I would miss that more."

There was a lot in that speech that I hadn't seen coming, least of all the end. It kind of overwhelmed me, but as none of it made me want to get up and run, I figured that I already had my answer there.

"I don't know exactly how I want to balance things between us," I told Simon, then included Jack in the conversation. "Or all three of us. Particularly if I move in with you and have to deal with your everyday bullshit every day." So maybe I wasn't at my most eloquent today, but what I was trying to say clearly came across when both of them shared a quick, amused look. I took a moment to finish my coffee, then set the mug on the table behind me before I turned back to the guys, first addressing Jack.

"My beef with you is pretty obvious, and I'm sure we'll find a way to resolve that. I hate to admit it, but there's not much you can do that I won't forgive, and since you got your head back out of your ass, I'd say we'll get back on track. Just don't do anything like that ever again to me, or even my puppy dog love for you won't help you a second time."

"Duly noted," Jack murmured, looking a lot more relieved than his dry remark made it sound.

Turning to Simon, I caught his gaze and leaned closer, not sure how to articulate my feelings about him.

"I think you're taking this way more seriously than I am, which, all things considered, makes sense, I guess. Just don't beat yourself up over it too much. It wasn't all your fault." He opened his mouth, ready to protest, but closed it again when I scowled. "Okay, let me rephrase that. Maybe it doesn't bother me that much because since our last scene together, I've been mulling over what to do about all that, and I guess

I've gone back to thinking of you more as my friend than my Dom."

I let that sink in, studying his features carefully. Like Jack, he seemed relieved, but also a little bothered. Why that gave me a hint of satisfaction, I wasn't sure, but it made going on much easier.

"We need to have that talk, no question. And I think we need to cut back on the intensity of what we do when we aren't just fooling around."

"But you want to continue," he clarified.

"I do. Very much so. But if I'm going to see you every day, things have to change. And, let's be honest—as much as I love what we do in the playroom, it pulled a number on me mentally, which in the end led to me ignoring Jack completely." As much as I hated to admit it, that part of his accusation had been true.

Simon considered that for a moment, but turned to Jack rather than me.

"Can you give us a minute?"

"Let the grownups talk while I sulk in the background. Sure, why not?" he grumbled, but got up and left for the back hallway.

Simon waited until he'd heard the door to Jack's room close before he started speaking again.

"How long do you intend to keep any sanctions up?"

I didn't like the implication of that.

"Do you think I'll let him off the hook just because I pretty much admitted that I've already forgiven him?"

Simon blinked, momentarily confused, then shook his head.

"I didn't mean that as an accusation. And it's not like you don't have reason enough to accuse me of the very same thing." He held my gaze while I considered that, then leaned back and hid his face in his hands. "I feel so fucking stupid it hurts. I also want to punch him like never before, but at the same time I'm so fucking glad that you're both still around and that we're having this conversation."

He seemed to wait for a reply from me but I honestly couldn't think of one, so I remained silent. Simon let his hands fall to his sides and stared at the ceiling for a few moments, then looked back at me.

"Are you backing down from our set schedule because you're afraid you will make him feel left out? Because I'm not sure—"

I interrupted him there before he could finish that sentence, simply because this once I didn't want to appear like the oblivious git.

"Did you know that he watched us? When we were in the attic, I mean."

I had my answer when Simon frowned, and it wasn't a contemplative expression.

"No. And he told you about that?"

"This afternoon," I admitted. Simon's frown deepened, but now there was pain in his eyes. I quickly went on, not wanting to linger on that. "Jack told me that he watched us, and he got off on it. Not the doing stuff to me part, but my reactions to it. And you obviously knew that he didn't believe a word of what he said when he accused you of abusing me, so it can't have bothered him all that much. To answer your question, I'm not backing down because of him, but because I'm afraid that I will completely lose myself if we step up the pace rather than slow down. It was easy to compartmentalize everything when it was all confined to one set time and one set place, with only a comfortable, sizzling reminder that you still own me even when I'm not kneeling at your feet in between. But if I'm around you all the time, that will drive me insane. Besides, do you really think you two horndogs can keep your hands to yourselves around me all the time so I can get away with a maximum of five orgasms outside of the playroom each week?"

I both hated and loved the typically male smile I got for that.

"I think you'd be sorely disappointed if we even tried. But no, I don't think that would work anymore. And I see where you're coming from."

"Glad you do. So can we agree on putting the kink on the back burner until we have everything else figured out, and confine that to random sessions we do when we're both up to it?"

He gave that some thought, but then shook his head.

"No."

I couldn't help get irritated at his reply.

"No? Why not?"

"Because I feel like that will just exacerbate the underlying problem. And because I'm a petty man who gets off on the thought that a part of you belongs just to me, a part that Jack can never have. He already has more than enough of you."

I didn't know what was stronger inside of me, confusion or annoyance.

"Did you forget my untimely confession from this morning? You already have a part of me that's just yours, as much as I'm currently hating to admit that."

He looked pleased, but not enough to appear smug.

"Of course I didn't forget about that. But can you honestly look me in the eyes and tell me that all you've ever felt for Jack were platonic feelings, and that at no point today you considered just holing up with him and ignoring that I even exist? Don't get me wrong—I'm not accusing you of anything, but you have to admit, the relationship between you and him goes a lot deeper than anything we have built so far. You've had twice the amount of time for it, too, but still. Is it so bad that I want a small, special part of you for myself? Something that I control?"

Maybe it was vanity that made his words sound appealing rather than offensive, or it was the fact that on some level I could understand him, because that very same connection he was talking about would also help set what we had apart from what was forming between him and Jack.

"Aren't you afraid this will just unbalance everything? If we really try to make some kind of triangle work, shouldn't all sides of it be equal?"

"They can never be equal. They have never been equal, and I think we would all lie to ourselves if we pretended they were. And that's not a bad thing. What you and I have doesn't stand in competition to your relationship with Jack. We all have our priorities, but they shift if they need to. We just have to be careful not to upset the balance too much. Do you understand what I'm trying to say? Because this is getting mighty esoteric for simply saying that I want to fuck both of you and never feel guilty about it."

That made me smile, and it was good to be able to do that again.

"So where exactly does that leave us? You and me and all that hair pulling and rough handling and making me do things I absolutely love doing?"

Leaning closer still, he reached for my chin, and it wasn't exactly a gentle gesture with which he held my head in place so he could kiss me deeply.

"I say we take it a step at a time and decide each day how we want to handle things. Might do you some good if you have to give me feedback all the time, and it leaves plenty of room for you to decide whether you just want to get your rocks off, or want me to drag you through hell and back. Considering how things were before we both veered off track, I'm not really worried that we never match each other's mood. Quite the contrary."

"And what about Jack? Right now, I mean. You were asking me about how long I wanted to hold a grudge, right?"

It was kind of funny to watch him drag himself out of the lust-induced haze, particularly as I could relate to him not wanting to.

"Right. Any objections to just ticking this off as a truly unpleasant but direly needed lesson we all had to learn, and admit that we'd only cut our own flesh if we decided to mope around for a week now until we're all just sick of it? Besides, he's right. We both know we'll find our own special ways of getting back at him, and considering that we should spend some time on defining and strengthening the bonds between us, I think that's an opportunity rather than a burden."

"Sounds good," I agreed, then deliberately dropped my eyes to his lips. "So can I go back there and tell him that we're not going to slaughter him right now, and bring him back here? Include him?"

Simon considered that while his fingers dug harder into my chin, forcing my gaze back up to his eyes.

"No, I'll do that. You go to the bathroom instead and prep yourself, so that by the time we're done talking, you're already waiting, kneeling naked, in my room. If last week was any indication, you've gotten a little lenient with your personal hygiene, and I think it's fair to give you a chance to catch up on that first."

"Not upstairs?"

He shook his head.

"Let's ease him into things. Besides, the bed's softer than the mats in the attic, and I'm not crazy about starting this weekend off with a bad case of rug burn."

I grinned as much as his grip would allow me to, and laughter sparked in his eyes as I remained silent.

"Do you really want to start this bent over my knee? Because I have no intention of going easy on you just because it might scare him off."

"No, Sir, I want to be your good little slut."

"That you always are," he breathed against my mouth before he kissed me again, and then sent me off running, giddy with excitement.

-19-

I heard them talking in the other room while I took care of business. Nothing in detail, but a few snippets came right through the wall, particularly when things got heated. That made me both curious and feel like an eavesdropper invading their privacy, a very strange feeling. I had to admit that I was happy not to be part of that conversation, whatever it entailed, but then I already had had my chance to start reconciling things with Jack, while Simon had not.

Even fighting with the disposable razor to the point of it getting ridiculous, I was still first to traipse into Simon's room, and because I didn't know how long they'd take, I took my position on the bed, then let my eyes droop closed just for a second. I must have started to doze off, excitement notwithstanding, because the sound of the door opening at my back startled me.

"Not that I'm complaining, but what is this?" I heard Jack say as I quickly straightened from my slumped position into an upright one, stealthily rolling my upper back and shoulders to get the kinks out of them.

"I thought I said you're stupid, not dumb," Simon remarked cryptically, laughter ringing clear in his voice.

"You just spent fifteen minutes tearing me a new one about how not to interfere where I'm not wanted, and then this?"

"Guess that means you are wanted in here after all," came Simon's reply. "Since you've apparently spent enough time lurking outside my playroom, you might as well make yourself useful. I need to fetch some things from upstairs. Be right back."

Silence fell once the sound of his footsteps had receded, making me guess that Jack was still standing in the doorway, his eyes glued to me. At least I thought he'd be staring, considering that naked women tended to draw the eyes of guys who wanted to screw them. I wondered for a moment if I should turn around, but I had no idea when Simon would return, and after two weeks of absence from the attic, I wasn't that keen on starting things with a hefty spanking I actually deserved.

A floorboard creaked when Jack finally moved, and I listened to him approach slowly. He stopped right at the edge of my vision, hovering cautiously. I didn't turn my head but glanced over until I caught his eyes. They were wide and he was licking his lips nervously, making it hard for me not to crack up.

"I'm not going to let him boss me around, just so that's clear," he said, more to himself than me.

"I don't think that's his intention," I replied, making him jump. Apparently he hadn't expected me to say anything.

Then his brows drew together as something occurred to him.

"Have you decided to torment me by screwing in front of me and making me watch?"

There was something that was strangely appealing about that thought, but my vindictive side was no match for my horniness.

"I don't have a clue what he has planned, besides the obvious. Unless you want to just watch, I think you're expected to get involved." Finally easing up, I turned my torso toward him, grinning when his eyes immediately flashed to my boobs. "At least I expect you to join. Vigorously."

Simon's return interrupted whatever else I might have said.

"Chatty, are we now? Guess I'll have to think of a way to shut you up," he said to me as he dumped a heap of rope coils on the bed beside me, then started to shuck his clothes unceremoniously. Jack was still standing by the bookshelf, ogling us hesitantly, until Simon stopped in mid-process of pulling off his jeans. "You're not gonna get much action if you just hover."

Jack didn't move until Simon was done undressing and walked over to him, clearly not caring at all that he was buck naked and the other guy still fully dressed. Reaching up, he put his hands to the back of Jack's neck, pulling his head closer to him in a nicely intimate gesture.

"I'm not going to make you do anything you don't want to, but the fact is, I'm kind of tired of always having to do everything on my own, and Erin can get pretty demanding when she's screaming at the top of her lungs."

My mouth was already open to deliver the scathing retort that deserved, but then I remembered where I was and what I was supposedly doing, and shut it again. Both guys sent me amused looks, but Simon resumed talking softly without commenting on it.

"You said you felt left out? Well, consider yourself included. Not every time and not in all things, but not everything kinky has to be so damn serious. Unless you want to keep sulking in the corner?"

"No, no, I'm done with that, I think." He hesitated for a moment, then reached up to pull Simon's fingers from his hair, but lingered a moment, their hands touching. It made me want to cheer them on to start kissing, but again, not my place. I could always do that later.

"Good," Simon said, then turned away from Jack and sauntered over to the bed, reaching for the first rope to uncoil it.

"I'm not going to take any orders from you," Jack repeated himself, finally pulling off his T-shirt.

"I'm not expecting you to," Simon replied, a light smile on his face. "You do remember how this works, right? I lead, you lend a hand where needed, unless you expressly want to take over, but in that event I would appreciate it if you'd check back with me before, because our little spitfire here—"

He paused to get a good grip on my hair and wrenched my head back, forcing me to bend my spine painfully while he briefly sneered into my face, "Has problems with accepting authority, and it would be too bad if you wimped out on her just because she's too successful provoking you. Is that not so?"

His hand pulled downward even harder, making me gasp, but at least not replying was not an option for me anymore.

"Yes, Sir!"

Simon eased his grip a little but didn't let go altogether as he resumed his banter with Jack.

"For the sake of everyone's sanity, we should maybe define a few boundaries. Obviously, she's my sub, and my responsibility to take care of. That means what I say, you do, and if it's something you're uncomfortable with, you back down but don't step in to save her. Trust me, she wouldn't appreciate it. If it gets too much for you, you leave the room and wait outside for me. I'll finish things with her, and then I'll come take care of you. She only needs to obey my commands, and unless we switch things up, she doesn't need to address you in any special way." Glancing down at me briefly, he smiled. "Otherwise we'd never get to any part that doesn't involve her punishment, am I right?"

"Yes, Sir," I offered in the fakest meek voice I could manage.

Simon gave me a pointed look but then let go, and I straightened with a contented sigh.

"Any objections?"

I held my tongue, while Jack shook his head, finally reaching his socks.

"Nope."

"Good."

Getting onto the bed in front of me, Simon doubled up the length of rope and set to work. With his usual calm efficiency, he quickly created a chest harness with rope running below and above my breasts, constricting and pushing together everything below my shoulders. And because he was feeling particularly gracious tonight, he also had me lean forward so he could wind yet more rope around each breast, the hemp digging in painfully as he tied off the ends. He had me cross my arms behind my back and tied them to the center point of the harness, effectively rendering me helpless as I wouldn't be able to get out of that on my own.

While he worked, he ignored everything around him, but once he set to tying the calf and thigh of each leg together, me still in the same kneeling position I'd started out in, he looked at my face briefly.

"Did Jack tell you what we were up to this morning? I think he set it up so you would walk in on us, but you were taking your sweet time coming over. What were you up to, anyway? Sentimental last morning?"

"He mentioned something, but no details." Which was kind of a lie, but I was sure that Simon wasn't just doing conversation, so I might as well give him the opportunity to enlighten me. "I was reading early reviews of your book in a coffee shop. Entertaining, but I'm sure you had more fun."

His smile was a sarcastic one, without a doubt tainted by what had happened later.

"Did you read the one where the critic called my writing style 'pedestrian'? My personal favorite."

"No, but that must be good for sales."

"You think?"

I nodded.

"I doubt that half the people reading that review will understand exactly what that means but get that the book might be easier to read than they expected, hence more something they'd be interested in if they aren't snotty book critics. But what were you up to?"

Still amused over my assessment, Simon bent to tying my other leg up.

"I'm surprised he didn't cough up any details, but then he was trying to talk you into running away with him, eh?" He looked to somewhere behind me, likely at Jack, before he went on. "Either he really was curious or he thought this was the way to make me forget all about how I suspected that he was acting like a manipulative asshole. He sucked me off, then quite liked me finger fucking him, although he did get squeamish at the end of that. Things ended with him screwing me again rather than the other way round. Don't you think that was unfair of him, leading me on like that, then not closing the deal?"

"I wouldn't know, lacking the anatomy myself to go any farther than that." Craning my neck, I looked over my shoulder at where Jack was standing, unsure what to do with himself, his cock starting to get hard. "But he does look kind of remorseful."

"Smartass," Simon murmured low enough that only I could hear, making me grin.

Finishing the last knot, he checked the ties again before he sat back, admiring his work. I couldn't help but push my shoulders back and press my already rather prominently displayed, bound breasts out. I couldn't believe how much I'd missed this! Also the physical side of it, but what was really making me wet was the quality of his gaze. Pride, admiration, lust, excitement, an unspoken promise to do unspeakable things to me—what more could a girl ask for?

Getting up, Simon turned to Jack, crossing his arms over his chest in a somewhat relaxed pose.

"So what am I going to do about feeling like you short-changed me on that? Any ideas?"

The look of suspicion on Jack's face was hilarious, and I suddenly understood why Simon enjoyed it so much when he set me up to dig my own hole like this. Then his eyes roved over to me and I quickly put a blank look on my face, but Jack likely saw through that mask.

"I don't know. Why don't you suggest something?"

"As you wish." I wondered if Jack knew that he'd just doomed himself, but then I personally never minded when that happened to me, so why should it bother him that much? "The obvious solution would be to go ahead now and shove my cock into your pert, tight ass. Think that's fair?"

Jack looked a little spooked, but his voice was even as he responded.

"I guess."

"Furthermore, I think Erin would feel neglected if she was the only one who wasn't getting anything up her ass today, so I think we should do something about that, right?"

I definitely liked where this was going, and so did Jack.

"I guess that's fair, too."

"The logical conclusion of that would mean that I fuck you while you fuck her, don't you think? It also comes with the benefit of you having to do most of the work because she's a truly insatiable cunt sometimes, and it's only fair that you start making up for screwing with us by screwing us."

Jack tried to hide a laugh with a loud snort, incapable of keeping a straight face.

"I think I like your idea of how I can redeem myself."

"I bet you do," Simon said and leaned in to steal a quick kiss, surprising Jack, but clearly not in a bad way. "Remember, she has to ask for permission before she comes, so if you feel like she's getting close, increase whatever you're doing to make it twice as hard for her to hold out. That's how you get her to scream the loudest."

I didn't even try to tone down the angry glare I sent them both, and they only had twin, nasty smiles for me.

Returning to the bed, Simon swept off the remaining pillows and blanket to make room, then slowly tipped me forward, one hand on my shoulder, the other supporting the weight of my torso in the middle of my stomach, until my body rested in a mostly horizontal position, the side of my head, shoulder, and knees balancing me, my toes now up in the air. I was suddenly glad that the pillows were gone—they might have been comfortable at first, but I didn't mind not accidentally suffocating myself this way.

"Hop up behind her," Simon directed, then grabbed the condoms and lube he'd also brought down from the attic.

The mattress dipped underneath Jack's weight as he knelt down behind me, gently running his hands up the insides of my thighs to help me spread them as much as I could. I would have loved for him to do more, but he obviously waited for Simon's instructions.

"I don't want your cock anywhere near her pussy. For now, that's mine. But feel free to use your fingers to work her into a frenzy—you know that she likes to be stuffed."

In my position it was easy to hide the inevitable eye-roll, but while Jack was busy liberally pouring lube over my anus and anything that might even remotely resemble an erogenous zone in the neighboring region, he couldn't stop himself from laughing softly.

"How do you manage to say shit like that without cracking up?"

"Practice," Simon offered, for once sounding a lot closer to laughing himself than I was used to. "If you want a good laugh, ask Beth about verbal the next time you see her. Erin takes to it like the needy little slut that she is, but I hated it. I think that's the only part of my training where she actually beat me into submission, and when she thinks I'm acting like a mopey whiner, she still whips it out randomly in conversations."

"Did you call her today?"

"And get insulted? No way. Besides, she would have thrashed my ass for slipping up like I did, and I'm not particularly fond of getting my balls handed to me like that." Suddenly Simon was leaning close to me, his breath warm against the side of my face. "But if, for whatever reason, you should develop a grudge against me, I'm more than happy to let you and my former Mistress hatch a plan of how to make sure it won't happen again."

That said, he crawled back until he was crouching behind Jack. My position didn't permit me to directly see any more than the left side of Jack's body from knee to shoulder, but the mirror on the outside of Simon's wardrobe gave me the perfect view of what was going on behind me. While Jack reached for me to spread my butt cheeks with one hand so he could easier toy with my anus, Simon pressed himself flush against Jack's back, one hand reaching up to his hair, the other wrapping around his cock to start stroking him slowly. The fact that I was incapable of moving anything except my hips back toward whatever Jack was going to do to me while I was forced to watch them was enough to make my vagina contract around the painful absence of anything stimulating.

Jack wasn't that much of a tease, though, and as soon as he started working one finger through my sphincter, his outer hand reached underneath me, sure fingers finding my clit and circling it in a slow, building rhythm. I forced myself to relax rather than tense with anticipation while I mulled over Simon's words.

What little he'd told me about this Beth woman made me both eager and scared to finally meet her, and while I didn't think that I had much of a sadistic streak myself, seeing Simon suffer at her hands while maybe playing a similar role as Jack did right now made me lick my lips in anticipation. Not because I felt like he really deserved it for being as human as the rest of us, but because I knew that it was something he'd like, too, and the competitive aspect of seeing just how hard he could be pushed before he yielded so I'd have something to compete with eventually was appealing, too.

Jack cut through my musing when he let out a low moan, apparently borne out of Simon kissing and licking along his shoulder, his free hand playing with Jack's nipples. Jack's cock looked almost ready for the next stage while he was still using only one finger inside of me, making me jerk my hips back as hard as I could when he pushed in the next time. A shudder ran through me when barely an inch deep became several all of a sudden, and Simon laughed softly when he looked for what had caused Jack to still.

"You're boring her, you know? What did I tell him, slut?"

"That I'm insatiable, Sir?"

"Right you are," Simon confirmed, then murmured something into Jack's ear that made him laugh, but also relax a little.

A second finger joined the first with much more enthusiastic motions, and for a little while I didn't give a shit about what was going on around me as I just let myself sink into the wonderful sensations created by Jack's hands.

Then they were gone, leaving me wanting for more, and when I saw him reach for the condoms, I knew I was going to get it very soon.

The last time Jack and I had been in a similar, if for me less restrictive, position, he'd been slow and careful, but whatever Simon had whispered to him earlier made him abandon the concept quickly—or maybe it was the fact that my ass wasn't painfully tight anymore, and while there was still the familiar burn of being stretched out as he thrust into me, it was a delicious burn now that made me arch my back and moan into the sheets underneath me. Strong hands gripped my hips for stability, then he pulled back out until only the head of his dick was still inside of me before he thrust back up, his balls slapping against my labia.

He set a slower pace than I would have liked, and I guessed that Simon was responsible for that, too, but I cared a little less about it when Simon left his post behind Jack and instead crawled over to me. Sitting down with his back against the headboard, legs to either side of my shoulders, he then shimmied down into a half-reclining position until his crotch was right in front of my face. I didn't need any directions to take his cock into my mouth, but when the angle remained awkward, I felt a sudden jerk at the ropes criss-crossing my back when Jack pulled my torso up. Simon slid down further, then grabbed my hair to steady my head so he could push himself deeper into my mouth, effectively fucking my face.

In short, I was in heaven.

Sadly, it was only a short duration soaring above the clouds as before long, Simon was hard enough to make the angle of his cock hitting the back of my throat uncomfortable, and the second time I gagged, he stopped. I must have looked rather disappointed because he laughed softly and leaned in to kiss me hungrily before he pulled back again.

"Don't worry. You'll get plenty more of that before we're done."

Then he returned to his previous perch behind Jack, in passing slapping Jack's ass playfully.

"Didn't I tell you to finger fuck her, too? It's been more than ten minutes now, and she hasn't even started panting. That's not really a performance up to my standards."

Jack was quick to remedy that, making me hold my breath for a few moments as I felt them slide into me. I still would have preferred Simon's cock, but when he rotated his hand so his thumb was back on my clit, I didn't really care all that much anymore.

Meanwhile, Simon reached for the lube, and Jack slowed down when he felt Simon's finger at his asshole. He earned himself a slap for that which was loud enough to make me guess that it had been a hard, real one, making Jack lose his rhythm for a second, but then pick up to his former speed.

"Ease up, then bear down on my finger. Unless you're too sore from earlier?"

"The only thing that's sore is my ego," Jack replied, pressing the words out between closed teeth.

"We'll see about that tomorrow," Simon told him, and used his other hand to cup Jack's balls.

Jack moaned, and his thrusts became erratic until he found a way not to hurt himself fucking me, which turned out to be using deeper thrusts than before, as deep as he would go. Taken together with what his fingers were doing inside me, I felt my orgasm swelling, a sweet, bright light on the horizon.

Jack really seemed to have less problems than I'd expected, judging from the way he obviously got worked up within minutes. Before long he was leaning further over me, panting into my ear in the most delicious way as he ceaselessly translated any of Simon's motions into pushing into me. Maybe it was the sheer physicality of the moment, with the restriction of bondage just adding to it, or it was the fact that I felt so relieved that we'd somehow managed to find a way out of what seemed like a massively tangled situation this morning, even with a long way ahead still; whatever it was, it made my resistance dwindle, and before long, the sounds leaving my throat drowned out Jack's.

"Please..." I started, low under my breath, but Jack must have picked up on it, because suddenly there was a third finger pushing into me, and the thrusts of his hips gained momentum. "Please may I come?"

"Already?" Simon asked, his usual teasing tone immediately making me bite the inside of my cheek to keep from groaning.

"Yes!"

"Oh, I don't know about that," he mused, taking his time with replying, all the while giving Jack time aplenty to increase everything he was doing to me.

"Please!"

It was easier this time to beg in Jack's presence, maybe because I now knew that he'd seen me do it even when I hadn't been aware of it, or because it had become a usual part of my routine. That didn't change the fact that I was very close to that razor sharp edge, and two weeks without any rougher kind of tumbling had taken their toll on my ability to hold back, too.

"What do you think? Shall I let her come already?"

I wanted to reply even though I knew he was asking Jack.

"I don't know. Do you usually let her come this fast?" Jack asked between pants, and I would have loved to kick him for it, but I couldn't even forcefully clench any muscles that would help him decide.

"No. But I feel generous tonight. How about this? Erin, you may come as soon as I have my cock up Jack's ass."

That made me want to throw a physical fit, but all I could really do was buck against Jack, who didn't seem opposed to the additional stimulation. The worst thing about it was that it was completely out of my control or influence. I had no way of telling how much Jack had loosened up already, or how much time Simon wanted to take. What I knew for sure was that I couldn't hold out much longer, although I tried my best to distract myself for the moment. Then even that failed, and I was getting frantic.

"Please, you can't do this to me, I can't hold it any longer! Please let me come!"

Simon just shook his head, grinning, making tears of frustration well in my eyes.

"You know the condition. You don't get to come unless Jack wants my cock in his ass. It's not my fault that he's too busy fucking you to give a shit."

Maybe if I'd not been half insane with the need for release, I might have thought of that earlier, but it took me another couple of seconds to decipher that.

"Jack? Stop being such an asshole and ask him to fuck you!"

"What, I don't even get a single nice word?" He grunted, then had the audacity of sinking his teeth into my shoulder, almost making me lose control from the extra sensation.

I gritted my teeth and closed my eyes, doing everything I could to hold out longer—rattling off lists in my mind, thinking about my octogenarian neighbor having sex—but Jack seemed determined to make me fail, judging from the way he practically ground the pad of his thumb into my clit.

I sailed past that point of no return and knew that now it was only a matter of time before my body would start to convulse. Forgetting all about propriety and how I usually acted around Jack, I started pleading with him at the top of my lungs.

I almost didn't make it when suddenly he went completely still above me and grabbed my bound left hand with his right that wasn't busy turning my genitals into the promised land. His forehead touched down on my shoulder, right where he'd bitten me moments ago, and he let out a low groan, followed by a rather emphatic, "Damn!"

It was pretty obvious what that meant, and the moment he pushed forward, into me again, I let go. Bound as I was, with Jack's fingers in my pussy and his cock in my ass, I couldn't evade, couldn't even move properly, which heightened the sensation of heat zooming through my entire body. Muscles locked and clenched, making me shake all over, while harsh breaths found their way out of my chest. It felt so fucking good that it was almost painful, and only got better when my mind cleared and I realized that Jack had started fucking me in earnest again.

A quick look in the mirror revealed than his motions where shorter than they felt to my hypersensitive body, but watching him pretty much fuck himself on Simon's cock, and thus also pushing into me, was mesmerizing and incredibly hot. My body calmed down a little but not much, the constant stimulation not letting the need inside of me ebb away. By the time I had caught my breath again, I was so fucking turned on that I likely would have had to start begging anew, only that Jack had ditched his manual stimulation so he could support himself better above me, lending me some matter of respite. Not that I necessarily wanted respite, but not feeling like I was about to explode any moment now let me appreciate the raw sensations every thrust brought with it, and that was satisfying on its own.

Then Jack's motions became less coordinated, and Simon finally took over, grabbing his hips and driving into him with slow, controlled rolls of his pelvis. I doubted that would have been enough to make me come, but then Jack was also getting massive stimulation from his cock still sheathed deep inside of me, and when he finally lost it, he came with a series of moans and grunts that was whipping my own libido back into a frenzy.

Simon pulled out of him as soon as Jack stilled, and pulled off the condom with one hand while he leaned into Jack and nuzzled his neck playfully. Jack grunted something incoherent and moved off me, rolling onto his back, eyes wide and his chest still heaving.

I half expected that Simon would just finish by jerking off, or maybe have me suck him off, but the telltale ripping noise of a new condom wrapper had me perk up and gave me about a five-second warning before Simon leaned over me, then picked me up and flipped me over onto my back. Normally he was pretty quick in undoing his own knots, but this time there was some extra needless jerking on ropes involved as he freed my legs, the bliss of being able to stretch those muscles the best thing I'd felt in a long time—until he pulled my hips toward him, put my raised legs up on his shoulders, and thrust into me hard enough that my entire body rocked into the mattress. Jack's fingers had felt great, but now having Simon's cock in my pussy was simply amazing, and he certainly didn't hold back.

He did lean further into me, forcing my legs to his sides and making my hips rock up to allow for deeper penetration, while one of his hands reached up and grabbed my breast, swollen, red, and sensitive from the ropes that had restricted blood flow for half an hour now. I started to moan, then cried out when he really dug his fingers in, squeezing hard enough to hurt, but not half as hard as I wanted him to. Grinning down at me, Simon increased his pace, fucking me harder, and before long he had me right where I needed to be again.

Instead of listening to my begging, he shifted himself further over me until his mouth could reach mine and drowned out his own orgasmic shout by thrusting his tongue into my mouth and sealing my lips with his. I took that as a sure sign that I might as well go ahead, but it was the same to me as I couldn't have staved off the second orgasm that rocked through me.

It took me a little while to gather my stray thoughts. Thinking was hard, moving was hard, too, and I wanted to do neither. I felt sweaty and gross and awesome and warm, with one hot body half lying on me, another pressed to my side.

Then there were eager lips seeking mine and I responded immediately by letting them in, then another mouth placing lazy, wet kisses all over my jaw and the side of my neck. Fingers moved, teased, explored, but for the most part stroked gently, and then Simon rolled me onto my side so he could start undoing the rest of the ropes. I complied automatically but never stopped devouring Jack's mouth until the restriction around my torso lessened, and a tingling, burning kind of sensation spread through my tormented tits.

I tried reaching up to cradle and massage them, but hands batted mine away, and when I tried again, Jack and Simon each grabbed one of my wrists and pushed them into the sheets next to my head, then went back to work, kissing and licking and sucking the pain away. It took a while, and they didn't stop when my hisses turned to needy moans. I was too tired and spent to keep my eyes open, so I had no idea whose hand reached between my thighs and started masturbating me to a third climax, one that I didn't even think to ask for.

I fell asleep cocooned by warm, sweaty bodies, the guys exchanging a few words before they settled down, but I was too out of it to catch them. The last thing I remembered was thinking that this was paradise, then my mind sunk into the dark land of dreams that, this once, couldn't hold a candle to reality.

-20-

I woke up the next morning alone in a bed that reeked of sex and sweat, a bright smile on my face. The sheets next to me were still warm, so whoever had spent the night heating up my back couldn't have been gone for long, but I didn't go forth to investigate until the heavenly smell of coffee gave me a good reason to abandon the languid laziness of just lying in bed and not giving a shit about the world.

I did hit the bathroom first, and then the shower because my own body grossed me out a little, before I made it into the front of the house. I didn't bother with grabbing any clothes, which was convenient, as Jack barely gave me enough time to grab a mug and fill it before he dragged me over to the couch and started going down on me.

Suffice it to say, I did not finish that cup, and by the time I remembered its existence, it was two hours later and I was in dire need of another shower as I climbed off Simon, Jack still leaning into my back. I was sore all over from simple physical friction and exertion, but didn't protest for a second when Simon joined me in the shower and did way more than just offer to wash my back. Although he did that, too, after making me tremble and clench and shout, and I was only too happy to stumble out of the stall to let Jack have the stage. At least then I finally got to drink my cold, stale coffee.

It was still the best coffee I'd ever had.

The doorbell rang when I was halfway through that cup, and I wondered if the universe was out to get me. Sighing, I ducked back into Simon's room and grabbed the first clothes I found—luckily my own panties, but the shirt I'd thought was Simon's turned out to be Jack's, and what could have been just an oversized tee pretty much dwarfed me. The bell rang again, decidedly unfriendly now, and I figured that whoever was intruding had it coming to need brain bleach after being confronted with my "outfit." In passing, I pounded on the bathroom door and yelled inside that someone was at the door, but the "I'm coming!" I got for a response could have meant anything, really.

With a smirk on my face I finally opened the door, coming face to face with a considerably startled looking Kara.

The range of expressions her face went through was so comical that it made me crack up before she even had a chance to say anything. She'd clearly come prepared to interrupt Simon's pity party, coffee in hand and a sympathetic look on her face. Then she saw me, and a line appeared between her eyebrows. Then she really *saw* me, making her eyes widen while a lazy grin curved her lips up.

"Hey, bitch. I feel like I should say I'm surprised to see you here, but I really am not."

Ignoring her brief scrutiny of the state I was in, I leaned out further to divest her of the coffee. It was strong, black, and scalding hot, an acceptable substitute for my now-abandoned cup.

"You're a lifesaver."

She watched me gulp down the better part of the cup, never minding the temperature, while a bemused look came to her face.

"I assume you're not alone?"

Just then shouts rang out behind me, thankfully not of an amorous nature, and a few seconds later Jack came barreling into my back, only the arm he wrapped around my middle keeping him from shoving me straight out the door. A moment later Simon followed, wedging the door open far enough to look out around us. Kara took the display in stride, her eyes flitting from one of us to the next before she regarded all three of us with something akin to satisfaction—as if she'd had anything to do with us getting things halfway sorted out again.

"I don't even dare to ask, but do you know what day it is?"

"Saturday, presumably," Simon offered, his eyes narrowing. "Why?"

"Because you're already one hour late for the brunch-slash-garden party your mom is holding, in honor of your big accomplishment. The book, not losing track of time screwing each other senseless."

"Oh, right," Simon muttered, scratching his head.

I vaguely remembered that Kara had said something about a party yesterday, but I had been too busy thinking about what to say to Simon once I got my hands on him to really listen. She always prattled on about parties and soirées, so it was hard to keep track of. Jack looked vaguely concerned, maybe because he was the only one of us who kept track of such things, and when he gave Simon a hard look, Simon shrugged.

"Forgot to tell you, too. It wasn't really important at the time."

"Anyway," Kara interrupted before Jack could do more than open his mouth. "Linda sent me over, telling me explicitly that I'm expected not to come back without you, but I'm not setting one foot into this house before it hasn't been thoroughly sanitized, so you can take yourselves over there on your own time. I'd advise soon—there's delicious, home-made punch, and Linda's excuses for why you're late might get more creative by the hour in direct relation to the disappearance of said punch. Oh, and you should shower, Erin. You have cum in your hair."

With that, she turned on her heel and sashayed back to the car that I just realized had been idling at the curb, a guy about five years younger than us giving us quizzical looks. I quickly shoved Jack back so I could close the door, then critically patted my hair down. There was something sticky up there, and I really didn't want to investigate what it was as I rolled my eyes and stalked toward the back hallway.

In passing, Jack leaned down to quickly tickle my sides, making me jump and shriek. When I glared at him, he just grinned at whatever was stuck in my hair.

"Ew."

"Yeah? Guess who put that there?"

His expression was completely innocent as he turned away, and I beat it to the bathroom. Just before I could close the door behind me—alone this time, to make sure I actually got some cleaning done—I heard Jack exclaim, his voice horrified, "What the fuck is this?"

"Judging from the consistency, it seems of a similar origin than whatever is matting Erin's hair," Simon observed, then started laughing at what I figured must have been Jack's horrified expression.

"I have to clean this up before we go or I'll never get the stains out."

"At this rate, we should just burn the couch and get a new one."

I silently agreed with Simon, although for sentimental reasons alone I hoped they'd opt to just have it deep cleaned or fitted with a new fabric, then closed the door before anyone could get between me and my shower again.

As I stepped under the hot spray, I couldn't help the smile spreading on my face.

Was everything perfect? No, of course not. Not by a long shot.

I knew that things wouldn't always be as easy as they were now—and we hadn't completely gotten over this first bump in the road yet, if I was honest and stopped ignoring the lingering feeling of resentment deep down in my chest. It was easy to ignore that we had a long road ahead to make this work when right now, just being together and forgetting about the world was so much easier.

Would our budding relationship last? I hoped so, but who could say?

The only thing I knew was that there was no one else in the world I'd rather spend my life with than Jack and Simon. And for now, that was enough.

THE END

The story continues in Tied Between - We Kinky Three #2

Thank you!

I cannot tell you how much it means to me that you picked up this book, read it to the end, and hopefully had a great time! If you have a moment, I would really appreciate a short review on Amazon and Goodreads. Reviews make a huge difference in helping readers find new authors and books.

Not quite ready to let go? There's more!
If you sign up for my newsletter, you'll get "Saturday Afternoon Special", a short story written from Simon's point of view, for free!

www.kirabarker.com/newsletter/

(or just head over to my website at kirabarker.com and click on the "newsletter" tab in the menu bar.)

Acknowledgements

I couldn't have done this without the help and support of more people than I can mention here. My trusty pre-readers— Christina, Tina, Izzie, Anca, Holly— because I'd be lost without you! My cover artist, my editor, my street team (I love you!), but also all the wonderful people who have been cheering me on for a long time now to embark on this crazy journey! Without you, Erin, Simon, and Jack would still be figments of my imagination that have kept me awake way too many nights.

THANK YOU!

If you're curious for more…

Hunter & Prey (Hunter & Prey #1)

Penelope Thompson loves her life. She has everything she wants. With her beauty, charm, and intelligence, she is at the top of her game and is one of the most sought after escorts in the city. She chooses her clients carefully and provides them with much more than just a great time between the sheets. Yet now at the age of 33, she is questioning just how much longer she has in the business. Life might be great, but sometimes it gets lonely to only ever be what others want to see in her, trading sex for true intimacy.

Darren Hunter has made a killing by being one of the best lawyers in Chicago. Renowned for winning any case, he has built up quite the reputation. He has a new beautiful woman attached to his arm every few months and is what every guy desires to be: wealthy, smart, successful, and has the looks to go with all that.

When it is time for Darren to choose his new "flavor of the season," Penelope catches his eye. As things heat up between them, Penelope starts to feel as if life is turning into a fairy tale—if not for the fact that, one by one, people are warning her about her Prince Charming, and evidence is mounting up that the elusive Mr. Hunter has his own skeletons in the closet. Will his past come to catch up with her? And why do all the women in his life suddenly disappear?

About the author

Kira Barker has always enjoyed telling stories. It has kept her sane through high school and college, and has become a true passion since. A geek gamer girl herself, she feels at home reading sci-fi and fantasy as much as writing romance. She likes her plots gritty, her smut realistic, and doesn't mind getting her hands dirty when it comes to research. When she's not writing, she loves annoying her cats or cruising country roads on her motorcycle.

You can sign up for Kira's newsletter and find out more about her books here:
http://www.kirabarker.com/newsletter/

Email: kira.e.barker@gmail.com
Twitter: @KiraEBarker
Website: http://www.kirabarker.com/

Other works

The Embassy - a collection of paranormal erotica novellas
Hunter & Prey
Tied Between - We Kinky Three #2